THE MIDWIFE AND THE ORC

A MONSTER FANTASY ROMANCE

FINLEY FENN

This is a work of fiction. Names, characters, places, and incidents are the product of the author's imagination or are used fictitiously. Any resemblance to actual persons living or dead, business establishments, events, or locales is entirely coincidental.

The Midwife and the Orc

Copyright © 2021 by Finley Fenn

info@finleyfenn.com

Cover artwork by Skadior Art

Cover design by Sylvia at The Book Brander

Visit www.finleyfenn.com for free bonus stories and epilogues, delicious orc artwork, complete content tags and warnings, news about upcoming books, and more!

ALSO BY FINLEY FENN

ORC SWORN

The Lady and the Orc

The Heiress and the Orc

The Librarian and the Orc

The Duchess and the Orc

The Midwife and the Orc

The Maid and the Orcs

The Governess and the Orc

The Beauty and the Orcs

The Widow and the Orcs

The Artist and the Orc

Offered by the Orc

Tryggred by the Orc

Yuled by the Orcs

Tales of Orc Sworn

ORC FORGED

The Sins of the Orc

The Fall of the Orc

THE MAGES

The Mage's Maid

The Mage's Match

The Mage's Master

The Mage's Groom

ABOUT THE MIDWIFE AND THE ORC

He's been watching her. Now he's going to ruin her.

In a world of recently warring orcs and men, Gwyn Garrett is a lord's daughter on a mission—to escape her lord father, dump her cheating betrothed, and pursue her true calling as a plant-obsessed midwife.

Until her quiet new cottage is invaded by an *orc*.

Joarr is a tall, taunting, treacherous orc spy, and ever since Gwyn moved in, he's been watching her. Studying her. Plotting how best to charm her, and gain her trust...

And then he'll claim her.

Compromise her.

Ruin her.

But Gwyn is far too clever to fall for a sneaky orc's schemes—right? Even if he makes her laugh. Even if he loves mushrooms and gardens. Even if he sparks something hot and reckless, deep in her soul...

It's a dangerous game, enough to destroy everything Gwyn has worked for—and enough to bind her to Joarr forever. To make her into his pawn, his plaything, his sacrifice in this war...

But maybe Joarr has been compromised, too. Maybe he's gotten closer than he wants to admit. And maybe, if Gwyn plays his game, she can win everything she's ever wanted...

Or lose her heart.

To Angie
With all my gratitude

~

Special thanks to the midwifery and health care professionals who
served as advisors on this book:

Line Vienneau
Rianna Nisbet-Roth
Twilla Love

1

One of these days, Gwyn Garrett was going to poison her lord father.

"I'm not changing my mind, Father," she told him, as she snapped apart the stalks of dried lavender with excessive force. "I'm moving. Next week."

Lord Anton of Dunburg had never been a small fellow, but his corpulent, sprawled-out body seemed to take up half Gwyn's kitchen, his bloodshot eyes reproachful on her face. "But that's *foolishness*, Gwynnie," he replied, in the petulant, exasperated tone of a man who hadn't yet had his morning drink. "You have a perfectly comfortable home right here, where it's *safe*. Where you can play at your little"—he waved a dismissive hand at her lavender—"*hobby* however you please."

Her little *hobby*. Gwyn audibly ground her teeth, and snatched for another handful of lavender. "It's not a hobby, Father, as I've repeatedly told you," she countered. "It's a profession that I've spent many, many years studying. A profession I'm *good* at."

Lord Anton cast a brief, skeptical look around at Gwyn's cramped apartment, and as she followed his eyes, she felt her shoulders sagging, her fingers slackening on the lavender. It was indeed a tiny apartment—she'd taken it more for the large windows than anything else—and every available space was crammed full of pots and jars and overflowing greenery, to the point where even walking through the room these days presented a significant challenge.

"And as you can see, I clearly need a bigger space," Gwyn continued, squaring her shoulders again. "With room for a proper garden. And Great-Aunt Agnes' place has those things, and now she's left it to me. And I am twenty-six years old, and I'm earning enough income with my *hobby* to live without your support. There is *no reason* for me not to move there."

Her father's frown deepened, his arms crossing over his stout chest. "There is every reason," he replied, "because that damned house is in Varrahan. In the damned shadow of bloody *Orc Mountain!*"

Gwyn drew in a deep breath through her nose, let it out. "Yes, I'm aware, Father," she snapped. "However, I'm sure you recall that you and your lord cronies also ratified an extensive *peace-treaty* with the orcs, well over a year ago. And since then, there hasn't been a single reliable account of a woman being forced or kidnapped by an orc. Not *one.*"

She raised her eyebrows toward her lord father, silently daring him to dispute that claim—because of course she'd already done her due diligence on this. And while the prospect of being stolen away by a vicious, hideous orc certainly still loomed large in her thoughts, her findings on that front had been far more reassuring than she'd expected. The orcs truly had seemed to take their new peace-treaty to heart, and as far as she'd been able to discern, there indeed hadn't been a single verifiable kidnapping case in almost two full years.

"Look, even if those ugly green bastards aren't still running around carting women off," Lord Anton shot back, "there's *plenty* else they'd like to do to a lone woman parked at the edge of their mountain. Lords, Gwynnie, you're a clever girl, can't you guess why those beasts have held so firm to the terms of that damned treaty? What they *really* want out of all this?"

Gwyn couldn't hide her wince, because curse him, her father wasn't wrong. Orcs *were* still orcs, after all—brutal, deadly, and deeply dangerous—and what was more, she'd seen firsthand the increase in certain... *situations* over the past year or two. Situations which had always existed, if her midwife mentors were to be believed—but which had certainly been exacerbated by the new freedoms the orcs had gained. Situations where women furtively whispered of huge powerful bodies, of deep voices and long slick tongues, of musky scents in the dark. Of choices foolishly made and then regretted, amidst panic and confusion and overpowering shame.

But Gwyn had long ago ceased judging other women for their mistakes—gods knew, she had no grounds to stand upon there—and she'd somehow even earned a reputation as someone to seek out, after landing in such a predicament. And while there was nothing even the strongest of Gwyn's herbs could do against an orc's impossibly powerful spawn, she still knew which midwives could offer other kinds of help, and which herbs could best prevent such outcomes in future.

And thus, not only had Great-Aunt Agnes gifted Gwyn a house—but the house was also in just the place where Gwyn was likely to be most needed. To be helpful. To be something, *anything*, other than the ruling lord's dotty, unfashionable, deeply disappointing daughter, who was best avoided unless one was ill, or knocked up by orcs.

"Yes, Father, I know what the orcs want," Gwyn said testily. "However, I have no intention whatsoever of being seduced or kidnapped. And even *should* the worst happen, I also know better than most how to prevent pregnancy, don't I? And in the meantime, you can happily launch into another war to rescue me, or make up some awful new laws, or whatever it is you're cooking up against the orcs these days."

Lord Anton had been scowling up at her, his mouth opening to reply—but then, oddly enough, he shut it again. His bloodshot eyes darting down to Gwyn's table full of herbs, his hand idly reaching to pick up a sprig of hyssop, as if he were actually interested.

And gods, Gwyn knew that look. It was the same look he'd given her fifteen years ago, when he'd told her that her mother wasn't likely to survive her lung infection. The same look he'd worn when he'd refused to pay for Gwyn's midwifery training, claiming it was no place for a lord's daughter. The same look as when he'd cut her monthly allowance, citing increased expenses from her four spendthrift half-brothers—and then had immediately turned around and begun begging her for a lead on a new opium supplier. And the same look as when, just three weeks past, he'd asked her to visit two of his mistresses, both suffering from "womanly complaints"—which, surprise surprise, had turned out to be the same insidious infection, transmitted by guess who.

"*Father*," Gwyn hissed, her patience already strained far too thin. "What is it now. What are you doing with the orcs."

And while she didn't particularly care what happened to the orcs—at least, beyond how it affected the women who came to her for help—again, that was surely something important in her father's shifty eyes. Something Gwyn was sure to thoroughly dislike, whatever the hell it was.

"Out with it, Father," she said, clipped. "If it's that bad, I'm sure to hear about it soon anyway, aren't I? What is it, some ghastly new law? You're trying to prevent women from travelling alone in public again?"

That horrid little plan had actually been raised by her father's awful Council last year, as a so-called attempt to offer women protection against the newly liberated orcs. It had thankfully prompted a vehement public outcry, and the realm's lords had shelved it for the time being—but Gwyn held no delusions about her lord father's capabilities for spectacular short-sightedness, or breathtaking cruelty, depending on what suited him best in that moment.

"Oh, it's nothing major, Gwynnie," he said now, with a nonchalance that suggested it was major indeed. "We've just decided to start gathering information from women, that's all."

Gathering information, from women. "About *what*," Gwyn replied, through clenched teeth. "About orcs?"

The look on her father's face confirmed as much, his thick fingers twisting the hyssop stem between them. But he didn't elaborate, and Gwyn stared at him over the table as her thoughts frantically choked and churned.

"You're planning to gather information from women about orcs," she repeated, her voice faint. "About their... encounters with orcs? Their... *intimate encounters* with orcs, you mean?"

Her father kept picking awkwardly at the hyssop, again suggesting that Gwyn surely had the right of it. And she felt her feet actually staggering as the implications of that slammed against her, burrowing deep and sickening into her belly.

"And how, exactly," she managed, "are you even *finding* these women, Father? How do you plan to collect this information from them? And"—she dragged in breath, her eyes searching his gradually reddening face—"are you establishing *consequences* around this, Father? For those poor desperate women, who are very likely to be *pregnant*?!"

Lord Anton gave an unmistakable grimace, a wary glance up at Gwyn's eyes. "Not *consequences*," he said quickly. "Of course we don't want to punish those orc-addled wenches for their honesty. But we'll offer... *solutions*, for those who willingly testify."

Good gods. Solutions... for those who *testified*?!

Gwyn gaped at her lord father for a long, horrible moment,

her hands crushing the forgotten lavender in her fists. "Do you mean to tell me," she breathed, "that you're putting these women on *public trial*, Father? And that you'll offer to help them... but *only* if they agree to testify? And let me guess, the only help you'll be offering them is *terminations*?"

Her father kept intently studying the hyssop stem, all but announcing his guilt, his horrifying brutality—and Gwyn felt the disbelief surging in her chest, flashing behind her eyes. "And what if those women *don't* agree to testify, Father?" she shouted. "What if they don't *want* to tell everyone they know that they made a stupid mistake, and bedded an *orc*?"

Her father grimaced again, waving his hand between them. "Quiet down, Gwynnie," he said. "We're sure the prospect of testifying will be enough to encourage those women to choose the... *solutions* instead. Otherwise..."

He shrugged, a casual, uncaring movement meant to cast those women to the wolves, to those in their communities who would devour them, *destroy* them, over a single foolish lapse of judgement. And Gwyn's legs suddenly couldn't seem to hold her up anymore, and she sank heavily down onto the wooden chair behind her, dragging her trembling hands through her hair.

Her father was essentially *coercing* the realm's women into terminating the orcs' offspring. Under the threat of making them publicly confess their intimate relations with an orc, no doubt before everyone they knew. Before their employers, their families, possibly their *husbands*.

And while Gwyn willingly supported the women who wanted to end their orc-induced pregnancies—and while they usually comprised the majority of those she helped—she'd also encountered a surprising number of women who *hadn't* wanted that. Women who were far more terrified for their own lives, for their health birthing the orcs' huge sons. Women who were willing to carry their offspring to term, if only they had the support and safety to do so. Women who needed the resources to run, or to hide their pregnancy's true nature from those around them.

Gwyn herself had never yet assisted with such a birth, but again, her mentors had whispered of astonishing tales. Tales of delivering the child, and then loudly proclaiming some fatal deformity or disease, and then leaving it out in the darkness. Tales of tiny wails fading into the distance, as their huge, hulking fathers carried them away to Orc Mountain.

They were dark stories, and even darker decisions for these desperate women to have to make, with devastating ramifications on the rest of their entire *lives*. And now Gwyn's selfish, bumbling lord father was going to throw himself into the midst of all that? With public trials, and blackmail, and forced *terminations*?! All, surely, as another ill-conceived attempt at warring against the orcs?!

"That," Gwyn said, once she'd somehow found her voice again, "is *vile*, Father. It is *abhorrent*. It is quite possibly the most *disgusting* thing you've ever done, and you must know, there is a *very* long list of possibilities in strong contention for that prize!"

Lord Anton winced, casting a furtive glance around at the apartment's too-close walls. "Settle down, Gwynnie," he said, moistening his lips with his tongue. "Look, it'll help those fool women in the end, all right? We'll likely even offer the termination service at a reduced cost. What's more, the rest of the Council is neck-deep in plans for this now, and it'll make no difference now whether if I cry off or not. My hands are tied."

Gwyn stared at him with a visceral, rapidly rising loathing, and she belatedly leapt to her tingling feet, and stalked over to her pot of candlewood. It was her worst plant to harvest, with tall spiky canes and fiendishly sharp barbs, and she almost wept at the relief of its painful spines pricking her fingers. Strong enough to drag her back from the edge of the all-consuming rage, from the desperate urge to shove a fistful of deadly wolfsbane into her father's wet, slack, lying mouth.

"This conversation is *over*, Father," she hissed, without looking over her shoulder. "And we will *not* be speaking again, until you find a way to stop this vile new law from proceeding. I mean that."

Lord Anton gave a resigned-sounding huff behind her, and she could hear him ponderously rising to his feet, and then accidentally kicking over a nearby pot, no doubt her priceless corncockle. "Now, now, Gwynnie," he said. "Don't be like that. You know what those orcs are. I'm only doing my job. Protecting my people. Protecting women like *you*, when you take it into your silly heads to abandon your *home*, your own *family*, so you can go live next to that damned dangerous mountain!"

Gwyn couldn't deny the earnest pleading in his familiar voice—or even worse, her own reaction to it. The way her shoulders dropped, her stomach sinking, her fingers twitching against the candlewood's spines. And when she felt her father's heavy hand settle on her shoulder, she couldn't even seem to move, or tell him to get out, or just *listen* to her for once in his life, or any of the other dozen things she should very well have said.

"You know you're my favourite girl, Gwynnie, even if we don't always see eye to eye," he said, and it sounded like he meant that, too. "I don't want to lose you to those vicious orcs, all right? I wouldn't want any father to have to face that, or to have to watch his daughter bear a deadly orc *spawn*, at the risk of her own *life*."

And again, Gwyn couldn't even seem to speak. Couldn't find a way to say, *It's not about you, Father, it's not about any of the men, or your damned war. It's about the women who will suffer from this, the women whose lives you're so thoughtlessly destroying—*

"Does all this have anything to do with Roy, Gwynnie?" her

father abruptly asked, in one of his all-too-disconcerting flashes of awareness. "You wanting to move to Varrahan, I mean?"

Gwyn betrayed a reflexive flinch, because he was referring, of course, to Royal Lindsay—his longtime ward, and now the captain of his elite household guards. Roy, with his lean body and laughing eyes, who'd years ago been promised to Gwyn, in some kind of nebulous betrothal arrangement she'd never properly understood. Roy, who had consistently shown himself perfectly content to postpone his supposedly forthcoming marriage to Gwyn for as long as possible, in order to continue carrying on as the province's most infamous rake.

"This has *nothing* to do with Roy, Father," Gwyn belatedly replied, though her voice damnably wavered. "I want a bigger place. And a garden. And Great-Aunt Agnes left the house to me, and now she's gone, and I want to honour her wishes."

But her father's low chuckle behind her was far too knowing, his hand giving her shoulder a gentle little shake. "Ah, *now* I see, you clever girl," he said. "Take off for Orc Mountain, and leave Roy here to stew without you, is that it? Light a much-needed fire under the boy? Let him worry about his best girl being stolen away by orcs?"

Gwyn's entire body had gone very stiff, her shoulder high and square under her father's hand. "This has *nothing* to do with Roy, Father," she repeated. "And I'm not his best girl, I'm a liability he'll be well pleased to have out of his way. It will be far better for both of us if I'm gone."

Lord Anton laughed again, low and tolerant. "Ah, you put on a good face, Gwynnie," he said, "but Roy told me he had you over just last week. Said you took a bit of a pet over something or other, though? Some silly chit who's been hanging off his purse-strings lately?"

Curse Roy, and curse her damned father, because Gwyn's throat had badly spasmed, the memories charging and trampling through her thoughts. The feel of Roy's silken skin under her hands. The sound of his husky voice in her ear. The sight of his half-lidded, long-lashed eyes on hers as he'd moved above her in the candlelight, filling her with his intensity, his beauty, his affection. Making himself hers, and her his, in that perfect, shining moment.

And then, of course, the aftermath. This time with an unfamiliar woman actually knocking at the door of his apartments, and blatantly asking if he might enjoy some company. To which Roy had laughed, and replied that he was presently occupied, but that she was welcome to try again later.

"You know Roy will come up to scratch sooner or later, Gwynnie," her father continued, his voice firm. "He's promised me that, and I know he cares for you. But, I suppose if you *are* twenty-six now, you're no doubt eager to move matters along…"

His voice trailed off, his fingers now drumming against Gwyn's stiff shoulder, and she desperately blinked back the wetness prickling behind her eyes. "I'm not eager to move matters along, Father," she said thickly. "I'm eager to end it, for good. Roy and I are *not* well suited for one another. And I want a bigger place, with a garden."

But she might as well have been talking to her candlewood, because her father only laughed again, and gave her shoulder another little shake. "You know what, Gwynnie, I'll allow it," he said. "But for only one month, you hear me? After that, I'm sending a band of men to bring you back, whether you want it or not. Oh, and look"—his voice brightened—"here's Roy now. We're going on a hunting trip for a few days, I told him to collect me here."

What? Gwyn whipped around, following her father's satisfied gaze out the nearest window. To where Royal Lindsay was indeed leaping gracefully down from a carriage on the street below them, and striding toward the door of Gwyn's building. And then there was the sound of his familiar footsteps, taking the stairs two at a time like always, while Gwyn's traitorous, scraped-up fingers wiped at her flushed-feeling face, and before she'd caught them, even straightened out her long black hair.

Her father had already flung open the door, a broad smile on his mouth—and now here was Roy in the flesh, tall and lithe and dressed in hunting clothes, lighting up the room with his grin. "Morning, Dunburg," he said, clapping Lord Anton on the back, though his sparkling brown eyes had already flicked to Gwyn beyond him. "And to you, my fair Gwynevere. How are you, love? Still miffed at me?"

Gwyn's voice was locked in her throat, her arms crossing tightly over her chest, and in return Roy threw back his handsome head and laughed, the sound warm and indulgent. "Ah, so that's a yes, then," he said, reaching a familiar hand to pat at her too-hot cheek. "What do you say I stop by once we're back, then? Try to make it up to you?"

Gwyn's cheeks flamed even hotter, and she raised her chin, and somehow spoke past the constriction in her throat. "That won't be necessary, thanks," she said. "I'm actually moving away, in a few days. To Varrahan."

It was a rare sight to see Royal Lindsay caught off guard, and Gwyn ought to have enjoyed the odd stillness in his eyes, the uncertain quirk on his mouth. "You're moving?" he repeated, his voice not quite as light as before. "To *Varrahan*?!"

He shot a brief, accusing glance at Lord Anton, who had now begun to look rather smug, his gaze flicking between Roy and Gwyn. "You know our Gwynnie, once she gets an idea into her head," he said cheerfully. "I've decided to allow it for now, but she'll change her mind soon enough, won't you?"

He actually had the audacity to *wink* at her, an action which Roy certainly didn't miss, his eyes narrowing toward Gwyn. "Varrahan, Gwyn?" he demanded at her. "You're serious? Next to fucking *Orc Mountain*?"

Gwyn twitched a nod, crossing her arms tighter, while an unmistakable anger flared through Roy's eyes. "That's *foolishness*, Gwynevere," he snapped. "Do you not know how horribly dangerous those beasts are? Gods, they've even been sneaking around *here* lately. One in particular"—his voice dropped—"who needs his ugly *head* impaled on a pike."

Gwyn grimaced at that lovely little image, and gritted her teeth so tightly it hurt. "Well, thanks to the peace-treaty *he* helped ratify," she said, jerking her head toward her father, "you're out of luck, Roy. And, if the orcs are actually sneaking around here in Dunburg too, then what conceivable difference does it make if I move to Varrahan?"

Roy stared at her for an instant too long, his jaw flexing in his cheek. "Don't think I don't know," he said, his voice very steady, "what you're doing with this, Gwynevere."

Good gods, these *men*, and suddenly Gwyn couldn't bear to look at them for a moment longer, or feel their infuriating, too-large presences crowding this tiny cramped room. "Indeed, Roy, moving to Varrahan, as I said," she snapped back. "And I'm *very* busy preparing, so please feel free to be on your way at once!"

Roy only kept staring at her, and then came a swift step closer—but thankfully Gwyn lurched backward just in time, and grasped for a bushy pot of fennel to thrust between them. "Very, *very* busy," she said loudly. "Goodbye, both of you. And Father, I meant what I said about that horrible law. We will *not* be speaking again, until you find a way to fix it. And *end* it. *Permanently*."

Lord Anton's mouth began babbling again, yet more nonsense about it all being out of his power, but Gwyn cut him off mid-sentence, wildly waving her pot in the air. "Goodbye," she said, her voice rising. "Goodbye. Both of you!"

Her father and Roy exchanged a brief, meaningful look— saying, perhaps, *We'll discuss this later*—while something sharp and shaky jerked in Gwyn's belly. Something she had to keep in check, these men couldn't keep *doing* this to her, she was an accomplished herbalist, a certified midwife, she'd borne everything these two had hurled at her all these years, and now they couldn't even leave her alone in her own *apartment*?!

"Will you both just *listen* to me for once in your damned lives?!" she shouted at them, before she could stop the words from escaping. "I said, goodbye. *Now!*"

Her voice scraped through the too-small room, shrill and shivering, while her father and Roy shared another dark, speaking look. Until finally, *finally*, Roy raised his hands, spun on his heel, and strode from the room. And after another frantic wave from Gwyn's pot, her father did the same, casting her one last pleading, reproachful frown over his shoulder.

Gwyn slammed the door shut behind them, leaning back against it, her chest heaving—but it was almost as though they were both still standing here, looming over her, careless and condescending, making her small and foolish and ashamed. A dotty, unfashionable, plant-obsessed lord's daughter, who couldn't even hold the attention of her own damned betrothed. Who couldn't even move away from her selfish, spoiled father for more than a damned month, without him sending his horrid minions to drag her back.

And without even noticing it, she'd lunged for her candlewood, grasping its painful green spines. Digging them deep and forceful into her palms, while the pain lanced and screamed, obliterating the whole of the room in its wake.

And finally, all was still. And Gwyn had somehow found how to breathe again, her eyes fluttering closed, the certainty swelling in her thoughts.

She was fighting her fate, and making her own way, and moving to gods-damned Varrahan. And even if she had to poison her own lord father, she was never, *ever* coming back.

2

A fortnight later, Gwyn stepped out of her new house in Varrahan, and shut the door behind her.

It had been two weeks full of exhausting, expensive work. Packing up all her plants and belongings, hiring a top-tier team of movers, and then hovering restlessly about as they'd loaded her precious plants into wagons. She'd had to intervene more than once, and her candlewood had bestowed multiple movers with minor injuries—but in the end, the three-day ordeal had gone as well as she could have hoped, with all her plants still mostly intact.

And gods, the *house*. Gwyn had only ever visited Great-Aunt Agnes a few times growing up—Varrahan was a full two-day ride south of Dunburg, and her father had never spared much thought for her mother's relations—but the house was even more perfect than she'd remembered. It was snug and well-built, with a kitchen, a sitting room, and a bedroom, and it boasted large, glazed windows that opened and closed, a reliable well, and a deep-dug outdoor privy.

And most importantly, it was surrounded by a truly breathtaking garden. One that had become somewhat overgrown in recent years, but which still held an astonishing variety of perennial herbs and flowers and shrubs, all protectively encircled by a tall yew hedge. Gwyn had already spent several thoroughly delightful days weeding and digging, followed by cozy lamplit evenings poring over her reference books, working to identify any unfamiliar plants, and developing plans for their care and use.

The house's only possible drawback, if there was one, was the location. It was technically in Varrahan, which was a busy little town in the middle of Sakkin Province, with a variety of shops and amenities—but in truth, the property stood well on the outskirts of town, and its south side sat directly on the thick green edge of the Sakkin forest.

Which meant, of course, that Gwyn's lovely new garden looked directly toward Orc Mountain.

And Orc Mountain, she could admit, had proven rather more alarming than she'd expected. Looming huge and grey and craggy over its surrounding forest, streaming steady plumes of dense black smoke into the sky. Silently speaking of bustling activity, of latent power, of a simmering, very real *threat*.

And Gwyn was sick to death of being intimidated by powerful males, especially in her own damned home. And thankfully—she squared her shoulders as she strode down her narrow front lane—there were simple, straightforward ways to deal with orcs, unlike with Roy and her wretched father.

"I want to buy a crossbow," she told the man at the little armoury, on Varrahan's bustling main street. "The strongest one that I'll still be able to fire myself."

The man gave Gwyn a critical once-over, lingering dubiously on her slim frame, and her unimpressive height. "What's a girl like you need a crossbow for?" he asked. "Not goin' off to war, are you?"

Gwyn ground her teeth, and fixed the man with her most

withering glare. "I'm new to the area, and I live alone," she snapped back. "And my house is in the bloody shadow of bloody *Orc Mountain*!"

Gods above, she sounded just like her father, but thankfully the crease in the man's brow had faded, his head nodding. "Ah, so you're the new girl at Agnes' place," he said, as he turned to pluck a crossbow off the wall behind him. "Her niece, or summat?"

"Great-niece," Gwyn said stiffly. "Through my father's side. I grew up in Talford."

None of that last bit was true, of course, but Gwyn was determined to cast away all connections to her lord father and Dunburg for as long as humanly possible. At least, until her father's men showed up in a month to drag her back—but over the past weeks, her resolve on that front had only deepened. No matter what it took, she would *not* go back to Dunburg. She would find a way to escape her father for good. And she would also find a way to forget Roy, who was no doubt hopping happily from one woman's bed to the next in her absence.

Gwyn's stomach had unpleasantly spasmed at the thought, and she belatedly forced her attention back to the man, who was demonstrating how to load the crossbow's bolt. "You put this here, and then pull," he said, yanking on the steel lever. "Here, you try."

Gwyn managed it, just barely, and next the man waved her around back, to where he helpfully had a target set up outside. And while loading and firing the crossbow was an awkward business, Gwyn's aim with it turned out to be quite good, enough that the man looked grudgingly impressed.

"Not bad, girl," he said, once she'd followed him back inside. "Thing is"—he rubbed at his bearded chin—"if you're meanin' to use that against an orc, you might as well not bother."

"Why not?" Gwyn asked, eyeing him sharply as she

counted out coins. "Surely orcs aren't impervious to crossbow-bolts?"

The man was looking amused, now, his eyes again flicking up and down Gwyn's form. "Look, girl, if an orc decides he wants you," he said, "you're already done for. That great green bastard will be swiving upon you and draining your lifeblood before you've even seen him coming. And by next spring, his foul spawn will be using its claws to tear its bloody way outta your belly."

Gwyn's heart skipped a beat, her throat swallowing hard. "That will *not* happen," she said, a little too loudly. "The orcs have signed a comprehensive *peace-treaty*, and they've held to its terms ever since. And what's more, orc-sons are born just the same way as human ones are. There are no claws involved. And *no tearing*."

But the man actually laughed at her, his eyes dropping down to linger on Gwyn's waist. "You don't think that'll tear you, girl?" he scoffed. "Good luck with your crossbow, then."

Gwyn stared at him for a long, thundering moment—and before she could say something she'd surely regret, she grasped her new crossbow, along with the bolts and leather sling she'd purchased, and stalked out the door without a single look back.

No. *No.* She would not allow some stupid man's baseless, uninformed drivel to make her small and afraid. She was finally on her own, fighting her fate, making her own way— and she was taking reasonable precautions against intruders, and that was *all*. And truly, if these were the kinds of ridiculous tales these people believed, it only stood to reason that any affected women must be isolated and terrified. And that surely, Gwyn could be of service here. Surely she could *help*.

With that firmly in mind, she slung her crossbow onto her back, and set out to meet some of her new neighbours. Stopping by various shops and inns, introducing herself, letting it be known that she was a practicing herbalist and midwife, with experience managing difficult situations, and a firm commitment to confidentiality. Not openly mentioning orcs, of course, but word would surely travel, as it always did. And indeed, most of the women gave her distinctly knowing glances, and several even cast wary looks toward the ever-smoking Orc Mountain to the south.

It also turned out that Varrahan didn't currently have a resident midwife, and that women had been obliged to seek support from Ashford, the next town over. All of which should have been highly encouraging news, and proof of an excellent day's work.

But as Gwyn walked back home again in the deepening darkness, something somehow felt... different. Something that had her repeatedly glancing over her shoulder, and twitching at small sounds from the surrounding forest. While that awful man's words kept echoing and jangling, raising prickling gooseflesh along the backs of her arms.

If an orc decides he wants you, you're already done for. And by next spring...

And gods, Gwyn should have been well inured to rumours about orcs by now. She'd heard so many of them in her line of work—everything from tales of the orcs wielding magical powers, to whispers of them drinking women's blood, to reports that the orcs had bewitched several of the realm's *noble-women*. Even today, an unfamiliar woman had muttered something about an orc-crazed heiress, wreaking havoc and debauchery throughout the nearby town of Ashford.

But Gwyn had always sought to accept only what was either before her own eyes, or shared by reliable, objective sources. People caught in stressful circumstances were always more likely to spread any number of lies and half-truths, and in Gwyn's experience, it did no one any good to fall prey to conjecture and gossip and fear. Especially when there was real work to be done, and real solutions to be found.

Even so, she felt herself exhale a shaky sigh of relief as she finally stepped into her house, and turned to bar the door behind her. Noticing, when she somehow hadn't before, that the bar was a thin, flimsy-looking wooden slide—odd, because hadn't Great-Aunt Agnes feared being attacked by orcs?—and after an instant's frowning at it, Gwyn resolved that her next trip into town would involve a visit to a quality locksmith. For several new locks and barricades, perhaps. And maybe some strong steel bars on the windows, as well...

"Foolishness," she snapped at herself, as she spun and strode away toward her little bedroom, yanking off her dress. "It's *nothing*. There's a treaty. There hasn't been a kidnapping in almost two *years*."

She kept silently repeating that truth as she changed into her sleeping shift, and then cooked herself a simple supper. It was barely edible, as usual—her love of plants had unfortunately never translated into a love of cooking—and she only felt her unease rising as she grimly chewed, and then cleaned up again. Glancing more and more toward the darkness beyond her windows, and desperately fighting to ignore the chills creeping down her back.

"Oh, *fine*," she groaned at the ceiling, as she finally stalked over to grab her new crossbow from beside the door. And after carefully arming it with one of its deadly steel bolts, she placed it on the kitchen table beside her, its sharpened tip aimed directly toward the door.

It was enough to stop her looking at the windows, at least, and she resolutely pulled over her thick notebook, as well as a few clippings she'd taken from the garden that morning. And now, thank the gods, there was only this. Running her fingers over the clippings, making detailed notes and drawings, flipping through one reference book, and then another—

When before her, the door banged open. Bringing a harsh gust of wind that fluttered her lamp flame, scattered herbs and papers across the room, and made Gwyn leap up so fast she nearly knocked over her table.

It was... an *orc*. Huge, menacing, horrifying. Stripped to the waist, towering in her doorframe, and staring at her with deadly black eyes.

An orc. Here. For *her*?!

And Gwyn didn't think, didn't hesitate. Just snatched for the crossbow, drew it up, and aimed straight for the orc's heart.

"Like hell, orc," she said, and fired.

3

That should have been the end of it.

But rather than remaining still, and allowing Gwyn's undeniably impressive shot to impale him in the heart, the orc dropped, and *rolled*. Moving so swiftly that her eyes only caught a large black blur, streaking across her floor.

And when the world came aright again, it was with the door slammed shut, and a crossbow bolt embedded deep into it. And a huge, bare-chested, thoroughly terrifying orc, now standing well inside her kitchen.

"*Damn* it," Gwyn said, pawing desperately at the table for another bolt, but her fingers were trembling too much to even hold onto it, let alone arm the damned thing onto the damned shaking crossbow. While the damned orc just kept standing there, gazing at her, apparently entirely unaffected by the fact that she'd almost nailed him to her front door.

"What the hell," Gwyn said now, and her voice was shaking, too. "How *dare* you break into my property, orc. This is *my* land. *My* house."

The orc just kept looking at her, giving Gwyn a good chance

to look back—and *gods*, he was horrifying. He was tall and broad-shouldered, and his skin was a strange shade of greenish-grey, marked all over with visible scars. His eyes were dark and glittering, his jaw and cheekbones sharp and square, and his hair was a shaggy mass of thick chaotic black, reaching nearly to his shoulders. Not only that, he appeared to be barefoot, with *clawed toenails*, and the only item of clothing on his scarred greenish body was a pair of trousers that had been brutally chopped off at the knee. Unless one counted the cord hanging around his neck, which boasted a single large, curving, deadly-looking *tooth*.

The orc seemed to be taking equal stock of Gwyn, his black eyes running up and down her frame, and far too late she recalled that she was only wearing her sleeping shift, and a rather transparent one at that. Which meant that the orc—this brutal, hideous, half-dressed orc—was openly *ogling* her. His eyes lingering first on the slight swell of her breasts, with their dark peaks clearly on display through the thin silk, and then down to the shift's too-short length. And there was a strange little ripple down her back, because all he would have to do was walk over, lift her shift, and—

"Don't come any closer," Gwyn gasped, and she did manage to grip a bolt this time, pointing its sharpened end in the orc's general direction. "In fact, get out. This is *my* house."

The orc's still-wandering eyes finally rose back to her face, and if she wasn't mistaken, he looked almost *amused*. "Ach, I ken," he said, the words coming out accented, dusky, hoarse. "But you no welcome guest?"

Guest? "Of course I don't welcome orc guests!" Gwyn snapped back, and in her irritation seemed to find the presence of mind—and hand—to reload the crossbow, pulling back the lever with all her strength, and then placing the new bolt, while the orc just watched. "Also, a proper guest would make proper arrangements, and perhaps bring a proper gift, and most importantly, properly *knock* on the damned *door!*"

She aimed the crossbow back at the orc, who just kept standing there, still with that amused look on his harsh face. "Here," he said, with a fluid flourish of his lean muscled arm toward her. "Gift."

What? Gwyn's grip on the heavy crossbow faltered, her gaze darting down to his outstretched hand. A large, capable-looking hand, with long fingers that ended in sharp black *claws*—but as appalling as that sight should have been, Gwyn's eyes were locked on what those fingers were holding.

It was a plant. A *living* plant. One that had clearly been dug up with care, its roots and earth concealed in a thick wrapping of damp paper. And without even noticing that she'd moved, Gwyn had somehow stepped around the table, in order to better peer at the plant's large, palmate leaves and distinctive spiked purple flowers.

Her breath clamped in her throat, her eyes widening—because this wasn't just any plant. It was *chasteberry*. A plant which grew far beyond the sea to the south, and which Gwyn had never before encountered in person. But it was well known to be an excellent midwifery herb, capable of regulating women's monthly courses and managing related pain, and its small round berries were often imported, at costs far too prohibitive for her to afford.

And now, an orc simply happened to be carrying about a live chasteberry plant? And offering it to her as a *gift*?!

Gwyn shot an accusing glare up at the orc's face, but he was still looking amused, or perhaps even smug. "Gift," he repeated, low and languid, as he came a smooth, graceful step closer. "You like, ach?"

Gwyn twitched, and belatedly jerked up her still-loaded crossbow between them—but the orc only raised a thick black eyebrow, and came another step forward. Moving like he was a prowling forest cat, stalking his prey, and surely orcs had no right to glide like that, they were supposed to be clumsy lumbering *beasts*. Weren't they?

But the orc only came another sinuous step nearer, his glinting black eyes mocking on hers, and Gwyn felt herself swallow, hard. She'd never actually seen an orc up close before, let alone spoken to one—and especially one who was still casually carrying a *chasteberry* plant in his clawed hand. But suddenly her thoughts were swarming with all those memories, with the hushed voices and flushed faces of multiple different women, whispering their shameful confessions with downcast eyes.

He wasn't at all what I expected. He was so... different. His hands. His smell. The way he tasted. The way he—

"Don't come any closer," Gwyn gasped at the orc, wildly brandishing her crossbow between them. "I *will* shoot you."

Thankfully the orc stopped moving, though his mouth had quirked up, flashing her a row of sharp white teeth. Complete with a set of unnerving, wolf-like *fangs*—and now here was the horrid memory of that horrid man today, speaking all those horrid words. *That great green bastard will be swiving upon you and draining your lifeblood before you've even seen him coming. And by next spring...*

Gwyn shivered all over, her heartbeat frantically skipping in her chest. "What the hell," she managed, "do you *want*, orc."

The orc gave a rolling shrug of his bare shoulder, and another blatant, lingering glance down at Gwyn's scantily clad form. "Wish to greet new neighbour," he said, in that smooth, accented voice. "See if she like orc *guest* as much as woman before her."

Wait. Gwyn's grip on her crossbow faltered again, her eyes narrowing on the orc's smug, still-smiling face. "You are *surely* not implying," she heard her distant voice say, "that my Great-Aunt Agnes welcomed *you* into this house! Or into her—"

She broke off there, her gaze darting reflexively toward her bedroom—and curse him, but the orc only flashed her another knowing, white-toothed grin. "*I* no knew her bed," he replied coolly, angling his shaggy head at the bedroom door, "but it yet *reek* of Bautul, ach?"

Good gods. Gwyn's already-unsteady body had badly staggered, and her shaky hand clutched for the table behind her, gripping at its solid wood with painful force. "Im-impossible," she countered. "G-great-Aunt Agnes was surely *eighty years old*, if she was a day!"

But the orc's grin looked even more mocking than before, and perhaps contemptuous, too. "Ach, and this was luck, you no ken?" he asked. "I no envy any woman who must grow and birth Bautul—"

But it was there, oddly enough, that he abruptly broke off. His mouth thinning, his thick brows furrowing close together, while his clawed hand slipped up to finger at the large tooth hanging around his neck. Almost as if he were—disconcerted, somehow, or even unguarded, for the first time since he'd broken into her damned house.

And rather than taking proper advantage of the moment, and shooting him, as she obviously ought to have done—Gwyn felt her grip further slackening on her crossbow, her head tilting sideways. "What's a *Bautul*?" she heard herself ask. "And more importantly, *why* would my eighty-year-old great-aunt tolerate it in her bedroom?!"

And gods, why had she even asked such a stupid question—surely she understood precisely what this orc was talking about—but curse her, perhaps this was why. The way his expression instantly cleared, his eyes back to amused again, the devious smile curling at his lips.

"You wish to learn, woman?" he murmured, as he came another smooth, rolling step closer. "Wish me to show you?"

Gwyn's mouth dropped open, her eyes gaping at his face—

and her heart was suddenly thundering in her chest, frantic and furious. "I wish for no such thing," she hissed, around her strangely tangled tongue. "In fact, my only wish at the moment is for you to vanish from my sight at *once!*"

The orc's black brows rose, his mouth still quirked into that mocking smile. "If this is truth," he drawled, "then why you no now shoot me, woman?"

Gwyn swallowed against her unnaturally dry throat, and yanked her crossbow back up between them. "Because I don't want to deal with your oversized dead body," she retorted, "or spend the rest of the night mopping up your *blood* from my clean new floor!"

The orc's grin broadened, more amusement sparkling in his dark eyes. "Ach, you are wiser than you look, woman," he said lightly. "Mayhap we then go into wood"—he jerked his head in the direction of the forest—"and you shoot me there instead?"

Gods *curse* the audacious bastard, because Gwyn actually felt her own mouth twitching up, enough that she had to press her lips tightly together. "You insolent *fiend*," she snapped, though there wasn't nearly enough heat in it. "You cannot call me wise one moment, and then ask me to go alone with you into a forest the next!"

She again flourished the crossbow toward him, perhaps to add some small semblance of threat to her words—but the orc only kept grinning at her, his eyes indulgent and appreciative, as though she were a particularly amusing kitten he'd happened to stumble upon. And as Gwyn watched, her heartbeat still furiously pounding, he came another slow, deliberate step closer—close enough that the armed crossbow was actually nudging him in the chest, the sharp bolt pricking slightly into his grey-green skin.

"Then mayhap I ask this," he murmured, and in a swift movement, his hand—his *orc hand*—had come up to stroke Gwyn's cheek. And it was huge, and warm, and *on her face*, its deadly claws gently scraping her *skin*. While he leaned in even closer, his nostrils flaring, his black tongue brushing against his lips...

"Mayhap I now show you all good guest may grant," he continued, his voice pitched even lower. "And if you no like, I shall go, and never come again. And thus, no heavy corpse. No blood. Naught to clean."

It was appalling logic, from an appalling orc, who still had an armed crossbow-bolt pointing straight at his heart—and gods, Gwyn should have shot him. It would have been so easy, the neat simple solution, precisely what any intelligent woman would do, when confronted with a shameless fearless orc in her own damned *house*—

But the orc's clawed thumb had slipped to Gwyn's mouth, stroking softly against her bottom lip. And against all reason, all possible fathoming, she felt her lips slightly parting at the touch, her breath expelling harsh against the orc's skin. An action that seemed to gain his immediate approval, judging by the fluttering of his black eyelashes, and the low, heated growl from his throat.

Damn. Gwyn's still-thundering heart skipped a beat, her breath drawing in—and suddenly she was swarmed with a rich, musky male scent. A scent that had perhaps been curling through the room ever since this orc had stepped inside it, all herbs and earth and growing green things...

Gwyn couldn't help another inhale, deeper this time, and another low, approving growl purred from the orc's mouth. While his tall, graceful body eased even closer, his eyes long-lashed and half-lidded, his thumb stroking firmer against her lips. And in this moment, there seemed no reason not to open her mouth a little more, to perhaps let that teasing warmth inside...

The orc took the opportunity without hesitation, his thumb slipping past her lips, finding its way within. And oh, he tasted just as good as he smelled, strong and savoury, curling deep into Gwyn's already-heated belly. And his touch was so gentle, his sharp claw so sweetly stroking at her tongue...

"Suck," he ordered, the word a hushed, harsh caress. "Show me what is mine."

His. Gwyn's breath gasped again, her thighs clenching—and without thinking, without following, she somehow... *obliged.* Sucking the orc's thumb as powerfully as she could, dragging it full into her mouth, feeling the impossible, inexplicable thrill of its claw nudging against the back of her throat—

And in that moment, if the orc had leaned forward, and pressed his foreign, dangerous, fang-toothed mouth to Gwyn's cheek, or her neck, she would surely have moaned, or even arched into his touch. She might have even let the crossbow fall harmlessly away, in favour of slipping her tingly hands around his shoulders, stroking that scarred grey-green skin, perhaps even curling her fingers into the mess of his dark hair—

But instead of coming closer, or kissing her, as Gwyn might have very much wished, the orc tipped back his shaggy head, and—*laughed.* The sound slicing bright and mocking through the hot thick air, and as Gwyn's hazy eyes blinked up at him, it occurred to her that this was... *triumph* in his laugh, in his eyes. It was *victory.* It was this outrageous orc clearly saying, without words, that she'd been a pushover, an easy target, ripe for the picking. That she was clearly willing to do whatever he wanted, even after he'd broken into her damned *house.*

And now that this brazen, belligerent orc had her in the palm of his hand—literally—he would use her as he pleased. He would use her exactly the way Roy always had, and casually toss her away afterward. And in the process, Gwyn risked becoming just like all those women she'd helped, with their anguished terrified whispers, their astonishing tales that suddenly felt far, far too vivid. Far too real.

And gods, she was finally on her own, fighting her fate, making her own way. And just because an orc, of all conceivable creatures, had barely even *touched* her, she was about to risk her entire future on him? On this? On an *orc*, who didn't even know her damned *name*?!

Gwyn frantically flung herself sideways, away from the orc's touch, well out of his reach—and thankfully, he didn't try to stop her. Only stood there and watched as she staggered across the room, one hand clutching at the nearest chair for support, the other gripping desperately at the crossbow.

"Nice try, asshole," she choked toward him. "Next time you want to seduce someone, you'd be wise to wait until *afterwards* to begin laughing at them."

The smile had fully faded from the orc's face, and his shaggy head cocked sideways, his clawed hand curling into a slow fist at his side. "I no laugh *at* you, woman," he said, with particular emphasis on the *at*. "I laugh—"

"*With* me?" Gwyn demanded, though her voice abominably cracked. "No. *Rubbish.* You thought you won, so you had a good chuckle, and thereby lost yourself an easy target. Better luck next time, you vile arrogant *scum*."

She'd somehow found the wherewithal to properly aim the bow again, but her hands were badly shaking, and gods, she could hardly see through the water swarming her blinking eyes. And what the hell even was this, she didn't give a toss about a filthy mocking orc, even if he smelled like plants and earth, even if her belly was still burning with abominable heat. Even if she could still taste him on her tongue...

The orc was still looking at her, his dark eyes now gone entirely unreadable, his hand again reaching for that tooth around his neck. Stroking it again and again, as though it somehow meant something to him, and Gwyn watched his lashes sweep closed, his throat visibly convulsing.

"Ach," he said, quiet. "I ought—"

But he was going to try to coax her, to use his voice and his smile and his lean, fluid body to beguile her again. And Gwyn knew how this went, she'd walked this dead-end road with Roy hundreds of times, and she was finally making her own way, away from these appalling, appealing males. Away from this foolishness, *forever*.

"No," Gwyn said again, her voice still wretchedly wavering. "No. I gave you a chance, orc, and you sure as hell didn't deserve it. Now get out."

The orc blinked at her, his eyes darting uneasily toward the door, and Gwyn wildly, heedlessly brandished her crossbow. "Did you not hear me?!" she shrieked. "Get *out*, orc, before I shoot you! Like I clearly should have done *long* ago, damn the bloody mess!"

The orc's watching eyes were very still, but his mouth slightly quirked, perhaps about to make another jest about blood and corpses—but a strange sound had escaped Gwyn's throat, almost half-growl, half-scream.

And finally, *finally*, the orc smoothly spun on his heel, and strode for the door. And with a sharp flourish of movement, the door slammed shut behind him, hard enough to shake the floor beneath Gwyn's feet.

He was gone.

4

leep refused to come that night.

Gwyn fretfully tossed and turned in her bed, alternately glaring at the ceiling in the moonlight, and reaching to grope for the still-armed crossbow lying on the bed beside her. No doubt a grave safety hazard, but she couldn't seem to bear the thought of putting it aside, away, out of her reach. And therefore possibly granting an orc—*that* orc—another opportunity to try to have his devious way with her.

And that was a very real risk, Gwyn now knew, because a careful post-orc inspection of the door—now with a crossbow-bolt embedded deep into it—had proven all her worst fears. The door's wooden slide had remained perfectly intact, meaning that the orc had somehow been able to open it from the outside, no doubt with one of those black claws. Perhaps the same claw that had slipped so sweetly into her mouth, nudging its velvet threat against her tongue, and...

Gwyn groaned aloud and rubbed at her eyes, flopping her head back on the pillow. Fighting, and failing, to rid her brain of the vision of the orc, so tall and lean and powerful, with that teasing smile always lurking at his mouth. And the sound of his voice, all low sultry honey, purring his audacious claims as though they were incontestable fact. Claims about Great-Aunt Agnes. About orcs in this damned *bedroom*.

And *surely* that had been a lie, craftily created to confound and convince her—and finally Gwyn shoved herself out of bed, and stalked back into the kitchen. To where she'd willingly touched an orc, and to where—she halted, and glowered toward it—he'd left the chasteberry plant he'd brought.

It was just sitting there on the table next to her notebook, silent and innocuous, as though it had always belonged there. And Gwyn was still cursing herself over that, because she hadn't even seen the orc put the plant down, and couldn't even remember when he must have done so. When he'd first touched her, perhaps, but his attention had been so thoroughly upon her, his warm hand caressing so softly against her cheek...

"Gods damn you, orc," she snapped into the darkness, but it didn't even slightly settle the chaos swarming her thoughts. And after another twitching, pulsing moment, she lurched over to her candlewood plant, yanked off a sprig of it, and dragged its sharp spine straight down her forearm.

The pain kicked and flashed, snapping white and vicious through her clamped-taut body—but curse her, it helped. Edging away the jangling jolting unease, returning the deep breaths to her lungs.

Yes, she'd been targeted by an orc. She'd even been slightly—*slightly*—compromised by an orc. But all things considered, she'd still managed the situation. She'd spotted the orc's lying, devious intent, and called him out on it, and escaped his slippery clutches.

And today—Gwyn frowned at the door—she would indeed make a much-needed visit to a locksmith, and put some proper barriers on that damned door, and the windows as well. And then she could rest easy, and sleep comfortably again, and everything would be fine. She was fighting her fate, making her own way. She was doing this.

Something warm and sticky was dripping down her palm—good gods, her *blood*—and she belatedly jerked toward the wash-basin, dabbing the scrape clean, wincing at the sight of the faded white scars beneath it. And sleeping was surely a lost cause at this point, so after a heavy sigh, she lit a candle, sank into her chair at the table, and pulled over her favourite reference book.

She spent the rest of the night reading about chasteberry, and making detailed notes about its care and harvesting. And as the sky gradually began to brighten, she finally replanted the chasteberry into a proper pot, furiously fighting to ignore the faint trace of the orc's distinctive rich scent upon it, and the obvious care with which its delicate roots had been wrapped.

But the more she thrust down thoughts of the orc, the more they seemed to bubble back up again. How had he known to bring a plant as a gift—and especially one so rare and useful as this? And how had he possibly managed to acquire it, so far out of its native habitat? Surely the realm's most prestigious herbalists wouldn't sell to orcs, so had he somehow brought it from the south himself? Or *grown* it himself?

Whatever the case, it certainly suggested some level of thought and planning on the orc's part, which seemed at utter odds with his breezy laughter, his flippant words, his disheveled appearance. With even the way he'd so casually broken into her house, clearly knowing how to work the door, knowing Gwyn was alone. Knowing she was a herbalist. Knowing Great-Aunt Agnes...

Gwyn loudly cursed under her breath, and finally washed and dressed, and made the short walk into town. And then waited, jumpy and jittery, outside the locksmith's closed shop, until he unlatched the door, and waved her inside.

"I need a new set of locks installed at my house," she told

him over his counter, her voice sharp. "The most secure ones you have. And some bars for my windows, as well."

The locksmith gave her undoubtedly frantic face a curious once-over, and reached for his nearby notebook. "You're the new midwife at Agnes', eh?" he replied. "Welcome to town. Here, I'll get you in for next week."

And while Gwyn should have been thoroughly gratified by the fact that even the locksmith already knew who she was— word was spreading, as it should—all she could feel was the urgency, sparking in her hands and feet. "Next *week*?" she heard herself echo. "No. I need it now. At once. *Today*."

The locksmith's lined brow furrowed, his hand hesitating on his charcoal. "Sorry, but I'm booked solid this week," he said. "What's your rush? Aren't having any trouble over there, are you?"

His gaze felt far too piercing for Gwyn's liking, and she felt her cheeks flooding with an abrupt, unnerving heat. *Any trouble*. Trouble with orcs, he meant, because his wary eyes had even glanced due south, in the direction of Orc Mountain. As if that particular information might spur him to action, or help launch some kind of investigation, or perhaps even send a ravenous armed mob to riot around Gwyn's house...

"No, no trouble at all," she heard herself say, far too quickly. "I'm—just a little nervous, I suppose."

And gods, why the *hell* had she just said that. Why wasn't she just telling this kind man the full truth, and welcoming the raging mob with open arms. She was finally making her own way, and she needed to stamp out the male rubbish from her life, *forever*.

But even as she opened her mouth to correct it—*actually, an orc broke into my house last night*—her throat oddly constricted, her fingernails digging into her palms. Her thoughts swarming, suddenly, with the too-vivid vision of that lean, fluid body, sprawled motionless in a pool of blood. His long limbs askew, his devious mouth permanently silenced, his laughing eyes forever gone dark and cold and empty...

"Next week it is, then," interjected the locksmith's satisfied voice. "Now, tell me what you need."

Gwyn somehow managed to reply, and accordingly set up the appointment for the following week. But as she walked back into the street again, her feet felt strangely wobbly, her brain unleashing a torrent of well-warranted protests and accusations. Didn't she *want* to bar the orc from her house? Didn't she *want* to see that laughing, manipulating asshole get exactly what he deserved?

Didn't she?

"Excuse me," said an unfamiliar, tentative voice behind her. "Are you the new midwife?"

Gwyn gratefully turned, and found herself faced with a pretty, plump, red-cheeked woman. "I am indeed," she replied, as steadily as she could. "Is there anything I can help you with?"

The woman stammered a flustered, incoherent-sounding reply, as she clinked what sounded like a few coins in her pocket—and thankfully Gwyn had been in this business long enough to easily discern her meaning, and flashed her a warm, reassuring smile. "I've certainly got just the thing," she said. "Why don't you come along to my place, and I'll do it up for you?"

The woman eagerly obliged, and soon she was comfortably seated at Gwyn's table, while Gwyn carefully crushed a bowl of fresh silphium seeds, and then poured the juice into a little vial. "You'll need to drink one of these each moon to prevent pregnancy," she told the woman, as she handed over the vial, and accepted her coins in exchange. "If you're consistent, it has a very high efficacy rate. However, to increase your chances, you need to have your man pull out as well. No 'mistakes' or 'just this once' nonsense, all right? We women need to watch ourselves with men, and be smarter than they are. No exceptions."

She felt herself wince at that last bit, but luckily the woman didn't seem to notice. And after thanking Gwyn effusively, she went cheerfully on her way, leaving Gwyn alone and unsettled again, and frowning darkly at the door. At that crossbow-bolt, and that damned flimsy wooden slide, which that damned devious orc could open at his leisure.

No mistakes. No exceptions. No trouble at all...

Gwyn's mouth barked out a noise much like a growl, and she finally fumbled for her silphium seeds, and made up another dose. Rather larger than her usual monthly amount, and rather early, too—but she could *not* afford to take any chances with this. She was making her own way. Getting rid of the rubbish, for good.

She swallowed down the bitter liquid with a grimace, and then forced herself to focus on her day's tasks. There were plants to water and attend to, seeds to harvest and prepare, stems and leaves to dry or crush or boil or steep. Not to mention the outdoor garden, too, and after several hours' productive work under the hot sun, she even set up an impromptu crossbow target beside her rose bush, and launched into some shooting practice, as well.

It should have helped. It should have thrust away all remaining thoughts of the orc, and Roy, and Gwyn's combined failures over the course of this past day. It should have made her far too tired to keep glancing over her shoulder, her heart-beat erratically skipping, while the occasional shudder quivered down her spine.

The orc wouldn't dare come back. Not after last night. Would he?

But once the sky had finally darkened to blackness, and Gwyn had washed, changed, eaten, and lit her reading lamp, it felt like an army of aphids was crawling under her skin, searching for a way out. Making her jump at tiny noises, her gaze constantly glancing toward the door, her clammy, trembly hands incessantly reaching to stroke the loaded crossbow. And she was both exhausted, and wide awake, and it was late, and what the hell was he waiting for, and perhaps she should go harvest her candlewood again, and—

"Where *are* you, orc," she groaned aloud, digging her palms into her eyes. "Just get it *over* with."

Nothing happened, of course, and finally Gwyn lost the battle with her flailing brain, and jerked toward her candle-wood. Her hands eagerly reaching for their cruel spines, the relief already ringing through her thoughts—

When behind her, something rapped on the door. Loud, quick, decisive.

Someone. Was—here.

Gwyn's heart surged in her chest, her legs staggering straight toward the door. And without calling out, without even thinking, she shoved aside the flimsy slide, and flung the door wide open.

It was the orc.

5

T he orc was here. Again. Standing tall and casual outside Gwyn's door, his eyes cool, his grey-green bare shoulder leaning against the doorframe.

And in his clawed hand, this time, he held a single, pure white rose. It was a variety Gwyn had never before seen, and she felt her frantic eyes briefly narrowing on it—where had he found *this* one?!—before darting back to his face. His harsh, angular, grey-green face, with its raised black brows, its ever-quirking mouth.

And as Gwyn gaped at him, her own mouth fallen entirely slack, his smile slightly broadened, showing more of those deadly gleaming teeth. "You no shoot me today, woman?" he asked, his low voice sparking something quick and warm in her belly. "Or you wish me to wait here, whilst you ready your bow?"

His amused eyes had glanced meaningfully behind her, toward where her crossbow was—Gwyn's hands clenched to fists—still lying uselessly on the table. And gods above, why hadn't she at least remembered to grab it before opening the door, what if it had been a whole *horde* of orcs come to loot and pillage and—

"No, you great arse," Gwyn loudly snapped, over that deeply alarming thought. "Now get in, before someone sees you."

She jerked her head toward the room behind her, even as her rioting rational brain loudly pointed out that the likelihood of the orc being seen here was surely almost nonexistent—but the orc's broad, sudden grin instantly set her thoughts scattering again, her heart wildly roaring in her chest.

"Ach, as you wish," he drawled, his voice and eyes brimming with mockery—but before Gwyn could protest that, or change her mind, he pushed off the doorframe, and strode straight toward her. His big hand reaching for her *face*, good *gods*—but she didn't move, didn't even try to argue. Only felt her lashes fluttering, her breath catching, as those warm fingers spread wide on her cheek, tilting her face up.

His brows had lifted, almost as if asking a silent question—and curse her, but Gwyn answered with an exhale, harsh and shuddering. Still not moving, not thinking, not even as the orc slowly bent his head, and... *kissed* her.

It was a rush of heat, a shouting storm of shock and sensation. A tilting, swirling unreality, with an orc's soft, heated lips teasing gentle against hers, his clawed hand sinking into her hair. While his musky green scent flooded the air between them, and his long, fluid, muscled body eased closer, fitting tall and effortless against hers...

Gwyn felt herself gasp into his mouth, her hand somehow clutching against the warm, silken skin of his arm. And in return he actually chuckled, his body sliding even closer, as a slick, slippery *tongue* brushed brief and hungry against her lips—

She was kissing an orc. She was... *kissing* an *orc*?!

Gwyn hurled herself backwards, far, *far* too late. Reeling

away from his warmth, his lean strength, his damned devious tongue. And oh, she could still *taste* him, could still feel the silk of his skin under her fingers, could still—

She could still see *outside*. Could see the night's darkness beyond him, through the propped-open door. And what the *hell*, she'd been kissing an orc with the door thrown wide open?! And good gods, she was going to *murder* this bastard, and clearly she should have eagerly welcomed the rioting mob, as well.

The orc was still smirking, as though flaunting his indisputable victory over her—and when Gwyn belatedly lurched to shut the door, she was disconcerted to discover he'd already somehow closed it. Even though his eyes hadn't once left hers, and his hand smoothly reached up to tuck the rose behind her ear.

Gwyn briefly braced herself, anticipating the certain prickling of thorns—but there was no scraping, no pain. Only the orc stepping slightly backwards, his warm hand again tilting her chin up, while his glinting eyes flicked down, and up, and down again.

And that, of course, was because Gwyn was wearing another sleeping shift. Another short, flimsy, entirely inappropriate sleeping shift, which blatantly hinted at everything beneath. And why in the gods' names had she dressed in this, rather than in multiple complicated layers of pantaloons and petticoats? What was she *thinking*?

But as the orc's eyes kept looking, *lingering*, their mockery slowly faded. And instead, there was an odd, quiet stillness in them, a quick, curious convulsing in his corded throat.

"You dress for me?" his low voice asked. "Wish me to come?"

The scent of him was again swarming Gwyn's lungs, all rich and musky and green—and it took far, far too much effort to shove herself away again. To stagger beyond the reach of that warm hand, that damned delicious smell.

"No," she snapped, tightly crossing her arms over her chest, valiantly fighting to ignore the appalling truth of her peaked nipples jutting against the fabric. "I want *answers* from you, orc. And that is *all*."

The amusement had instantly returned to the orc's eyes, his brows rising. Clearly waiting for her to continue, so Gwyn squared her shoulders, and dragged in breath. "Where did you get the chasteberry plant," she said. "How did you keep it alive in a climate that's so unsuited for it. And how the *hell*"—her eyes narrowed—"did you know I wanted one."

The orc's brows ticked higher, while something Gwyn couldn't read moved across his eyes. And when he smiled again, it looked a little too practiced, a little too easy, almost as if it were a mask he'd assumed at will.

"Ach, any wise woman should wish for this," he replied. "And orcs have long learnt the ways of the earth, ach?"

But it wasn't really an answer, and Gwyn felt her eyes narrowing further, searching the sharp lines of his face. "Do you mean to say *you* grew and cared for it?" she demanded. "And surely you don't mean me to believe that you honestly think *any* woman would welcome such a gift?"

His smile twitched a little higher, quick and casual, and it distantly occurred to Gwyn that he had an unfairly appealing smile—and also, that it was again hiding something. Hinting, surely, that he knew more than he was letting on. And since it wasn't like orcs could just publicly saunter about, collecting information from random townspeople and passersby, that had to mean...

"You *have* been spying on me," Gwyn said, slow, but certain. "Maybe even *targeting* me. Haven't you? For how long? *Why*?"

The orc's eyes blinked, once, his head cocked sideways, the casual smile still pasted on his face—and then he stepped forward, swift and graceful. "Your kinswoman took my kind into her bed," he said coolly. "Why no you, also?"

Gods, not that again, and Gwyn couldn't help a reflexive grimace, a hard shake of her head. "You don't get to pin this on my great-aunt, asshole," she countered. "Sure, she liked plants, but she likely wouldn't have known chasteberry from pipe-weed. How the hell did you know *I* would?"

The orc blinked again, his head still tilted, and for the briefest of instants, that might have been almost appreciation in his dark eyes. "Little house now *reek* of herbs," he said lightly. "Smell a full league away, ach?"

Gwyn's arms tightened over her chest, and she jerked another sharp shake of her head. "Oh, so now you're claiming that you could identify all the herbs currently in my house with smell alone?" she demanded. "And what, then you determined that chasteberry was missing, so you decided to magically procure one from your secret stash at Orc Mountain, and give it to me? All in hopes of weaselling your sneaky way into my *bed*?!"

The amusement had flicked back across the orc's eyes, while a more genuine-looking smile curled at his lips. "This seems good account, woman," he murmured. "Now we mate, or no?"

Gwyn was struck momentarily speechless, her mouth uselessly opening and closing—this orc didn't truly think she was *buying* his rubbish?!—and he took advantage of the opportunity to come another step closer. His glittering eyes again flicking up and down Gwyn's scantily-clad form, while his clawed hand dropped to casually stroke at the front of his *trousers*.

"The—the *hell*, orc," Gwyn sputtered, but oh gods, he was *still doing it*. That easy, audacious hand gripping tighter against the fabric, slowly stroking up and down. Showing her the truly shocking length of him, reaching fully to his trousers' *waist*.

And she could even see it pulsing, *flexing*, as if eagerly twitching into his fingers' touch...

The whispers of one particular client had been relentlessly rising in Gwyn's head—*His prick was that of a god*, she'd said—and Gwyn belatedly forced her eyes back up to the orc's face. Which still bore that sharp-toothed grin, devious and smug and hungry, as his other hand came up to rake through his shaggy black hair. His head tilting slightly backward, his eyes half-lidded, the movement sensuous and graceful. Showing off his glistening bare chest, the hard ripples of his abdomen, the shifting muscle in that long fluid arm...

Wait. The orc was actually—*flaunting* himself to her. Doing this on *purpose*. Trying to distract Gwyn from her questions, very important questions, but now he was shaking out his hair, showing her the long line of his corded neck, the elegant taper of his pointed ears...

"You like," his low voice murmured, his hooded eyes far too knowing on hers. "Wish for more, ach?"

Gwyn twitched all over, and her mouth snapped open to protest—but curse her, no words would seem to come out. And in return, the orc actually *laughed*, all swaggering obnoxious insolence, as his other hand dropped to join the first on his trousers, unloosing the tie at his waist with an easy flick of his claw...

And then, slow, deliberate, arrogant, those clawed hands slid down inside the trousers, and smoothly guided them downwards. Until the fabric sagged low on the sharp muscled cut of his hips, and showed Gwyn... *everything*.

She was blatantly staring, but there seemed no possible way to stop, because—well—*damn*. Those women hadn't been lying. He was—he was—

"You are—disrobed," she somehow squeaked, her voice high-pitched and very far away. "In my *house*."

The orc's grin was surely genuine now, likely because Gwyn

still couldn't stop staring, her gaze and her thoughts seemingly attached—arrested—on this orc's audacious bare prick. Long, grey, smooth, swollen, jutting out straight toward her. Wanting her. *Claiming* her.

The bollocks below it were just as impressive, thick and hairy and bulging, and as Gwyn stared, one of the orc's hands—now somehow minus the claws?!—came down to caress their heavy weights. Rolling them between familiar fingers, brazenly displaying them for her, while his other hand circled around the base of his hard grey length, and slowly slid upwards.

Gwyn gulped aloud, and the orc gave a low, breathy chuckle as he did it again, and again. Playing with himself in her kitchen, like an utterly debauched *heathen*. And while it occurred to Gwyn that she should surely shout at him, or perhaps lunge for her crossbow—she somehow found that she didn't, in fact, want him to stop. Especially not now, not with that thick bead of white already pooling at his blunt tip...

"You like," he said again, hoarse, husky, as that hand pumped up again, and again. Doing it as smoothly and fluidly as he did everything else, as if bringing himself off in a strange woman's kitchen was an art form, or a dance, and not the shockingly grievous imposition that it actually was.

Or was it, because Gwyn's tongue had brushed against her lips, and her thoughts had somehow become twisted, disjointed, vague. Lingering less on the fact that an orc was doing such things in her kitchen, and more on the heat pooling in her own belly, the tight snap of tension in the musky-smelling air. On the way the orc's lithe, self-assured graceful-ness had seemed to stutter, hitching on his suddenly harsh-sounding breaths...

And as she looked, it distantly occurred to her that in this moment, the orc didn't seem casual or effortless at all. That his easy, fluid movements were all tight, brutal control, and that beneath those half-lidded eyes, he was watching her. Weighing her. Applying considerable focus and skill to sway her, to seduce her, to *compromise* her...

"Why," she heard herself say, her voice rasping. "Why me."

The orc lurched a step closer, the movement oddly harsh and jerky—while the hand on that long grey heft had begun pumping faster, stronger. Coaxing out more liquid from the tip, until it had become a dangling string of thick, viscous white. Which—Gwyn's throat spasmed—he reached to catch in easy fingers, and then kept stroking, rubbing himself all over with it, until his length was shining, slick, dripping.

But he was still watching her like that, still evaluating her, still not answering her questions. Just like he hadn't truly answered *any* of her earlier questions, either, had he? And here in the fog, pinned in the power of his focus, breathing the dizzying green scent of him, Gwyn almost, almost didn't care...

Almost.

"Why me," she repeated, the words a croak. "Tell me."

He came another step closer, and it was sheer relief in the haze, a swarming cloud of heat and hunger. His tall, powerful body so close, so resolved, his fluttering eyes drinking her up like that, his control cracking, slipping—

"Why," she insisted, and this time she thrust a hand to his bare chest, stopping him, blocking him—and he visibly shivered at the touch, his heartbeat thundering against her fingers. His black eyes snapped wide, his body entirely still against her, his scent somehow just slightly sharper than before...

"No more," she choked, to those eyes, "until you tell me."

His body under her hand shivered again, as though Gwyn had just wielded some unspeakable power over him—and when his eyes squeezed shut, there was a sudden, inexplicable heave in her belly. He was going to refuse. He was going to ruin this. He was going to leave...

"Please," she whispered, and without at all meaning to, she

jerked closer. Deeper into that shuddering heat, that swirling rich scent—and into that brazen, audacious, dripping-white part of him, now nudging hard and strong against her. But she didn't care, perhaps she even wanted it there, streaking its warm wetness against her too-thin sleeping shift...

And the orc *knew*. He knew it all, in one swift glance downwards from those intent black eyes. And Gwyn could see his throat bobbing, his black tongue slipping against his lips, while his other hand lifted to absently stroke that tooth around his neck. Again, as if it meant something, as if it might answer for him, or even come to his rescue...

But she didn't drop her eyes, didn't relent. And finally the orc groaned, the sound quiet and hissing, almost like a sigh. Almost like... capitulation.

"You are... quick," he said, his voice very low, somehow different than before. "Sharp. Wise. Careful. You learn from the earth and its ways. And below all this"—his hand slid up, nudged under her chin—"you are hungry. So hungry. Ach?"

Oh. Gwyn was frozen beneath his eyes, in the astonishing awareness behind his words, in the distant realization that his hand on her chin was still wet with his own slick. In his rich scent swarming her, part of her, just like his eyes, his knowing, his understanding. His sure admission that he *had* been watching her, wanting her, and now...

"Now we mate," he murmured, his voice a heated caress, low and sweet. "We sate all our hunger this night. Ach?"

And in that moment, in the heady weight of his voice his eyes his touch, there seemed no other recourse. Only holding her eyes to the truth in his—and then closing that last little space between them. Filling it with heat and power and craving, with the bare honesty of an orc's bared body, his bared-open soul, pressed pure and powerful to hers.

"Yes," she whispered. "We will."

6

Gwyn's words were met with a growl. A loud, guttural growl, deep and hoarse and objectively terrifying, rumbling from the orc's mouth.

"Yes," he breathed, his powerful body shifting closer against Gwyn's, his huge heated hands dropping to grip her waist over her shift. "*Mine.*"

But Gwyn wasn't alarmed, or terrified, or any of the other available appropriate responses. Not even with this audacious orc now *here*, his big hands running strong and possessive down her sides, while his face bent to bury itself in her neck, inhaling deep.

"Mine," he said again, pulling away long enough to flash her one of those sudden grins, wicked and sharp. "I claim. Tonight."

There was no arguing with the bastard, especially with Gwyn's eyes fluttering like this, her breath gasping short and shallow. While the orc's big hands kept roving, running over her too-thin shift, and then hesitating on the slight swell of her breasts, cupping one with warm heat, stroking the other's hard nipple with his thumb.

"Comely woman," he said, quiet, and in that instant the smile abruptly vanished, leaving only a hushed, steady intentness. "Ripe. I like."

He liked. And that was oddly disconcerting, perhaps even beyond those hungry hands now gripping Gwyn's bare hips below her shift, and sliding the flimsy fabric upwards. Undressing her, her distant thoughts shouted, an *orc* was *undressing* her—but she could only seem to choke for breath, arch her body into the warmth of his touch, raise her arms so he could slide the shift over her head.

It left her standing fully naked and exposed in her kitchen, faced with an equally naked and exposed orc. An orc whose swollen heft—Gwyn shot a heated glance downwards—was currently leaking even more thick white, dripping it copiously onto the floor between them.

He saw her looking, of course he did, and one of those big hands went down to pump himself again, slow, fluid, slick. Coating himself even more with it, the scent of earth and green rising ever stronger between them.

"You like," he murmured again, that lazy smile back on his mouth. "You welcome in you."

In you. Gwyn's naked body gave a hard, thrilling shudder, perhaps with fear or something else entirely, and suddenly here were the orc's hands again, one of them still slick and sticky, sliding over her skin. Caressing strong and purposeful over her bare belly, her breasts, her arse, all sheer sensation and smooth, supple heat, and his face was in her neck again, his muscled strength so close, his deep inhale filling his chest.

He was speaking again, this time a harsh, fluent string of words that Gwyn didn't even slightly recognize, and her jolting, scrabbling thoughts pointed out that this was the orcs' blacktongue. Because this was an orc, an honest-to-gods *orc*, and he was easily lifting her, and setting her on the hard kitchen table behind her. And—she couldn't help a strangled moan—

guiding her knees wide apart, exposing her to his greedy, glittering eyes.

But she didn't even try fighting it, and she could feel her traitorous body clenching as he looked, could hear its wetness, perhaps just as slick as his. Brazen and utterly shameful, surely, but the orc's watching eyes showed only hunger, or maybe even appreciation, as another low, heated growl burned from his throat.

He spoke in the black-tongue again, the words a grating beautiful melody in Gwyn's ears—and in a single, silent movement, he sunk to his knees before the table. His warm hands spreading her thighs even wider—exposing her to his face, his eyes, so *close*   and leaned in, and inhaled, sharp and deep. He was—*smelling* her.

It was entirely illogical, both the doing of it, and Gwyn's body's response to it. Trembling and twitching before his eyes, and then almost seeming to open more, willingly, eagerly, as if her most secret parts were flowering for him. Inviting him, beseeching him, to come closer, to breathe deep, to drink.

And then, oh *hell*, he did. The touch of his sinuous black orc-tongue gentle at first, delicate, as though tasting a delicious morsel, savouring it—and then smoother, broader, deeper. Almost as if he had suddenly determined to lick her all over, to taste every petal of her, and oh it felt good, shockingly good, the pleasure wheeling and jolting and skittering down Gwyn's spine.

"Fuck," she choked out, and in reply the orc laughed again, the movement vibrating his slick, licking tongue. Making her clench and gasp even harder, louder, while that invading orc-tongue explored further, deeper. Actually delving itself into her now, drinking her from the inside out, while those lips kissed and suckled her, oh *gods*.

There were prickles firing in Gwyn's hands and feet, light sparking behind her eyes, and her hazy gaze was trapped on the sight, on the impossible truth of this moment. Of her own thighs spread wide apart, held there by an orc's clawed hands, while his harsh grey face eagerly buried itself between. Licking and sucking with shameless abandon, even as his glinting, half-lidded eyes held to hers, still studying her, learning her. And now gleaming with mischief as he briefly drew away, spread her wider, higher—

And in one deep, strong movement, he licked from one end of her crease, all the way to the other. Slow, succulent, merciless, as she scrabbled and choked, pushing and pulling, needing more, more, *more*. While the orc just held her there, mocking her with his satisfied black eyes as he did it again, again, *again*.

It was unthinkable, it was *impossible*, and it was without question the most thrilling, most arousing moment of Gwyn's entire damned *life*. And her hands had somehow even found the chaotic mess of his hair, her fingers sinking deep within it, dragging him closer while the hunger staggered and soared—

But then, without warning, he stopped. Leaving Gwyn panting and quivering, while he lazily pulled himself up, and looked at her. His taunting black eyes lingering on her too-flushed face, and then to her hard, peaked nipples, and then down between her sprawled legs, where it felt heavy, swollen, bereft.

"Good," he said, through his decidedly wet-looking mouth, and Gwyn replied with a helpless, frantic groan. Making him laugh again, the arrogant bastard, and one of those hands slipped up to tweak her nipple, rolling it between deft, familiar fingers. "Now we mate."

He said it like it was a fact, a foregone conclusion, and Gwyn couldn't help another helpless moan, a glance down at that long, sleek, dripping prick. So close now, jutting between her spread legs, aiming toward her wet, hungry heat as though compelled. And maybe it was, or she was, because she couldn't stop watching as their bodies slowly, finally came together. As that slick smooth head settled just slightly against her, just beginning to part her around him...

"Oh," she gasped, as he let out another string of black-tongue, low and guttural and hoarse. Because oh, it felt good, it felt like a rampant mad euphoria, and somehow Gwyn's sparking hands had dropped to touch him, grasping at the smooth skin of his lean hips, needing him closer, oh *gods*—

But he didn't come closer, his eyes still held to the sight of it, black lashes blinking, his mop of black hair hanging low over his forehead. His big hands now gripping the table on either side of her, his shoulders lithe and defined, the muscles clenched taut all through his chest and abdomen. And it occurred to her, disjointed but certain, that he wasn't nearly as hideous as she'd first supposed, and also—

Her unthinking hand had snapped to his face, tilting his chin up to look at her, and without hesitation or resistance, he did. His eyes oddly still, liquid, deep enough to get lost in, blinking at her under those eyelashes, so thick and black against his scarred, sharp cheekbones.

Gwyn's words seemed to have escaped her entirely, floating away into the night, but suddenly, there seemed no need of them. Only this, two hungry lonely bodies in the dark, relief and pleasure finally fusing, her hand on his face, his strength between her legs.

And without thought, without intent, Gwyn pulled that face down, and pressed her lips to his. Kissing him, again, kissing an *orc*, on *purpose*—but in this moment these were the only words she had, spoken through silent lips and tongue. And he was speaking back, his mouth so clever and surprisingly gentle on hers, whispering of pleasure, of kindness, of regard.

You are quick. Sharp. Wise. Hungry...

When he pulled away Gwyn was breathing hard, and so was he, those eyes locked to hers. And then one of those black brows rising, asking, *Still?* And her head nodding in return, her hands pulling on his hips, *Yes, please, please.*

He nodded too, those eyes blinking one more time—and then in a surge of burning, blazing movement, he was there. *Here.* Taking her, plunging into her, impaling the open flushed flower of her body all around his huge, raging orc-prick.

It was pain and bliss and deliverance, it was the unalloyed power of a lithe, sensuous, virile body taking its greedy pleasure from her. Now arching forward and back, curving and driving into her without thought, without control. Only frantic fluid desperation, green and life and shouting ecstasy inside her...

Gwyn was meeting it, meeting him, her arms and legs clutching against his back, yanking herself onto his battering invading heat with a frenzy she couldn't understand or explain. Only needing this, craving this like she'd been starving for it, like breaking herself on the hot huge poker of his prick was her life's one true salvation...

The fluid body over her moved faster and faster, harder and rougher, every muscle standing out from his skin as he burned and raged inside her. Feeling even tighter, closer, friction rising and pulling, her body shouting for relief, for release, white stars behind her eyes as he plunged in one final time, the world pitching and screaming—

And then he exploded inside her. Spraying out fierce and raw and wild, all pulsing chasing fury to every nerve under Gwyn's skin. Filling her with power, with hot surging life, with a flood of sobbing, soaring pleasure.

When it finally stilled, it was Gwyn who was still shaking. Still quivering around his slowly softening heat, while his body above hers remained solid, unmoving, but for the slow rise and fall of his breath.

He wasn't looking at her now, his eyes dropped down to their joined bodies—and with an easy, unhurried movement, he slid himself out of her. His length smaller now, spent, the sight of it distracting enough that it took her an instant to notice that he'd put his hand flat between her legs where he had been, almost as if to hold the mess inside.

It felt very full, Gwyn realized, and sore. Increasingly so, in fact, and no wonder, because he hadn't been gentle, and neither had she. And what was he doing with this, holding that hand there against her, while his other hand reached to the side, snatched for something from the nearby shelf, and sniffed it.

It was one of the cloths she used for compresses—usually soaked in a herbal tincture of some sort—and she stared blankly as the orc's hand tossed it onto the table, and next snapped for one of her bottles. It was diluted chamomile, which Gwyn often used to soothe injuries and lacerations— and after another long sniff at the bottle, the orc yanked out the stopper with his teeth, and dumped the tincture onto the cloth. And then he drew away his hand from between her legs, and gently pressed the damp cloth there instead.

Gwyn's already-hazy thoughts were distantly protesting— surely orcs didn't know how to use *tinctures*?!—but she couldn't seem to protest, or even move. Just kept staring, blinking, while the orc's surprisingly careful hands brought her thighs back together, holding the cloth in place.

With that, he leaned slightly backward, his gaze flicking up and down her still-naked body. Not betraying even a trace of hunger or interest now, but only that same intense focus, that watchful control. As if Gwyn were a problem to be solved, a challenge to be conquered. A target that he'd been watching, and studying, and... and...

Wait. *Wait.* Had the orc had a... motive with this? A *plan*?

Gwyn's heartbeat kicked into speed, her breath catching in her throat—and the orc shot a furtive, betraying glance toward her face, and then away again. Purposefully away, almost as if he were... *guilty*?

"Y-you," Gwyn began, her voice thick and hoarse. "You said you..."

But good gods, he hadn't truly said anything, had he? He hadn't answered a single one of her questions. He'd spouted that bit about her being quick and wise, yes, but *had* it even been an answer? Or had it been yet another deflection, carefully calculated to help him gain his ends? To gain him—this? Whatever the hell this had been?

The orc's head had slightly ducked, his shaggy hair hanging over his eyes, hiding him away. And that was on purpose too, he didn't *want* her to suspect, to know—and before Gwyn could give voice to the thoughts now screaming through her skull, he'd slid his hands beneath her naked body, and effortlessly plucked her off the table. And then, with her in his arms, he strode off toward the bedroom, his gait smooth and easy, his body warm, close, powerful.

And gods, Gwyn wanted to sink into it, to drown in it. To believe that this truly had been about hungry lonely longing, about an inexplicable mutual understanding, about finding relief together in the night. About being known, *seen*, and yet still wanted, just as she was. *Quick. Wise. Hungry...*

But already the orc was placing her down onto her bed, his movements so careful, so controlled—and then the warm strength was gone, replaced by the feel of her heavy blanket settling over her. And when her hazy eyes blinked up toward him, he was looking back, his gaze very still, almost as if arrested on hers...

But then it was gone again, hidden behind the fall of his hair, guilty, *guilty*. And when Gwyn's cursed hand somehow snapped from beneath the blanket, groping for him, he actually leapt backwards, swift and instinctive, his eyes still averted, his clawed hands clenching to fists.

Something brittle seemed to crack, deep in her chest, and there was an odd, quivering constriction in her throat. And good gods, she was not going to weep over an orc, and especially not while the orc dispassionately stood there and watched, and behaved as though this had meant nothing to him at all. As though *she* had meant nothing.

"So—you got—all you wanted, then?" she heard herself say, her voice a rush of choked breath. "I won't see you again?"

And it didn't matter, it didn't. Gwyn was betrothed to Royal Lindsay, and she was used to this rubbish, to the wash of beautiful soaring pleasure, to the inevitable crash of disappointment afterwards. It was always the same, and it was what she'd sought to escape in coming here—and now it had cornered her again, in the form of this arrogant, gods-forsaken orc.

And the orc wasn't speaking. Wasn't even about to give Gwyn the courtesy of a reply, let alone an explanation, or answers to all the questions still trampling through her thoughts. And before she could start sobbing—before she could betray to this distant, mocking orc the strength of what he'd done, what this had somehow been—she twisted around in the bed, facing away from him, yanking the blanket up to her face. Trying and failing to keep her breaths steady, to keep the prickling wetness from escaping her squeezed-shut eyes.

She needed to watch herself. To be smarter than he was. And that meant, she needed to face the truth that she'd just been brutally, thoroughly outmatched. That the orc had clearly had a motive, and a plan. That he'd obviously been spying on Gwyn. Targeting her. For a reason.

And when it came to reasons why an orc would be targeting a plant-obsessed midwife... well, there was only one.

"Was this—about my father, then?" Gwyn made her voice say, wooden and cracked. "You know he's Lord Anton of Dunburg, I suppose?"

There was utter silence behind her, not even the sound of a

breath. So quiet that she whipped around again in the bed, fully expecting the orc to have vanished entirely—but no. No. He was still standing there, his lean body perfectly still, his eyes fixed blankly to her face. To where—Gwyn wiped an angry hand at her wet cheek—she was truly *weeping*, weeping over a horrid lying orc, curse her wasted life to hell and back.

"Get out," she croaked, because it was all she could find, all she had left in the barrenness of this moment. "Leave me alone, and get the hell out of my life, forever. *Now!*"

And in that instant, it was as though the mask had slipped back across the orc's too-still face. Replacing whatever that had been—surprise, guilt, regret?—with a cool, distant insolence. And if he immediately backed away from her, the movement absurdly graceful, why did Gwyn notice, why the hell did she care?

But part of her did, even now, because the orc was still facing her, and she belatedly realized that his trousers were still hanging down around his hips, his groin still fully visible in the dusky light. His grey length still jutting out slightly, still slick and shiny from what they'd just done—and when he put a deliberate hand to it, and slid up, Gwyn's betraying gasp was still audible, enough to carry through the room.

And that was what this awful orc had wanted, what he'd expected, because he barked out a hard, triumphant laugh, and slowly, purposely, tucked himself away. Saying too much, too many things, and Gwyn's swimming head couldn't think, couldn't bear it.

"Get the hell out," she croaked again. "Go!"

And thank the gods, he spun on his heel and strode away, without a single look back. And when Gwyn heard the door slam shut behind him, she finally buried her face in her blanket, and wept.

7

It was another endless, sleepless night.

Gwyn tossed and turned in the bed, throwing the blanket off, yanking it back on again. Furiously shoving away the visions, the memories, the feel of that hot graceful body moving over her, that slick tongue tasting her, the heat of his growl.

You are sharp. Wise. Hungry…

But no. *Hell*, no. The orc had all but admitted it, he might as well have shouted it, hurled it out into the open between them. He'd come to Gwyn with a goal. A goal of seducing her… on account of her *father*.

And gods, it didn't take a genius to figure it out, did it? Because the shit her father had been stirring up lately had *everything* to do with orcs. That damned law, those coerced terminations, those blatant targeted threats toward any women the orcs touched.

And now, Lord Anton's only daughter had been compromised by an orc. And if she were to become pregnant with an orc's child, she would be obliged to testify. To publicly humiliate her lord father, while the entire realm watched and laughed.

Or, perhaps more likely, the orc had expected Gwyn to run weeping to her lord father, and beg him to protect her, or change his awful new law. To weaken it, perhaps, or create loopholes that could then be fully exploited by others. To set a precedent that any affected women after her could follow. To find a way to save the orcs' unborn sons.

And if it hadn't been her—if it hadn't been *him*—Gwyn might have almost appreciated the cleverness, and the insight, behind such a plan. Her father's new law was utterly and horribly foul, and deserved drastic measures to abate it. Her father should have expected drastic measures. Gods, *Gwyn* should have expected drastic measures. She should have taken one look at that smooth, lying orc bastard, and known exactly what he was about.

"Stupid," she choked at her ceiling, digging her palms into her still-wet eyes. "Stupid. So damned *stupid*."

She finally shoved herself out of bed, staggering toward the kitchen—but then realized, far too late, that the orc's chamomile compress had fallen away. And in its place, there was a sudden surge of liquid heat, pouring thick and pungent down her bare thighs. Reeking of orc, of *him*, and Gwyn silently and vehemently cursed herself as she waited for it to end, her eyes scrunched shut, her hands in painful fists.

And once it was mostly done, she stumbled awkwardly across the room, snatched for a piece of candlewood, and drove it deep into her forearm. Spurting out a hot stream of blood, its pain streaking straight through her shouting thoughts, flooding over the anger and the shame and the gods-damned *misery*.

And as always, it was enough. Enough for Gwyn to numbly light her lamp, grab for some rags, and clean up first herself, and then the floor. And then she mixed up another dose of silphium, grimacing as she swallowed its bitterness, and finally, blankly turned her attention to the white flower lying innocuously on the table. The orc's rose.

It must have fallen there while they'd been—well. But roses had many restorative properties, and Gwyn still didn't recognize this variety, and it would likely propagate if she attempted it. So with a heavy sigh, she once again sat down at her table, and set to work.

She didn't return to bed until the sun had started to rise, but thankfully she was exhausted enough that her eyes instantly closed, her thoughts twisting off into the distance. Curling into visions of a sharp-toothed grin, fluttering black lashes, a musky scent of green...

No, she told herself, as she slipped into sleep. *No. Stupid. Never again...*

Bang-bang-bang.

Gwyn immediately jerked back to wakefulness, her sweaty hands clutching at the bed, her heart pummelling against her chest. Bright mid-morning sunlight was streaming through the window, her head felt like someone had bludgeoned it, and surely this couldn't be the orc again, surely—

Bang-bang-bang.

"Gwyn!" hollered a voice—a deep, devastatingly familiar voice. "I know you're in there. Open up!"

Gods *damn* it. Gwyn's cursed heart skipped a beat, a ragged groan escaping her throat—but she was already scrambling out of bed, and clutching for her dressing-gown. Making sure to drag the sleeve down over her still-raw forearm, and then tying the sash painfully tight as she lurched toward the door.

"Gwyn!" the voice shouted again, alarmingly close, and Gwyn fumbled for the latch, thrusting aside the wooden slide. Which had somehow been closed again, curse that orc bastard, and Gwyn's stomach clutched as she yanked the door open, and stared at the sight standing behind it.

It was Roy. Royal Lindsay, her betrothed, in the flesh. Tall and handsome and rakishly disheveled, wearing mud-spattered riding clothes, and flashing Gwyn his broad, breathtaking grin as he strode past her into the room, and shut the door behind him.

Gwyn stared at him for a hurtling, frozen moment, while her traitorous heart careened back into a gallop again, and an icy chill streaked up her spine. Roy was here, in *Varrahan*. What in the ever-loving *hell*, how could this week possibly get any worse—

"Why," she bit out, with creditable steadiness, "are you *here*, Roy."

Roy's eyes flicked down Gwyn's front and back up again, narrowing on her face. "What, I can't pay a visit to my own betrothed?" he said lightly, stepping closer—and before Gwyn could move, he'd bent down to press a warm, familiar kiss to her cheek. "How've you been holding up, my fair Gwynevere? Missed me?"

Gwyn belatedly jerked backwards, crossing her arms over the front of her dressing-gown. "I've been busy," she said, voice flat. "Very, *very* busy."

Roy's eyes were sweeping across the room, passing over Gwyn's masses of lush plants in favour of lingering on the admittedly ancient-looking stove, and the slightly crumbling masonry of the fireplace. "I can see that," he said, his voice still light, though his eyes settling back on Gwyn's face had darkened, looking troubled, or perhaps even concerned. "You look like you haven't slept in a week, love. Everything all right?"

Gwyn's throat convulsively constricted, but she twitched a sharp nod, and tightened her arms over her chest. This was how it always went with Roy, how she'd been roped back into his clutches again and again. He would smile at her, disarm her with his easy kindness, his care, his *regard*. And then, once she'd devolved into a gasping mess in his arms, the knife-blade would appear, and skewer her in the heart with agonizing, deadly precision.

Just like with a certain orc last night, her scattered thoughts unhelpfully pointed out, as Roy's forehead furrowed, and he came a step closer. "You sure, Gwyn?" he asked. "You haven't had any trouble with the orcs, have you?"

Gwyn's throat convulsed again, and she wildly shook her head, hard enough to whip her hair into her face. "No trouble at all," she replied. "I've been perfectly fine. I'm only a bit tired from all the work to get settled, that's all."

But she was speaking too fast, her voice high-pitched, and of course Roy caught that, the worry again darkening his lovely eyes. "Then why don't we go rest up for a while?" he said, cocking his head toward where Gwyn's messy bed was just visible through the bedroom door. "And you can tell me all about it?"

And for the first time in months, or perhaps years, there wasn't even the slightest trace of hunger in Gwyn's belly. Not even a twitch of temptation, or longing, or regret. Because instead, her flailing, still-addled brain was full of that cursed orc. The ease of his tall body, the brush of his tongue, the hot sticky scent of what he'd left inside her, which was currently seeping steadily down her thigh...

"No," she snapped, maybe at Roy, or the orc, or both. "Look, I told you last time, Roy, and the time before that. I'm finished with this. With us. For good."

Roy's brows rose, and that was surely a hint of a smile on his mouth, amused and indulgent. "You're really working to punish me with all this, aren't you, Gwyn?" he asked, with infuriating calm. "What is it you want from me, then? A good grovel? A glut of expensive gifts? Or maybe I spend the rest of the morning making good use of my mouth?"

His teasing smile ticked up further, matching the meaningful heat in his eyes—but again, there was no responding spark in Gwyn's belly, none of the familiar dragging weakness. No, because there was only the damned orc again, kneeling on the floor before her, his long lashes fluttering, while his slick, shameless tongue drank her from the inside out...

Gwyn briefly squeezed her eyes shut, and rubbed at her aching temples. "It's not about punishing you, Roy," she replied thickly. "Or gaining compensation from you, or whatever. We're just not good together, and we never have been. And that's never going to change."

Roy's head tilted, his smile slightly fading. "Nice try, Gwyn, but we both know that's rubbish," he said, flatter than before. "We've known each other all our lives. We *understand* each other. And, even after all these years, we're still damn good in bed together. Aren't we?"

Gwyn couldn't hide her sigh, or her reflexive, bitter wince. "Yes, Roy," she said wearily. "You and me, and every other woman who happens to wander across your path. I've put up with your explanations and justifications and empty promises for far too many years, and I'm sick of it. I'm *finished* with it, Roy. For good."

Roy's head tilted further, and his gloved hand dropped to fiddle with the shining rapier hanging at his side. "Oh, come now, Gwyn," he said, with a rather forced-feeling cheerfulness. "You know that's all only harmless fun, right? It doesn't mean anything. It's what everyone does. I just don't hide it from you like most fellows do, that's all."

Gwyn felt her shoulders squaring, her chin lifting. "So if I were to do the same," she said, voice clipped, "and go off and have a little *harmless fun* of my own, you'd be perfectly fine with that?"

She already knew his answer, because they'd already had this entire infuriating argument multiple times before—and even as Roy opened his mouth, Gwyn snapped her hand up between them, and gave a furious shake of her head. "Or," she continued loudly, "you'd be perfectly fine with me having my own life here in Varrahan, just as you do back home in Dunburg? You'll leave me in peace here, to do as I wish?"

Something flared in Roy's eyes, and he shot a quick, meaningful glance toward the south. "Look, Gwyn," he said, "Your father and I, we give you a hell of a lot of leeway, all right? You can have your little plant obsession, your playing at being a commoner, your running off at all hours to birth random strangers' *children*. But parking yourself here, in the shadow of Orc Mountain, where you could be attacked by those vicious brutes at any moment? It's on the outside of enough. It's putting your entire damned *life* at risk."

The concern was there again on his face, thinning his mouth, flashing like that in his eyes. Hinting that he did really care, that he was truly worried about her—and that had always been the worst part, hadn't it? Knowing that to Roy, Gwyn *did* matter. She'd always been special, his betrothed, his *favourite*. He was one of the most popular, most handsome, most desired men in the realm, and he was here, for *her*...

Or was he? And Gwyn felt her gaze sharpening on his face, and then flicking down to that rapier at his side. As if he were here in some official capacity, and—Gwyn's eyes narrowed— yes, that was her father's muddy *regalia* on his back, which had to mean—

"Wait," she snapped at him, as she rushed toward the nearest window. "Surely you aren't here with *soldiers,* Roy?!"

But yes, good gods, there was an entire group of armed fighting-men, milling about outside Gwyn's house. Stretching their legs, talking to one another, and brushing down their stamping horses. And there had to be at least a dozen of them, and some of them were even looking toward the house with obvious impatience. Clearly waiting for their captain to finish his morning tryst, so they could get back to doing their damned *jobs.*

"You are *unbelievable*, Roy," Gwyn breathed, rounding on him again, her hands in stiff fists at her sides. "You were going to leave all those men waiting for you out there, while you pretended as though you'd come here alone, and then spent the rest of the morning in my *bed*?"

Roy grimaced, his uneasy gaze darting toward the window. "Oh, calm down, love," he said, in that soothing, patronizing tone Gwyn knew all too well. "We needed to rest the horses for a while anyway, all right? They're happy to have a break."

The rage was bright and bristling, flaring behind Gwyn's eyes, pulsing against her ribs. "And you think I want a band of soldiers camped outside my house for half a day?" she shouted at him, her voice shrill. "I'm trying to get away from you, Roy! I'm trying to start a new life! What the hell do you expect all these townspeople will think, when they see Lord Anton's household guards parked on my damned *doorstep*?!"

Roy's jaw flexed in his cheek, but he was smiling again, chilly and brittle. "Maybe they'll think you're a lord's daughter, Gwynevere," he said. "Maybe they'll realize you're not, in fact, a commoner, or a midwife, or a barmy plant lady, or whatever the hell you're pretending to be this week!"

The bastard. Gwyn's breaths were coming in harsh little pants, her head pounding in her skull. "I *am* a midwife, you prick," she hissed. "And I am a barmy plant lady, too. And my father promised me at least a month of freedom here, so you can get the hell out, and get these soldiers off my damned *lawn*!"

But she knew it was a waste of breath, even before she'd finished speaking—her father had always been far too willing to revoke his promises, whenever it better suited him—and Roy rolled his eyes, and huffed a heavy sigh. "For gods' sakes, Gwyn," he replied testily. "Do you hear me telling you to pack up, and come home with me this minute? No. I'm just stopping by to make sure you're still *alive*, while you live out your ridiculous little commoner fantasy under the shadow of bloody *Orc Mountain!*"

"And you think my little commoner *fantasy*," Gwyn snarled back, "will last the rest of this morning, with a dozen armed men stationed outside my house? With *you* here?!"

Her hand flapped furiously toward Roy's tall, handsome form, which despite the mud, still radiated wealth, standing, command. And even if the soldiers' presence alone didn't give it away, it would only take one meal at a tavern before everyone in town knew that Roy was Lord Anton's much-loved ward, mysteriously appeared from Dunburg to court the mysterious new midwife.

"Look, I'm riding back out today, Gwyn, if that's such a concern," Roy replied, voice sharp. "And none of my men even know why we came here, because I *understood*"—his hand snapped to Gwyn's chin, giving it a proprietary little shake— "that you wanted to keep this secret. I *understood* what you wanted, and I wanted to make you happy. All right?"

And curse her, but Gwyn felt her shoulders sagging, her throat swallowing. And of course Roy saw that, and he eased a step closer, his gloved fingers gently drumming on her cheek. "I didn't even tell them who you are," he added, his voice dropping. "As far as they know, you're just another side-piece of mine, all right?"

And gods, Gwyn might have forgiven it. Might have accepted his words as truth, or even leaned into his familiar touch—if not for that damned betraying line, escaping so easy from his mouth. Another side-piece of mine. *Another.*

Gwyn's suddenly narrowed eyes darted up and down Roy's muddy body, not thinking, not even knowing what she was searching for—or did she. Because there, on his stubbled neck, there was a distinctive, fresh red splotch... and what might have even been a set of *teeth-marks.*

Gwyn whipped away from him so fast she felt faint, and she

furiously shook her head, squeezing her eyes shut. "You're not *understanding*, Roy," she breathed. "I keep telling you, I'm finished with our betrothal, *forever*. And if you truly want to make me happy"—she dragged in air, made her prickling eyes meet his—"you'll respect that, and move on with one of your many convenient side-pieces, and leave me alone here in *peace!*"

But something new, something unfamiliar, had flashed in Roy's eyes. Something that curled on his lip, and contorted his handsome face. "No, Gwynevere," he said, voice hard. "You don't get to pretend your way out of this. You're a lord's daughter. You're my *betrothed*. You need to grow the hell up, and do what's expected of you, and stop behaving like a spoiled, immature, petty little *brat!*"

And with those words still ringing through the air, he strode for the door, and yanked it open—and then spun back around, fixing Gwyn with the force of his furious eyes.

"You have twenty-two days left, Gwynevere," he hissed. "And then you're coming home with me, as per your father's orders. And if you *dare* try this bullshit with me again then, you will fucking *regret* it."

Gwyn's throat badly convulsed, her blinking eyes fixed to his enraged, distorted face. "Will I?" she replied, her voice curiously hollow. "Whatever will you do, Roy? Judge me and mock my interests? Ignore my wishes? Or perhaps you'll put off our marriage indefinitely, while you take your pleasure with every other woman in sight? However shall I acclimatize myself?"

But Roy's answering bark of a laugh was again like nothing she'd ever heard before, curdling beneath her skin. "No, Gwyn," he purred, cold, vicious, deadly. "I will drag you out of this shithole house, and then I will burn it all to the *ground*."

8

After Roy left, Gwyn couldn't stop shaking.

She wandered aimlessly around the house for far too long, stumbling over nothing, her trembly fingers stroking at her plants' beloved leaves and spines. Her passion. Her livelihood. Her *calling*. All held here in this one isolated, unguarded little house, and suddenly feeling impossibly precarious. Vulnerable. *Flammable.*

I will drag you out of this shithole house, and burn it all to the ground.

And while Gwyn had seen Roy's darker side before—and had heard many more tales—until now, she'd never actually been the target of it. Roy had always treated her with indulgence, amusement, affection. They'd known one another for so long, they'd spent so many hungry nights together, and yes, perhaps they even understood one another—or so Gwyn had thought.

But now her father's words were scraping through her head, over and over again. *Leave Roy here to stew without you. Light a much-needed fire under the boy...*

Gwyn groaned aloud, and rubbed her still-shaking hands

over her prickling eyes. Good gods, did Roy truly think this was some kind of test? A challenge? An attempted retaliation on her part, to spur him on to commitment? To *marriage*?

Her stomach was badly churning, the room feeling far too stuffy and hot—and she stumbled for the front door, and swung it open. The men had disappeared, at least, and she gulped in deep breaths as she staggered around to the garden, and sank to her knees amidst a patch of overgrown comfrey. This would burn too, this whole garden would be destroyed, and she would be—

Her twirling vision caught on a clump of field thistle, growing among the dense clusters of comfrey, and she wildly lunged for it, and yanked it out. Its prickly spines nicked painfully at her skin, but she kept grabbing for more, and more, and more. Frantically, furiously weeding, until her hands were bright red and full of tiny thistle-spines, and the sweat was streaming off her brow.

Gods, what was she going to do. First her father, and then the orc, and now Roy. All trapping her, manipulating her, trying to steal away her freedom for their own damned ends. And now, what options did she have left? Abandon her lovely new house? Run for the hills, and leave her entire livelihood behind? Marry the man who'd just threatened to destroy *every-thing* she cared about?

"Stupid," she hissed at the thistles, dragging her stinging hand against her dripping-wet forehead. "So damned *stupid*."

There was no answer, of course—but even so, Gwyn suddenly felt a vivid, overpowering sense of... something. Something here. Something... *listening*.

A hard, furious chill flared up her spine, and she whirled around, fully expecting to see Roy standing behind her. Or maybe one of his soldiers, come to loom and threaten and *burn*—

But no. It was—the *orc*.

He was sitting casually sprawled on the garden's single wooden bench, tucked close against the dense encircling hedge. His chest and shoulders were still bare, his limbs long and lean, his face a stark mass of light and shadow in the bright sun. And his eyes on Gwyn were amused, *mocking*, as though he'd been sitting there all this time, just waiting for her to notice.

Something dangerously plunged in Gwyn's chest, and her head was suddenly pounding, her hands uncontrollably trembling on the thistles. While somewhere deep in her brain, a vague, distant screaming had begun. This asshole orc had targeted her. *Used* her. And she'd told him to get out of her life forever, and now here he was again? Not even a full day later? And directly on Roy's heels, no less?!

"Why the *hell*," she said, her voice badly wavering, "are you back here, orc."

The amusement had slightly faded from the orc's eyes, but he didn't answer. Only kept looking at her, his head cocked, his dark gaze flicking up and down her kneeling form. Lingering first on her reddened hands, and then—Gwyn twitched— narrowing on the still-raw cuts in her scarred forearm, clearly visible beneath the thrust-up sleeve of her dressing-gown.

She yanked the sleeve down, far too late, and her stomach again plummeted in her belly, her heartbeat thundering louder in her ears. "What, are you here to laugh at me some more?" she demanded at him. "Or maybe to see if your little ploy against my father worked? If I'm already pregnant with your spawn?"

Something tightened on the orc's mouth, faint but unmis- takable, but he still didn't answer. Only kept looking at her like that, surely still mocking her, and Gwyn heard herself make an odd, choked noise, not quite a laugh.

"Well, just so you know," she spat, "I'm on an extra-strong dose of silphium, which has been consistently proven to be effective, even against your kind. And therefore, despite your best efforts, I will *not* be bearing you any children, or making your case to my father, or publicly testifying before an angry mob, or whatever other life-altering ordeals you had planned for me to endure on your behalf!"

The orc's hand had again risen to that tooth hanging around his neck, stroking it with his claws—but he still didn't speak. Not even attempting to explain himself, or gods forbid, apologize. And surely, Gwyn would never want such an apology from him anyway—would never accept an apology, after all he'd done—so why did she still feel so worn, so sick, so *broken*.

"I grant you, it was a clever plan," she heard her cracked voice continue, all on its own. "And my father's new law is *unspeakably* foul. Gods know, I might have even gone along with you willingly, if you hadn't—"

And wait, what was she saying—she surely hadn't once *thought* about actually *helping* this orc?!—and she rubbed at her prickling eyes with her stinging palms. Forgetting all about the thistle-spines still stuck in them, and then wincing at their sharp scrape against her eyelids—

When suddenly, something snatched at her wrist, and yanked it downwards. Something new, something warm and surprisingly powerful, and wait, it was—the orc's *hand*?!

Gwyn flinched all over, blinking her bleary eyes—and yes, the orc was—*here*. Crouching directly before her in the garden-bed, his eyes dark and disapproving, his long fingers flexing tight and familiar around her wrist.

"No," he said flatly. "You keep eyes *safe*. These are no easy to heal. Ach?"

She flinched again, but didn't move. Couldn't seem to move, somehow, as the orc slowly, carefully turned her wrist over, exposing her raw, reddened palm to the sunlight. And exposing, too, all the clusters of tiny thistle-spines, caught in her inflamed skin.

The pain had been fairly negligible, but the disapproval again flared in the orc's watching eyes. And as Gwyn kept staring, unmoving, he began plucking the spines out, one by one, with rapid, efficient flicks of his sharp black claws.

Gwyn's brain was wildly stuttering, but she didn't jerk away, even as his warm hand snatched for her other wrist, and proceeded to do it all over again. And gods, she should not be allowing this, she should be shouting at him, demanding why the hell he was pretending to care, why he was even *here*—

But she just kept staring at him, blank and bewildered, as he frowned down at her still-inflamed palm, and tilted it toward the light. And without warning, he pulled her hand up to his mouth, and... *licked* it?!

But yes, yes, now this incomprehensible orc was *licking* her. His long, sinuous black tongue stroking soft and smooth against her reddened skin, lingering against the worst cuts, even curving around her fingers. The movements deft and certain, almost as though he wanted this, perhaps even *needed* to do this...

And then he grasped again for her other hand, and set upon it with equal intensity. That sinuous orc-tongue tasting, swirling, almost caressing—and flashing across Gwyn's thoughts was an abrupt, absurdly powerful vision of last night. Of this lithe, graceful orc on his knees before her, black lashes fluttering, as this same slick, supple tongue curled deep inside her...

But then the vision scattered, because the orc's hand had somehow slid up the sleeve of her dressing-gown, and his tongue was now trailing up her *arm*. Lapping against the still-painful cuts she'd made with her candlewood, and as her dazed eyes blinked down at him, it occurred to her that he—*knew*. Good gods, he knew, and was that *reproach* in his black eyes? *Disapproval*? After all he had done? And was still currently doing?!

Gwyn yanked her arm away from him, so forceful that she nearly fell backward, and she stumbled up to her feet, while the garden spun powerfully around her. "What the hell, orc," she croaked. "You have no right. *None*. Don't you *remember* what you did to me last night?!"

Her voice came out sharp and shrill, not unlike a scream, and before her the orc had risen too. And Gwyn belatedly realized how damned *tall* he was, his lean powerful body towering deadly and dangerous above her. And she'd left her crossbow inside the house, and was he going to take advantage, was he going to—

"Ach, I ken," he cut in, the words cursory and stiff. "But you"—he hesitated, his head tilting—"you no... you no betrayed me, this day. No spoke of me, to this man."

To this man. To *Roy*? And Gwyn couldn't stop squinting up at the orc's face in the bright sunlight, searching his dark eyes, grasping at her spiralling thoughts. He'd come back here because... he'd been *spying* on her, again? And waiting for her to report his devious arse to Roy? To claim, perhaps, that she'd been tricked by an orc? Accosted? Attacked?

And wait, *wait*, how had this not yet occurred to her? Because yes, surely, she could have easily done such a thing. She could have made up any number of ghastly, terrifying tales about what this horrid orc had done to her, and thrown his horrid plan straight back into his horrid face. She could have single-handedly dismantled that entire peace-treaty, and *destroyed* him.

Should the worst happen, she'd told her father that day, *you can happily launch into another war to rescue me...*

"But," she began, and then hesitated, frowning suspiciously at the orc's guarded eyes. "But—you can't mean to tell me that was actually your *plan*, when you came here? That you were willing to risk another *war*, for a few minutes over my kitchen table?"

The orc blinked, once, and that might have been a wince, tightening his mouth. "I no *plan* to risk all this," he said, voice flat. "I no saw all this. I never saw you—"

He broke off there, definitely wincing this time, and Gwyn considered that for an instant—and heard herself bark a laugh, bitter and cold. "Oh, so I wasn't supposed to figure out your little scheme, is that it?" she retorted. "I was supposed to dangle along after you for weeks or months on end, growing your child, until I was too compromised to escape? To be *believed*?"

She was somehow shouting again, the words ringing through the suddenly small-feeling garden all around them— and the orc took a hasty, reflexive step backwards, his face gone rather pale. "So *now* you do this," he said, in a monotone. "Now you go find this *betrothed*, and speak this to him."

What? Gwyn's throat was making a strangled sound, her hands dragging through her hair. "Of course I'm not going to go find Roy, or tell him *anything*," she snapped back. "I've been trying to shake him off for *months* now, and I came here with the express intent of getting the hell away from him, permanently, *forever!*"

The orc kept blinking at her, clearly nonplussed, and Gwyn rubbed at her eyes again, fighting to ignore the fact that doing so felt far less painful this time. "And to finally start my own life," she added, her voice hollow. "To escape my fate as a lord's daughter, and make my own way, apart from Roy and my father. But now—"

She couldn't seem to finish over the constriction in her throat, and gods, why was she even telling such things to an orc? To *this* orc? Why was she giving him even more to wield against her, after what he'd done?

"Just—forget it," she heard herself say, her shoulders sagging. "You tried to use me for your purposes, you failed, and now you can even rest assured that I'm not going to report you. So if you'll kindly go away, I have more important things to address right now, without adding in your awful manipulative *rubbish*. Goodbye."

With that, she spun around and lurched in the direction of the house, silently cursing herself with every step. Stupid. So damned stupid. And her eyes were even prickling again, and she would not shed more tears over this bastard, she would *not*—

Until before her, something flashed into place, tall and dark and impossibly swift. Sending Gwyn reeling backwards, cursing aloud this time—because of course, it was the orc again. Now fully blocking her path, looming over her, looking down at her with unreadable black eyes.

"Wait," he said, his voice low and urgent. "I wish—"

But he broke off there, his throat bobbing—so Gwyn jerked a hard shake of her head, and swerved to step around him. But again he leapt to block her, the movement again almost instant, his shaggy hair glinting as it settled in the sunlight.

"I wish to offer amends," he said, in a rush. "To... you."

Amends? To *her*? Gwyn heard herself bark a disbelieving laugh, and veered in the other direction—but again the orc was far too fast, his tall body easing into place before her. "You are... under threat," he continued. "This fool man swore to burn your goods. Your herbs. Your *garden*."

His eyes flicked darkly toward the garden around them, almost as though he'd been personally insulted by that—and then he glowered back down at her, his long arms gracefully folding over his bare chest.

"Have you funds or help to hire guards, to keep all this safe?" he demanded. "Or to hire new lands, and to move all your goods there in secret? Or"—his fingers flexed against his arms—"to make second garden, in safe place, to serve as surety if this one is lost?"

Gwyn felt her frustration simmering as he spoke, seething for escape—but then it seemed to plummet again, dragging down her head and her shoulders. No, she didn't have enough extra money for such things. And this asshole had very aptly summarized the totality of the possible options that had already been swarming her thoughts, all of them with deeply depressing finality.

She needed to protect her life's work. So many of her plants were costly or rare—some were irreplaceable—which meant that rebuilding would take years, and would be exorbitantly expensive, as well. But without her plants, her ability to earn her living would be significantly reduced, perhaps enough to destroy her career forever.

No. She had to find a way to keep her plants safe, or move them elsewhere. And to make that happen, she again needed either large sums of money, or considerable support from others. And she had no friends or family here, and this entire move had already consumed most of her savings, and—and—

"Look, I'm likely worrying over nothing," she said, too quickly, though she couldn't hide her grimace. "Roy obviously just lost his temper, and was making entirely empty threats. He and my father are both quite fond of me, and I'm sure I can bring one of them around on this. Roy wouldn't truly want to hurt me like that. We—understand one another."

But the orc's scoffing laugh was immediate and unapologetic, his eyes sparking with dangerous amusement. "This man no *understand* you," he drawled, "if he believe *this* threat, of all means, shall gain him your vow, or your fealty. If he believe woman like you shall sit still and *wait* for this threat to become truth?"

Gwyn's mouth had opened, surely to make some kind of appropriate counter-argument—but nothing came. And instead, there was an odd little prickle up her back, a tight swallow in her closed-off throat. Because yes, good gods, again, this too-astute bastard had the truth of it. Now that Roy had made that threat, Gwyn would never, ever forget it. And as long as it retained even the slightest possibility of coming true, she surely wouldn't be able to rest until she'd dealt with it. Permanently.

The orc was smirking at her again, as though he'd read the words from her very thoughts. "You are under threat," he said firmly. "You have no funds to face this. Thus, you need help."

Gwyn felt her teeth grinding together, her hands again pulling at her hair. "Help from *you*?!" she demanded. "And what, exactly, do you think you can offer me, orc? And why the *hell* would I accept it, after how you've treated me?!"

Her voice had gone shrill again, echoing through the air between them, but the orc seemed entirely unaffected, his eyes steady and cool on hers. "You are no fool enough to spurn help when you need this," he said smoothly. "I have long followed the ways of the earth. I help you move whole garden to safety, or I grow you new garden as surety, from your seeds and seedlings, and any plants you may spare. Ach?"

Gwyn's words had entirely vanished again, her eyes staring at the orc's impassive face. Surely he couldn't possibly have the knowledge to *move* her garden? Let alone grow her a *new* one?

But the vision of that carefully wrapped chasteberry plant had flashed through her thoughts, and she felt her breath exhaling, her fists clenching at her sides. While a slow, smug smile curled across the orc's mouth, his black brows rising. Waiting for her to argue, clearly—but curse her, the argument still wouldn't come. And instead, her traitorous brain was swarming with implications and possibilities, and even, gods forbid, with *hope*.

"Where would you do this?" she heard herself ask, before she could stop it. "Do you have a safe place in mind? With plenty of extra space, and adequate sun, and wind protection?"

The orc's nod was just as smug as his smile, and if Gwyn wasn't mistaken, his shoulders might have slightly relaxed, too. "Ach," he said. "Now safe against any man, also."

Wait. There was something about the way he'd said that, and Gwyn felt her eyes narrowing, and reflexively glancing toward the south. Toward *Orc Mountain*, still towering abominably close beyond the hedge, streaming its black plumes of smoke to the sky...

"You are *surely* not suggesting," she replied, her voice rising with every word, "that you move my precious, priceless plants—and my whole garden—to *Orc Mountain*?!"

But the orc's face remained implacable, his eyes steady. "Ach, why should I not?" he asked. "It is safe, and well guarded. My kin are there, and shall tend it when I am away. And, it is only a half-day's walk from this house, upon an easy path."

Gwyn sputtered some kind of incomprehensible reply, and she had to gulp for air, thrust it deep into her lungs. "I will not," she countered, "trust you with my entire *livelihood*, orc! And I will certainly not move it into some deadly, likely poisonous place at *Orc Mountain*!"

Something shifted in the orc's eyes, and he gave an overly casual shrug, his gaze fixing slightly beyond her. "It is no deadly, or *poison*," he said. "Your garden shall flourish there. It shall be *safe*."

"Safe?!" Gwyn echoed, her voice painfully shrill. "At *Orc Mountain*?! With the likes of *you*?!"

And suddenly, it was as though that mask had slid back over the orc's face, hiding him away. And the smile curling at his mouth was practiced and cool, his shoulder rolling in a casual, dismissive shrug.

"Ach, as you wish," he said, his voice very even. "Then I

have naught else to offer you, woman. I wish you"—his eyes shifted, changed—"all luck against this man. Farewell."

And with that, he turned around, and strode toward the garden's exit. Just leaving, walking away, just like that—and Gwyn felt herself leap into motion after him, her hand scrabbling at his arm.

"So what, now you're just going to *leave*?!" she demanded at his back. "What the hell happened to making amends to me?"

The orc had slowly turned around to look down at her, his expression still unreadable, his eyes carefully distant. "I offer all I am able," he replied curtly. "What more do you wish from me? You no ken I shall seek to *stop* this man, when he come here to burn your house?"

Gwyn stared at him an instant too long, her hands again dragging through her hair. "Well, why not?" she demanded. "Surely you would be *more* than a match for Roy?"

And wait, she wasn't truly expecting this orc to *fight* Roy, was she? Wasn't envisioning his lean, agile body darting and twisting, defending her house and her safety with smooth, capable ease, and then...

"Ach," the orc replied, voice clipped. "I should easily break this man's tiny neck, woman. But in this, I only call down yet more war for my kin, you ken? We have yet much to face from your curst father, and his fool Council's cruel laws. And I"—his eyes flicked away—"I have yet risked enough this day, ach? I shall no throw this man's death into the fray. No even for your garden, or my guilt."

Oh. Gwyn's mouth spasmed, and she somehow felt her head nodding, her shoulders sagging. Of course she didn't want this orc to *kill* Roy, and she didn't want to give her father any more justification for his horrible laws, either. But what did that leave now, what would come next, how in the gods' names would she ever get out of this mess—

But there was nothing, *nothing*, and she dragged her shaky

hands harder against her hair, pulling, twisting, fighting to think. Until she suddenly felt something snap, the pain flashing white behind her eyes, while a hoarse, broken gasp choked from her already-trembling mouth.

The orc had actually been turning away again, clearly finished with this for good—but at the sound of Gwyn's gasp, his disapproving gaze darted back over his shoulder, his eyes narrowing. And with a sharp, fluid flare of movement, he was once again standing close before her, both his hands clamping tight and warm around her wrists.

"Ach, woman," he hissed at her, as he dragged her hands upwards, away from her hair. "You are healer, no? You ken it is no always easy to grow hair back, ach?"

He sounded genuinely exasperated, and in another swift shuffle of movement, he'd snatched both her wrists into one hand, and yanked something out of Gwyn's still-clutched fingers. A clump of her long black hair, now dangling before her eyes in his sharp claws.

"*No*," he ordered her, waving it in front of her face. "You no do this. You are wiser than this."

Gwyn's mouth opened to protest, again—and in another too-swift movement, his hand tossed the hair aside, and dropped to cover her mouth. And that hand was huge, and warm, and with it was that smell again. Heated, husky, whispering of earth and green…

"No," he insisted, his voice slightly deepening. "Now kneel, and I shall tend to this, before I go."

He would *what*? Gwyn attempted some kind of enraged response, the words muffled against the orc's hand—but he entirely ignored it, jabbing his clawed finger downward. "Kneel," he repeated. "You have *more important things to address*, beyond needless wounds. You no take my offer of help, you at least grant me this. Ach?"

And gods, Gwyn should have kept arguing. And surely she

would have, if at that very moment, she hadn't wiped her sweaty, still-shaky hands on her dressing-gown. And thereby discovered, to her genuine astonishment, that her hands... didn't hurt. Didn't sting, or smart, or however they ought to have felt, after stupidly attacking a patch of field thistle without wearing any proper gloves.

The realization was enough to jolt her to stillness, her disbelieving eyes wide on the orc's face—and the too-perceptive bastard smirked at her again, and once more jabbed his claw toward the ground. "Kneel, woman," he repeated. "*Now.*"

And finally, foolishly, without at all intending to, Gwyn jerked a shaky little nod, and... obliged. Dropping awkwardly to the earth, and shifting so that she was indeed crouched on her knees before this tall, commanding, enraging orc.

There was an instant's caught stillness between them, and Gwyn blinked up, glaring, perhaps daring him to mock or gloat—but his eyes on hers were strangely still, and she could see his chest expand, and hollow again. And his clawed hand, which had been hovering in the vicinity of her face, slowly lifted up, and smoothed against her hair.

The touch was surprisingly careful, or even gentle, guiding her hair back. Perhaps searching for the place she'd injured, and after a moment's silent stroking, his other hand moved to join the first. His claws lightly trailing against her scalp as they parted her hair, as she felt a warm finger brush against a decisively sore spot...

And before she could possibly stop it, Gwyn felt her breath catch in her throat, a hard shudder wrenching down her back. A movement that abruptly stilled the orc's hands, while a peculiar awareness rippled through the air—and Gwyn bit her lip, and squeezed her eyes shut. This utter bastard, he needed to get the hell on with this, whatever the hell this even *was*, and...

And then he grasped at a large handful of hair, and—*pulled.* Gentle, but surely purposeful, enough to slightly yank Gwyn's head back. Firing a fierce, exquisite thrill down her already-shivery spine, and her loud gasp escaped before she could stop it, in perfect time with the harsh hiss of breath from the orc above her.

Damn, damn, *damn*. Gwyn flinched all over, and belatedly made to jerk away from him, out of that too-aware touch—but of course he'd anticipated that, and his long fingers against her head had spread wide, holding her still. Sending another furious flare of heat down her back, and she couldn't help a furtive, fearful glance up at his face. Fully expecting his mockery now, his judgement, his triumph...

But no. No, he was still just looking down at her, his head tilted sideways, while the oddest look sparked through his too-intent eyes. A look that might have been... *comprehension*. As though he suddenly understood something he hadn't before, as though a question had been answered, a puzzle decisively solved.

Something dark and shameful was churning in Gwyn's belly, and she felt her throat convulsively swallow, her eyes dropping back to the earth. And what the hell was she doing, why was she still here, why in the gods' names had she ever, *ever* agreed to this—

Until there was another abrupt, close movement, as the orc bent over her—and then the feel of a big hand curling against the nape of her neck. And then—Gwyn's shiver wracked her entire body this time—she felt the sure, staggering touch of his warm mouth, kissing her tender scalp with soft, careful gentleness.

Gods, it felt good. And even more so when those claws again carded smoothly through her hair, his kiss giving way to that slick, licking tongue. But it all stayed careful this time, cautious, gentle. As if he didn't want to go further, didn't want to take advantage of what he'd just learned...

And gods curse her, *condemn* her, because Gwyn felt herself yank slightly away from him, tightening his grip on her hair. Sparking another furious flare of heat up her spine, even as the shame flashed and burned, as her head ducked even lower. And suddenly there was the jolting, overwhelming urge to spit at him, to rage at him, to leap up and run for her life—

But she did none of those things. Only stayed there in place, pinned and exposed, as the orc's warm hand slid around to her chin, and tilted her face up. Snapping her blinking, ashamed eyes to his, her cheeks burning, her lips shamefully parting...

But again, there was no triumph in his eyes. No mockery. Only the quiet, steady intentness. Seeing. *Knowing.*

And with another smooth, silent movement, his still-stroking hand dropped from Gwyn's hair, and reached for his trousers. His tight, straining trousers, streaked with visible dampness, directly before Gwyn's wildly blinking eyes...

And oh, hell, he was doing this. Slipping down inside, easy and shameless, and bringing out—*that.* That swollen, jutting length of him, tall and grey and smooth, with those twin weights bulging out beneath.

And as Gwyn stared, her heart thundering in her ears, the orc's long-fingered hand brazenly ran over them. Stroking them, *flaunting* them, before sliding further up, and circling around that hard base of him. And then his hand slowly, smoothly dragged up, pumping himself, milking out a thick, glistening bead of white.

Damn. Gwyn's groan was loud, desperate, utterly humiliating—but the orc's other hand kept gripping against her chin, now giving it a meaningful little shake. Dragging her gaze up, wanting her to look at him, to drown in the truth of her shame...

"You like," he murmured, low but sure, his black brows raised, his nostrils flaring. "You wish me to tend you. Ach?"

And gods, Gwyn couldn't even argue. Couldn't pretend to

resist or refuse. Not with her lashes so desperately fluttering, her throat swallowing, her tongue flicking out to brush against her lips. Yes, she liked. Yes, she wished. To taste. To know. To be... *tended?*

"Yes," she whispered. "Please, orc. Tend me."

9

Wait. What the hell was Gwyn saying. What was she *thinking*. Tend me. *Tend* me?!

It was unbelievable, it was appalling, it was utter and complete *absurdity*. He was an orc, he was supposed to be staying away from her forever, and he was—he was—

Growling. Yes, growling, low and steady and deep in his throat. Perhaps even more like a purr, as his big warm hand gently caressed Gwyn's hot face, tilting her chin further upwards. While his other hand slid back into her hair, catching on a generous handful, tugging it back, oh, oh—

And as that beautiful flash of tension soared down her spine, the orc leaned forward. Not quite all the way, but just enough that the hard, slick, now-dripping head of him was nearly brushing her lips. And gods, the smell of him was everywhere, so rich and deep, and surely he was taunting her now, surely—

But his eyes upon her face were pure liquid black, somehow both shimmering and still. And then his growl suddenly broke off, as if he'd perhaps stopped breathing. In favour of just watching this, wanting this, craving it with just as much strength as she did—

The first lick of her tongue toward him was furtive, tentative, ashamed. Nudging with trembling, breathless uncertainty at that slicked smooth head—but oh, the *taste* of him. Sparking across her tongue like sweet spring sap from a sugar maple, all slippery perfect wonder, swarming her from the inside out...

Her moan was hoarse, helpless, heavy with hunger—and gods, surely the orc was laughing now. But she didn't look, didn't even care, because he'd also eased further forward, jutting that slick, sweet head directly between her parted, gasping lips.

Fuck. Gwyn jolted at the shock of it, the truth of an orc's prick kissing at her mouth, pulsing its sweetness inside her— and then, oh hell, she was sucking. Dragging him deeper, drinking him up, lavishing him with her tongue. Needing more of this, more of him, whatever he would give her...

And oh, gods, he was giving it. Bearing down hard and hungry, opening her wide around him, seeking his way toward the back of her mouth. Until that smooth, slippery head was delving close against her convulsing throat, tight, hot, dangerous.

But Roy had taught Gwyn very thoroughly, for far too many years—and she drew in a fortifying breath through her nose, and then took the orc even deeper. Opening her throat, angling her head to make it easier, and the orc's next nudge forward felt almost tentative, uncertain, as though afraid she might retch, or refuse...

Gwyn's blocked throat made a noise that might have been a snarl, her hands somehow clutching the firm backs of his thighs, dragging him closer. Nearly shoving her face into the mass of coarse hair at his groin, and groaning again at the silent answer of a long, shuddering pulse down the full length of him, while a twinge of sweet heat slipped out deep in her throat.

The orc's hand gently tugged at Gwyn's hair again, sparking more screaming hunger in its wake—and it was only after another gentle pull that she realized he was pulling her off, back, away. So she went, moaning again at the draw of that hand on her hair, at the slight sputter of that impossibly sweet syrup on her tongue...

But he was holding her there, waiting, wanting something. Wanting to see her, perhaps, so she blinked upwards, held his glimmering eyes as she again slowly, deliberately sucked him deep. Almost revelling in the answering shudder against her throat this time, in the return of his steady growl, surely more menacing than before.

"Witch woman," he gasped, the words husky and harsh. "You wish me to take this from you?"

Yes, yes, *hell* yes, and somehow Gwyn even managed a nod, even with his full length still jammed deep in her throat. And in return, his growl cracked into something more like a roar, both his clawed hands clutching hard into her hair, as he drew her off, holding there for a frozen, glorious instant—and then slammed himself deep, filling her throat with one swift, devastating plunge.

But Gwyn didn't even gag, and only sucked harder, feeling her throat clamp and convulse upon him. And gods, he liked that, he *wanted* that, his eyes fluttering as he dragged out, and again rammed back inside.

Gwyn's moan was more like a cry, her tingling hands clutching desperately at his hard arse, gouging him even deeper—and with another ragged-sounding groan he complied, grinding and circling into her throat. And then yanking out again, his claws scraping sharp at her scalp, before driving back in, again, and again, and again.

And it was chaos, it was splendour, it was delirium. It was a furious, trammelling mash of pain and pleasure and sweetness, of twirling triumph and palpable power. Of this orc craving her, devouring her, his control utterly lost, the lust and the bare greed flashing in his deadly black eyes, and he was going to, he was, he was—

The blast came without warning, slick hot syrup surging into Gwyn's mouth, flooding down her throat. Pulsing into her again and again, filling her with him, so sudden and so overpowering that she had to fight to breathe and swallow, to choke his thick liquid into her belly...

But gods, it was so much, so heavy, so sweet. Too much to possibly keep inside, and already it was bubbling out her swollen lips around him, dripping down her chin...

And gods, the orc. Just standing there unmoving, not breathing, his eyes fixed blankly to the sight. To his prick still filling Gwyn's mouth, while his mess streamed from between her lips. Almost as though he were awed by it, as though it couldn't truly be real...

But in a quick, fluid movement, his hand dropped down, and streaked his messy slick wide against her cheek. Almost as if to mock her for her failure, and Gwyn's stomach briefly caught, her eyes trapped on his—and gods, he did it again. Streaking it on the other cheek, too, covering his hand in it, and then—she swallowed hard against the softened flesh still filling her mouth—carding his dripping-wet fingers deep into her hair.

"Mine," he whispered, the word so low, almost inaudible. "You bear *my* scent now. Ach?"

Oh. Gwyn couldn't move, couldn't speak, couldn't take her eyes off his—but somehow, somehow, she was nodding. Nodding, saying *yes*, with an orc still in her mouth—and his hand again came to her face, wiping at the mess, streaking it through her hair.

And it should have been shocking. Repulsive. *Laughable.*

But in this shivering, silent moment, it felt like something else. Something important. Something... sacred.

But even as that awareness hurtled through Gwyn's thoughts, the orc's eyes shifted. And then blinked, multiple times—and suddenly the hazy hunger had entirely vanished, and in its place was... surprise. Shock. *Horror*?

And in a single flashing movement, he snapped away from her. His head ducked low, his long fingers yanking up his trousers, hiding himself from her blinking eyes. As if he were disgusted with himself... or with *her*?

And then he spun on his heel, as if he were about to leave, *again*. He was going to abandon her again, after all that. And Gwyn couldn't stop her shaking hand from reaching after him, while a choked, bitter noise croaked from her throat.

"What the hell," she gasped toward his bare back, in a voice not her own. "You said you—you would *help*."

The orc's tall body had gone perfectly still, his hands in fists at his sides—but then Gwyn could see him making himself relax, his shoulders dropping, his clawed fingers unfurling one by one. And when he turned around, slow and sinuous, the familiar coolness was back in his eyes, the easy smile on his mouth.

"Ach, I did," he said smoothly. "And then, you spurned this. You said you should never trust me, or move your priceless garden into this *deadly, poisonous place* at Orc Mountain."

Right. She had. And the orc was looking almost satisfied by that, almost *relieved*. Almost as though he couldn't wait to leave her, *forever*, and he was already turning away, she would never see him *again*—

"Could you—show it to me," Gwyn's voice gasped, all on its own. "Take me there. So I can make an—informed decision."

The orc's form instantly froze, and even half-tilted away from her like this, she could see the grim clench on his mouth, the slow, resigned close of his eyes. As if he'd so nearly escaped, and now he was trapped, cornered, doomed...

"You wish me to take you to *Orc Mountain*," he said, his voice mocking, bone-dry. "*You.* Daughter to Lord Anton of Dunburg."

And if that was supposed to remind Gwyn of her place, or of the total inappropriateness of such a plan, it failed utterly, because her chin jerked up, the rebellion flashing behind her eyes.

"Yes, me," she snapped back. "And you knew very well who I was when you offered it, *and* when you made yourself at home in my mouth just now. So are you going to keep your word? Or are you going to run off again like a frightened sneaking *coward*?!"

And when the orc slowly turned to face her again, that mask had slipped back over his eyes, making them cool and empty. And his smile was so practiced, so brittle, that Gwyn actually flinched under the strength of it, her body again shivering at his feet.

"Ach, woman, I always keep my word," he said, his voice light, glittering, deadly. "Should you truly wish to witness this, then come."

10

Gwyn was losing her mind.

It was the only possible explanation, she thought grimly, as she dashed around her house, tidying up the table, yanking on a sturdy dress and boots. She'd clearly been driven round the bend by all the rubbish from her father, and Roy, and now this damned orc.

But she didn't stop, either. Just kept churning through tasks, one after another. Watering the necessary plants, harvesting the necessary seeds, and even—she hesitated for an instant, but then did it anyway—slinging her crossbow onto her back, and ensuring her bolts were properly fastened into the sling, as well.

"You said it was a half-day's journey, right?" she asked the orc, who had followed her inside the house, and was now leaning against the closed door with deceptive casualness. "I'll be back by tonight?"

The chilly distance hadn't once left the orc's eyes, and he gave a careless, dismissive shrug. "Mayhap," he said. "This hangs upon how weary you become."

Gwyn couldn't help a snort—some midwife she would be,

if she couldn't handle a day's walking—but after a moment's consideration, she snatched for a sheet of paper, and dashed out a note to leave on her kitchen table.

Gone to care for a client, she wrote. *May be complications.*

It wasn't much, but it should cover her if anyone came by needing help, or gods forbid, if Roy or his minions should decide to return. And with that sorted, Gwyn squared her shoulders, hoisted her crossbow on her back, and turned to face the orc.

He was looking pained again, his eyes fixed to the note on the table, and for an instant, she had the oddest suspicion that he'd somehow *read* it, even at that distance. But surely orcs couldn't read, and perhaps that explained the tightness on his face, the flex of his long fingers at his side.

"Well, I'm ready," she said, suddenly feeling strangely self-conscious. "Unless you can think of anything else I'll need?"

Her gaze had darted back to her plants—perhaps she should bring some chamomile, or some wort to soothe the anxiety this journey was sure to bestow—but the orc shrugged again, and spun for the door. Not even looking to see if anyone was beyond as he yanked it open and strode away, without a single glance toward her.

Gwyn made a face at his retreating back, but accordingly followed, shutting the door tightly behind her. And then rushing to catch up to where the orc was already disappearing around the house, his strides swift, impatient, annoyed.

And as she followed him toward the nearby forest, her unease only surged stronger, lowering her head, heating her cheeks. Gods, what the hell was she doing. Cajoling a clearly unwilling orc into taking her to Orc Mountain, so that she could potentially move her *garden* there? After what they'd just done in her own garden?

She rubbed at her face, fighting to shove the memory back—but it was still so vivid, so unnervingly powerful. The way he'd tasted. The way he'd growled. The way he'd gripped those handfuls of her hair, easy and purposeful, and...

Her vision had briefly blurred, enough that she tripped over a highly avoidable root, jutting up out of the path. A bit of stupidity that earned her a dark glance from the orc over his shoulder, obviously even more annoyed than he'd already been before.

Gwyn gritted her teeth together, and forced her attention back to the path under her feet, and the forest all around them. This indeed seemed a straightforward route, easy and unobstructed, and it occurred to her that it was clearly familiar to the orc, too. Not only that, but it had seemed to lead directly to her garden, suggesting several obvious implications that she'd been very intently avoiding, until this moment.

"I know you said you weren't... close with my Great-Aunt Agnes," Gwyn ventured, toward the orc's stiff-looking back. "But did you ever... meet her?"

It suddenly felt like a crucially important question, and one that Gwyn should have surely asked upon their very first acquaintance. But her stomach was unpleasantly twisting, her clammy hands rubbing at her skirts, almost as if she were afraid of the answer. Afraid of what it might mean.

"Ach," the orc finally said, his voice thin, as though he hadn't wanted to answer, either. "I met her."

Gwyn heard herself exhale, and she dropped her gaze back to the path, stepping over rocks and roots. "What... was she like?"

The question felt choked in her throat, and she kept her head ducked low, her steps careful. Surely betraying even more of her many failures to this orc, and she could almost feel the added weight of his disapproval, his mockery. Because while Great-Aunt Agnes had shown Gwyn shocking generosity, in leaving her an entire house, Gwyn honestly knew very little of her, beyond those long-ago childhood visits. And even though she surely could have made an effort to visit in recent years, or at least written letters, it had never seemed a priority, not with all the other chaos that had constantly seemed to plague her existence.

And now Great-Aunt Agnes was dead. And Gwyn would never be able to sit with her, or work together in her garden, or ask all the questions that had been piling up in her brain these past days. Had Agnes truly been intimate with an orc? Had she somehow *supported* the orcs? And worst of all, had she *known* that Gwyn would be confronted by orcs, in coming here? By *this* orc?

"Your kinswoman was... wise," the orc replied finally, without inflection in his voice. "Quick. Kind. She... granted me freedom to use her garden, as I wished."

She *what*? Gwyn's footsteps stumbled again on the path, her wide eyes blinking at the orc's stiff back. Not only had Great-Aunt Agnes *known* this orc—but she'd known him well enough to let him freely use her garden? The *hell*?!

But the orc didn't hesitate, or elaborate, or even look back. And as Gwyn clambered to catch up again, a new, surprisingly lowering suspicion flashed through her thoughts, grim and bitter and cold.

"Wait," she gasped at him. "So you offering to move my garden—it *wasn't* because you felt guilty about trying to ruin my life? It was because you—you saw that garden as *yours*?!"

And gods, the orc didn't even reply. Just kept walking, distant and silent, as though he couldn't care less that he'd blatantly lied to Gwyn, again. That he'd used her—and was currently still using her—to gain his own ends. His own goals. What he saw as his own damned *garden*.

And now—Gwyn's feet slowed, halted—she'd once again fallen for it. She'd once again decided, beyond all reason, to trust this sly, slippery bastard at his word. After he'd again mocked her, and spied on her, and blatantly used her mouth for his pleasure? What the *hell* was wrong with her?

She dragged her hands against her hair, fighting for breath, fighting to ignore the infuriating fact that neither her hands nor her head hurt anymore. Because no. *No.* This was *ludicrous.* Ridiculous. She could not be voluntarily going to Orc Mountain. And not with this orc, of all orcs. Not when he kept lying to her like this. Not after all he'd done.

Gods, this had been stupid. So, *so* stupid.

The orc had finally hesitated ahead of her, glancing warily over his shoulder, and Gwyn squeezed her eyes shut, and stiffly made herself turn around. Facing back in the direction she'd come, and taking one unsteady step, and then another. She would go home. She would find another way to save her livelihood, to escape Roy and her father forever. There had to be some solution, some way she hadn't yet considered. There had to be…

Until something gripped at her shoulder, strong and certain. Halting her firmly in place, and Gwyn felt her body sag against it, her eyes blinking toward the earth at her feet.

"If I only wanted garden," the orc's flat voice said, far too close, "I should have stolen this before you came, or whilst you slept. I should never offer you *help* in this. Ach?"

Gwyn's swallow was audible, and she breathed in deep, wincing at the too-familiar scent of him swarming her nostrils. "But you obviously don't *want* to help me," she replied, her voice pathetically plaintive. "You *wanted* me to refuse your offer. So why the hell did you even bother?"

There was more silence behind her, and she could feel his exhale, fluttering at her hair. "You showed me much… kindness, this day," he said finally. "You no only kept me secret from this man, but you no even *touched* him, also. You no tainted my scent with his. You had all right to do this, and yet, you… *honoured* me."

Oh. Gwyn swallowed again, and then made herself scoff, the sound thick and hoarse. "And then I sucked you off," she shot back, "and it was disappointing enough that you realized your mistake!"

The orc's hand flexed on her shoulder, a low growl hissing through the air. "I *realize*," he countered, "you are yet daughter of Lord Anton. And now I am tangled with you, and my scent broods heavy upon you, with yet no trace of my son. And next I am bound to bring you to my home, and proclaim to all my kin who you are, and how I have failed?"

For a stiff, stilted instant, Gwyn stood frozen, digesting that—and then she whirled around to look at him. To search those dark, glittering eyes, which suddenly looked just as frustrated as she felt. Because yes, this orc had come to her with a goal. A mission. A plan. Gwyn had been a target, one he'd clearly invested in for some time.

And now she was... what? A public sign of his failure. A risk. A *liability*.

"Well, surely even orcs understand," she snapped, without at all meaning to, "that a woman's pregnancy isn't guaranteed after one isolated instance. Which, by the way, is sure *never* to be repeated!"

The orc shrugged, his mouth curling in a faint sneer. "Mayhap," he said coolly. "But we also *understand* that lord's daughter in mountain brings great risk. Most of all when she has sworn no vows, bears no son, and knows she is a tool we wished to gain!"

Gods, this *orc*, and Gwyn felt her anger sparking, her hands again dragging through her hair. "So because *you've* been spying on me, and trying to use me as your pawn," she retorted, "you still think *I'm* planning to do the same? That I'm coming to Orc Mountain to spy on you, and wreak my revenge upon you? And then I'll run back and tell my father and Roy how you've kidnapped and tortured me, and urge them to gather all their horrid lord cronies, and come here to obliterate you at once?"

The orc looked at her for a beat too long, his eyes glinting—but then he shrugged again, cool and uncaring. "Why should you not?" he asked. "I have brought you risk and threat, for my own gain. In your place, I should also seek vengeance against me, without regret."

Oh. So because *he* was a vengeful lying bastard, he expected Gwyn to be the same. And she couldn't even seem to argue it, dragging her hands deeper through her hair—at least, until the orc's brief, exasperated growl, together with a sharply disapproving look, made her drop them again.

"And I suppose it won't do any good," she said irritably, "for me to just tell you otherwise? To insist I have no interest in revenge, and I only care about saving my garden?"

"No," he snapped back, "it shall not. No human care about garden this much. Humans care about own self. Care about *own way.*"

Own way. Those were her words, Gwyn realized with a wince, as the orc stalked a smooth step closer. "Even if you now *think* you only care for garden," he continued, "this no always hold true, ach? Mayhap father or betrothed make new offer. Mayhap they pay for new way, if you help them against us. Or mayhap they bribe you, or press you, or bring new threats against you."

Gwyn surely should have tried to argue that, but Roy's actions of just that morning presented a strong deterrent, and the orc's eyes flashed with palpable awareness. "Or," he added, even flatter now, "mayhap my mountain or my kin bring you fear or anger, and you then seek vengeance. Mayhap *I* further harm you, and thus spark this. Ach?"

Oh, so again it was about *him*, the asshole, and how *he* couldn't be trusted. And again, Gwyn certainly should have tried to argue that—but now the abrupt, incongruous vision of that incident in the garden was flooding her thoughts. How he'd been fully about to leave, before that whole stupid situation with her hair. How he hadn't wanted to keep going, but he'd then been caught in it, perhaps, just as she had, and he…

"I no *wished* to take your throat," he said, his voice lowering, as if he'd precisely followed her thoughts. "I no *wished* to know the truth of this, or what more you might welcome from me. Ach?"

His black gaze had briefly settled on Gwyn's hair, and then dropped to her mouth, lingering there with unnerving intensity. Enough that she couldn't seem to hide her shiver, or stop her tongue from flicking to wet her lips. An action which drew a brief, betraying hiss from the orc, before he purposefully looked away, his eyes frowning toward the trees beyond her.

It suddenly felt hard to breathe, to think, especially with that rich musky sweetness still flooding Gwyn's lungs. Smelling perhaps even more delectable than it had before, and perhaps that was because she *knew* how it tasted, and…

"Very well, then," she said, far too loudly. "We've established that you don't trust me, and that *neither* of us can trust you. I'm glad that's settled. Now"—she narrowed her eyes on his still-distant face—"are you going to take your offer back, or not?"

The orc's eyes flicked back toward hers, and for an instant, they might have looked almost amused—but then they darkened again, his mouth thinning. "No," he replied. "I shall not."

There was a sensation much like relief in Gwyn's gut, and she jerked a firm nod, raising her chin. "Well, then I'm not turning back either," she said flatly. "So lead on, orc."

The orc accordingly shrugged, and then spun and strode off again. While Gwyn quietly followed, her gaze oddly fixed to his still-stiff shoulders, his clenched-tight fists at his sides. The long, powerful-looking muscles in his back, shifting beneath his skin with every smooth, purposeful step.

He was—keeping his word to her. Helping her save her garden. Even if he didn't trust her, even if she was public proof of his failure. Even if she would never touch him again—which she most assuredly would *not*, because he was a devious lying asshole, he'd manipulated her, he'd been trying to ruin her *life*, and...

"Are there," she heard herself say, into the taut silence, "any other women at your mountain, presently? I'm quite sure I've heard tales...?"

She'd more than heard tales, of course, though until this moment, she'd paid them very little heed—and that might have been a nod from the orc, despite the careless shrug of his shoulder. "Ach," he replied. "Some."

Gwyn drew in more breath, let it out through her teeth. "Then would it help," she said, "if I were to visit them, and offer my services? If you were to introduce me as a midwife, rather than as Lord Anton's daughter?"

There was an odd, inscrutable stillness from the orc ahead of her, even as his strides stayed steady, and Gwyn grimaced at his back. "Or maybe they'll all know who I am anyway," she said, her voice dropping. "I mean, how many of you orcs were actually involved with this little destroy-my-life plan? There must have been a few of you, at least, if you've been planning this over the course of months?"

The orc's shrug seemed even more casual this time, his steps still unnaturally steady. "A few," he said. "No many."

Gwyn's glower at his back deepened, and she clambered over a large rock blocking the path. "So would that help, then?" she demanded. "Or would you rather I just walk in and announce that I'm Lord Anton's daughter, here to unleash my devious revenge upon your unsuspecting mountain, by means of insinuating myself into your garden?"

The orc actually glanced over his shoulder this time, reflexive and quick—and to Gwyn's genuine surprise, that might have been a hint of a smile, pulling at his mouth. "Ach, no," he said, turning away again. "If you should... help our women, I should be... grateful."

Something hot swarmed low in Gwyn's belly, and she somehow found herself half-smiling at his back, too. "You *should* be grateful, asshole," she said. "Not used to not getting your way, are you?"

That was definitely a quirk on the orc's lips this time, his eyes again angling toward her. "No," he said. "No *used to* witch women with such deft mouth, also."

Gwyn's face instantly flushed—he was trying to discomfit her, the bastard—and she made a rude gesture at his stupidly muscular back. "I am a midwife, *not* a witch, you wily prick," she said. "And when do we talk about *your* mouth? It was pretty damned deft, too."

But if she'd hoped to discomfit him in return, she'd utterly failed, because he actually laughed, the low sound carrying through the trees around them. "Ach, I ken," he replied over his shoulder. "You liked. Wish for more."

Gwyn did *not* wish for more, would *never* wish for more from him, *ever*—but even as she shook her head, she still couldn't stop smiling at his back. "Like hell I do, asshole," she countered. "I don't know you. I don't trust you. I don't *like* you. Gods, I don't even know your damned *name*."

And it was that, strangely enough, that finally slowed the orc's steady steps. That made him first hesitate, his shoulders rising and falling, before turning around to face her. His eyes dark, inscrutable, oddly piercing on hers.

"I am... Joarr," he said. "Of Clan... Bautul."

oarr, of Clan... Bautul.

There was something in the way he said it, in the heaviness of his voice. In how his clawed hand reflexively lifted to stroke that tooth, still hanging around his neck.

Gwyn's head had tilted, studying it, studying him, while various words from various women flashed through her thoughts. *His clan was like his family, his pack. They did everything together. Everything...*

"Is there something wrong with that?" Gwyn asked, again without at all meaning to. "I thought you orcs were supposed to like your clans?"

The orc's wince was unmistakable, and he briefly shook his head, as if to thrust something out of it. "Ach," he said, though his voice sounded odd, almost uncertain. "My clan has my... *like.*"

It wasn't even slightly convincing, and Gwyn put her hands to her hips, and raised her eyebrows at him. "So what's the issue, then?" she demanded. "Did you just discover your clan's secret dark side? Or did you have a massive fight? Or maybe they threw you out for being such a smug, snarky asshole?"

And gods, she had no idea why she was harping on this—or did she, because the orc still hadn't turned away, his hand repeatedly stroking at that tooth. "Clan can no *throw out*," he countered. "It is no *choice*. It is birth that marks this, always."

That fact bothered him too, that much was clear. And while Gwyn surely didn't care about this orc's family problems, she still couldn't seem to stop searching his eyes, either. Seeing the strange hesitancy there, the unease, the unhappiness. So at odds with the rest of his cool, careless confidence, and with those brief moments of pointed, focused intensity, too. No, this felt almost... wrong, somehow, like it didn't fit properly on his face.

"So what happened, then?" Gwyn asked, quieter than before. "Something with your birth? What, did they lie to you?"

The orc's eyes snapped to sudden, visceral stillness, almost as if she'd struck him—and in a jerky, impossibly swift movement, he spun around, and began walking again. Even faster than before, leaving Gwyn to scramble to catch up, her eyes fixed to his back.

"They no lie," he finally said over his shoulder, his voice clipped. "They no *knew*. I no knew."

Oh. Gwyn grimaced toward his back, toward that stiff set of his shoulders. While her brain twisted and twirled, and something caught in her belly that might have almost been... sympathy.

"You know, that actually happened to my third-eldest half-brother," she heard herself say, again before she could stop her mouth. "Robert. He grew up thinking his mother was my father's first wife—she died when he was little—but it turned out, his mother was actually one of Father's mistresses, who didn't want to keep him, so Father took him in as a baby. Quite a shock for Robert, to discover himself not even in the line of succession anymore."

The orc—Joarr—didn't make any acknowledgement of this, but for some reason Gwyn kept talking, her eyes still held to his back. "Of course, Robert's never forgiven Father, and things were never the same between them. Though to be fair"—she couldn't help a dry-sounding chuckle—"I don't even think Father remembered. It certainly isn't the kind of thing he would spend time thinking about. And Robert's a complete blighter anyway, so I must say, I didn't feel too badly for him at the time."

The orc still didn't reply, but if Gwyn wasn't mistaken, some of the tightness had perhaps slipped from his shoulders. And his long strides had slowed, too, almost as if giving her time to catch up again.

"So what's this Bautul clan like, then?" she asked. "Different than your old one, no doubt?"

The orc—Joarr, damn it, *Joarr*—shot her a suspicious look over his shoulder, and for a long moment he didn't reply. But Gwyn kept waiting, following, and finally he shrugged. "Ach," he said. "Bautul are oft... the horde. The hungry orcs you humans so fear. They fight, and take, and think as one."

Well, that sounded horrifying, and Gwyn couldn't deny the compulsive shiver down her back. "Lovely," she said thinly. "So how do *you* fit in, then?"

The orc's shoulders stiffened again, and too late Gwyn realized what she'd just implied. That this orc—Joarr—was somehow different than that. Better than that, even. Because he'd refused to fight Roy. He hadn't taken anything from Gwyn that she hadn't wanted to give. He'd cared for her great-aunt's garden. And he certainly seemed like an independent type, more than willing to operate and think for himself.

"I'm not suggesting that there's anything wrong with not fitting in," Gwyn continued, flatter than before. "I mean, if you've truly been spying on me for months, you've obviously encountered *my* family, right? Or my many close friends?"

Joarr didn't reply, but again, Gwyn almost thought she saw his shoulders settle, his steps slowing. His head lifting, almost as if he were smelling the air—and then, without warning, he abruptly veered sideways, off the path, toward a distant clump of trees.

Gwyn blinked, but accordingly followed, and soon found him standing beneath an old oak tree, and slicing something off the trunk with his claws. Something lush and yellow, growing in horizontal fronds upon the tree, and—wait, those were mushrooms. *Sulphur shelf* mushrooms, in fact, notoriously difficult to find, and also extremely delicious.

"How did you know those were there?" Gwyn asked breathlessly, her mouth already watering. "Surely you couldn't *smell* them, at that distance?"

The orc—Joarr—was smirking at her, apparently fully back to his smug self again. And before Gwyn could follow, he'd dumped the yellow fronds into her hands, and then snapped around behind her, tugging at her sling. And when he stepped away again—*wait*—he was holding her *crossbow*. Not only that, but he'd somehow swiped all the bolts too, which were now sticking out from between his long fingers in a deadly-looking fan of pointy steel.

"Wait," Gwyn snapped. "That's *my* crossbow, orc. What are you—"

But before she could finish, Joarr had—*vanished*. Or wait, not vanished, because there was a distinctive rustling sound from above—and when Gwyn's head jerked up, he was up in the *tree*. And not only in it, but standing tall and easy on a thin trembling branch, directly above her head.

Gwyn yelped and leapt sideways, before the fool fell on her—but as she stared, he took one long, flying leap, and landed in the next tree over. Balancing just as effortlessly on that branch, and then closing his eyes, and visibly inhaling. As if he were again... smelling. As if he were... *hunting*?

But yes, surely, that was what he was doing. Leaping from branch to branch above her, as easily as if it were solid earth beneath his feet. Moving further and further away, until all she saw was a distant shadow, and a trembling spray of pine—

And then she heard the distinctive *snap* of the bow firing— and then the sight of the branch wildly waving, as Joarr leapt out of the tree, onto the ground below. And when Gwyn rushed over, still clutching the mushrooms to her unsteadily thumping heart, he was kneeling over what looked like a dead grouse, and deftly skinning it with his sharp black claws.

"Need dry wood for fire," he said, without glancing up, as his bloody fingers tossed a disgusting-looking morsel into his mouth. "Lest you wish to eat this fresh?"

Gwyn made a face, and again, likely should have protested—but she *was* hungry, and if he was offering to cook for her, she certainly didn't need to complain. So she carefully set aside her mushrooms, and went to work. Collecting dry twigs and roots from around the nearby trees, and piling them together on a large, flat stone.

Joarr soon joined her, now carrying a fully-skinned bird carcass in his claws. And though he offered no comment on Gwyn's wood, he promptly knelt beside her little pyre, and after a few sharp snaps of his claws in the sunlight, it somehow sparked into sputtering flame.

Gwyn gasped aloud, her eyes wide, and that was surely another smirk on Joarr's face as he set to making an impromptu little spit. And then he skewered the mushrooms together with the grouse on the spit, and soon was casually spinning it all over the fire, while the mouthwatering scent of cooking poultry wafted through the air.

"I smell sage, to the east," he said, with a meaningful jerk of his head. "You find, ach?"

Gwyn didn't even think about protesting this time, and instead just nodded, and went to search in the direction he'd indicated. Scanning all around for the conditions sage best liked—decent elevation, lots of sun—and sure enough, finding a clump of it in a grassy little clearing.

She returned to Joarr in good time, and he accepted the bunch of sage without comment. And then, to her vague astonishment, he promptly raised a handful to his mouth, tore off a large chunk, and began *chewing*.

Gwyn watched with uncertain fascination—did orcs truly enjoy eating raw herbs, too?—until he actually spat out a clump of chewed-up sage into his hand, and then began *rubbing* it onto the cooking *food*.

"Oh, *disgusting*," she muttered, and in return Joarr shot her a disapproving look, and purposefully bit off more sage. Showing rather more of his sharp teeth than was necessary as he chewed, and then deliberately spitting out another mouthful of mushy green into his hand, and rubbing it onto the grouse.

"I cook for you, you *eat*," he said, jabbing a claw toward her. "You no yet eat this day, ach?"

Gwyn opened her mouth to counter that, but then belatedly realized that no, in fact, she hadn't yet eaten today. And Joarr surely caught that, and he rubbed more chewed-up sage on the grouse, which now smelled so damned delicious that her stomach audibly growled.

"Ach?" he repeated, now pointing his finger toward her waist. "Also, you already taste my mouth. You kiss and drink me dry with own *tongue*. You can no be fool enough to say *food* is worse?"

Gods curse the smug asshole, and his delicious-smelling cooking, and the way Gwyn's stomach was flopping with something that wasn't entirely hunger. The way she *again* couldn't even seem to argue, not even as Joarr peeled off a piece of steaming meat with his claws, and handed it over the fire toward her.

She made a face at him, but when he kept waiting, his black brows raised, she finally reached out, and snatched the meat into her fingers. And before she could properly consider what was on it, she stuffed it into her mouth, and chewed.

And *oh*, it was good. Tender and juicy and succulent, the flavours made even richer with the sage's seasoning. So delectable that she actually moaned as she swallowed, her mouth watering, her eyes fluttering closed.

Joarr's laugh broke through her thoughts, the sound low and mocking and close—but when Gwyn jerked to glare at him, the look in his eyes was more amused than scornful, and he was holding out a piece of mushroom, dangling it toward her. And she eagerly snatched and ate it this time, revelling in its rich, savoury flavour, and fighting back the odious, rising temptation to return Joarr's smug, teasing smile.

But then she was somehow smiling anyway, her fingers brushing his claws as she accepted another chunk of meat across the fire. And then they were just eating together, their gazes occasionally catching, almost feeling—easy. Companionable, even. As though that same mutual understanding had slipped over them, drawing them closer together, and next...

Joarr's head jerked up and sideways, his breath dragging in deep—and in a blur of urgent movement, he sprang to his feet. Grasping for the remnants of the grouse before scattering the spit and the fire with his bare foot, and then—Gwyn twitched and stared—he yanked down his trousers, grabbed himself with deft familiarity, and relieved himself all over the orange embers until they fizzled into grey smoke.

Gwyn belatedly jerked backwards, scrunching her eyes shut, shoving that vision away—but it was still there, streaming through her thoughts. And so was the truth of the orc, kicking more leaves over the fire, entirely hiding it from view. And then, before she even realized he'd moved, he grasped her crossbow, fastened it into the sling, and hung it over his own shoulder.

"What is it?" Gwyn demanded at him, but she'd already dropped her voice, her gaze darting toward the thick forest all around them. And Joarr's answer was already there, in the way he spun to face her again, his hands clutching tight to her arms. In the way his eyes had darted toward the north, and held there, while another sharp, purposeful inhale filled his bare chest.

"Men come," he breathed, the words low and intent, his gaze snapping back down to hers. "They shall soon be upon us. You wish to stay and meet them, and go safe back to your home? Or run with me?"

Go safe back home, or... *run* with him. Gwyn's frantic eyes were searching his face, her heart hammering, her throat spasming. And somehow her hand was grasping at his taut arm, her nails digging into his skin. Holding him here while she studied him, searched for the truth hiding behind the urgency of his eyes.

He'd cooked for her. He'd fed her. He'd offered to help her save her garden. And now he was asking again, and waiting, and for some ridiculous, unfathomable reason, Gwyn's other hand snapped up, jittery and cold, to stroke at that tooth, still hanging around his neck.

She needed to save her garden. She needed to find her own fate, her own way. She needed to...

"Run with you," she whispered. "Now."

12

Joarr's curt nod was a blaring, inexplicable relief. Thudding with impossible weight through Gwyn's chest, steadying her trembling hands and feet.

They would run. Together.

And when he swiftly turned and crouched before her, and jerked his head toward his bare back—the bow now hanging at his side—Gwyn instantly caught his meaning, and clambered on. Fighting to ignore the shift of warm skin and powerful muscle against her as he stood tall again, one hand clamping on her arm, the other gripping at her thigh, hoisting her closer, his weight bobbing on his feet—

And then he kicked off, and ran. Sprinting with staggering speed away from the path, deep into the suddenly close-feeling trees. Dashing and dodging and leaping, his long steps almost entirely silent on the forest floor beneath them, as Gwyn desperately clung to his flexing back, and fought to remember how to breathe.

She could hear distant noises behind them now, the telltale sound of voices and crackling brush, but Joarr didn't spare a single glance back. Only kept sprinting through the trees, his shaggy hair streaking out behind him, tickling at Gwyn's cheek and ear. Because somehow, her face was buried in the crook of his warm neck, her eyes peering up ahead over his shoulder. Almost as if drinking in the sight of the forest sweeping by, in flashing swells of deep grey and green.

And even as her heart kept thundering, her hands hot and sweaty against Joarr's bare skin, there was an odd, hurtling whisper of... eagerness. Or, perhaps, even appreciation. Not only for the beauty of the soaring forest around her, but for the agile strength beneath her, the easy drive and certainty of his steps. The way his body smoothly shifted into one movement, and then the next, as though running barefoot through a dense forest—while carrying her extra weight on his back—was boundlessly simple, something he'd done his entire life.

And surely, he *must* have done it all his life, to acquire this level of grace and skill? And for the first time, it occurred to Gwyn that she should rather enjoy learning more about this orc's past. About what had happened with his clan, and how he'd learned to cook, and why he knew so much about plants and mushrooms. And why he'd been the one spying on her, the one to come to her, when surely there were hundreds—or even thousands—of orcs at Orc Mountain?

A shout from behind them sliced through Gwyn's thoughts, and she somehow felt more tension charging through Joarr's body against her, more power and focus beneath his feet. As if this were one last push, driving him forward, and her heart skittered at the sight of what looked like a *ravine* up ahead. And surely he wasn't going to jump, surely—

But he wasn't balking, wasn't slowing down. And the distinctive sound of rushing water was coming closer and closer, and with it, more shouts from behind them. And even the sound of barking dogs, good gods, and were these unknown men truly *hunting* Joarr, as though he were prey? As if he were an *animal*? Weren't they supposed to be keeping a damned *peace-treaty*?!

But the ravine kept rushing ever closer, Joarr's feet pounding the earth, his focus a single driving point. And Gwyn's hands were digging into him, her heart screaming in her throat, he was going to jump, he was going to *kill* them—

His leap into the air was pure barrelling terror, Gwyn's face buried into his neck, her body clamped against his—until suddenly, her stomach was wildly surging, the world flashing upside-down, the sky charging toward her. And it took all her furiously shattering focus not to shriek aloud, to keep holding on, Joarr's hands clutching painfully against her, oh gods oh gods oh *gods*—

Until all at once, it stopped. Stopped, with Gwyn right-side up again, her vision violently spinning, her heart hollering, her trembly body somehow still fastened to Joarr's back. While beneath her, his body began moving again, but this time, walking with perfect balance on a very thin, very shaky *tree-branch*.

He'd hurled them into a *tree*?!

But yes, yes, they were in a tree. A dense, towering pine tree, and Joarr was already climbing them higher, his clawed hands gripping the branches above, his feet stepping with smooth, silent care. And below them, the distinctive sounds of dogs and men and crackling brush came ever closer, surely they would be discovered, surely—

But Joarr just kept climbing, stepping very slowly now, shifting his weight from branch to branch, moving steadily closer to the tree's thick trunk. Until finally he was close enough to touch it, his hands spreading wide against the rough bark, his shoulders heaving with his soundless breaths.

They were well over halfway up the tree, and surely concealed by the dense branches below—but Gwyn still froze all over as the barks and voices surged all around them.

Suggesting several dogs, and multiple men, and the clanking metal had to be armour, *weapons*—and wait, surely they hadn't truly been ready to *kill* Joarr? For what, making a fire in a *forest*?!

"The slippery bastard jumped!" one of the men called, his voice so close that Gwyn badly flinched, almost losing her grip on Joarr's back. Earning what actually felt like a sigh from his taut body beneath her, and in a flash of deft, silent movement, he twisted and shifted her weight, easing her around him.

It meant that she was clutching at his front, rather than his back, her arms and legs still circled around him, and he hoisted her up a little higher, one of his big hands spreading wide under her arse. And then, with unexpected gentleness, he leaned her back into the tree-trunk, enclosing her between its solid bark, and the still-shuddering heat of his body.

"The orc jumped into *that*?!" another male voice demanded, from far too close beneath them. "Then maybe he's already dead."

Gwyn's indignation flared with surprising strength, and with it was a sudden, powerful urge to glance downward, to try to identify these assholes—but before she could even blink, Joarr's warm hand had clapped against her mouth. Jerking her back to stillness, her eyes snapped to his, his rich scent swirling into her lungs...

His head silently moved from side to side—clearly saying, *No, don't risk it*—and Gwyn swallowed hard, and then nodded back. Earning what might have been a twitch of approval in his eyes, but he didn't move his hand, or glance downwards, either. Just kept standing there, pinning her to a tree, his shoulders still rising and falling with his heavy, silent breaths.

"He might be hiding down on the cliffside," said another new voice, deeper than the last two. "You two, look that way, we'll go this way."

So there were at least four men, possibly more. And surely

there was no denying that they truly *were* hunting Joarr, right? But why? Wasn't the peace-treaty supposed to prevent such things? And surely Gwyn would have heard of it, if orcs were still being hunted and attacked, or even *killed*?

But then again—she felt her head tilting—there had been all those women's whispers, full of so many fears. And while most of those fears had been focused on themselves, Gwyn belatedly recalled that there had also been fears around this, too. Fears for the safety of the orcs, and their unborn sons. Whispers of aggression, of injuries, of war.

Gwyn's eyes were searching Joarr's, her forehead furrowed—and he kept gazing straight back, cool, unflinching, despite his still-heaving breaths. As if to say, no, this wasn't unusual, no, he wasn't surprised. No, the men weren't keeping their peace-treaty, and perhaps... perhaps they never had been?

Gwyn's thoughts flashed to her father and his horrid Council, to the foul laws they kept attempting to implement—and then to her great-aunt, who against all reasoning, had seemingly chosen to ally herself with the orcs. With this orc. This orc, whose steady eyes were still watching her, his head tilted, as though he could read her very thoughts as they passed.

And without intending to, Gwyn felt herself wince against his hand, her eyes almost... apologetic on his. Almost as if to say, *I'm sorry you've had to deal with this. I didn't know. I didn't... care.*

And how Joarr followed it, she couldn't quite say—but he did, and that was another wry twist on his mouth, a shrug from his bare shoulder under her hand. *Whatever*, it might have said. *I'm used to it.*

And perhaps it was the sheer casual bravery in such a dismissal, or the way his shoulder blade had shifted against Gwyn's still-clutching fingers. Or, perhaps, the ongoing truth of his hand still over her mouth, his scent furling so heavy, so rich...

But whatever it was, something streaked through Gwyn's belly, burning deep and low. Something that made her throat hitch, her lips slightly parting against his warm hand. Her eyes belatedly darting away, beyond him, seeking safety, perhaps an escape—

But there was no escaping this damned orc, especially when she was still clinging to him like this, her body trapped between his lean strength and a tree. And especially with his shoulder slightly shaking like that, as though—Gwyn's mortified eyes darted back to his smirking face—he was *laughing* at her, the bastard.

Gwyn grimaced into his hand, and attempted to elbow him, as well as she could with both arms around his shoulders—and gained for her trouble an even broader smirk, a spread of his long fingers under her arse as he hoisted her higher against him. The movement purposeful, almost proprietary, grinding her already-open groin closer against his belly. As if he had every right to do so, as if Gwyn were his to do with as he wished...

Mine, he'd said, back in the garden, with that certainty blazing in his eyes. *You bear my scent now.*

Gwyn's breath had dangerously caught, her eyes furtive and shameful on his—and his smirk curled higher, into what might have been an actual grin. Crinkling the corners of his glittering eyes, showing all his sharp white teeth, as his hand smoothly dropped from Gwyn's face, and went to grasp at her bunched-up *skirts*. Her skirts, which were now the only thing between her bare groin and his bare belly, and—

"There's no sign of him this way!" called a nearby voice. "Do we keep going, or come back?"

Gwyn's whole body froze rigid, white ice streaking up her spine, and she scarcely heard the other man's return call from the south, something about doing another sweep. Because

Joarr's easy, audacious hand had kept working at her skirts, and was now smoothly, purposely, dragging them *upwards*.

Gwyn gaped at his laughing eyes, his mocking, curving mouth—because good gods above, he was *not* truly suggesting this, was he? Suggesting this, here, now, while a band of men swarmed just below them, surely set on *killing* him?!

But the cool air currently tickling at Gwyn's bare arse clearly said otherwise, and so did the way Joarr's other hand grasped around her waist, supporting her tightly against him. So that his hand on her arse—which had previously been over her skirts—could slip up beneath, now palming hot and strong against fully bare skin.

An outraged gasp nearly escaped Gwyn's mouth—damn, *damn*—but she bit her lip just in time, and purposefully dug her fingernails into Joarr's shoulders instead. To which he shot her an approving, conspiratorial look—wait, he thought she *wanted* this?!—as his hand now dropped to the front of his own trousers, and slid down inside.

Good *gods*. Gwyn elbowed him again, hard enough to slightly knock him off balance—but his hand instantly snapped for the tree-trunk, steadying them again. His shaggy head now tilting as he studied her, and as the men's voices called out again, even closer than before.

Gwyn furiously jerked her head toward the voices below, her brows raised high, as if to demand, *Now? Really?* Which Joarr met with another smirk, even more challenging this time, his own brows raised to match hers.

Yes, really, it meant. *You don't want to?*

And this, surely, was where Gwyn needed to refuse, with wild and raging indignation. To attempt the silent equivalent of *Hell no, you audacious bastard, I am not copulating with you in a tree, these men are hunting you, they might very well hear us and kill you—*

But instead, she held still, and looked at him. Looked at those fearless waiting eyes, all bright glittering black, speaking of clear provocation, of danger, of threat. Of... *eagerness.*

Because of course he wanted this. Of course he wanted to take a lord's daughter in a tree, right above the noses of the men hunting him. That was just the kind of smug asshole he was, ready to leap at any opportunity, to take advantage, to stake his claim.

Mine.

And his mouth was quirking up again, betraying even more of that conspiratorial eagerness, light and teasing and alarmingly contagious. As if he and Gwyn were on a rare, exhilarating adventure together, and if she only followed along, she would find herself...

Smiling at him, like this. Rueful, and maybe disapproving, but eager, too. Saying, without speaking, *Fine, you devilish snake. Prove it. Show me.*

His replying flash of a grin was quick and genuine, lighting up his face. Turning it into something new, something that stole away Gwyn's breath, firing a sharp, shuddering thrill of heat deep into her belly—at least, until another too-close shout from directly below froze her to stillness again, her eyes frantic on Joarr's face.

But he didn't even look slightly concerned, the bastard, and his free hand had again dropped, moving below Gwyn's bunched-up skirts, tugging the last of them out of the way. And all at once, there was the blaring realization that her lower half was fully exposed under there, her legs spread shamefully wide, and that—her breath caught—he was—he was—

There. Touching her.

Gwyn's gasp nearly choked her throat, a full-body shudder rippling her to stillness. Because this wasn't his hand, wasn't a precursor or a tease. No, this was already *that*, slick and hard and demanding. Its smooth head nudging her apart, opening her around it, seeking its way inside.

Gwyn shuddered again, her body clamping tight against him, halting him there—and gods, he was so *much*, even just slightly jutted inside her like this. Stretching her so wide apart, invading her softness with his solid, uncompromising heat, swelling even fuller against her...

Gwyn's gasp almost escaped her mouth this time, but Joarr's warm hand clamped back over it, quick and meaningful. His eyes still gleaming, still speaking of amusement and anticipation, his head giving a slow, purposeful shake.

Be quiet, woman, it meant, *whilst I take you.*

More heat streaked to Gwyn's already-convulsing groin, clamping it tighter against that jutting head—but she somehow nodded, sharp and fervent against his hand. *I know. Don't stop.*

His grin flashed white, the sight again clutching at Gwyn's belly, wrenching her closer. Even as she froze again at the sound of another man's voice, almost directly beneath them.

"Any sign of him?" it called. "Should we come back that way?"

Gwyn's heart thundered louder, her fingernails digging deeper into Joarr's bare back, but his eyes on hers kept glimmering, hungry, fearless. And those eyes kept holding hers, that hand flexing over her mouth, as his hardness swelled again, and then slowly, surely, pushed inside.

Fuck. It was beautiful torture, exquisite agony, her still-inflamed heat once again crushed open around a piercing, plunging orc. An orc who didn't care if she was wildly shivering against him, her nails dragging at his back, her mouth gasping into the press of his strong hand. Because no, that was still only hunger in his eyes, only triumph, as he finally sank all the way inside her, settling her bare, swollen, split-open groin tight against his.

She felt his exhale rather than heard it, his breath hot and sweet against her face. His hand clenching on her arse as he ground his hips against her, wrenching her deeper, dragging another choked, desperate gasp from her still-covered mouth.

And he liked that too, his lashes fluttering, his lips parting—and when the men below shouted again, still far too close, Gwyn felt another exhale of his breath, harsh against her skin. And then an unmistakable flare of challenge across his eyes as that hand on her arse gripped tighter, drawing him out, leaving her trembly and empty in his wake...

But then he sank back in, smoother this time, faster. His hooded eyes still watching Gwyn as he did so, his hand tightening on her mouth. Perhaps testing her, taunting her, seeing if she would stay quiet, how much she would take...

But this time she bit back her gasp, pressing it down into the convulsive shivering of her body impaled upon him—and yes, that was surely approval, answering on his face. And when he dragged out again, his thrust back inside was even faster, harder, smoother, driving Gwyn full and deep upon him.

But somehow she still kept quiet, now biting at her lip behind his hand. And his approval came in a very slight smile this time, as he held her pinned against him, circling his hips, making her feel it, perhaps even rewarding her—

The men's voices were calling again, but perhaps now from further away, and of course Joarr took full advantage, dragging out, and plunging back inside in one deep, devastating stroke. Hard enough to shake Gwyn all over, nearly rattling her teeth, but she only bit her lip harder, choked back her scream into her throat—

And yes, that was more approval, more greed, kindling bright in his gleaming eyes—and he slipped his hand away from Gwyn's mouth, and instead grasped a thick, careful handful of her *hair*. Pulling back just enough to expose her neck, while she seized and flailed upon him, her eyes shocked and wide and staring, he wouldn't, he—he—

He was. Slamming deep and deadly inside her, again and again, that hand gently yanking at her hair with every thrust. Whirling up a roaring, rioting mass of light and sheer sensation, her entire body struck and scrabbling upon him. Silently shouting at him, raging at him, her teeth biting so hard that the tang of blood filled her mouth. *Don't stop you asshole, don't stop, more more more—*

The ecstasy flashed like a flood, blazing beneath Gwyn's trampling skin, bubbling and burning for escape. Consuming every last drop of her willpower in the charge to stay silent, to not betray this, pierced and clamped and arching upon an orc, her rapture raging to the sky—

And then it was Joarr arching, his throat and teeth bared, his hand in Gwyn's hair yanking hard enough to be painful. And that driving heft inside her suddenly locked to shuddering stillness, buried as deep as it would go—and then, oh *hell*, it released. Surging out pulse after pulse of hot molten euphoria, flooding her with the pure power of his hunger, his approval. Of his bright, burning *triumph*, fused and sealed within her, reborn again as one. As... *hers.*

She could feel her conquered, swollen heat still clutching against him, as if milking him, dragging out every last drop— and him silently answering, squeezing it out, wringing himself dry. His head tilted back, his eyes closed, his throat bobbing, his jaw sharp and striking in the dappled sunlight.

And when it finally ended, Gwyn couldn't move, couldn't stop staring, couldn't breathe. Could only wait, and watch, and feel the truth of him still inside her, his hard strength slowly softening. His breaths silently heaving through his chest against her, his hand releasing her hair—and then even giving her head a quick, almost apologetic caress.

And then, finally, were his eyes. His hazy, unguarded eyes, blinking back to hers again. And speaking, so bare and clear, of his deep satisfaction, his approval, his triumph. *Ach, yes. Well done, woman.*

Gwyn felt herself sag against him—had she perhaps been expecting his censure, his distance?—and belatedly released her tooth's still-sharp bite on her lip. Scarcely even noticing as a trickle of blood slipped down her chin, but Joarr's eyes immediately dropped to it, his body tensing against hers—

And before she'd even seen him move, his mouth was there. Brushing heated and eager against her bloody lip, his tongue lingering at the wound with astonishing gentleness. And gods, he smelled good, tasted so good, so close—and when Gwyn's own traitorous tongue slipped out, perhaps to test this, to meet this, he instantly met her in return. His kiss long and languorous, his slippery tongue twining against hers, easing her into his warm mouth—

And curse her, but it was that, of all things, that drew the low, betraying moan from Gwyn's throat. Not loud, not piercing—but still enough that Joarr utterly froze against her, his head and his kiss whipping away, his full attention fixed toward the east. Toward the... *men.*

"Did you hear that?" came one of their voices, far too audible in the twirling, crackling silence. "Came from this way."

No. *No.* Gwyn's body was shivering again, gooseflesh breaking out on her arms, her breaths heaving in harsh little pants—and Joarr spun back toward her, his brow furrowing. And in another flash of movement, his hand had tightly clasped over her mouth again, his eyes sharp with warning.

Be silent, they said. *Be still.*

Gwyn didn't even dare a nod, but just held those eyes with her own, her body locked tight against him. Waiting, waiting, as the men's steps crunched closer, and with them the distinctive sound of snuffling, sniffing dogs.

"Any sign of him?" one of the voices asked. "There was definitely a noise around here."

There were more stomping feet, a yelping dog, an unmistakable shirr of weapons. "No, but keep looking," one said. "Maybe he's up in a tree?"

Gwyn's heart faltered, her sweaty hands sliding dangerously on Joarr's back—and in return he gripped her closer, pressing her tighter against the tree. His eyes glancing quickly around, searching above and below, and then narrowing as they settled on something. On a cluster of... pinecones?

They were dangling several branches above, well out of reach, but Joarr's gaze stayed fixed upon them for a long, calculating instant. And then dropped back to Gwyn again, focused and urgent, and she felt both his hands shifting against her arse, guiding her away, releasing the hold of his slick, softened length between them—

But as he drew out, leaving Gwyn's still-spread groin quivering and hovering over the tree, there was a sudden, surging flood. A rush of hot, forceful, scented heat, pouring from inside Gwyn, and straight out onto the tree-branch below. Where it splashed and scattered in all directions, already coating the bark below, and dripping off toward the earth.

"It's not raining, is it?" came one of the men's voices from directly below, as one of the dogs began abruptly, frantically barking. And the panic was washing through Gwyn's form now, streaming with terrifying desperation, and wrenching even higher as Joarr thrust her fully away from him, pushing her back flat against the tree-trunk, his eyes dark with purposeful intent.

You stay here, they said, *and wait.*

Gwyn silently shouted her protest at him, even as her

trembly legs scrabbled for purchase on the narrow branch below. *No*, she wanted to say. *I can't. I'll fall.*

You won't, he said back, his eyes glinting, as he pried both her hands from where they were still clinging at his back, and pressed them against something above. Another branch, Gwyn's screaming thoughts noted, and she frantically clung to it, her feet skittering on the narrow branch beneath her, as Joarr steadily backed away, his eyes piercing, his finger pressed to his lips.

Do this, it said. *Trust me.*

And without waiting to see her answer, he crouched, his eyes focused on the pinecones above—and then leapt. Flying an astonishing distance upwards, his hair streaking out behind him—and as Gwyn's scream again choked in her throat, his fingers barely grasped the next branch above, his black claws scrabbling to hold on—

But somehow he did, even as the branch dipped and waved, earning another shout below from the men. And in one more flash of movement, Joarr had wrenched himself up onto it, his long leg swinging over, his hands shoving himself upwards— and then another desperate, mind-spinning leap, his lean form flying through the air, while the men's voices gathered and rose, even closer than before. And they were surely looking up, they had to see him, his body wrangling and twisting like that against the wildly waving branch, hanging upside-down as his hand snatched for a pinecone—

There was an instant's stillness as he lightly tossed it up, as if testing its weight in his hand—and with a jerk of his head, a sharp snap of his arm, he *threw* it. Hurling it hard and high toward the north, and after an instant Gwyn could hear it landing in multiple thunks, perhaps pinging off the branches of a faraway tree.

"What was that?" demanded one of the men's voices, but Joarr had already grasped another pinecone, and hurled it in the exact same direction. Resulting in another series of impressively loud thunks, resonating through the suddenly silent forest.

"Go!" shouted one of the men, amidst a swarm of crunching and rushing below—and then their combined footfalls and dog-yelps dashed northward, the sounds slowly fading as they went.

Gwyn felt herself badly slumping against the tree-trunk, her heart still clanging, her eyes desperately blinking at where Joarr had leapt back down from above, landing on the narrow branch with atypical unsteadiness. But then he swiftly caught his balance as he strode down the branch toward her, his eyes unreadable on hers.

All right? they seemed to ask, one hand reaching to lift her chin, the other circling close and familiar around her waist—and somehow Gwyn nodded, again and again, releasing her trembling grip from the branch above, and clinging back to the safety of his warm shoulders.

She felt him nod too, his hand briefly patting at her hair—and in another heave of movement, he'd again lifted her up, this time hoisting her against his side. And then, with perfectly silent steps, he again began climbing down the tree, using his free hand to guide his steps.

He finally landed on the ground in a heavy crouch, his eyes casting all around, lingering toward the north—but then he smoothly stood again, hoisting Gwyn higher against his hip as he silently strode along the ravine. Moving with a careful, quiet urgency, frequently glancing over his shoulder.

Finally he reached a place where the ravine narrowed, and a tree had fallen across its gaping width—and without even the slightest hesitation, he leapt up onto the tree, and strode across. Walking with breathtaking ease over the harrowing chasm, with a river rushing far below, and while Gwyn couldn't seem to stop shivering, she couldn't stop staring, either, drinking up the majestic, terrifying sight beneath them.

It felt like an eternity before they reached the other side, and Joarr finally leapt off onto solid ground again. But it suddenly seemed as though all the tension had slipped from his body at once, and when he settled Gwyn's trembly body back to her feet, there was an odd clutching sensation in his chest, shuddering rhythmically against her still-clinging hands.

Gwyn grasped for focus, blinking up toward him with dazed, uncertain eyes—and found him... laughing? Yes, *laughing*, his shoulders shaking, his eyes bright with crackling mirth. And his mouth broadly grinning down toward her, easy and contagious and brimming with irresistible life.

"Band defeated by *pinecone*," he said, between guffaws. "And *dripped* on with fresh *orc-seed*."

Gwyn had been fighting back an oddly uncontrollable urge to smile, and found that she'd already lost the battle, her mouth quirking up, her eyes dancing on his. "*What's that?*" she said, in her best impression of a deep male voice. "*It isn't raining, is it?*"

Joarr's hoot of laughter echoed through the ravine, far too loud—but he clearly didn't care, his shaggy head thrown back, his clawed hand clutching at his shaking belly. "And this *dog*," he added, his voice unsteady, his bright eyes dancing on Gwyn's. "Knowing this was my scent dripped clean upon his head, and these fool men no even *notice*?!"

And despite everything, Gwyn was laughing too, the sound warm and rich, her shoulders shaking. Which somehow ramped Joarr's laugh even more contagious than before, lighting up his eyes. "Raining," he said again, and those were truly tears, streaking down his cheeks. "*Raining!*"

And when he slid down onto his arse on the ground, his head bowed, his shoulders still shaking, Gwyn somehow slid down, too. Finding herself inexplicably tucked between his knees, his long legs close on either side of her, while more occasional gales of laughter rolled through his body against her.

"Ach, witch," he said finally, his voice still irresistibly warm, his head lifting to meet her eyes. "This was well met. I no even *think* to mate in tree, before this."

And while that perhaps should have been a dampening thought—did he often do such things in *other* places, then?—Gwyn still felt herself smiling back, warm and rueful. "Just had to wait until you had a lord's daughter in your clutches, right?" she asked lightly. "Take full advantage of the situation?"

His twinkling eyes on hers slightly stilled, his head tilting, considering her. Almost as if he were weighing her, deciding whether to tell her the truth.

"Mayhap I no think of lord's daughter, or *advantage*, in this," he said finally, with a shrug. "Mayhap I think only of *fun*. Ach?"

Oh. And while that was surely exactly what a devious orc would say—wasn't it?—it almost felt like truth, glimmering like that in his eyes. And somehow Gwyn was smiling at him again, her cheeks oddly heating, her own eyes dropping. "Right," she said, low. "Me, too."

There was a heartbeat's silence, a strange tightness furling through the air—and then Joarr rose to his feet again, drawing her up behind him. "Come, witch," he said, his voice deceptively casual. "After all this, mayhap my mountain shall mean naught to you, ach? Mayhap no even *frighten* you?"

Gwyn had been intently brushing off her skirts, fighting to ignore both the heat still swarming her cheeks, and the streak of telltale thick liquid now pooling down her thigh. Not to mention the truth of what they'd just done, she'd just copulated with an orc in a tree, a half-hour after she'd sworn never to touch the devious bastard again...

"Ach?" Joarr said again, a distinct note of challenge threading his voice—and when Gwyn furtively glanced up, the challenge was there in his eyes too, his brows lifted, the provocation curling at his too-expressive mouth. "You ken you face my mountain with such mettle, also? Show again how you are no only lord's daughter?"

Gwyn's eyes instantly narrowed, her fingers fisting at her skirts. "We've already agreed, for the purposes of this little exercise," she replied stiffly, "that I'm not a lord's daughter. I'm a *midwife*. Remember?"

But Joarr kept gazing at her, those brows raised, his mouth quirked. "Ach, I ken," he said, voice cool. "But mayhap we leap one branch beyond this? Mayhap when you come to my mountain, you show more of your true heart, and your hunger? Mayhap you freely flaunt this before me, and all my kin?"

Wait. He wanted Gwyn to flaunt her hunger... before his *kin*?! Meaning, of course, that this manipulative bastard was once again trying to manage the situation, and turn it to his advantage. Not only wanting to hide his defeat from his fellow orcs, now, but instead to show it as a *victory*. To show himself a clever, superior orc, who had recruited Orc Mountain a midwife... *and* who still held said midwife firmly in his clutches. In his *thrall*.

"And why, exactly," Gwyn said, clipped, "should I go even further out of my way to oblige you, orc? When I've already committed to one ruse to help you save face before your kin? Which was already an *excessive* kindness on my part, and which, you must realize, you already didn't deserve?"

Her voice had risen as she'd spoken, her eyes hard and demanding on his face. And for an instant, he just looked back at her, while something much like appreciation flicked through his eyes.

"You prove this to me," he finally replied, his voice smooth, "and I shall prove more to you. You show me your mettle and your wits and your hunger for me, as you walk amongst my kin—then I show you more of this *fun*. I give you fine frolic at my mountain you *never* forget, even after you go north to wed this man. Ach?"

Gwyn immediately opened her mouth to protest again—she was never marrying Roy, *ever,* and she was still returning to Varrahan tonight, wasn't she?—but Joarr's quick hand had already clapped against her mouth, its close weight feeling abominably familiar. Warm. Perhaps even... welcome.

"I give you more *deft tongue*," he said, his voice low, as its slick, sinuous length blatantly slipped out, and curled at his lips. "I give you more deep relief inside you. Mayhap I even give you"—his other hand snaked up, and calmly, deliberately grasped a handful of Gwyn's hair—"more of *this.*"

He'd very gently pulled, tilting her head back, driving a reflexive, helpless moan from Gwyn's mouth—even as her blinking eyes caught something, something new, flicking across his face. Something almost like... *reluctance*?

And that *wasn't* actually new, Gwyn realized, was it? And her stomach had suddenly seemed to plunge in her belly, the tingling hunger pooling away into uncertainty, into *shame.* Remembering how he hadn't intended to do it in the garden, either. How it had been her who'd pushed. Her who'd wanted more.

"But maybe—maybe you don't actually *want* to do more of that, with me," she breathed. "Do you?"

That was surely surprise, now, flaring in Joarr's eyes—and then vanishing just as quickly as he twitched an overly careless shrug. "Ach, I wish it," he said. "Only no wish to be part of... *this.*"

His hand had dropped from Gwyn's hair, and now stroked casually down her arm, the claw of his thumb faintly tracing against her still-tender skin. The touch light, gentle, but still enough to make her wince, as more shame swirled up into her cheeks.

"It's not the same," she said in a rush, before she could stop it. "It's not. At *all*. I *swear* to you."

And gods, why did it matter so much, why was she frantically searching his watching eyes for his mockery, his distaste, his *judgement*. And why was she so damned relieved when he finally shrugged again, his head briefly nodding. His hand sliding up her arm again, over her shoulder, sinking back into her hair...

"Ach, then," he murmured, as he again tilted her head back, the movement slow, careful, *wonderful*. "Mayhap I even give you *this*."

With that, he ducked his shaggy head down, and bent his face into her *neck*. Brushing her too-sensitive skin with hot breath, warm lips, his slick, twisting tongue, his...

His *teeth*. Sharp, shocking, deadly *teeth*, dragging against her vulnerable skin with gentle, painful, meaningful intent. Wrenching Gwyn's breath into a loud, desperate, betraying cry, while the heat flashed to her groin, craving for more, more, *more*—

Until just as quickly, it vanished. Because Joarr had eased abruptly backwards, well out of her reach, both hands dropping slack to his sides. His brows again raised in a silent challenge, his eyes now studiously blank, as if he hadn't been affected by that in the least.

"You like, ach?" he said, and his voice was all taunt, all insolence. "Wish for more?"

And gods, Gwyn couldn't even slightly pretend to deny it. Not after all she'd just betrayed, and surely not with her breaths still heaving like this, her heart hammering, her face red-hot. And her eyes, her eyes searching his face, how it was so cautiously distant again, hidden beneath his mask...

And without thought, Gwyn lowered her gaze from his eyes, and instead found... *that*. That long, rigid hardness, flagrantly swelling against the front of his trousers. Saying, *betraying*, that yes, he surely wanted it too...

But wait. *No.* He still wanted more than that. He was seeking an angle in this, an advantage, a *victory*. This was all about him, always about him, and Gwyn had to think, why couldn't she *think*—

"This garden of yours," she finally managed, between breaths. "Does it have other plants like chasteberry? Or any more mushrooms like the sulphur shelf?"

Something that again might have been appreciation flashed in Joarr's eyes, and he slowly inclined his head. Finally betraying that *yes*, the bastard, he'd grown that chasteberry plant himself—and that was another truth, another revelation, from this infuriating deceitful orc.

"Then these are my terms, orc," Gwyn said, as firmly as she could, "I'll do my damnedest to put on a good show for you at your mountain, but you also need to give *me* free rein in *your* garden, like my great-aunt gave you. I get to do whatever the hell I want with it, and take back whatever seeds and cuttings I please. And"—her eyes narrowed at him, her traitorous brain suddenly lingering on that *deceitful* point—"as long as you are touching me, you are *not* touching anyone else. No one, *nowhere.* You got that?"

An unmistakable amusement twinkled in his eyes, and he again inclined his head—but not before Gwyn caught the flash of triumph there, too. Because wait, had she just implied that this *wasn't* only about today? That this terribly ill-advised deal with this terribly manipulative orc might extend until... when? Not her remaining twenty-two days until her father's deadline, surely?

"Ach, I follow," Joarr said, his voice cool, as if they were discussing the weather or dinner plans, rather than a tangled, twisted, tit-for-tat transaction that surely flouted all good sense. "You shall thus stay true to me also, ach?"

Oh. Something clutched tight in Gwyn's belly—he cared about her loyalty, too?—and she couldn't seem to raise her eyes as she jerked a curt, quick nod. Saying, surely, *Yes. Only you.*

There was an unintelligible sound from Joarr, deep and low—but when Gwyn glanced up, his eyes were all light again, sparkling down toward her. And his hand had once again slipped to her face, tilting it up, so easy, so proprietary. As if she truly were his, for now. For today. And surely, that was all...

"Then come to my home, my fierce little witch," he purred, "and show me all you can do."

13

If Gwyn's primary goal was to take Orc Mountain in stride, she utterly failed at her first attempt.

The rest of their journey had taken them through ever-thicker forest, blocking the sight of Orc Mountain above—and when Joarr finally led her out of the trees, and halted at a solid-looking rock wall, she found herself looking up, and up, and up. At a sheer, craggy, deadly stone monstrosity, looming over them like a brooding giant, blasting its black smoke to the sky.

"Well," Gwyn said, rubbing at her mouth, fighting to wrestle down the sudden waves of rolling, rioting panic. "I don't suppose—your garden—might be, um, out here, somewhere?"

She flapped her hands at the thick forest around them, which was obviously horribly suited for a garden, and Joarr smirked at her as he strode undaunted toward the stone wall. "My garden is under the sun, ach," he said coolly, "but it is only found from inside."

Of course it was, and Gwyn made a face, and squared her

shoulders. "Right," she replied, her voice thick. "How do we get in, then."

For an instant, Joarr didn't answer, and she could feel the weight of his eyes, prickling her skin beneath them. "My orc brothers no harm you," he said. "My scent now hangs heavy upon you, ach?"

Right. So he'd made some kind of... *claim* on her, then, through what they'd done. And while Gwyn had been trying quite desperately to shove down her memory of what had happened in the tree, it had hovered over the rest of their journey with a nagging, twisting tenacity. The way he'd looked. The way he'd felt. And of all things, the way he'd *laughed*.

"Come," he said, and that was the unmistakable feel of his warm hand, spreading easy and proprietary against Gwyn's arse. "Find more *fun* with me. Ach?"

Something hot and hungry swelled in Gwyn's belly, and she couldn't quite look at him as she twitched a jerky nod. But that hand gave her a satisfied little pat before he strode the rest of the way to the sheer wall of the mountain, and heaved his shoulder against it.

And to Gwyn's gaping astonishment, it moved. *Tilted.* As though the rough, jagged stone were installed on some sort of hinge, turning to reveal a narrow sliver of blackness beyond.

Joarr glanced back at her, brows raised, his typical taunting smile curling at his mouth—and somehow, Gwyn mustered the courage to follow him toward that inscrutable darkness. Toward Orc Mountain.

She was doing this for her garden, she told herself, as she stepped inside, and the rock crunched shut behind her. Making her own way.

But as she stood there, suddenly enclosed in cool pitch-darkness, the panic began flailing again, clawing at her ribs. Good gods, she was in *Orc Mountain*, she couldn't see a damned thing, what if they were surrounded by vicious deadly orcs at this very moment—

"Come," Joarr's voice repeated, close in the darkness, as his warm hand again found her arse, and nudged her forward. "I no walk you into wall, ach?"

The sound of his voice was unnervingly comforting, and Gwyn dragged in breath, and took a tentative step forward. Finding, indeed, only more empty air before her in the blackness, and earning another approving pat of Joarr's hand.

"Where are you walking me, then?" she asked, perhaps out of curiosity, perhaps out of a shameful need to hear his voice again. "To your garden, right?"

There was an instant's hesitation, even as Joarr's hand nudged her into another cautious step, and another. "No yet," he said, his voice distinctly casual. "Must first bring you to Captain, and next my clan. Show them new midwife, come to care for women. *After* this, we find fun in garden, ach?"

Oh. Of course. Because that was the highly ill-advised plan Gwyn had foolishly signed onto, wasn't it? *Show me your mettle and your wits and your hunger,* he'd said, *then I show you more fun.*

And as she allowed herself to be ushered down a pitch-black corridor, ever deeper into Orc Mountain, she couldn't at all recall why she'd ever agreed to such a ridiculous scheme. Especially when it clearly worked almost entirely to Joarr's advantage, if he decided to walk away right now she would be trapped, lost, *doomed*—

"No all our paths are so dark," his voice cut in again. "Many now bear lamps, to help guide humans' eyes. But we are sure to meet other orcs in those, ach? I wish my captain to learn of you first."

Gwyn's panic had slightly settled again, her thoughts fixed on the damnable comfort of his voice. "And who is your captain?" she asked, perhaps just to keep him talking. "And is he captain of your clan? Of the... *Bautul*? Or of all the orcs?"

"Of all this mountain," Joarr replied, with another approving—and infuriatingly comforting—pat of his hand. "And he is Grimarr, of Clan Ash-Kai. He has my fealty, and my favour."

Gwyn couldn't help mentally comparing that to his tepid praise for his own clan—*they have my like*, he'd said—but before she could ask what made this Grimarr so superior, Joarr had guided her sideways, and suddenly into *light*.

Or rather, a room. A snug, stone-walled room, with a low table in the middle of it, and a fire merrily crackling in the opposite wall. And in the dancing firelight, there were—*orcs*. Three huge, vicious, deadly-looking orcs, all sitting on the floor around the table, and staring at her with glittering black eyes.

And even if Gwyn had somehow become accustomed to Joarr—to his greenish skin, his harsh features, the sheer height of him—the sight of these new orcs still seemed to fire fresh ice through her veins. One orc was just as lean and sharp-looking as Joarr, his eyes already narrow with dislike, his sinewy arms crossing over his bare chest. While the shorter, bulkier orc beside him looked far less alarming, his gaze curious rather than hostile—but wait, were those *teeth-marks* in his neck, dripping *blood* onto his tunic? And the last orc—Gwyn's heart had perhaps stopped beating—was a scarred, massive, hulking beast, so huge that she hadn't even noticed the fourth person curled into his lap. The... *woman*?

But yes, good gods, that was a woman. And not only that, but tucked into the woman's arms was a small, black-haired bundle... with a tiny, pointed *green ear* just visible through that thatch of hair.

For a single, frozen breath, Gwyn couldn't move, or blink, or tear her eyes away. She'd never encountered an orc child in person before, and while she knew—intellectually, at least—that they were much like human ones, there was still something about how small it was, how vulnerable, how its tiny hand was clutched into the woman's dark braid. And how the woman was cradling it, close and clearly affectionate, as any mother might, and—Gwyn's brain latched onto something in the chaos, her eyes peering closer—how the woman was surely sound *asleep* in the circle of the orc's huge arms, with her baby also asleep upon her.

There was truly no way to speak, no way out of the stunned silence in Gwyn's throat, or the memories of her clients' whispers now swarming her thoughts—and thank the gods Joarr coughed, snapping her blinking gaze up toward him. Toward where he was looking entirely unconcerned, his brow raised, his eyes speaking again of that challenge, that promise. *Show me your mettle and your wits, as you walk amongst my kin, and I show you...*

"This is our captain," he told her, his brow still lifted, as he inclined his head toward the huge orc with the woman in his arms. "Grimarr, of Clan Ash-Kai. And his Right Hand"—Joarr nodded toward the lean, glowering orc—"Drafli, of Clan Skai. And his Left Hand is Baldr, of Clan Grisk. Drafli's mate."

Joarr's eyes had settled on the least alarming of the three orcs, who was currently giving Gwyn a cheerful, if rather sheepish, smile, his hand absently rubbing at his bloody neck. A startling fact that Joarr didn't even seem to notice, as he waved back toward the big orc—or rather, the sleeping woman in his lap. "And this is Grimarr's mate, called Jule, and their son Tengil. Jule was once Lady Norr of Yarwood, before she chose to swear vows to our captain."

Gwyn's brain was shouting even louder, her eyes now desperately flicking between Joarr and the subjects of these thoroughly shocking disclosures. This woman had once been an actual *lady*, in Yarwood? And she'd willingly sworn vows to an *orc*? And good gods, Gwyn had surely heard—and ignored—tales of this too, hadn't she? Of the Yarwood lord's mistreatment of his wife, and then an attack by orcs, and then the wife's disappearance, and now... *this*?

And not only that, but—Gwyn's glance at Joarr was more of a glare this time—had he just said this Baldr and Drafli were *mated*, too, as in married, as in a clear repudiation of all the realm's firmly held laws? As casually as he might point out that his mountain was made of *stone*?

But yes, yes, he had. And as the bastard stared back at Gwyn, brows still slightly raised, it occurred to her that this was another challenge. It was him throwing the pinecone toward her, seeing what she would do next. Whether she would show him her mettle and her wits, or turn tail and run, like the craven coward he himself was wont to be.

And curse him, but Gwyn could surely do better than that, and surely wasn't about to be defeated by a round of introductions, either. So she somehow squared her shoulders, and even dropped a little curtsey as she turned back toward the strange orcs.

"It's a pleasure to meet you all," she said, her voice only slightly faltering. "I'm Gwyn, from Varrahan. I'm a herbalist, and a trained midwife. Joarr tells me"—she had to drag in breath—"you might have some need of a midwife here?"

The angry orc—Drafli—didn't show any acknowledgement that Gwyn had spoken, but the neck-bitten orc—Baldr— smiled again, even warmer this time. And the huge captain orc nodded back toward her, his mouth slightly curving up, though it occurred to her that his glittering eyes were far more knowing than she might have liked.

"We welcome you to our mountain, woman," he said, his voice deep and unhurried, his clawed hand stroking the still-sleeping woman in his arms. "My mate shall be well pleased to meet you, once she wakes. Our son now grows new teeth, and thus scarce slept, this night past."

There was both pride and ruefulness in his voice,

something Gwyn had often encountered in bewildered new fathers—and she felt her unease slightly thawing, her own mouth softening into a little smile, too. "Teething is always so difficult, isn't it?" she replied. "That said, there's a helpful herb—chamomile—and if you apply a paste to his gums, that ought to soothe the pain, at least long enough for him to fall asleep. I'd be happy to make you some, if—"

She bit off the familiar spiel there, disconcerted—not only by her own offhanded offer to *help* this horrifying orc, but also by the unmistakable flare of interest in his watchful eyes. And also by the undeniable fact that her chamomile was back in Varrahan, and therefore entirely unavailable to support this thoroughly ill-thought plan.

"Ach, I ken I have some of this," said Joarr's voice beside Gwyn, "should you wish for it, Captain."

Gwyn's head snapped back toward Joarr, her eyes narrowing—but the bastard just gazed down at her, utterly unruffled. Telling her, without words, that he *did* have chamomile in his garden? Truly?!

"Thank you, brother," Grimarr replied. "I shall speak with my mate upon this once she wakes, and send you word."

Joarr briefly nodded toward Grimarr, before settling his eyes back on Gwyn. "Also, Captain," he continued, his voice deceptively light, "I have altered our plan, with this woman."

Their plan. Gwyn blinked at him, and then at this captain, whose gaze looked even more piercing than before. "Ach, I see this," he said, his voice deliberate, heavy with meaning. "What have you altered, brother?"

And for an unmistakable instant, that was surely *uncertainty* in Joarr's eyes. In the way his hand reflexively snapped to that tooth around his neck, concealing it in his fingers' grip.

"This woman knows," he replied, after a too-long silence, "that I wish to whelp a son upon the daughter of Lord Anton of Dunburg, as a strike against the lords' foul new law."

An odd, scraping shiver hurtled up Gwyn's spine—these orcs *all* knew who she was, then? And Joarr had concocted this dastardly little ruin-her-life plan with his *captain*, the leader of their entire *mountain*? And also—her eyes darted between the captain and Joarr—had Joarr just said he *still* wished for a son with her? *Present tense?*

"Ach, this would alter much, I ken," replied the captain's deadpan voice, and it distantly occurred to Gwyn that his glinting eyes looked almost *amused*. "And yet, this woman willingly comes to us, bearing your fresh scent?"

His gaze had shifted to something more speculative as it slipped back to Gwyn, clearly giving her an opportunity to speak—but her thoughts were clamouring far too loudly in her skull, drowning out her voice. And finally it was Joarr who spoke again, his hand still absently stroking the tooth at his neck.

"You ken I always run with what the gods drop upon me," he told Grimarr. "Thus, I seek new way in this. Seek to help this woman, mayhap, and regain her trust. Lest you wish to stop me, Captain?"

That was an unmistakable challenge in his voice, but Gwyn's uncertain glance at the captain showed him looking thoroughly unprovoked, his eyes steady on Joarr's. "No, I shall not stop you," he said finally. "But you must make sure there can be no claim of kidnapping or guile. No cause for men to cast blame upon us. Ach?"

Right. He thought Gwyn's disappearance would lead to accusations of abduction, or worse. And Gwyn found herself again looking between them, twitching her head back and forth. "I left a note," she said. "And I'm only staying here for a day. Right?"

But Joarr's glance at her was quick, quelling, his eyes flicking back to his captain. "Ach, you ken I shall address this, should she stay longer," he said. "My scouts shall leave more notes, and traces of her there. And spread word of her many travels, mayhap."

Gwyn was now eyeing Joarr suspiciously—this seemed a lot of forethought, for a one-day trip—but the captain was looking distinctly pleased, and gave a satisfied grunt. "Good," he said. "And whilst this woman stays, we speak not of her father nor Dunburg before our kin, ach?"

He was obviously including Gwyn in that directive, his focus again shifting toward her—and she saw Joarr nod at the same time she did, his shoulders visibly relaxing. "Ach, she has agreed to this," Joarr said lightly. "Whilst she is here, she is solely a midwife who wishes to gain my garden, and my hungry tongue."

Gwyn's face flushed with sudden, powerful heat, which was only made worse by Joarr's jaunty, knowing grin down toward her. "Best of all, this is all truth," he purred. "Is it not, woman?"

Gwyn shot him a black look, but her retort was forestalled by the warm, appreciative chuckle from the captain at the table. "Ach, you must well meet her wishes, then, brother," he said. "We shall speak again soon."

It was clearly a dismissal, and Joarr answered it with an easy nod, the smile still lingering at his mouth. And then, with an already-familiar clutch of his hand to Gwyn's arse, he steered her out the door, and back into the pitch-black corridor.

Gwyn's brain was still frantically churning, pulling pieces together, so distracted that the close blackness didn't feel nearly as oppressive as it had before. And perhaps it was her imagination, but Joarr's body beside her felt easier than before too, his long arm all but embracing her, his graceful steps moving in time with hers.

"So you didn't only want me to *meet* your captain," Gwyn said finally, frowning up in the general direction of Joarr's face, "but you wanted to *test* me, while he watched. You wanted to show him how thoroughly I'd stick to our midwife story. And also"—she felt her frown deepen—"you wanted to pitch your revised plan to him, didn't you? Because you actually had no idea if he'd approve of you single-handedly tossing out your original plan to destroy my life, and deciding to bring me here instead?"

There was a brief, almost imperceptible flash of tension through the warm body against her—and then the sound of his laugh, rich and appreciative in the darkness. "Witch woman," he said lightly. "I knew you should show your mettle in this, ach?"

So her suspicions were entirely correct, the bastard, and Gwyn huffed a groan, even as she fought back the twitch of a smile on her mouth. "What if your captain had decided to kick me out on the spot?" she demanded. "Or to imprison me, or hold me for ransom, or something?"

And gods, why hadn't she been more concerned about this, why had she just taken Joarr at his word, *again*—but his next bright, genuine-sounding laugh seemed to scatter her tension, his hand briefly abandoning her arse to ruffle against her hair. "Ach, he no do such a thing against woman *I* bring here," he said lightly. "And even if this come to pass, mayhap you find *fun* in this prison, ach? Mayhap I bind you in shackles, and pull your hair, and punish you?"

His voice was teasing, testing, *searching* her on this—and Gwyn halted mid-step, her breath catching, her heart wildly beating. "No," she hissed, before she could stop it. "*Never*. My father, one time he forgot me in the family crypt, and—"

She broke off there, far too late, while certain horrible, mostly repressed memories threatened to surge up, to swallow her—and suddenly it was Joarr surrounding her, his arm on her back pulling her close, his other hand sunk into her hair. "Then we no do this," he said, softer than she expected. "I only ask, ach? Wish to know."

Oh. Gwyn felt herself oddly sagging, her head nodding, her eyes fluttering closed. "Is that—something *you* want, though?" she heard her wretched voice ask. "Something you'd miss, if I—"

And good gods, what was she even asking with this? Surely she was still only spending a day here? *Surely?*

But Joarr hadn't laughed at the question, or dismissed it, and he was somehow still here against her, his body so solid, so damned reassuring. "Ach, no, woman," he replied, without a trace of mockery in his voice. "I no need locks or chains to spill my seed. I may no more belong to Skai clan, but I am no yet Ka-esh, ach?"

With that, he drew away, his hand again ruffling her hair as he guided her back down the corridor. While it occurred to Gwyn's still-scattered thoughts that this was another pinecone, another opening. *No more Skai, no yet Ka-esh…*

"So the Skai were your old clan, then?" she asked, though her voice still sounded damnably thin. "And the Ka-esh clan enjoys, um, *games of intimacy?*"

It was a term some women had furtively used for it, when they'd come to Gwyn with unexpected injuries, and Joarr gave her another approving little pat. "Ach, the Ka-esh even have a secret room for this, down in the bowels of the mountain," he said lightly. "But when you meet them, they shall only speak of their books and their learning and their *science*, ach? And so long as you listen, they shall speak, and speak, and *speak.*"

He sounded genuinely amused by this, and Gwyn felt her interest catching, her thoughts indeed chasing this damned pinecone where he willed. "And the Skai?" she asked. "What are they like?"

Joarr had to have known it was coming, but that was surely another flare of telltale tension through his body, in his hand against her. "Skai no like to keep secrets, or to hide our hunger away," he replied slowly. "Skai give no room for shame. And

Skai *do*, instead of read and speak, ach? We hunt, we fight, we mate, and we flaunt our *joy* in this."

We. It had obviously slipped out without him catching it, and Gwyn again felt that twitch of tension through his body. Strong enough that she twitched too, her eyes seeking his face, despite the still-inscrutable darkness.

"Well, it certainly sounds like you'd fit right in," she said, and she meant it. "You must miss them."

There was another beat of silence, another breath of tightness against her. "Ach, they are still here," Joarr replied, and even in the darkness, Gwyn could envision that mask, slipping over his eyes. "Naught to miss, ach?"

He might as well have not bothered, but Gwyn didn't try to argue. And after another moment's silent walking in the blackness, he abruptly drew her toward the right, and then around a sharp turn, and then another.

"Wait here, woman," he said, as both his big hands gripped at her hips, holding her in place. "Whilst I trade for lamp."

Wait, he was trading for a *lamp*? But yes, his touch had vanished, and was almost instantly replaced by the sounds of voices. His voice, yes, low and rolling, speaking the orcs' blacktongue, and with it another voice, higher-pitched, and unmistakably combative. But Joarr's voice didn't rise, and after a distinctive clank of metal—of coins?—he was back beside Gwyn again, and a sudden blinding light lit up the black corridor around them.

"Here," he said, thrusting the lamp's metal handle into her fingers. "Better?"

Better. And as Gwyn squinted at him in the too-bright light, it occurred to her that his head was tilted, his brows furrowed... and that it might actually have been *concern* in his eyes. Concern, because of what? That stupid little disclosure about the crypt?

But yes, surely, that was what he meant, and his eyes slid

purposefully away from hers, his shoulder shrugging, as though she'd somehow asked aloud. "I no followed why you tasted of fear toward this mountain, when you have feared so little else," he said, his voice light. "I no count this against you, ach?"

Right. Because Gwyn was supposed to be impressing him, showing him her mettle—and she'd already failed, because he'd known she was afraid of a giant hunk of rock. And so he'd bought her a damned lamp, as some sort of *consolation*, and—

"Also," he continued, louder than before, his head angling toward the dark shadow of a nearby door in the wall, "it is good that I remind Uglak that I have *right* to Bautul trading-post, ach? That he must deal *fair* with me, lest I come *steal* what I wish whilst he sleeps?"

There was the distinctive sound of a retort, barking back from beyond the door's blackness, and while it was all again in the gnarled black-tongue, Gwyn was sure she caught the unmistakable word *Skai*. Spat out like a curse. Like an *insult*.

And despite everything, she felt her indignation rising, her eyes disbelieving on Joarr's face. That orc—that *Bautul* orc—had called Joarr a Skai, and tried to prevent him from buying a *lamp* for his guest? Truly?

But yes, truly, that was what Joarr had meant. And while it was surely also another pinecone—another distraction, hurled into the sky—Gwyn again felt herself chasing it, following it where it led.

"Why wouldn't your new clan deal fairly with you?" she demanded at him. "I thought you said this was bound at birth, so it couldn't be changed. Why on earth would they hold something like that against you, when it's so far beyond your control, and obviously not something you wished or asked for?!"

And again, though Joarr had clearly wanted Gwyn to run down that path, she didn't miss his reflexive wince, or the clutch of his hand back to that tooth around his neck. And the way he smiled at her, like it was an attempt at his mask, that had instead faltered into a brittle, defeated bleakness.

"You wish to learn my clan's ways?" he asked, in a voice just as bleak as his eyes. "Wish to face these with me?"

There was surely some kind of meaning there—some unspoken truth, or perhaps even a warning. But even so, Gwyn already felt herself nodding, sharp and certain, toward those empty eyes. She'd promised to do this. To show him her mettle, and help him. For her garden. Her future.

"Ach, then, witch," he said, his throat convulsing, his mouth curling into another blank, broken smile. "Next, we meet the Bautul."

14

Joarr led Gwyn down the corridor in a stilted, dangling silence. His hands now not touching her, but instead hanging stiff at his sides, his steps smooth and controlled, his eyes staring straight ahead.

And up ahead, there was another light, gradually brightening the walls around them. And as they approached, Gwyn could hear a rising murmur of voices, and perhaps other sounds, too. Hinting at something she wasn't sure she wanted to identify, and Joarr's grim face was certainly no comfort, and—

And with one last step, the surrounding stone corridor suddenly broadened into a room. A large, circular stone room, with low stone benches cut into the walls, and wooden tables and chairs scattered about. And in the room's very middle, there was a tall, cylindrical stone chimney, rising all the way up into the stone ceiling, and boasting a lively, crackling fire at its base.

Under other circumstances, the fire—and the relative normalcy of the room it illuminated—should have been a welcome surprise. But once again, Gwyn's body felt irrevocably struck to stillness, her eyes fixed wide and stunned to the sight before her. To the dozen-odd orcs filling the room, and... *debauching* one another.

One orc had another orc pinned to the nearest wall, his trousers yanked low, his hips snapping powerfully against the first orc's bare backside. Another orc was sprawled spread-legged on a bench, while yet another one knelt before him, working over his groin with his mouth. And another pair were fully bared and furiously wrestling on the floor, perhaps fighting for dominance, until—Gwyn startled—one finally pinned the other, and then drove inside, while the defeated orc kicked and moaned beneath him.

Gods. Gwyn had never considered herself much of a prude—her line of work generally involved far more familiarity with the human body than most—but even so, this was certainly multiple leagues beyond her current realm of experience. So far beyond that her brain couldn't quite seem to accept it, and had instead decided to fixate upon the only orc in the room—beyond Joarr—who was not currently lost in the throes of passion. A huge, deeply hideous orc who was sitting across from someone on a bench, and... *sewing*?

Gwyn blinked again at the sight, because not only was the orc indeed sewing, but the person across from him was a *woman*. And the woman was sewing, too, both of them intently frowning down at what looked to be a single piece of cloth between them.

Gwyn's blatant staring had finally seemed to catch the hideous orc's attention, because his big head snapped up, his eyes narrowing toward her. And then his gaze flicked to Joarr beside her, and held there with something that had to be astonishment, or perhaps even disbelief.

Joarr surely saw it too, and when Gwyn glanced up toward him, that mask was already firmly in place, hiding away his eyes. And without a word, or a single look back toward her, he ushered her into the room, and straight into the midst of its groaning, growling, completely shameless orcs.

Gwyn's steps slightly stumbled, her eyes darting furtively at the shocking sights still unfolding around them—but Joarr's hand had thankfully gripped her again, holding her steady. And while many of the orcs hadn't yet seemed to notice her, she could still feel several pairs of eyes settling on her as they passed, followed by multiple voices quieting to watchful, wondering whispers.

Joarr still hadn't even spared a glance toward them, and just kept guiding Gwyn across the room, his steps purposeful, his hand firm on her back. Until he drew her to a halt before the ugly, incredulous-looking orc, who slowly set his sewing aside, and rose to his feet.

And. This orc was *massive*. Perhaps just as large as the captain orc, with a thick corded neck, a huge barrel chest, and powerful, sloping shoulders. And he was entirely undressed, his muscled body heavily dusted with dense black hair, and— Gwyn tried to stop herself from looking, too late—the sight at his groin was blatantly bared, though thankfully pointing slack toward the floor.

But even more daunting, by far, was his face. It was harsh and badly scarred, with a ruined nose, and bulging, battered ears that scarcely retained their pointed tips. His mouth was cruel and thin, and his eyes under their heavy brows were truly vicious, glowering at Joarr with visible, palpable loathing.

"Ach, our *brother* has returned," the orc said, his lip curling. "And what is *this*?"

His frankly terrifying gaze had snapped to Gwyn's face, before sliding deliberately down toward her waist. Almost as if peering *inside* her, somehow, and she couldn't deny the irrational urge to cover herself, or perhaps even hide behind Joarr's tall form beside her.

But she was supposed to be proving this to Joarr, and

surely this exact moment was a crucial part of what he'd wanted from that. And while the bastard surely could have taken a minute to better warn her about this—whatever the hell it was—there was also something about the stillness of his hand on her back, the cool blankness of his eyes on this orc's face.

"My *name*," Gwyn finally replied, when Joarr still didn't speak, "is *Gwyn*. And I'm a practicing midwife, and with Joarr's help, I've come to offer my services to the women here."

The disbelief again flared across the frowning orc's eyes, his cruel mouth snarling toward her—when suddenly, the woman who'd been sitting across from him staggered up to her feet, and grasped his huge arm. "Silfast," she gasped. "*Please.*"

Gwyn blinked at the woman, who bore a head of thick dark hair, and a pair of large dark eyes—and whose plump, scantily clad form was visibly *pregnant*, perhaps five or six months along. Not only that, but the woman also looked unmistakably exhausted, her eyes shot with red, with deep blue circles beneath.

"It's so nice to meet you, Gwyn," she said, her voice soft, her mouth curving in a wan but genuine smile. "I'm Stella, of Clan Bautul. And this is my mate, Silfast. He's one of our mountain's fiercest warriors, and serves as a captain of the Bautul clan."

Her fingers were digging into the orc's muscled arm, clearly sending some kind of silent message—and while the orc's glance down toward her was still dark with displeasure, his other hand moved to rest over hers, holding it against his skin.

"And thus, I must hold our kin to account," the orc replied, his deep voice a growl, his eyes glowering back at Joarr's face. "And most of all those who make vows, and then flaunt their *failure* to keep them!"

Gwyn felt Joarr's hand clutching against her back, but his eyes remained impassive, his face expressionless. "I no *fail*," he said, voice clipped. "I only alter my means. And I spoke of this to the captain today, and he has granted me leave upon this. So why no you?"

Gwyn's eyes narrowed, darting back and forth between the two orcs, while her whirling brain fought to catch up again. So this Silfast orc had been involved in that destroy-her-life plan too? And not only that, but Joarr had made some kind of *vow* about it? To *him*?

"Ach, the *captain*," Silfast sneered at Joarr, baring a row of deadly white teeth. "You ken the captain's leave absolves you of your vow? Again, you show you have learnt nothing of your clan, or your goddess!"

His *goddess*? But yes, Joarr's hand had again clenched on Gwyn's back, again suggesting that there was some truth to this, some weight he surely didn't welcome. "I no dishonour the goddess," he replied, without inflection. "I oft seek her, in this."

He had? Gwyn's surprise must have shown on her face, because this Silfast's snarl had twitched into a chilly smile, his eyes now glinting on hers. "Ach, is this truth, woman?" he demanded. "Has our *brother* oft spoken of his goddess to you, as a true Bautul would? Has he taught you her ways, and what shall be expected of you, now that he has placed his scent upon you, and brought you here, to our sacred hearth?"

Gwyn's heart skipped a beat, her eyes again darting up at Joarr's face—but again, he was looking straight ahead, impassive, unmoving. As though his mask had consumed him whole, emptied him of his life and his laughter, and there was an odd, inexplicable pang of sympathy, jolting in her belly.

"Joarr did speak of his goddess, several times," she belatedly replied, lifting her chin toward Silfast. "But my decision to accompany him here was quite sudden, and then we were almost instantly pursued by men. So there was very little time to delve into specifics."

But if she thought that would help, she'd utterly miscalculated, because the rage in Silfast's eyes only kindled higher, his huge body rounding back toward Joarr, his growl rising in his throat. But again Stella clutched at her mate's arm, her eyes wide, her agitated urgency even more palpable than before.

"We are *happy* to have you here, Gwyn," she said meaningfully, fixing her tired eyes back on Gwyn's face. "And if you're new to the clan, of course you're new to the goddess as well. She is the Goddess of Bautul—of this clan—and though she's best found in the moon, she often meets us in other forms, as well."

Stella's hand fluttered purposefully beyond them, toward the middle of the room—and when Gwyn spun to look, it was to the unnerving realization that nearly all the room's orcs had stopped their cavorting, in favour of watching them. Watching all this, no doubt, and listening, and *judging*. Judging her, and clearly judging Joarr, as well.

But Joarr was still offering no help whatsoever, the mask still firmly in place over his eyes, all life locked beneath. Except... except for that brief, telling glance toward the tall chimney in the middle of the room, with the fire crackling at its base.

It surely meant something, something important—so Gwyn studied the chimney again, more carefully this time. Looking at the rounded weight of its stone base, filled with that lively fire, and then narrowing as it rose. As it then swelled again, curving out and in before blending into the stone ceiling.

Oh. *Ohhhh.* It was a woman's figure, with a fire in its belly. Or rather, perhaps, life. A child.

And Gwyn could readily appreciate the symbolism in that, and she nodded as she turned back toward Stella, and even attempted a smile. "It's a lovely representation," she said. "And I presume you have specific practices around the Goddess of Bautul? Or certain rituals, and such?"

Stella immediately smiled again, obvious relief flaring in

her tired eyes. "Yes, exactly," she said. "And one of these"—she shot Silfast a swift, unreadable look, her face slightly reddening—"guides how newcomers are brought into the clan."

Gwyn couldn't help another glance up at Joarr, who still remained infuriatingly useless, locked like that behind his mask. "I see," she replied, and after another instant's awkward silence, fumbled for a polite question. "And how does that ritual work, exactly?"

Stella's face had flushed even deeper, and beside her Silfast huffed a satisfied-sounding snort, settling his huge, heavy arm around Stella's shoulders. "Anyone seeking to join our clan," he said, "must first seek the goddess' favour here, upon our sacred altar."

His gaze had also slid purposefully behind them, and when Gwyn again turned to look, she indeed found a large, circular stone table she hadn't noticed before, placed close before the crackling fire. It was covered with a heavy helping of furs, and it had the look of something very ancient, something that might have stood here long before the orcs had arrived.

"I see," Gwyn said again, in the absence of anything else to add. "And the newcomer speaks some sort of prayer here, asking the goddess' favour?"

But the Silfast orc barked a heavy laugh, his taunting eyes again fixed on Joarr. "The *seeker* does not speak," he said flatly. "The seeker is bared, and opened, and offered before the clan. The seeker then anoints the altar with fresh, rightfully earned Bautul seed, drawn from her orc, whilst his clan bears witness. And after this, her *Bautul* begs for her welcome."

Oh. Well, damn. Because of course this awful orc would be talking about a ritual like *that*. And of course he'd be eyeing Gwyn like that, too, all smug triumphant *superiority*. Like he was just waiting for her to be shocked and appalled, and to perhaps excoriate Joarr for associating with such degenerates, before turning tail and running out of his mountain forever.

But instead, Gwyn's hands had somehow come to her hips, her eyes narrowing on Silfast's hideous face. Because she certainly wasn't about to give this asshole the satisfaction of being shocked, was she? Especially at the oh-so-profound revelation that a clan apparently chock-full of exhibitionist orcs would obviously want newcomers to also embrace their exhibitionist ways? All while wielding some highly convenient divine directive to ensure ready compliance?

"Sounds like quite the welcome party," she said, as smoothly as she could. "Now, as I mentioned, I'm a midwife, and I've come here to work, so"—her eyes settled back to Stella's tired face, her tone reflexively softening—"if you might have any interest in a brief consultation, I would be happy to oblige? Or perhaps you'd like to hear more about my experience and qualifications first, and give it some thought?"

But instead of replying, Stella winced, and angled a wary look up at Silfast. Who had stepped slightly forward, his clawed finger pointing at Joarr's chest, his eyes flinty on Joarr's impassive face. "No," he said, his voice hard. "You shall not escape this, *brother*, nor again slip away from what is your due. You bring a woman here who bears your scent, you next honour your clan's ways with her. Most of all if you claim you do not deny your vow before the goddess, and yet swear you mean to keep your word!"

Gwyn again surely wasn't following, her eyes darting back and forth between them. "Excuse me," she said, her voice unmistakably sharp. "I told you, Joarr brought me here to work. To *help* you. This has *nothing* to do with him."

But Silfast barked a loud, mocking laugh, and suddenly Gwyn was again far too aware of all the watching orcs, their eyes prickling on her back. "You are wrong, woman," he growled at her. "We do not need help. We have a gifted healer here, and many clever Ka-esh, who offer good care for our mates. And a Bautul *never* brings a woman here to our hearth without claiming her before the goddess and his clan, and *he* full knows this!"

Wait. So Silfast was truly saying they *had* to do this ridiculous exhibitionist ritual, then? And, Gwyn's role as a midwife didn't matter here, because they already had a healer? Multiple healers? And Joarr... *knew* this?

But Gwyn's quick, uneasy look up at Joarr's face told her nothing, *nothing*. As though he was fully gone, vanished, hidden away, lost. Leaving her here all alone, with a room full of deadly watching orcs, and her own foolish vow that she'd so foolishly made.

Show me your mettle and your wits and your hunger for me, as you walk amongst my kin.

And yes, he'd specifically included *hunger* in that. And that meant—Gwyn sighed, felt her eyes briefly close—Joarr surely *had* known about this ridiculous ritual. He'd known what would be expected of them, in this. And good gods, perhaps he'd even hinted at it, earlier, hadn't he?

You wish to learn my clan's ways? Wish to face these with me?

And now, this craven, manipulative coward had cornered her. Trapped her. As if this were truly some kind of vicious trial by fire, a catapult's worth of pinecones hurled straight into her face. And her choices were either to walk out, to condemn the bastard as the useless spineless swindler he was, an utter ignorant failure of a Bautul, a lying piece of *rubbish*, or...

Or, to throw his rubbish back toward him. To be the bigger person here, by virtue of being debauched on an altar, before an entire clan of equally debauched orcs.

And it should have been an easy choice. It should have been the only choice. It should have been Gwyn putting her foot down, stalking away from here, and getting the hell out of this gods-damned encroaching mountain, forever.

But at that very instant, Joarr finally looked at her. And it was as though his mask had briefly slipped, betraying him—

and his eyes were suddenly brimming with frustration, and with *rage*. With helplessness, because he felt trapped by this too, whatever absurdity it was, that had eaten him alive, and longed to chew him up and spit him away like so much bile.

And curse her wasted life to hell and back, because Gwyn felt her shoulders sagging, her breath exhaling. Her eyes holding to Joarr's, and glaring daggers into their depths.

"Well, if that is what's required of us," she said, her voice echoing in the silence, "then surely, we'll oblige."

15

Surely, we'll oblige.

And as Gwyn stood there, glaring at Joarr in this foreign fraught room, the words didn't feel like a concession, or an offering. No, they were a challenge. An attack.

And Joarr's tall, still body surely knew that, the mask snapped back in its place, hiding away his eyes. And all that was left on his face was the smile, curling up slow, empty, deadly.

"You ken, woman?" he asked, his voice brittle, as his hand once again slipped up to touch that tooth around his neck. "You shall bend to this, to honour my *captain*?"

The last word was pure poison, and Gwyn made herself smile back at it, even as she shot a poisonous glance of her own toward the odious Silfast, who was watching them with unreadable eyes. "I do nothing for *him*," she replied, her voice just as thin. "I do it to keep my word to *you*. And"—she couldn't help a quick, dark look at the room full of watching orcs—"to honour the Goddess of Bautul, upon her sacred hearth, as she asks."

Something stilled in Joarr's eyes, freezing his already-empty face. And for a breathless, airless instant, she could almost feel his surprise. His... *guilt*.

"You are... sure, of this," he said finally, low. "*All* of this."

His gaze had glanced down, brief but telling, toward Gwyn's dress, and she felt herself sigh again, her throat swallowing. Because of course it was too much to hope for that she could at least remain clothed—or half-clothed—in this. When proving points to the shameless, surely one would be expected to abandon shame.

"Yes," she said, through her clenched-tight teeth. "I'm sure."

There was another instant's stillness, but then Joarr slowly inclined his head, offering his agreement. And when his eyes rose again, the mask had again fully returned, the cool smile still curving at his mouth.

"Then come," he said, his voice so smooth, as his already-familiar hand spread on her back, and guided her around toward the middle of the room. Toward where—Gwyn's feet faltered—many more strange orcs had somehow appeared, all standing curious and watchful around the room, waiting in bated silence.

But Joarr's eyes didn't look, and his steps didn't hesitate. Only kept driving Gwyn closer, closer, until they'd reached that large, fur-covered stone, directly before the crackling fire.

The stone stood higher than a table, reaching past Gwyn's waist, and in an easy shift of movement, Joarr plucked her up to sit on the edge of it. Bringing her face almost perfectly in line with his, still giving that practiced, empty smile.

And in another quick, fluid flare of movement, he leaned in, and *kissed* her. His lips warm and succulent on hers, his breath sweet, his rich scent unfurling between them...

But for a single horrible instant, Gwyn couldn't seem to follow. Couldn't sink into it, or even *feel* it, through the awareness of all these strange orcs watching, their eyes prickling into her skin. Waiting, because next...

Joarr drew back again, his brows furrowed, his head tilting. While Gwyn only stared at him, her eyes wide, her heart suddenly knocking fierce and powerful against her ribs. She had to do this, she *would* do this, how the *fuck* was she supposed to do this...

There was an almost imperceptible movement on Joarr's mouth, perhaps a grimace—but just as swiftly, it vanished. And in its place, once again, was his smile, though this time it was teasing and rueful, warming his empty eyes.

"You faced this in *tree*," he murmured at her, his brows lifting. "Under open sky, in cold air, on rough narrow *trunk*. Now you balk at soft stone, before warm fire?"

It was enough to drag up Gwyn's disbelief, and even a wavering snort. "That is *not* the problem at hand," she hissed back, "and you damn well know it, orc."

Joarr's smile twitched up more, quick and conspiratorial. "Ah, I no know this," he purred. "I ken mayhap my witch find *like* in this. Find *fun*."

Gwyn made a face at him, but his eyes were all challenge now, his body leaning closer, his mouth warm and wicked. "I show you fun in this, ach?" he whispered, lips almost to her ear. "If you think only of me. Look only upon me."

And Gwyn *knew* full well what he was doing, the bastard, but she still felt her throat swallow hard, her tongue reflexively brushing her lips. And in return Joarr chuckled, close in her ear, as his warm hand somehow found her bare knee beneath her skirts, and slowly, surely, began slipping upwards.

Gwyn twitched, her eyes again darting toward the room full of watching orcs—but in a breath, Joarr's other hand snapped up to her face, and spread to cover her eyes. "No," his hot voice hissed in her ear. "Me. *Only* me."

The words had deepened to almost a growl, and somehow, Gwyn found herself jerking a short, furtive nod in return.

Earning a slow exhale against her ear, an approving clutch of his claws against her bare thigh.

"You like," he murmured, so soft—and oh *hell*, that was a gentle, purposeful nip of *teeth*, against the skin of her earlobe. Firing a streak of damnable heat into her lower belly, followed by another low laugh in her ear, a slow slide upwards of that hand beneath her skirts...

"You hunger," he whispered, as that wandering hand brushed at the join of her thighs, which were still pressed tightly together. Still safely concealed under the weight of her skirts, because Joarr hadn't yet lifted them, or made even the slightest attempt to undress her. And there was a twitch of hazy gratefulness, a slow exhale of her own breath, perhaps even a tilt of her head toward his lingering mouth...

He rewarded it with another brush of teeth against her earlobe, harder this time. Making her entire body shiver, and his answering laugh felt like a shiver too, a ripple of silvery light in the darkness.

"You like," he breathed again, as that audacious hand purposefully gripped her thigh, and slid it sideways. Opening her, exposing her for his touch—but Gwyn's jolt of stillness was instantly chased by another gentle tug on her ear, a featherlight touch of claws against the parted, quivering heat between her legs.

"You wish for more," he said, or perhaps taunted, as those sharp, deadly claws brushed against her, teasing their velvet threat against her most vulnerable places. "Wish me in you."

Gwyn's answering shudder wracked down her spine, and Joarr's nip at her ear was even harder this time, just edging at pain. "Keep still," he breathed. "Keep eyes upon me. *Only* me."

Gwyn's head was nodding, jerking against his other hand, still over her eyes—and after another bated breath, that hand slowly slid away. Bringing back the room, the watching orcs, him.

But *only* him, he'd ordered her, and her blinking eyes were already catching on his. Drinking up the heat in them, the hunger, the *adventure*.

And his smile was surely genuine this time, all quicksilver impishness and deadly white teeth. While his hand slipped down to the front of her dress—to her buttons—and with an easy flick of his claws, he deftly tugged the top button open.

Gwyn's dazed eyes instantly froze on his, her breath catching—but then, curse the bastard, his claws still under her skirts traced her again. Slowly teasing up and down, lingering sharp and dangerous against her parted, frantically clenching heat...

"You undress," he whispered, those eyes flashing light, "and I tend you."

Tend her. Gwyn's breath came in a shuddering gasp, a desperate flutter of eyelids. And Joarr's devilish smile only twitched up more, his amused gaze pointedly dropping back to that row of buttons, all the way down the front of her dress.

Gwyn groaned aloud this time, but the bastard was relentless, his claws settling even closer, stroking her slightly harder. As if to sink inside her, just like this, oh hell—and somehow, *somehow*, her shivering fingers were skittering to her dress. Yanking open one button, and then the next, and the next, what was she doing, she couldn't be doing this, she was...

She *was*. And her reward was already here, in those fingers nudging so careful against her, opening her, spreading her further apart. While a knee—his knee?—settled close beside hers, purposefully guiding it wider...

And by the time Gwyn's trembling, traitorous fingers had finished unbuttoning her dress, Joarr's lean, muscled body— still wearing his trousers—was kneeling on the stone between her thighs, his free hand whisking the dress fully aside. Moving so swiftly that she didn't protest, perhaps didn't even notice—at least, until she somehow found herself sprawled naked on her back, with a tall, shaggy-haired orc hovering over her on one arm, his other hand still toying between her legs.

Damn. Something hot and shameful was creeping up Gwyn's bare chest, heating her neck and her cheeks. And suddenly the temptation to look at the room was almost over-powering, what did they see, what in the gods' names was she doing—

But then, from above her, Joarr *growled*. The sound raw and rich and close, and when Gwyn blinked up, there was pure danger in those eyes on hers, in the command that she felt even before it escaped his lips.

"Me," he hissed, the word rolling in his mouth, in her ringing ears. "In you."

Oh *hell*, yes, and Gwyn was nodding, jerky and wild, her eyes furiously blinking—and then following Joarr's other hand as it dropped, and shoved down his trousers. Releasing that long, powerful, swollen-solid hardness, jutting straight toward her over bulging bollocks, dripping a thick string of delectable white from its slit...

And the bastard was watching her look, he *wanted* her to look, and he made a show of drawing away from her, up onto his knees. So he could circle his other hand so shamelessly around it, pumping himself up firm and slow. Oozing out more thick white, dangling it down toward her...

"You like," he breathed. "Wish to milk more from me. Drink me into you. Ach?"

And it was utter insolent arrogance, it was *abominable*—but Gwyn couldn't look away, couldn't breathe. Couldn't deny her head nodding, *nodding*, needing him, needing more...

"Yes," she choked back. "Yes, Joarr. *Please*."

There was another deep, guttural groan from his throat, a hiss of words in his incomprehensible black-tongue. And in another flashing rush of movement, he'd grasped for both her hips, and easily flipped her over on the soft stone. So that

Gwyn was on her hands and knees on the altar, facing toward the crackling fire, her cheeks flooding with its steady warmth.

And behind her, she could feel Joarr's body shifting, rising up—and then, oh hell, *that*. That slick, dripping-wet hardness, nudging its smooth head just up against her open, clutching heat.

Gwyn cried out, loud and shameful, and behind her Joarr actually laughed, his delving heft vibrating with the movement—but before she could turn, look, follow that, she felt both his hands gripping her arse-cheeks, pulling her wider apart. Perhaps exposing her more for his eyes, for the room's eyes, and even as she shuddered with shame, the heat rolled higher, hotter. Her greedy body shivering and clamping, as if indeed fighting to drink him, to milk him, to swallow him whole...

And then, as if she'd shouted her thoughts aloud, Joarr sank inside. Carving into her in one single, fluid stroke, plunging himself to the hilt. Hurling a sheer, shouting furor down Gwyn's back, across her eyes, and she felt her whole body desperately arching up, the shout tearing from her throat—

But he was already drawing out again, taking his power away, almost slipping free of her—and then he slammed back inside. With even more fluent driving purpose than before, her body again snapping at the impact, oh gods, more, more, *please*—

And had she said that aloud, or perhaps even shouted it, because there was another dark, thrilling laugh behind her. And then the distinctive feel of a hand on her neck, gently gathering up her loose hair, while that driving heat ground in a harsh circle inside her—

And this time when he drew out, slow and deliberate, he also drew her *head* back. Because yes, he had a handful of her *hair*, oh gods, and he was just holding it like this, holding her like this, her head up, her face toward the fire. Her eyes wildly blinking, her mouth making a choked, broken sound as he popped himself fully free of her this time, leaving her empty, wide-open, bereft—

His plunge back inside was a shock of sensation, a strike of sheer ecstasy. His hard strength buried all the way inside her, his groin grinding against her arse, his fist gripping her hair. Spiralling out the whirling pleasure, towering over the tease of rising pain, plundering her, hurtling her toward the depths—

And then he dragged out, and rammed in again. And then again and again and again, wringing first more shouts from Gwyn's gasping mouth, and then rising to screams. That hand pulling harder, her entire body arched up and back, his hips slamming against her in a ruthless, raging rhythm. Riding her like he owned her, like he was spurring her faster and faster, like he was going to drive her until she broke—

And then, somehow, she did. The tension catching, crackling—and then reverberating out from her, from them, in blazing streams of vicious, clamping euphoria. Seizing him in it, crumpling his flowing rhythm, dragging him so hard it hurt—until he finally, finally capitulated, curling over her, crashing her full of his hot molten seed in spurt after shuddering, straining spurt.

Gwyn had no sense of how long it lasted, his taut body slick and sticky over her, squeezing out the dregs of its bounty in ever-slower, ever-longer pulses. Until finally he was empty, his strength gone soft inside her, his previously bulging bollocks hanging slack against her still-shivering heat.

And for an instant, it almost felt like she was floating, like the rest of the room had winked fully away. Like it was only this, her orc's sweaty, sated, heaving body curled over hers, his hand still clutched in her hair, his own dangling hair tickling at her back. Like they'd battled through this trial together, and gained triumph, and truth, and perhaps even... *peace.*

Until. Until a heavy sigh skated against the skin of her neck, and she felt his grip abruptly releasing her hair, letting her head drop. And that warm sweaty body was easing up and off, he was pulling away from her, holding her hips in place, no, *no*—

But it was too late. Too late, because where his softened heft had been, there was suddenly—shame. Hot, sticky, liquid shame, spurting out strong from between Gwyn's spread legs, streaking down her thighs, pooling on the furs below her. While Joarr's hands just kept holding her there, as if he'd wanted to see this, wanted to show it to them...

To them. *Them*, the sea of unfamiliar terrifying orcs, standing close all around, and watching with glinting, eager eyes. Watching her. Watching everything, *everything*...

A sharp slash of ice streaked down Gwyn's spine, choking her breaths, wrenching her to stillness. This couldn't be happening. This hadn't been happening. She hadn't truly done this, like this, she *hadn't*—

But yes, it was still happening, *still*, and Joarr's clammy hands were still gripping her hips, still holding her where all the others could see. And she could hear him clearing his throat, could feel the unsteadiness of his breath on her back.

"Goddess of Bautul," he said, in a voice that wasn't quite his. "I... bring this woman before you. I offer her, as you ask. I... seek your favour... upon her."

There was a quivering, suffocating silence in return, as though the room, the world, dangled on a knife-edge, waiting for a fall. Until before Gwyn's blinking, streaming eyes, something in the fire loudly flickered and cracked, sending a bright shower of sparks out onto the stone floor beneath it.

It was as though the room collectively exhaled at once, its tension snapping away—and suddenly there was a rising hum of shifting bodies and murmuring voices, and even a few relieved-sounding laughs. And Gwyn twitched at the sight of a strange, hideous orc stepping closer toward her, oh *gods*—but no, he was looking at Joarr, and reaching a huge hand to clap at Joarr's bare *shoulder*.

"Well done, Seer," the new orc said, with visible satisfaction in his glinting eyes. "You have gained strong favour in this, ach?"

Joarr's hands had slackened on Gwyn's hips, and she felt herself reflexively flinch away from him, her tingling hands scrabbling for her dress, which had thankfully still been lying close by. And as she awkwardly yanked it on, fighting to hide her bared form as best she could, even more orcs approached, several of them smiling toward her this time.

"Welcome to our clan, woman," said one hulking grey orc, with genuine-sounding warmth in his deep voice. "Bautul is honoured to count you among our own."

"Ach, and mayhap next your son," said another orc, with a toothy, teasing grin. "The goddess is sure to grant you this next favour also."

Gwyn fought to stammer some sort of coherent reply, while her shaky fingers kept desperately fastening buttons. Did these orcs truly think she was part of their *clan* now? And had that— had that been Joarr's *intention* in this?

Or—her prickling eyes snapped to where Joarr was now standing surrounded by strange orcs, accepting their congratulations with a cool smile—had it been about *this*? About Joarr's own reputation in his new clan? His own status?

Show me your hunger for me, as you walk amongst my kin.

More biting chills were shivering down Gwyn's back, and she felt herself hunch as she crossed her arms over her now-clothed chest, as if to belatedly hide from the surrounding orcs' view. Because yes, this had surely been Joarr's plan, his own goal. Him blatantly using her to his advantage, for his own gain among his clan.

And as her brain swept back over it, her cheeks burned

with even more heat, more shame. Gods, he'd barely even touched her in it, had he? There'd been very little kissing or caressing, no affection, no vulnerability. No, it had been Joarr getting his way, as rapidly and efficiently as possible, all while wielding all Gwyn's most mortifying weaknesses against her. The claws. The teasing. The *hair*.

"Are you all right, Gwyn?" asked a soft voice, and when Gwyn's bleary eyes darted up, it was Stella. Standing here next to her horrid mate Silfast, her brow creased, her large eyes dark with worry. "Can we... help? Bring you anything?"

But Gwyn could feel this Silfast asshole watching her, his eyes glinting with too-keen awareness. As if he were just waiting for her to crumple and weep, or to tearfully call Joarr out on yet more of his miserable rubbish—and somehow, Gwyn managed to square her shoulders, and even paste a smile on her face.

"No, I'm quite all right," she said, in her brightest voice. "Just taking it all in. Things are quite different here, you know?"

Stella's worry vanished into a relieved-looking smile, and beside her, Silfast even gave Gwyn a curt little nod. Almost as if she'd somehow gained his *approval* in this, though his dark, frowning look toward Joarr suggested that this sentiment clearly didn't extend toward him.

And now Gwyn was looking at Joarr too, at his easy smile, his relaxed stance. At how he hadn't even bothered pulling up his trousers, and how that part of him was still slick and dripping with what they'd done. Still flaunting her, even now. Still wielding her weakness for his gain.

And gods, her eyes were prickling again, her smile feeling almost painful on her face. And she was trapped here, buried under this dark imposing mountain, surrounded by this sea of strange speaking orcs. While her heart began frantically skipping beats, her eyes now desperately blinking, and she would not weep here, she would *not*—

"Come, woman," cut in a clipped voice, and when Gwyn whipped toward it, it was Joarr. Still with that empty smile on his face, though he'd at least pulled up his trousers, and his arm was circling around her shoulders, guiding her off the altar. "You are sure to be weary, ach?"

Gwyn somehow managed a nod, while still keeping the painful smile pasted to her own face. "Yes, I suppose, thank you," she said, her voice bright, her eyes casting unseeing at the still-watching orcs around them. "Thank you all for welcoming me so kindly. And"—she glanced at the crackling fire—"I offer my thanks to the goddess, as well."

There were multiple nods and murmurs of approval, suggesting that this had at least been the proper response. And did that mean it was over, please let it be over, she'd damn well done it, and now...

Joarr was saying more words in the black-tongue, purring smooth from his throat, and then finally, *finally*, he ushered Gwyn back toward the corridor, in the direction they'd come. And he'd somehow even grabbed her lamp, which she'd entirely forgotten about, until this moment.

Gwyn numbly walked beside him, the noise fading behind them, the only light now from the lamp in his hand. Revealing a variety of square doors cut into the stone corridor, and several forking branches off both sides, but she couldn't even seem to make herself notice, or find a way to stop the misery pooling behind her eyes.

"Is there somewhere we could talk for a moment?" she heard her distant voice croak. "In private? Preferably near a latrine?"

The fact that Orc Mountain had latrines was pure presumption on her part, but Joarr didn't argue it, and accordingly guided her toward one of the nearby doors. Into a small, stone-walled room that appeared to be empty, but turned out to have a hole cut into the floor at the back, with steps circling downwards. And when Joarr silently gestured toward these, Gwyn staggered down them, moving so fast she tripped—but Joarr had swiftly snapped forward, catching her arm in his iron grip.

"Take care, woman," he muttered, the first words he'd said since they'd left that damned degrading room. And once they'd reached the bottom of the staircase—opening up into yet another empty stone room—Gwyn finally spun her shaky body to face him, her hands in fists, her chest heaving with her shallow, straining breaths.

"What," she gasped, "the *hell*, asshole. Why didn't you *tell* me?!"

Joarr's face was all stark shadows in the lamplight, his mouth tight, his eyes unreadable. "I tell you," he said, voice thin. "*Told* you."

Gwyn gaped at him, her heart still stuttering, while something new seemed to clutch at her chest, wrenching powerfully against it. Because of course he wasn't wrong, the utter bastard. He *had* told her. *Wish to learn my clan's ways? Show me your hunger, before all my kin.*

And yes, Gwyn had accepted it, agreed to it, and hadn't even asked a single damned question. Because maybe—maybe she hadn't wanted to know. Or maybe—she dragged her shivering hands against her hair—she'd wanted to trust him. Curse her cursed life, she'd wanted to trust him.

"You still could have said," she finally replied, her voice plaintive. "There was a *hell* of a lot more you could have said. How about, '*Hey Gwyn, by the way, this means I'm going to pound you naked on an altar, while thirty terrifying strangers leer at us. And also, they're even going to judge our performance, by the nebulous standards of some godawful deity you've never even heard of before!*"

Something shifted in Joarr's eyes, and he barked a low, bitter laugh—but he didn't actually reply. Not even making an attempt, the insufferable prick, and Gwyn felt the tightness in her chest skittering, tilting toward incredulity, toward *rage*.

"Why didn't you tell me," she hissed at him. "You thought I'd refuse? You thought I wouldn't go through with it? Is that why?"

Joarr's eyes shifted again, hinting at something almost like *amusement*, biting and grim. "No," he replied, short. "I saw you would do this. I knew."

He *knew*. And for an instant, Gwyn could only stare at him, her mouth agape, while the cool, careless arrogance in those words kept shuddering through her brain, stealing her breath. He'd *expected* all that, then. He'd known exactly what he'd been walking her into. He'd *known*.

She had to drag for air, gulp it down, press her clammy hands to her burning-hot cheeks. "Then *why*," she gritted out. "It was another test? You wanted to see how I would react?"

Joarr replied with a shrug this time, his eyes flicking to something beyond her head—but it wasn't a yes, it *wasn't*. And Gwyn kept staring at him, searching him, while that tightness seemed to yank even harder in her chest.

"Then you wanted to humiliate me," she said, slow, empty. "You wanted to show a spoiled lord's daughter just what you thought of her. Just where she belonged."

Her voice cracked at the last bit, snapping Joarr's gaze back toward her, his clawed hand rubbing at his mouth. "No," he countered. "I no seek to shame you. No even *think* of this."

Gwyn stared at him for another long, painful breath, and then heard her own laugh, echoing far too loud against the stone. "Rubbish, asshole," she barked back. "You *wanted* me on my knees and begging for you. You wanted me completely in your thrall. And you worked damn *hard* for that. *Why*."

Joarr's body was very still now, his eyes so deliberately blank—and the clench in Gwyn's chest swerved, lurching for escape. "Tell me, Joarr," she gasped. "Or else I will walk back into that room, and do *everything* I possibly can to destroy whatever the hell it was that I just gained for you! Whatever the hell you *really* wanted out of this!"

A palpable flare of tension snapped across Joarr's shoulders, and for an instant it was like his mask briefly slipped, his face contorting into something ugly and broken. "You ken I *wish* for this?" he demanded at her. "You ken I wish to follow this fool *goddess*, who so oft is equal to whatever words spew from Silfast's mouth? Bautul has long been *his* clan to rule, and he *yearns* to see me fall, to see me crushed and spurned at his feet. But *you*—"

His voice broke off there, and he squeezed his eyes shut, his mouth clenching tight. Not finishing that statement, not even looking at her—but the comprehension was finally flickering through Gwyn's thoughts, driving the breath from her chest.

"So this was all a play against *Silfast*, then?" she said, her voice hollow. "Because he doesn't want you in his clan? And you don't want to be in his clan, either? At all?"

Joarr's laugh scraped down her spine, jagged and hoarse. "Ach, no," he snarled back at her. "I wish for *naught* of this. All I wish is to bend Silfast over this curst altar, and drive all the pious words from his lying mouth!"

Oh. *Oh.* And the full truth of that was there, finally, shouting in Joarr's bitter, raging eyes. While Gwyn's damned betraying brain suddenly swarmed with visions of it, with Joarr bending another orc over that altar, driving against another orc's arse, his hand caught in thick black hair. And wait, he'd all but just admitted that, he wanted that, he *did* that?!

And yes, yes, Gwyn's vision was now flooding with the vivid images from that room, with how Joarr had scarcely even *blinked*. Because *that* was what he did, when he wasn't spying on lords' daughters, and manipulating them, and seducing them in trees?

And worse, why the hell was Gwyn fixating on this, given

everything else he'd just admitted? He'd been on another *mission* with this. He'd had a victory to gain, a pawn to manipulate. A target to work toward. A patsy.

And gods, Gwyn was so stupid. So, so damned stupid. And her eyes were prickling again, something dangerously lurking in her throat, her breaths dragging in painful gulps...

"I need," she choked, "a latrine. Please."

Joarr didn't answer, but silently turned on his heel, and strode toward the far wall. Where there was a small opening tucked into the stone, and Gwyn wordlessly grasped the lamp from his hand, and ducked inside.

It was another little room, surprisingly well-outfitted with a covered bench, and even a spout of fresh-looking water trickling down the wall—but Gwyn scarcely noticed through the silent screaming in her thoughts, the shallow panic of her breaths. She was trapped here, gods knew where under the earth, and Joarr hadn't even truly wanted her, she was only a tool in his ridiculous feud, and she couldn't start sobbing, she would not weep here, not where he would mock her, he would know—

Her desperate bleary eyes had been searching, searching, *please*—and there, the lamp handle, held in place by its two sharp ends. And when Gwyn's shaking hand yanked at it, thank the gods it came off, its pointy metal tip glinting in the flickering light, settling against her wrist.

And then she dragged it deep and relentless down her forearm, drawing a beautiful line of thick red blood behind it. And finally, *finally*, the pain screamed to life, and devoured her whole in its wake.

16

For a sickening, silent moment, there was only the pain. Shuddering and shrieking from Gwyn's already-bleeding arm, escaping in a clutched gasp from her throat.

But at least it wasn't weeping, it wasn't the regret, it wasn't the gods-damned *grief*. It was just pain, and Gwyn could face this, could understand this, could even wipe away the wetness streaking down her cheek—

Until in a breath, Joarr jerked into place before her. Looming tall and deadly, bobbing on his feet, like he'd flashed there out of *nothing*.

"What," he growled, his gaze snapping down to her arm, "is *this*?!"

Gwyn yelped and stumbled backwards, dropping the lamp handle onto the stone floor with a clatter, and clamping her hand over the betraying cut on her arm. Wincing at the renewed flare of pain, while frantically shaking her head, fighting to ignore the pulsing stickiness under her fingers, the pungent scent of blood filling the air—

"No," Joarr hissed, as his hand closed on hers, yanking it away. "You no do this."

Gwyn's breaths were shuddering again, perhaps even worse than before. Because he'd ruined it, the bastard, the misery was rearing up again, the *loneliness*, jostling, choking, dragging her beneath—

"You," she gulped back, "do *not* get to tell me what to do, asshole! And if you think I'm going to *listen* to you, or care what you think, now that you've made yourself *very* clear to me, you—you—"

And oh gods, she was losing it, she was going to break down bawling right here in front of him, and she wrenched out of his grip, and reeled over toward the covered bench. Crumpling down onto it, burying her face in her sticky hands, desperately choking back the ever-rising sobs in her throat.

"Stupid," she gasped into her hands, wildly shaking her head. "Stupid. *Stupid!*"

But it wasn't helping, wasn't working, the bitter misery still swelling, fighting to explode from her quivering mouth. And what happened now, what was left, she was trapped under Orc Mountain, she was going to lose her garden, lose *everything*, and this stupid, *stupid* hope she'd somehow been clinging to was scattered to *dust*—

"No," said a voice, low and fervent, far too close—and when Gwyn flinched to look, it was Joarr again. Now crouching low before her, his body still slightly bobbing, his eyes glinting dark and oddly fierce on her face.

"No," he said again. "You are no *stupid*, woman. *No.*"

And curse him, but it was something to cling to, *anything*, and Gwyn barked a laugh, hoarse and shrill. "Aren't I?" she demanded at him. "Let's see. I didn't shoot you. I copulated with you in a *tree*. I covered for you. I made *excuses* for you. I trusted you to bring me here, and treat me fairly, and show me a garden, and—and *fun*. Like you *promised*."

Her wet eyes were fixed to his face, glaring at him, accusing him—and of course he didn't even reply, damn him, his mouth gone thin, his swallow audible in his throat.

"And instead, *this*," Gwyn continued, her voice cracking, her hand flapping at the stone latrine around them. "You used me to make a point. You—you turned my weaknesses against me. You didn't even bother to tell me what to expect, even after you decided I'd probably go along with it anyway. And then you tell me you'd have liked it better if it was *him*?!"

The tension seemed to spiral even tighter between them with every word, but Joarr *still* didn't speak—and Gwyn gasped another laugh, or perhaps a sob. "I don't understand," she breathed, "*why*. What I've *done* to you."

The tightness somehow shuddered, choked—and then escaped in a bitter, broken laugh. Not her laugh, this time, but Joarr's. His mouth twitching both up and down, his eyes unnervingly bright in his strangely pale face.

"Mayhap," he began, his voice halting, "you *bewitch* me, woman. Ach? Cast spell. *Entrap* me."

What? Gwyn glared at him through hazy eyes, the room skittering around her—and Joarr laughed again, darker this time. "You ken how I—*spy* on you," he said bitterly. "You ken this is also my... *work*. How in this, I serve my kin, and my mountain. Ach?"

Gwyn couldn't find a reply, but yes, she supposed she had known that. And Joarr jerked a nod, his mouth twisting, as if she'd spoken her agreement aloud.

"No only this," he said, even flatter. "But I am no just any spy, ach? I am"—his shoulders rose and fell—"this mountain's Chief Scout. Chief spy. For all five clans. Ach?"

Chief spy? Gwyn's brain seemed to sputter again, and Joarr barked another low, brittle laugh. "I hold this place for many, many summers," he said, "and watch many, many humans. Most of all these fool lords, and their hollow, greedy spawn. I work against them again and again, and I *never* catch care for them. Never catch *guilt*."

Gwyn still couldn't think through the chaos, the constant clutch in her chest, and Joarr's gaze dropped, to where his hand was flexing on his knee. "I *never* break plan. Never seek to make amends for my work. Never wish to stay close, to watch, to know. To *help*."

Oh. Gwyn felt herself swallowing, perhaps loosening the tightness in her throat—but no, no, this made no difference, this wasn't even an apology, whatever the hell it was. Was it?

"Never find another so quick to learn," Joarr continued, and suddenly he sounded angry, his eyes frowning at his knees. "So easy to follow, to catch, to see. You watch me, you *know* me, ach? As if I speak to you, when only I *look*."

Gwyn still wasn't justifying this, wasn't—and Joarr barked yet another laugh, thick in his throat. "As if," he said, "I am no more alone. No more without a true clan. As if you shall fight beside me, even when I no ask you, or warn you. You shall spurn Silfast, and throw his fool goddess in his face, and smile all this while. You shall follow all this, and face all this"—his throat convulsed, his voice dropping—"with *me*."

Oh. So maybe—maybe it hadn't been about Joarr using her, mocking her, to gain his ends. Maybe it had been about him wanting—*help*. Someone by his side. At his back. Someone who... understood.

And even as that stab of comprehension flashed through Gwyn's chest, she still felt her head shaking, her eyes glowering toward him. "Even if you expect me to believe that," she said, her voice hollow, "that you just wanted help, someone to trust—then why the hell does it only benefit you? You don't think I wouldn't like to be able to trust someone, too?"

The silence seemed to again echo between them, taut and grating, and Gwyn made herself continue, fighting to ignore the rising throbbing pain in her arm. "I went above and beyond for you back there. Gave you a hell of a lot more than you deserved, *again*. And in return, you couldn't even look at me? Or maybe even explain what it was all about, instead of telling me that you *really* just want to have your way with that smug hideous bastard?"

Her voice had badly wavered at the end, hinting at something abominably like jealousy—and Joarr's eyes finally flicked back to hers, his mouth twisting. "You no ken I... *hunger* for Silfast?" he said, incredulous. "After you scream for my hard ploughing on this altar, and milk me dry before all my kin? After you take me in tree, and rain my seed upon my enemies? After you even no *shoot* me, on account of this bloody mess I leave behind?"

Oh. It was a confession, maybe, though surely not one he'd wanted to make—and his eyes were glittering on hers now, his brow furrowed. "Yet, you are lord's daughter," he hissed at her. "You wish to soon go away from here, and take all this with you, and never come back. So why ought I grant you yet *more* power to cast your spells upon me?"

He sounded angry again, and maybe despairing, too. And Gwyn couldn't seem to find a reply, her hand again clutching at her still-stinging arm—a foolish, ill-thought action that drove a harsh gasp of pain from her mouth.

"Ach," Joarr said, with a wince, his head whipping back and forth—and in a swift, fluid movement, he'd grasped for both her hands, and yanked them apart. His gaze dropping to the cut on her arm, which was still slightly bleeding, dripping red onto the floor.

"Ach," he said again, more displeased this time, his eyes glaring brief toward hers. "This scent, of your blood and suffering, it—"

He shook his head again, tugging her hand toward him— and before Gwyn could speak, or even think, he ducked his head, and... *licked* her. His long black tongue lapping against her arm, deft, gentle, purposeful. Just like in the garden, as if this were something he needed to do, twisting her pain into a surprising, disconcerting warmth...

"What," Gwyn somehow managed, "are you *doing*."

But he didn't hesitate, didn't even look at her, and for some bizarre reason, she didn't pull away, either. Just sat there and watched this incomprehensible, infuriating orc, now crouching low before her, his hands cradling her arm. While that warm, sinuous tongue kept stroked and tasted, lapped and licked, as though she were something prized, something precious.

And once he'd finally finished, he still didn't look at her—but instead, grasped for her other hand, which still felt sticky from where she'd touched her arm. And then, just as intently, he began licking it, too, his strokes firmer this time, curling and caressing hot against her fingers.

Gwyn had to bite back her gasp, clamping her lips together, and perhaps her thighs, as well. Finally earning a dark, knowing glance from Joarr's eyes—and for an instant, there was the irrational, impossibly absurd temptation to spread her legs again, to perhaps guide that slithering tongue to where it surely most mattered—

But no, no, *gods* no. He'd admitted to lying to her, to not *wanting* to trust her—and Gwyn belatedly jerked her hand away, and clutched it to a tight fist. Not missing the way those eyes followed it, before angling up brief toward her face, and away again.

"You no again draw your blood thus," he said, in a tone she couldn't quite read. "No if you wish me to *ever* tend you thus again. Tease you with pain thus. Ach?"

Wait, what the *hell*? Now he was calling her out on *that*? And essentially *blackmailing* her with it?! Gods, as if she even cared, as if she would fall for his latest gods-damned audacity. For this cursed orc once again twisting the situation to suit himself, to gain what he wanted...

But before Gwyn could answer, or spout any of the crucially important retorts swarming her thoughts, Joarr's warm, infuriating hand again clapped over her mouth. His body rising to his knees, his face on a level with hers, his gaze dark and serious.

"No, woman," he said again, harder this time. "You find other way, in this. Seek other relief. Stay *safe*. I never again wish to scent your blood, lest it is *me* who draws it. Ach?"

Him who drew it. Gwyn felt herself inhale sharply, her eyes pinned to his—but then she squeezed them shut, shook her head against his hand. Damn him, this was so absurd, especially when he'd been the whole reason she'd been craving relief like that in the first place. He'd lied to her, he'd flaunted her to his entire clan, and he hadn't even *warned* her—

"Listen, asshole," Gwyn mumbled into his palm, stupidly—and then shoved his hand away, fighting to ignore how easily it went. "I am *not* yours to order around, most of all when you're the one who made me so miserable in the first place! Why the hell would I listen to *anything* you have to say? Especially when"—she hauled in breath—"you *still* haven't actually apologized? And, you still haven't told me *crucially* important information about all this?!"

Joarr's eyes blinked, once, and Gwyn didn't miss the brief, reflexive grimace, contorting his mouth. Or the tension snapped all through his taut body, holding him unmoving before her. And for a breath, she was sure he was about to refuse, keep arguing, leap up and walk away...

Until he... didn't. His shoulders sagging, his clawed hand dragging through his hair, his eyes fixed unseeing to the wall behind her.

"Ach," he said, slow, on a sigh. "Ach. I ought to ask your—your mercy, for how I threw this upon you. I was"—his shoulders rose, fell—"selfish. Unjust. I... grieve this pain I have wrought upon you."

Oh. It felt genuine, looked genuine, like it almost hurt him to speak it. Like each word was a tentative, uncertain offering, from an orc entirely unaccustomed to ever being in the wrong, or facing his own regret.

But surely it still didn't compensate for what he'd done back there, did it? And surely Gwyn couldn't just forget this and carry on... could she?

And as if she'd spoken that aloud, Joarr grimaced again, and lurched a little forward. Both his hands now gripping at the stone bench on either side of her, trapping her in place before him.

"Now," he continued, clipped, "you shall tell me what more you wish to learn from me. And I shall answer this with truth."

Gwyn exhaled, her heart skipping in her chest, her eyes still locked to his. To the glinting determination in them, perhaps even the challenge, as if he was daring her to test him on this, to play his latest game, follow his newest pinecone...

And instead of roundly refusing, as she surely should have done, she sucked back more breath, huffed it out again. "I want to know the truth about you and your clan," she snapped at him. "The entire story of what led you to this. Why the Bautul don't want you. Why Silfast hates you. And why you needed to make that ridiculous public *statement* to that ridiculous damned goddess!"

Joarr's throat visibly spasmed, his chest hollowing—but his eyes remained fixed to hers, glinting with that grim determination. As if he would tell her. As if it might even be truth.

"This tale," he began, with an unmistakable edge on his voice, "began in days long past. With my father's father, Joakim of Clan Bautul. Joakim was Seer of the Bautul clans, in Tomor."

Tomor was the small, swampy, mostly uninhabited province south of Sakkin province, on the very edge of the southern sea. And while Gwyn couldn't recall hearing of orcs there, she felt herself nodding, all the same.

"What's a… Seer?" she asked, before she could stop the question. "And how did your grandfather become one?"

Joarr shrugged, his eyes sliding away from hers. "It is an old Bautul calling," he replied, curt. "A leader. Passed through blood, from son to son. But in this"—he drew in breath—"Joakim failed his clan. He failed to see an attack by men, and this led to many deaths, and much strife. So to escape this, he planned what seemed his death, and next fled west. To Osada."

Osada was northwest of Sakkin, next to Dunburg—and Gwyn nodded again, waiting, while Joarr took another heavy breath. "There, Joakim hid his true name," he continued. "And found means to hide his true scent, also. And there he whelped a son—my father—and claimed himself a Skai. The clan most like Bautul, mayhap, and with no strong leader, and no books or old accounts to say he no belonged there. Joakim also bore the height and air of a Skai, I ken, with more speed than strength. And thus—"

Joarr broke off there, shrugging again, as though that were the end of it—but that surely wasn't the end, was it? And despite everything this damned enraging orc had done today, Gwyn found herself sitting up straighter, her attention caught, her eyes searching his.

"And thus *what*?" she demanded. "You were born—up in Osada, or here? And did your father know the truth? Or your mother? And how did you finally learn you weren't Skai, after all?"

Joarr's eyes had shuttered, and he shrugged again, even more careless this time. "I was birthed in Osada," he said coolly. "I never knew my mother, and if my father knew this truth of the Bautul, he no spoke of it to me. I have only now learnt it, these past moons, thanks to the work of our Ka-esh kin, who seek to help all our mountain with their learning."

Right. The Ka-esh clan, the literary ones, who didn't stop talking. And who, Gwyn couldn't deny, were currently sparking an undeniable, jolting indignation in her already jumbled thoughts.

"And the Ka-esh thought it was *helpful*, to expose you like that?" she said sharply. "To cut you off from the Skai clan you'd believed to be your own for your entire *life*?!"

Joarr's mouth might have winced, but he gave another too-casual shrug, his gaze once more slipping past her. "The Ka-esh are no at fault for this," he said, voice flat. "And they no *expose* me, ach? They only speak of what they learn to me alone, in secret. But"—that was without question a wince this time—"this is no a burden I wish to keep, ach? No a falsehood I wish to carry, for my own son to face alone after me."

Oh. Of course. Because as little as Gwyn truly knew about this orc, she still knew, somehow, that he wouldn't choose to live a lie. He wouldn't choose to pretend that he belonged, where he didn't. He wouldn't pass that on to his son.

His... *son*?

"You don't," Gwyn gasped at him, her thoughts flailing in a dozen new directions at once, "*have* a son. Do you?"

Joarr stared at her for a breath, his brow knitting—but then he choked a laugh, bitter and hoarse. "Ach, no," he said. "Had I one of these, you no ken I should leave him to go all this time without his father?"

Right. And blinking at his deeply disgruntled face, Gwyn realized that perhaps she'd known that, too. That if one could somehow hold Joarr's loyalty, it would be a fearsome thing, unshakeable, inviolable. *Mine.*

An odd, hurtling shiver rippled up her back, but she held her eyes to his, grasped for the next question. "So *why*," she said, "doesn't Bautul want you. I mean, they surely can't fault you for what your grandfather did, can they? And if you're truly the Chief Scout of this entire mountain, that's surely an enviable position, isn't it? A gain for them? A mark in their favour?"

She couldn't read the shift in Joarr's eyes, the jerkiness in his shrug this time. "The Bautul have long ago learnt," he said, his voice wooden, "to live without this Seer, ach? They now follow their battle-captains, the strongest orcs among them, who flaunt the power they prize. One of these captains is Silfast, who thinks himself the goddess' voice come to earth, and who no wishes for a rival, most of all in me. And the other is Olarr—he was the first to greet me after this today—who no cares to fight against his brother, or against what he believes is his goddess' voice. And until this day"—Joarr sighed—"I held no claim to this goddess, ach? No blessing."

Gwyn fought to digest all that, to search the hard set of Joarr's face. To pull all the bits together, to find the way through...

"So that whole farce on the altar, back there," she said slowly, "that was *huge* for you. It was you striking back at Silfast's resistance against you. Claiming your rightful place among your own clan."

Joarr's mouth clenched, his eyes glinting—but his shrug might as well have been a nod this time, swift and furtive. "It should... help, I ken," he said, quiet. "For this, I... thank you."

Well. Gwyn felt something catch, deep in her throat, and somehow she was the one shrugging, her eyes blinking down at his bare chest. "You're welcome," she replied, just as quiet. "I'm... glad it helped."

There was an instant's fraught stillness, a visible flinch of Joarr's still-crouching body before hers—and then another choke of a laugh, too close. "Ach, witch," he said, with a sigh. "Now flood me with your kindness, so I may yet drown in my guilt, and long to make more amends, ach? Mayhap next you speak of the deep joy you found in this? And how your lone regret is that you no found a means to spray my good seed all over Silfast's limp prick?"

Gwyn twitched to stare at him, while the gods-damned vivid vision of it swarmed through her brain—and then, somehow, she... *laughed.* Yes, laughed, her shoulders shaking, the mirth escaping her mouth in shrill, irrational gulps.

"Can you imagine," she gasped, "the look on his face? While it's... *dripping*, all onto the floor, and then you could say..."

Joarr's lips quirked, and suddenly the mirth was dancing in his eyes, too. "'*Is it raining?*'" he asked, in so much the voice of that hunter from the forest that Gwyn gasped another too-loud peal of laughter, her head shaking, her hands somehow skittering to find his shoulders. His warm, powerful shoulders, so close, and his face was even closer, and if he were to just lean forward, he would...

"Look, I still don't forgive you, asshole," Gwyn said abruptly, but there was very little heat in her voice, and her hands were still spreading wide on his skin. "You were supposed to give me *fun*, remember? And instead, I've been dragged into your ridiculous clan drama, and all but *sacrificed* to some ridiculous exhibitionist deity, and there isn't a single garden in sight. And now here I am, fruitlessly arguing with the most enraging orc in existence, all while feeling exhausted enough to collapse, and being trapped under Orc Mountain, and sitting in a gods-damned *latrine.*"

Joarr's eyes on hers were still warm, and he was even still smiling, flashing her his sharp white teeth. "Ach, I have failed you in this, woman," he murmured. "Should you... mayhap... sleep here this night, and then grant me one more day? And in this, we shall do all that you wish, and frolic in my garden? And only seek this fun I swore to grant you?"

And surely, it was a terrible plan. It was surely only Joarr wanting more from her, dragging this out, getting his own damned way, *again.* One more day, in Orc Mountain, after all Gwyn had already endured here? After all he'd already done?

But gods, his eyes. The warmth of his skin under her hands.

The way he was smiling at her, tentative, rueful, uncertain. *Hopeful.*

"This shall be good fun," he murmured. "Good *rain.* Ach?"

And curse Gwyn's foolish judgement, her instincts, her sheer stupidity—because she was smiling back. *Smiling*, slow, approving, true.

"One more day, orc," she whispered. "And it had better be *spectacular.*"

<h1 style="text-align:center">17</h1>

oarr guided Gwyn back through Orc Mountain with silent steps, one hand warm against her back, the other still carrying his lamp.

It somehow felt easier to look around this time, to drink up the maze of twisty, clever corridors. And when they passed multiple unfamiliar new orcs, all of them eyeing Gwyn with blatant curiosity, she managed to meet their eyes, and even offer a careful little smile.

Joarr nodded to the new orcs as they passed, but didn't bother to hesitate or make introductions. Just kept walking, tall and silent beside her, until they'd reached what seemed like a dead end—but when he heaved his shoulder against it, it proved to be another exit, tilting open with a grating crunch. Flooding Gwyn with the sweet scent of fresh, cool air, and the faint sight of stars, glimmering in the black sky beyond.

"Oh, *gods*," she gasped, lurching out into the open, dragging in long breaths of the beautiful clean air. While behind her, Joarr heaved the door shut again, and then doused his lamp, plunging them into deep, dark starlight.

"Come," he said, as his hand clasped hers, guiding her further into the darkness. "We shall sleep in my garden."

His garden, *finally*. However, Gwyn couldn't see a damned thing, and she frowned up toward where she could scarcely make out his shadow beside her. "You're not going to show it to me first?"

"No in the night," he said, as he kept walking, leading her along what felt like a stone path beneath her feet. "You see this best in sun, ach? Until this, you *rest*. You *heal*."

Gwyn was apparently even more exhausted than she'd thought, because she couldn't seem to muster even a tepid argument. And after a few more steps, Joarr halted before her, and turned to clasp both hands to her waist. Fully ignoring her squeak of protest as he plucked her up, and set her upon something soft and... *swinging*?

"What's this?" she demanded, as she felt Joarr's warm body settle close within it, stretching out long. "And why is it *moving*?"

"It is my bed," Joarr's low voice replied, as his hand circled her waist, and tugged her down beside him. "It is hung between the trees, and thus rocks with the wind, ach?"

Oh. His bed was a *hammock*. And it did feel surprisingly inviting, his body smooth and warm, and Gwyn felt herself sliding down into the crook of his arm, tentatively resting her head against his shoulder. Feeling the slow, steady sway of the hammock as she drew in more fresh air, now blended with Joarr's already-familiar scent, so close, so safe...

And instead of sleep eluding or taunting her, as it so often did, it somehow eased over her in gentle waves, twining into the night. Into the light nudges of wind, the warmth of the solid orc beneath her. The rhythmic rise and fall of his breath, the spread of strong fingers against her back...

And when Gwyn's eyes blinked open again, there was light.

Golden and dappled and stunning, peeking over that stone wall, pouring its warmth within.

She startled and sat up, making the hammock rock and judder beneath her, and she grasped at it for balance, holding herself upright. She seemed to be alone, with no hint of Joarr to be seen—but before her brain could properly belabour that point, she felt her breath catch, her eyes staring wide at the new world all around her.

It was indeed a garden. One tucked up close against what must have been Orc Mountain's south side, its solid stone soaring sheer and deadly above, painted with long shadows from the morning sun. While the rest of the garden was closed in with massive stone walls, rising several fathoms high, and boasting a thick cover of ivy.

And within the walls, there was *chaos*. Beautiful, bursting green chaos, trees and shrubs and herbs and grasses and flowers all rioting together, flooding all available space with their bounty. Almost looking as though they'd been hurled there by the gods, and then entirely forgotten, and left to run rampant under the sky.

But the more Gwyn stared, her breath locked in her lungs, the more the chaos began to resolve into some kind of sense. Into trees mostly clustered along the north side, ensuring their shade didn't cover the entire garden. Into herbs and flowers in cheerful little clearings, where the sun would be brightest. Into—she squinted downwards—what looked like a maze of narrow, stone-paved paths, meandering haphazardly through the green, in a delightfully odd echo of the twisting corridors within the nearby mountain.

And while Gwyn couldn't make out all the plants around her, she could certainly make out some. The hammock's thick rope ends were both tied to tall, sprawling apple trees, and the common ivy covering the walls was much prized for its anti-inflammatory properties. That cluster of green was most definitely more sage, the flowers were poppy and mugwort and feverfew, those bushes blackthorn and cranberry, those shrubs holly and silverthorn. And that—Gwyn choked an audible gasp—was surely a rare bloodroot, a prize that she'd long sought and failed to acquire.

The urge to explore felt all-consuming, and she finally turned her attention to the swinging hammock beneath her. It was made out of heavy brown leather, and it was slung high between the trees, perhaps on a level with Gwyn's chest. There was no obvious way down, and she glanced uncertainly around, eyeing the apple trees' twisty trunks—

When suddenly, there was Joarr. Dropping down from one of the apple trees with astonishing ease, and landing in a fluid, silent crouch below.

"Here," he said, as he rose tall again, and tossed something toward her. And when Gwyn reflexively reached to catch it, she found herself holding not an apple, but rather a ripe, blush-brown plum.

Her empty stomach immediately growled, and she brought the plum to her mouth, took a tentative bite—and good *gods*, it was delectable. Pure, bursting rich sweetness, exploding across her tongue, and she couldn't help her moan as she chewed, or her sheepish smile toward Joarr's amused eyes.

And now, finally, she was properly looking at him, for the first time since yesterday. All lean height and hard muscular edges, his cropped trousers hanging low on the cut of his hips, his messy hair glinting blue-black in the morning sun. His brow slightly lifting as he looked back at her, and for a jolting, dangling instant, there was the memory of herself on her knees on that Bautul altar, his hand caught in her hair, while that hungry strength pounded into her again and again—

Gwyn ducked her head, took another too-large bite of plum—but she could still feel that awareness snapped between them, taut and shimmering. And surely Joarr felt it too, and when she risked a glance up he was striding toward her with deceptively easy steps, his eyes glittering on her too-hot face.

"Come," he said, reaching both hands toward her—and when she carefully edged closer, those hands grasped warm and familiar to her waist, and plucked her down. Standing her gently onto her feet before him, his bare chest brushing hers, his fingers spreading wider against her hips...

Gwyn's eyes caught on his again, on the glinting, too-hot meaning within them. And for a bizarre, irrational breath, there was the completely ridiculous urge to put her hands to that chest, to follow the ripples of muscle in his torso. Even, perhaps, to slide lower, to acknowledge that rapidly swelling ridge at his groin, nudging into her belly. To stroke it, or maybe even to kneel down and taste, to flood her tongue with even more rich sweetness...

The knowing glint had sharpened in Joarr's eyes, and Gwyn could feel his hand trailing away from her hip, toward his own trousers. Surely about to tug them down, so he could nudge her down too, and—

Gwyn belatedly jerked backwards, reeling into the hammock behind her. No. *No.* This orc could not be trusted. He'd lied to her, he'd manipulated her again and again, and she'd given him one more chance. One *last* chance. And he was supposed to be using it to show her fun, and to prove that he could help her save her garden, and outsmart Roy. *Not* to gain himself some gratuitous morning servicing, when he'd barely even offered her a hello.

And even more infuriating was the fact that Joarr had almost seemed to *follow* all that. His eyes gone rueful, his shoulder giving one of those careless, rolling shrugs. And then he glanced sideways toward another tree-branch, his knees crouching—and in a graceful movement, he'd leapt up, grasped the branch with one hand, and swiped for a high dangling peach with the other. And then tossed it toward

Gwyn, his brows still raised, a hint of a challenge now lurking at his mouth.

"You wish first for fun, then?" he asked coolly. "Or first my garden?"

His garden. The words already snapping Gwyn's attention back toward it again, her greedy eyes drinking up the bursting greenery all around them. "The garden," she said firmly. "I want to see *everything*."

Joarr shrugged again, but accordingly waved her ahead of him, toward one of the twisting stone paths. And soon she was darting from one plant to the next, touching and smelling and marvelling, and casting delighted glances at Joarr's watching form behind her.

"You have lungwort!" she exclaimed, as she gently stroked a pure-white flower. "And betony! And four different varieties of rue! Though this one might be happier if you moved it away from the mustard—they don't like growing together, you know—and wait, are these strawberries under the sage? Those would be worth moving too, and your sage is overdue to be harvested and dried. Do you have a place where you do such things? Or do you mostly use them fresh?"

Joarr's face was now wearing a reluctantly amused half-smile, and he jerked his head toward the nearest corner, beneath a tall pine tree. And when Gwyn rushed over to look, she discovered a cozy hidden hut tucked into the tree's bottom branches, built out of carefully placed stones and sticks, and covered over in multiple layers of ivy. And inside—she gasped as she stepped through its little door—there was a broad wooden worktable, scattered with an assortment of tools and jars and chipped pots, and surrounded by clusters of hanging, fragrant herbs.

And like the rest of the garden, it was a completely chaotic mess—but it still seemed perfectly functional, as well. And it was a considerable size, too, and appeared watertight, and even had what looked like a little *burner* on the worktable—and Gwyn couldn't seem to stop grinning around at it all, or drifting over to smell the nearest bunch of hanging herbs.

"Rosemary," she said, "and that's angelica, right? And comfrey—I didn't see that out there—and wait, are these dried *mushrooms*? Are you growing those out here as well?"

Joarr's eyes were still unmistakably amused, and he gave yet another casual shrug. "Ach, some," he said. "Shall I show you where I shall keep your plants?"

Her plants. Because yes, right, that was the major objective of this entire endeavour, and Gwyn eagerly nodded, and followed him out of the hut. Back onto the twisty stone paths, now going toward the very middle of the garden.

And here—Gwyn's body stilled, her gaze casting upwards— was another tree. A variety she didn't immediately recognize, and it appeared very old, twisting gnarled and knotty toward the sky, and scarcely boasting a single leaf. And beneath it, spread wide around its trunk, there was a sea of tall unkempt grasses, suggesting that this had once been a little meadow to frolic in, here in the heart of the garden.

There were even a few large low stones scattered about the meadow, as if meant for sitting or playing upon, and directly before the tree stood a particularly large stone, broad and flat, and covered over with a generous helping of moss. Looking, perhaps, not unlike...

"See?" Joarr's voice interrupted, his hand giving a fluid wave around them. "Fresh earth, mayhap never before planted. Good for new garden."

He wasn't wrong, and something was oddly tugging at Gwyn's chest—he was offering her prime space, in the middle of his truly dazzling garden?—even as her eyes flicked back to the old tree, its wizened grey branches, the moss-covered stone beneath.

"Do you think," she said, low, "it's appropriate, though?

How"—she shot him an uncertain look—"how old is this garden, Joarr?"

Joarr's shrug was certainly too careless this time, a hint of that mask shifting over his eyes. "I no ken. Long before my days. But if you no want this place, pick aught else you wish."

Gwyn cast another furtive glance around at the clearing, and felt herself swallow. "Of course I want it," she said quietly. "If you really mean to move my garden here—or even part of it—and keep it as insurance for me, I would be deeply grateful."

For an instant, there was silence, broken only by the morning call of a sparrow—and Gwyn couldn't at all read the look on Joarr's face, the distance in his eyes. "Ach," he said, his mouth curving up in not quite a smile. "And how long until you are raiding *my* garden, and stealing away all you wish?"

His eyes had angled purposely toward the edge of the little meadow, to where—she froze in place—there were more chasteberry plants, grown into full-sized *shrubs*. Many of them, in fact, all clustered together in an unruly mess, with a protective frame around them—and Gwyn gasped, and clutched her hands to her heart. "Joarr!" she crowed. "You have so *many* of them! And"—she gasped again, her eyes darting to the distinctive, spiny seed capsules—"thornapple! How did you get it to grow in the shade like that?"

Joarr returned this with a surprisingly comprehensive reply, and soon they were embroiled in a detailed debate about nightshade propagation, while Gwyn kept dashing around the garden, and drinking up its wonders. Discovering dittany, hops, and mandrakes, an excellent compost-pile, and even, in the garden's northwestern corner, a little waterfall pooling into a stream, providing a convenient irrigation source.

And once Gwyn had happily washed her hands and face in the fresh water, Joarr drew her up again, and led her toward the mass of oak, plum, and apple trees lining the garden's north side. "Come," he said, as he grasped what looked like a hanging rope, and stepped onto a low branch. "Teach you to climb, ach?"

Gwyn surely had no need to learn how to climb trees, but she couldn't find the will to argue, either. And she even found herself intently watching as Joarr took his time stepping from branch to branch, moving higher and higher into the canopy of leaves above, all while using the rope for balance. Not as if he needed the assistance, clearly, but Gwyn could certainly see how it would be helpful. And after a bracing breath, she carefully began following him up, toward where he was now watching from a wooden platform above, his hand outstretched down toward her.

It was far more difficult than he'd made it look, and the ground below soon seemed very far away. But despite Gwyn's sweaty hands and hammering heartbeat, she kept working her way upwards, and finally reached Joarr's proffered hand, clasping it tight. And once he'd yanked her up, standing her on the wooden platform beside him, she couldn't hide her triumphant grin, or her awestruck gasp at the new sights before her.

It was a whole maze of little ropes and wooden platforms, curling and twining up and down through the trees. Likely meant to make picking their fruit easier, Gwyn's brain absently noted, even as she grasped for the nearest rope, and stepped onto the next platform, and the next. Until she was surrounded by a cloud of leaves, fully enclosed by their green shimmering life, while birdsong lit up the clear morning air around her.

Joarr had followed close behind her, his movements silent, his face dappled in warm glints of sunlight through the leaves. And by the time Gwyn finally reached the last tree in the row, there was an odd lump in her throat, her eyes blinking at the world of surrounding green.

"You like?" Joarr finally said, his voice gruff—and when

Gwyn glanced back toward him, he was holding out another plum, his brows raised. "Please you?"

Gwyn blinked at him, and then felt herself give a raspy, incredulous laugh. "Of course," she said, as she numbly took the plum from his hand. "I—I *love* it, Joarr. It's *wonderful.*"

His sudden grin seemed to flash even more light through the green around them, and he kept his gaze on hers as he grasped for another dangling plum, brought it to his own mouth, and tore off a sharp bite. Spurting a trail of juice down his chin, which he licked off with a languorous swirl of his tongue, before tossing the rest of the plum into his mouth, and swallowing it whole.

"Then mayhap now some fun?" he asked, coming a slow, meaningful step closer, and jerking his head toward his back. "Come. Hold me."

Gwyn again didn't even try to protest, and instead finished eating her own plum as quickly as possible. And then climbed up onto his warm, powerful back, wrapping her arms and legs around his solid strength, just like she'd done when they'd been running in the forest.

And then, Joarr grinned over his shoulder, grasped for a nearby branch, and... *jumped.* Swinging with heart-stopping speed toward the next tree, and landing with perfect balance on a thin, moss-covered branch.

Gwyn's arms and legs had spasmed around him, even as she gasped a breathless laugh into his ear—and after another grin over his shoulder, he leapt again. Almost as if they were weightless for an instant, hanging in empty air, before he caught the next branch, and again shuddered them to a halt.

His next leap took them higher, further up into the tree— and next out of the tree entirely, flying straight toward the nearby sheer wall of the mountain. Terrifying enough that Gwyn yelped into his hair, her eyes squeezing shut—but when they stilled again, he was balanced on a little stone precipice, his hand clutching a sturdy-looking vine twining up the mountain from below. And then he leapt off again, back into the wash of surrounding green, while Gwyn shivered, and stared, and marvelled.

She was truly disappointed when they finally returned to the ground—at least, until Joarr somehow produced a tiny, dark blue huckleberry, and popped it into her mouth. Swarming her tongue with its impossibly rich sweetness— gods, she hadn't tasted one of these in *years*—and she eagerly ate it, and then glanced around at the nearby plants. Because surely, this meant there had to be more?

"Wish for another?" Joarr cut in, the challenge sparking through his eyes. "Then come find me, ach?"

With that, he spun and sped off into the garden, disappearing behind a cranberry bush. Leaving Gwyn to huff a breathless laugh, shaking her head—but when he didn't reappear, she accordingly followed after him, and peered behind the bush.

But wait, he—wasn't there? Because somehow, that was him over there, multiple steps away, casually leaning against the garden's ivy-covered wall. And actually *winking* at her, the bastard, as he tossed another deep blue berry into the air.

Gwyn loudly groaned, but rushed off after him again—and this time, he scuttled up the wall, and disappeared into a thatch of overhanging leaves. And when she darted over to frown up toward them, she caught a movement well off to her right—and good gods, that was him, now standing in a patch of feverfew. Waiting there, grinning, as she stalked up toward him, and tried not to smile back at his smug, infuriating face.

But he only kept grinning as he popped the berry into her mouth—and then somehow produced another one, brandishing it in front of her eyes before turning and running off. Obliging Gwyn to chase after him again, truly panting with the effort now, while the amusement bubbled higher and higher in her chest. And when she finally caught him—crouching behind a rose bush—she couldn't suppress her gale of laughter, or her full-body shiver as he rewarded her with another berry, his warm hand lingering against her lips.

The next time she caught him, she was still laughing, and his hand lingered even longer, his fingers slipping into her mouth. His gaze sweeping over her flushed cheeks, her heaving chest, her surely sparkling eyes. And then dropping to where her hand had somehow gripped his forearm, almost as if needing to touch him, to keep him here before her...

"Once more," he murmured. "And then"—his voice dropped—"*more* fun, ach?"

Gwyn's breath hitched, her throat convulsing, and Joarr flashed her one more teasing, too-knowing grin before taking off again. And after another merry chase all through the garden, she finally found him leaning lazily against his hammock, and holding out his last precious huckleberry. His brows raised, his eyes intent on her mouth, waiting.

It meant he wanted her to come get it, oh gods. And instead of even trying to argue, Gwyn just nodded and stepped closer, and closer. Until she could gently bite the berry out from between his fingers, her lips brushing against his claws.

Joarr's eyes seemed to darken in the bright sunlight, long lashes fluttering as he watched her swallow. And then he wordlessly reached both hands to grasp her waist, sweeping her up and around into the hammock behind him.

Gwyn's heart kicked into speed, her eyes wide on his face— because yes, she knew exactly what he wanted, what he was doing. His hands already catching on her bare calves beneath her skirts, tugging her arse close to the hammock's edge, spreading her legs apart...

"You devious *snake*," she breathed, but she didn't even try to resist, let alone attempt an escape. As if all her willpower from earlier that morning had crumbled into dust, and all the excellent reasons to avoid his—his *pinecones*—felt thin and murky and very far away. She couldn't trust him. He'd lied to her. He had one last chance. And...

And he was smirking as he stepped closer between her parted legs, his brows raised, his hands sliding steadily up her thighs. Moving up her skirts with them, exposing her bare skin to the warm dappled sunlight.

"You like," he purred, his hands now skating over her hips, pushing the dress up further. "Wish me inside you. Ach?"

Gwyn sputtered, or tried to—but was utterly, abruptly silenced by the realization that she was already bared to the waist, with an orc standing close between her parted thighs. An orc whose clawed hand was casually dropping to his own trousers, shoving them downwards—until his long, swollen heft bobbed free, jutting out toward her.

It was at a perfect height like this, oh gods, and already easing closer—because wait, he was *moving* her. Because *she* was the one in the hammock, and both his hands were spreading wide on her bare hips, swinging her straight toward his waiting, pulsing prick.

Gwyn braced herself, anticipating it—but just before it made contact, he swung her away again. Leaving her gasping, shuddering, untouched, while her disbelieving eyes caught and stuttered on the sight. On her own bare lower half, spread wide open for an orc, aimed straight for the protruding, dripping-wet pole of him. And perhaps even waiting for him to swing her back toward him, yes, oh gods, just like that. Just close enough to feel that slick silken head brushing just slightly against her, pulsing, seeking its way deeper—

But then he swung her away again, far too soon. His expression still impossibly cool, his brazen eyes flicking between her hot face, and her waiting, exposed, wide-open heat. Because he was clearly taunting her with this, the bastard, taking his time swinging her forward again, casually nocking that swollen head back against her starving wet heat. Playing with her, *amusing* himself with her, his lips quirking up at her choked, breathless groan.

"You like," he murmured again, as he held her there just a little longer, watching her wet, desperate folds clutching at the slick, jutting crown of him. "Wish me deeper in you. Wish to drain me dry."

Gwyn's mouth made a noise much like a growl, which only twisted his smirk higher as he deliberately swung her away again. "You speak what you wish," he said lightly, "and then, mayhap, I give more."

Gods, he was enraging, devious, not to be trusted—and Gwyn growled again as he thrust her legs wider, and again swung her close. Digging himself just a little deeper as he kept watching, mocking, with those cool, half-lidded eyes. *Waiting.*

Her breath was coming in sharp pants, her body crawling with heat, with the prodding, pulsing heft jutted against her core. And she needed more, she was going to explode if she didn't have more, and all she had to do was speak, speak...

"Closer," she heard herself gasp, earning an indulgent smile from his mouth, a sustained flex of that hardness brushing against her. And then, oh, he indeed let her settle closer, let her feel even more of him, his head just spreading her apart around it...

Gwyn cried out long and loud as she convulsed upon him, craving him—and the bastard actually *laughed* as he pushed her away this time, the sound bright and warm, his head tilted back. Mocking her, *again*, and she belatedly bit at her lip, squeezed her eyes shut. Gods, why was she giving him this, why was she playing along with his ridiculous game, his gods-damned pinecones...

And then, oh hell, the bite of *claws*, digging gentle but purposeful into her thighs. Snapping her gaze back toward him, his laughter now vanished, his eyes purposefully distant again. As his fingertips kept carefully pricking those claws into her skin, sparking delicious pain beneath them, while her open heat kept clutching at nothing, *nothing*...

"Look upon me," he said, his voice dark, "and speak more. And *then* I tend you, as you wish."

Gwyn's ragged moan escaped on its own, and she felt her traitorous head somehow nodding, *nodding*. While Joarr's eyes flared with chilly satisfaction, his brows rising, waiting. Wanting her to speak.

"Inside me," her betraying mouth choked. "All the way. *Please.*"

And yes, there, there was his approval, his twist of a smile. But still no laughter this time, as his claws on her thighs slowly, purposefully drew her closer, jutting his swollen heft back against her. Lining her up, holding her there, his grip flexing against her skin...

And in a single, devastating stroke, he drove her deep. Slamming all the way into her, skewering her, *impaling* her upon his huge, powerful prick.

Gwyn's shout rang through the garden, the mingled shock and thrill ringing up her spine, and Joarr's mouth quirked as he watched her, his hands holding her tight upon him, his groin pressed flush to hers, his strength buried to the hilt inside her. And already pulsing, filling further, leaking its seed deep within...

His hooded eyes dropped to watch as he slid her back again, and this time Gwyn was watching, too. That long heft now slick and glossy, its every vein and ridge shining in the sunlight as it slowly emerged from between her legs. As his hands pushed her just a little further away, enough that he slipped fully out of her, hovering between them. So he could again watch her greedy, empty heat gripping for him, begging for him, please...

"Again," she gasped, and again he smirked as he slowly

brought her forward again—and then rammed her full and deep upon him. The feeling just as powerful, just as impossible, dragging another hoarse shout from her choked, gulping throat.

"You like," he purred, challenged, all cold control, as he again swung her away, his slick length once more bobbing free of her. "Wish to suck my strong seed inside you."

Gwyn desperately nodded, frantic, far too hungry to be ashamed. And in reward he again lined her up, sank her deep while she shouted and clamped against him. While he kept watching with half-lidded eyes, so cool, so insolent, so *wicked*.

The hunger kept spiralling, pooling tighter and deeper in her belly, radiating out from his every plunge inside her. From where he was finally moving faster, guiding her smoothly up and down upon him, his claws sinking sharper into her thighs. Tangling more sparkling, exquisite pain into the wheeling whirling pleasure, ramping it higher, screaming it into her soul…

Gwyn was babbling and begging now, her hands and legs fighting to drag him close, to keep him there—and she could feel his full-body shudder as he picked up speed, slamming her down onto him, plunging her full again and again. Driving them raging and relentless toward the edge, to the precipice, closer, closer, trembling, teetering…

Her relief tore from her with a scream, with the fierce, shattering flares of her pierced-open heat upon him. Gripping him, milking him, dragging him to stillness—until he finally flashed out inside her, flooding her with burst after burst of his molten liquid seed. His low growl burning from his throat, his eyes clenched shut, his claws crushing her close against him as his hips circled, ground, emptied himself fully within.

When it finally stopped, Gwyn felt like the earth was swirling around them—or perhaps that was the hammock, still slightly swinging beneath her. Still moving with him, maybe, and she felt her dazed eyes searching his face, drinking up his closed eyes, the sheen of sweat on his cheeks, the heave of his breath. And there was the hope, swift and strangely powerful, that he would look at her, caress her, or even lean down and kiss her...

There was a beat of stillness, of Joarr's eyes blinking open, catching on hers. And for an instant, she was sure he would touch her, tell her she was a good little witch, *mine—*

When without warning, he pushed her away. Thrusting her fully free of him, the hammock tilted high, so that—she gasped, fluttered her hands downwards—the mess he'd left between her legs would pour down toward the ground below, streaking thick white against the long grasses, even spattering onto his bare *feet.*

And he was watching it with visible amusement, his lips again quirking up, his cool eyes finally flicking back to hers. "Ach, witch," he said, his voice light. "Raining again, you ken?"

Gwyn's mouth made a noise much like a laugh, her head giving a wry shake—but something was clutching at her belly, at the emptiness he'd left behind. At how this was clearly over already, because it had just been... *fun*, for him. It had been this devious, manipulative, entirely untrustworthy orc remaining utterly in control of the situation, and giving her exactly what she'd wanted. Again.

And the worst part was, Gwyn *had* wanted it. Gods, she'd even demanded he show her more fun, hadn't she? So why did she care? Why was it hard to make herself smile, or even to look at him?

She could hear him clearing his throat, perhaps about to speak—when behind them, there was a telltale crunching of stone. The door to the *mountain*, Gwyn realized, with a horrified glance toward it, her body flinching to stillness in the hammock.

But Joarr didn't even blink, and briskly yanked down

Gwyn's skirts, and tied up his own trousers. And then reached to lift her off the hammock before striding toward the mountain, pulling her along after him.

The new arrival turned out to be another orc—in fact, the bulky, friendly, neck-bitten one she'd met the day before, with the captain. Baldr, his name had been.

"Greetings again, new woman," Baldr said, with a quick little bow toward her. "And Joarr. Please forgive my intruding, but some orcs have gained new wounds in the Skai arena, so Efterar seeks some henbane—if you might have some to spare?"

Joarr jerked a nod, and then spun on his heel toward the hut, leaving Gwyn to follow behind with Baldr. And despite Baldr's warm, apologetic smile toward her, she couldn't seem to smile back, or drag her stuttering brain away from this newest onslaught. *Henbane*, Baldr had said. For injured orcs. For this... Efterar?

"Who did you say was administering the henbane?" she asked Baldr, once Joarr had gone into the hut, leaving them both waiting outside. "A healer of some sort, I presume?"

Her thoughts were suddenly racing, crashing together all at once, because gods, how had she forgotten about this? About how Joarr had told her—yes, quite clearly—that Orc Mountain needed a midwife. But how back in that Bautul room, Silfast had insisted that they already had strong healers here. That Stella already had good care...

"And would that be the same healer," Gwyn continued, speaking faster now, "who's taking care of Stella?"

Baldr nodded, and glanced toward where Joarr was already striding back out of the hut, a small bottle in hand. "Yes, our Chief Healer is Efterar, of Clan Ash-Kai," Baldr said brightly, as he took the bottle from Joarr. "He bears much skill, and is mayhap the best healer in the realm. Enough that he does not always use herbs this way, but the Ka-esh have been a good influence upon him, I think."

With that, he gave them both a friendly wave, and then turned back toward the mountain. Leaving Gwyn alone with Joarr again, who hadn't spoken a word to her since Baldr's arrival—and who was once again wearing that mask over his eyes, hiding himself away. Hiding the truth.

Because what exactly had Silfast said, back in that room? *We do not need help*, he'd claimed. *We have a strong healer here, and many clever Ka-esh, who take good care of our mates.*

And whatever mental justification Gwyn had been harbouring around that—that Silfast had been exaggerating, or posturing at Joarr's expense—was now decisively dashed. And in its place, even more dark thoughts were swarming, dragging down her head, her heart. They already had healers here. She wasn't needed here. And Joarr had lied to her, *again*.

"So when you said," she began, her eyes not fully meeting Joarr's now, "that it would be helpful to bring a midwife here— was that just more manipulation from you, then? More half-truths, to help you get what you wanted from me?"

There was an instant's silence in return, surely betraying that she'd struck close to the truth—and she heard herself laugh, the sound grating in her ears. "And maybe you never truly intended for me to do any real midwifery work here at all," she continued, her voice brittle. "Because a lord's daughter can't be a real midwife, right? Not even if I paid for all my training myself, or did it all with no support, because no one else cared, they thought it was a stupid, self-indulgent *fantasy*. A whim of a dotty, plant-obsessed lord's daughter, who can't even—"

She belatedly broke off there, pressing her hands painfully against her eyes, because gods, where had she been going with that? A lord's daughter who couldn't even keep an orc's attention, beyond his *fun*? Who kept playing into his slippery fingers, and believing his lies, and making herself his *pawn*?

Stupid. So, so *stupid*.

But suddenly Joarr's tall body was here, snapped close before her, his strong hands clamping around her wrists. Yanking them away from her eyes, wanting her to look at him, to meet the... the *disbelief* in his glittering gaze.

"No, woman," he said, his voice firm. "No. You no speak all this. You *are* midwife. And you ought to be here, for our mountain lacks this. We *need* this."

Gwyn blankly blinked at him, and had to fight through the fog for a reply. "But you apparently have the best healer in the *realm* working here," she countered, too shrill. "And Silfast said—"

The rest of that thought was muffled by the abrupt clap of Joarr's hand over her mouth, his eyes flashing with sharp, surprising fervour. "You *never* speak to me of what Silfast say," he shot back. "Silfast know *naught* of this, and he think he say truth, when he have none. He say Stella have good care, but you meet her, ach? You see her? You ken she is happy here? You ken she stay here to bear Silfast this son he longs for?"

Gwyn blinked again, while her scattering thoughts twisted back toward Stella, toward her reddened, tired eyes, her wan smile, her soft voice. How she'd looked at Silfast. How she'd seemed almost... sad. Uncertain. Alone.

"No," Joarr continued, his eyes hard. "Silfast push his mate away, so she go. And she is no quick, wilful woman like you, ach? She no find own way, with no help. She walk straight into this new law. Into these men. Into *death*."

Oh. A horrible little shiver snaked up Gwyn's back, and Joarr twitched a nod, as if she'd somehow spoken her agreement aloud. "Stella have *good care*," he said, his lip curling. "She have Efterar, and the Ka-esh medics also. They bear much skill, ach—but they are yet orcs, and no human. They are no close enough to gain her trust. And"—his eyes shifted in the brightening sunlight—"they see only her flesh, ach? They seek to heal only this. They say she is weary. Must rest. Grow son. This is all."

Gwyn winced against Joarr's hand, digesting all that, because yes, actually, he did have a point. Her best midwifery mentors—and the ones with the most successful outcomes, as well—had repeatedly spoken of how prenatal care needed to extend beyond just physical needs, and consider the woman as a whole.

It was a truth that Gwyn had taken fully to heart, and had seen bear out in her own practice, too. Women needed to feel safe, comfortable, prepared. They needed to know they were supported, and had options. And sometimes, they needed help against their families and intimate partners most of all.

"But," Gwyn belatedly said, pulling at Joarr's hand on her mouth, feeling it easily slide downwards at her touch. "Has it never occurred to you that perhaps it *would* be better for Stella to leave? That if Silfast is cruel to her here, she may very well be better off away from him?"

Joarr grimaced, and his eyes shifted again, gone distant behind his mask. "Silfast is no cruel, he is a fool," he snapped. "This is no the same. And Stella is no *better off* if she is *dead!*"

There was more surprising vehemence in his voice, firing another uneasy chill up Gwyn's back, and Joarr jerked a hard shake of his head, as if to jolt something out of it. "You ken these *solutions* your father wields against these woman are safe?" he sneered, his eyes again sharp on hers. "You ken these human *physicians* shall take good care, most of all when this woman bears an orc son?"

Gwyn's stomach was unpleasantly roiling, and Joarr barked a bitter laugh, the sound at awful, scraping odds with the lush greenery and sunlight all around them. "And you ken Stella is only one?" he hissed at her. "Only woman who shall meet death at the hands of this? Even only *Bautul* woman?"

Gwyn swallowed hard, her eyes desperately searching Joarr's cold, strangely hostile face. Catching on that inexplicable certainty in his eyes on hers, glittering, *accusing*. Not without reason, because her very own lord father was doing this. Putting women at risk. Endangering them.

Killing them.

Gwyn swallowed again, raised her chin. "Do you think," she began, her voice hoarse, "that Stella might see me today?"

Joarr's eyes again shifted, slipped behind his mask—but then he nodded, curt and quick. "Mayhap," he said. "She may no yet agree to midwife, but I ken she wish for *friend*. Also"— he briefly touched his hand to the tooth around his neck, his voice tellingly casual—"whilst you sleep last eve, I also send away yet two more orcs, who wish you to see their mates today."

He *what*?! "Why," Gwyn demanded at him, her own anger rapidly rising, "would you do such a thing?!"

Joarr blinked at her, but then shrugged, not nearly as careless as it looked. "I owe you only *fun*, this day," he said, voice clipped. "Only *after* this, shall you stay and help."

Oh, good *gods*. Gwyn barely suppressed a growl, yanking her hands through her hair, and glaring at his enraging face. "I didn't mean at the expense of these women's *well-being*, you prick," she snapped at him. "How could you possibly think I would prioritize my own entertainment over their health? Haven't you been spying on me for months? Surely enough to know something like that?!"

Joarr didn't reply, but the look in his eyes clearly betrayed him. Suggesting that no, he didn't think Gwyn would place others' *survival* before her own damned amusement, being the spoiled lord's daughter that she was, with a gods-damned *murderer* for a father.

And suddenly there was only a chilly, flat determination, filling her chest, swirling to her feet. She would do her job. She would help. She would do whatever the hell she could to thwart her accursed father and his horrible looming law,— even if it was one woman, one meeting, at a time. And damn this slippery orc and his unwarranted judgement, she would start here, now, today.

"Then forget the fun," she said, cold, calm, utterly certain. "And take me where I'm most needed. Now."

18

After the wild, cheery brightness of the garden, it felt even more difficult to enter the mountain this time. More daunting, somehow, knowing that all those dark corridors awaited, close and cloying and crammed full of dangerous, unfamiliar orcs.

But Gwyn certainly wasn't turning back, either, and she strode through the corridor as smoothly as she could. Putting one foot in front of the other, fighting down her racing heartbeat, glancing regularly at the burning lamp grasped in Joarr's hand. Trying to ignore the sound of his heavy sigh, and the infuriatingly reassuring feel of his warm fingers, again settling wide to her back.

Because even if Gwyn had slept in his arms in a hammock, and had had further *relations* with him, and had even found genuine fun in his chaotic, glorious garden—she was still vividly, irrationally angry with him. With how—yes—he'd kept the truth from her, again. He hadn't explained, again. And he'd even had the gall to be snappy with *her*, as if he'd expected her to read his gods-damned mind, or know that people had needed her while she'd slept.

"For future reference," she said into the taut darkness, "if there's *ever* an emergency while I'm sleeping, you wake me up. *Always.*"

And gods, why was she even saying this, surely she wasn't possibly staying here long enough for this to happen *again*—and beside her there was an instant's silence, then the sound of another sigh. "It was no *emergency*," he said, voice flat. "And this is the first night you sleep through since we meet. You are human. You need this."

And wait, was he implying that he'd been spying on her in Varrahan while she'd *slept*? And even more enraging, the asshole wasn't wrong about Gwyn's chronic inability to sleep, or the fact that she currently felt more well-rested than she had in weeks, or perhaps months.

"Where are we going again?" she demanded, her voice unmistakably testy, as Joarr guided her around another corner, past a huge, block-like orc who blatantly gaped at her. "I would appreciate some kind of mountain-navigating instructions, in case I ever need to find my way in this confounded maze without you?!"

And curse her, because again, surely she didn't intend to stay, or do any solo navigating of this dark unnerving mountain whatsoever—and she certainly didn't feel *relieved* when Joarr drew in breath beside her, and finally began to speak.

"Our mountain is split into five parts, for each of our five clans," he said. "This part—where my garden is, and where you met the Bautul—is all for the Bautul, on the south and east of the mountain. I take you again to their common-room—their hearth—which lies at the heart of this."

Their hearth. Still as if it didn't belong to him, even as the garden somehow did. "So your garden is actually part of the Bautul wing, too, then?" Gwyn asked, still with an edge on her voice. "How did it end up being yours? Was it a gift from them, or something, when you learned the truth about your clan?"

A glance up at Joarr showed his brow furrowing, his mouth tight. "No," he said, voice thin. "The Bautul of old followed the ways of the earth, but there are none among them now with the learning to lead this. Thus, I alone tended this garden, most of all after the war with the men ended, and this became safe again. This was my own *fun*, when I was no away with my work. And now…"

And now, oddly enough, he really *was* Bautul, after all. And despite Gwyn's still-present frustration toward him, her curiosity was even stronger, her eyes glancing at his tense face. "And where did you first learn about plants and gardens?" she asked. "Your father?"

Joarr briefly nodded, before jerking his head toward a wide corridor to the left. "This way," he said, louder than before, "leads to the Ash-Kai, high up in the mountain. And the Skai"—he gave a dismissive wave toward the stone wall on the right—"are beyond, thus. Next to Bautul."

There was an audible shift in his voice as he spoke, and for an instant, Gwyn might have felt a stab of sympathy—when from up ahead, she heard a rising swell of noise. Noise that she now surely recognized, along with that flickering firelight— and she braced herself as Joarr guided her back into the room. Into the Bautul *hearth*.

And despite the earliness of the hour, it was once again filled with a swarm of shocking sights. With multiple orcs grinding and groaning together, taking their pleasure with blatant, unrepentant openness. There were orcs against the walls, orcs on the benches, even orcs rocking on the altar where she and Joarr had—well.

But at least Gwyn was prepared this time, and she somehow found herself taking better stock of the rest of the room, as well. There was a table set up to the side, where several orcs seemed to be playing a game of chance together, entirely ignoring the heated goings-on around them. Off to another side, an orc was beating a large hidebound drum, while before him two orcs stomped out a complex-looking dance. And carved into the walls, there was a variety of detailed artwork Gwyn hadn't noticed before—battle scenes, hunting scenes, and yet more scenes of brazen intimacy, featuring orcs, and women, and even what appeared to be human *men*.

"Welcome back, woman," interrupted a voice, and when Gwyn blinked to look, it was one of the orcs she vaguely recognized from yesterday, tall and charcoal-skinned, and fixing her with a cautious, careful smile. "It is joy to have you among us. I am Kalfr, one of Bautul's chief hunters. I seek to learn the ways of our gardens, also."

Gwyn attempted a smile in return, though a glance up at Joarr showed his mask had slipped back into place, hiding away his eyes. Suggesting some sort of discomfort with this, then, so Gwyn quickly and politely introduced herself, and then made to move toward where she'd caught a glimpse of Stella, on the other side of the room. But before she'd taken a single step, another familiar-looking orc had lumbered over, this one huge and craggy-faced, flashing her a broad, sharp-toothed grin.

"Greetings, woman," he said firmly. "Welcome to our clan. I am Olarr, one of our battle-captains. We are honoured to count you as Joarr's mate."

Wait. As Joarr's *mate*?! Gwyn tried to reply, but already here was another younger-looking orc, jostling his way in front of Olarr. "I am Eyolf," he said brightly. "I have just reached nineteen summers, but I am already a fierce and strong Bautul warrior. Ach, Olarr?"

To Gwyn's vague surprise, the Olarr orc shot a tolerant smile toward Eyolf, and even rustled his black hair with a big clawed hand. "Ach," he said, reaching to pull over another nearby orc, who had been skulking behind Eyolf. "And this is his bond-brother Iyolf, who is also a strong warrior, but shall not boast so proudly of it, ach?"

The new orc's squarish, sharp-jawed face visibly flushed with pink, and Gwyn smiled again, more genuine this time. And once she'd again introduced herself, she found herself being half-guided, half-crowded, toward the next orc in the line, a hunter named Egil. And then toward more warriors, called Thorvald and Arne and Matuk and Grum, and then the drummer and the dancers, Magni and Thrand and Leif. And more, and more, far too many names for her to remember, until her brain was desperately floundering, and Joarr had finally yanked her away, his hand tense on her arm, his smile markedly tight.

"Meet more later, ach?" he said, his eyes distant, his voice carrying. Suggesting, again, some level of discomfort with this, even though he was the one who supposedly needed to mend relations with his new clan. But Gwyn didn't protest, and even attempted a conciliatory wave back toward all her new acquaintances as Joarr pulled her across the room.

"Are you all right?" she muttered at him, but he ignored the question, and drew her toward where Stella was indeed, again, sitting on the bench. She was dressed in a heavy shawl, her dark head bent over what appeared to be more sewing, and thankfully there was no hint of Silfast to be seen. However, Stella still looked unmistakably exhausted, her bleary eyes blinking down at her work—and it wasn't until Joarr loudly cleared his throat that she glanced up, and then visibly startled at the sight of them.

"Gwyn!" she exclaimed, setting down her sewing with eager-seeming relief. "You've returned. How are you faring so far? I heard you spent the night in the Bautul garden?"

The *Bautul* garden. A glance up at Joarr showed him looking patently irritated by this—but Gwyn was still irritated by him at the moment, and therefore decided to ignore him, in favour of dropping down onto the bench beside Stella. "Yes, and it was very lovely," she replied, stretching her arms over her head. "I slept better than I have in weeks! How about you?"

Stella's answering smile was surely part grimace, and she dropped her eyes back to her sewing. "Oh, you know," she said, a little too offhandedly, her hand rubbing at her generously rounded waist. "This little fellow never sleeps, do you?"

Gwyn felt her mouth opening, about to ask the usual litany of questions—had Stella tried matching her sleep patterns to the baby's, or perhaps cutting out certain foods—but thankfully she bit back the words, just in time. Stella needed a friend, Joarr had said. And truth be told, Gwyn could probably use a friend, too.

"I'm so sorry to hear that," she said instead, and she meant it. "Not being able to sleep is awful. One time, I stayed awake for three days in a row, and by the end of it I was having visions of giant slugs invading my apartment, and eating all my favourite plants. It was *harrowing*."

Stella's half-smile was creeping upwards, a faint warmth sparking in her tired eyes. "Because of the slugs?" she asked. "Or your doomed plants?"

"Oh, definitely the plants," Gwyn said, with a shudder that wasn't at all put-upon. "Slugs, I can deal with. Losing my priceless garden, *no*."

She couldn't help a furtive, betraying look toward Joarr, who'd dropped to sit beside her on the bench. And in return, he nudged her elbow with his, in a gesture that might have been approving—or, perhaps, even comforting.

"I've always liked plants too," Stella said now, her eyes fixed back to her hands. "And gardens, and just being busy out in the fresh air and sun. Although these days..."

Her voice trailed off, but her implication was far too clear— and this time, Gwyn's mouth was running before she could stop it. "You don't get outside, Stella?" she demanded. "But you're pregnant. It's a basic *requirement!*"

Stella winced, and jerked her head back and forth. "I mean, I get *outside,*" she said, very quickly. "Silfast doesn't feel it's safe for me to be out above ground right now, but there's a little bluff up off the Ash-Kai wing, and a cozy Ka-esh sunroom, as well. Silfast makes sure I go to one of them every day to rest. He's *very* rigorous about his son's needs."

Her voice sounded bright, but her face looked even more miserable than before. And Gwyn's indignation was much too strong to ignore at this point, and she frowned over at Stella, and perhaps the entire room, as well. "Well, his efforts would be far better spent on *your* needs," she snapped. "And there's absolutely no reason for a pregnant woman not to be busy and active outside, as long as she feels up to it. And if your partner is that concerned about your safety, why can't he just accompany you?!"

Stella winced again, and this time her head dropped further, her shoulders sagging. "He used to, but there have been so many men around lately," she said, quiet. "*Hunting* us. Some even with long-range crossbows. Last month, two men dug a hole—during a heavy rain—and hid themselves so well, that even *Joarr* didn't see they were there."

She attempted an apologetic smile over toward Joarr, who was indeed looking distinctly disgruntled, staring darkly across the room. While Gwyn's twisting thoughts flicked back to the men in the woods, the dogs, the pinecone. The *orc-hunting,* in blatant defiance of their own damned treaty. Of Gwyn's *father's* treaty.

"Right," Gwyn replied, with a grimace. "But surely"—she shot Joarr a furtive glance—"there's no reason you can't come out to Joarr's garden, at least? It seems quite secure, and perhaps you could even take on some work there, if you like? There's *always* something that needs doing in a garden."

She was purposely avoiding Joarr's eyes now, though she could feel his gaze boring into her, his disapproval prickling under her skin. But he'd given her leave to use his garden as she wished, and he wanted her to make friends, and maybe help Stella as well—and therefore, in what world could he possibly justify refusing Stella entry into his garden? And even more ridiculous, refusing Stella's *help*?

"It's so kind of you to offer," Stella replied, with a too-aware glance of her own toward Joarr. "But I'm sure Joarr doesn't need intruders, and I don't think Silfast—"

She broke off there, just as Gwyn felt another pointed nudge of Joarr's elbow in her side. And that was because—her eyes snapped upward—here, indeed, was Silfast himself. Looming in the doorway opposite, glowering balefully toward them—and then striding across the room with powerful, angry-looking steps.

"What is this?" Silfast demanded down at Joarr, once he'd swept to a halt before them. "You wait until the *one* time I am away, before you come here and pounce upon my mate? When you *know* she does not need more care for our son?!"

Joarr slowly unfolded his body from beside Gwyn, and smoothly rose to his feet before Silfast. And to Gwyn's vague surprise, this close Joarr was actually the taller of the two, looking down his nose toward Silfast's angry eyes.

"We no *pounce*," Joarr replied, his voice deceptively casual. "We come to see Bautul kin. And woman wish to make friends."

Silfast looked deeply unconvinced, his eyes still dark and narrow on Joarr's. "I see your slippery ways, *brother*," he said flatly. "You have scorned our sacred hearth for three whole moons, and *now* you wish to see Bautul kin? Wish to make *friends*?"

"Indeed," Gwyn piped up from the bench. "Just today, I've already met Kalfr, and Olarr, and Eyolf and Iyolf, and Egil and

Thorvald and Arne and Matuk and Grum. And Magni, and his dancer friends, too."

Grum, who was currently grinding against another orc's arse nearby, had glanced over his shoulder at the sound of his name—and Gwyn even smiled, and gave him a cheerful little wave. "They've all been so lovely and welcoming," she said, shifting her smile back toward Silfast's face. "I suppose earning the goddess' blessing like we did yesterday has probably helped, don't you think?"

Silfast's jaw jumped in his cheek, but he didn't comment, and dropped his gaze to Stella, who was currently clutching her sewing, her knuckles white. "Come, woman," he said flatly. "You must eat. I have your meal waiting in our room."

Stella quickly nodded, and leapt to her feet—a sudden movement that set her staggering sideways, and Silfast instantly caught her, his big hands spreading gentle against her rounded waist. "Ach, woman," he murmured, his tone softer than before. "Mayhap we shall again rest, also."

Stella nodded again, angling an uneasy glance toward Gwyn as Silfast steered her away—but then she pulled back, biting her lip. "Um, Silfast," she said, her voice thready, "Gwyn invited me to come see the B—, er, Joarr's garden. Or perhaps even to help work in it, a little. What do you think?"

Silfast's huge body froze in place, his dark eyes snapping back toward Joarr, his rage all too visible on his face—but Gwyn could see his effort to clear his expression, the purpose in his hand stroking Stella's back. "I think this is hard work, in the hot sun," he said flatly. "You are yet so weary, woman. You ought to rest, not fritter about in foolish *gardens*."

"But—Gwyn thinks it might be healthy for our son," Stella said, very quickly, as though seeking to finish before she lost her courage. "And good for—for me. And she's a trained midwife, so she should know, shouldn't she? And we can have

Efterar monitor our son's health after, right? It might be—nice. Just to—try."

She winced as she spoke, her gaze dropping, and even as Silfast shot Joarr another accusing look, his hand kept stroking her back, his mouth tight. "Ach, if this is what you wish," he said, "then this is what shall be done."

Stella twitched a shaky, relieved-looking nod, and gave Gwyn a wavering, apologetic smile. "How about tomorrow morning, then?" she asked. "If you're still sure, Gwyn, that is?"

"Of course I'm sure," Gwyn replied firmly. "We'd love to see you both there. Wouldn't we, Joarr?"

Joarr's replying nod was terse and unimpressed, but thankfully he didn't argue. And once Silfast was guiding Stella away, Joarr also marched Gwyn toward the opposite exit, his steps long and fast and clearly disapproving.

"What?" Gwyn demanded at him, once they were back in the dark corridor again. "I thought you *wanted* me to make friends? And are they not allowed to visit us in your garden? Even when it used to be the *Bautul* garden?"

Joarr didn't answer, though his scowl visibly deepened. Suggesting that again, this was a point of some difficulty, and Gwyn sighed, and rubbed at her face. "And are they... always like that?" she asked. "Silfast snarling and raging, while pretending he isn't? And Stella tiptoeing around him, as if to prevent some devastating catastrophe from occurring?"

Joarr twitched an unreadable look at her, and then barked a sudden laugh. "No," he said. "Before this, you were more like to see Stella taunt and tease him, with all eager sweetness. Until he threw her over his lap, and struck her whilst she screeched for his mercy. Or his prick."

He looked faintly amused by that, and Gwyn made herself consider it as they turned into another corridor, now tilting steadily downwards. So Stella and Silfast had once enjoyed those *games of intimacy* too, then. And while such things of course needed to be modified with pregnancy, there was no reason to stop if both partners were still enjoying it—but then again, a difficult pregnancy could certainly have an effect on one's enjoyment, too. And if Stella truly took Gwyn up on her offer about the garden tomorrow, perhaps that might help, and—

Gwyn belatedly startled, her steps faltering, her hand rubbing at her face. Because had she really just promised to see Stella *tomorrow*? To spend yet *another* day in this damned mountain, with this damned infuriating orc?!

But Joarr's sidelong smirk at her suggested that yes, she had indeed committed to such a thing, and he hadn't missed it, either. "This way," he said coolly, nudging her toward another corridor, with an even steeper angle to the floor. "I take you next down to the Ka-esh, ach?"

The Ka-esh. The reading orcs, Gwyn recalled, the ones who'd discovered the truth about Joarr's clan, and who supposedly never stopped talking. And as she was fighting to reorient her still-spinning brain toward this new objective, someone whirled out of a nearby room, and rushed over to bounce before them in the corridor.

"Oh, here they are!" exclaimed a bright, enthusiastic voice. "Oh, how *exciting*! Welcome!"

Gwyn jerked to a halt, blinking—and found herself staring at a *woman*. Yes, a woman, small and blonde and pert-looking, her blue eyes sparkling with anticipation, her hands clasped over her chest. And she, too, was visibly pregnant, her rounded belly very obvious against her otherwise slight form.

"I'm Rosa, of Clan Ka-esh," the woman continued cheerfully. "And you must be Gwyn! It's such a *thrill* to finally have a real midwife join us! We always knew Joarr was a clever orc, and fully on board with the cause, but—I hope you don't mind me saying, Joarr—this is a fate-changing feat! A *master-stroke* on your part! Don't you agree, John-Ka?"

With that, she'd dashed back into the room, and returned dragging someone else behind her. Another orc, it turned out—and this one was strangely, surprisingly handsome. His body more human-sized, his features almost elf-like, his grey-green face entirely unmarked by scars. And he was also clearly involved with this blonde woman, his clawed hands catching easy and familiar at her full waist as he nodded toward Joarr and Gwyn.

"Ach, we have greatly needed this," he said, his voice and eyes grave on Gwyn's. "We welcome you among us, woman, and look forward to your work here."

He spoke as though this were some sort of long-term arrangement, rather than a two-day—or three-day—visit, but Gwyn thrust away that awareness for now, and attempted a smile. "Er, thank you," she said. "It's a pleasure to meet you both."

The orc returned this with a brief nod, while Rosa positively beamed. "*So* exciting," she said again. "Now come, come! I hope you'll give me a *complete* examination? Also, I've just finished a new copy of *A Treatise on the Gainful Birthing of Orclings* for you. You'll want to read it at once, I'm sure!"

She was eagerly gesturing toward the nearby door, and Gwyn felt herself inexplicably hesitating, angling another glance up at Joarr. At where he was twitching a wry, reassuring half-smile back down toward her, almost as if to say, *I warned you about these Ka-esh, didn't I?*

And despite Gwyn's still-present irritation toward him, it helped, somehow. Settling the tension in her shoulders, bringing a more sincere smile to her mouth. "Of course," she said to Rosa, as she followed her inside. "I'm happy to do whatever I can."

The new room was also made of stone, not dissimilar to the others Gwyn had seen so far—but it also had stone workbenches cut into nearly all the walls, as well as several stone tables rising from the floor in the middle of the room. And upon the workbenches, there stood neat rows of mismatched opaque bottles, multiple thick books and piles of paper, and a variety of familiar-looking steel implements. Of... *medical tools*?

"It's a... clinic?" Gwyn's astonished voice asked, as Rosa hopped up to sit upon the nearest table. "A medical clinic?"

"Yes, and you're more than welcome to make use of it as you need," Rosa replied. "Our approach to healing is a collaborative one, isn't it, John-Ka? Oh, and speaking of which, Gwyn"—her bright eyes flicked toward the door—"surely you don't mind if a few of our medics observe our consultation, as well?"

Gwyn whipped around, and discovered that there were indeed three more orcs striding into the room—all of them again surprisingly handsome, and all eyeing her with wary curiosity. "This is Salvi, and Eben, and Aaron, all of Clan Ka-esh," Rosa announced from the table. "And this is our new midwife, Gwyn, of Clan Bautul!"

Gwyn, of *Clan Bautul*?! Gwyn couldn't hide her reflexive twitch, or her sharp look toward Joarr—but he was conveniently looking elsewhere, his mouth thin. Leaving Gwyn to attempt a smile at these new orcs, while desperately grasping for some kind of focus. "Lovely to meet you," she said. "Though I'll warn you, my consultations aren't very exciting. Mostly talking, I'm afraid."

The orcs gave a variety of nods and hand-waves, apparently undaunted, so Gwyn drew in a breath, and returned her attention to Rosa's expectant eyes. And then, while intently fighting to ignore her watching orc audience, she launched into her usual list of questions from the top.

The list was of course very thorough, built over years of practice, and encompassed everything from dates to diet to moods to symptoms to sleep. And while it soon became clear that Rosa and these orcs were very well-informed about many facets of pregnancy and childbirth, they also seemed to have surprising gaps in their knowledge, several in deeply crucial areas.

"No, I'm afraid your birth can't happen here," she told Rosa, glancing around at the room, once Rosa had announced this as her plan. "Not unless you can bring in a large basin of hot water, and keep regularly refreshing it. You'll most certainly want to plan for a water birth—and the option to remain mostly vertical—especially with your first, and with the inherent size difference in cross-species births like this. Perhaps we should look into getting you a birthing chair, as well."

"Truly?" Rosa asked, glancing uncertainly at the orcs around her. "We brought in a human midwife for Jule's birth, and she didn't mention anything about water. Or being upright."

"Well, every midwife has their own set of practices," Gwyn replied, with a shrug. "But in my experience, having these options available improves outcomes considerably—as well as your comfort. I can certainly direct you to a few reliable references, if you like."

"Oh, yes, please," Rosa said, with genuine-seeming relish. "As many as possible, if you don't mind. And what do you think about pain management during the birth?"

Gwyn of course had extensive thoughts on that front, and talked Rosa through the best available options, and the assets and drawbacks of each one. And once Rosa and the orcs seemed satisfied, Gwyn finally proceeded with the actual physical examination, in which she checked Rosa's pulse, breasts, and pelvis, listened to the baby's heartbeat, determined the baby's current position, and thankfully ruled out any obvious infections or concerns.

"You and the baby both seem to be doing very well," she said, once she'd finally finished. "Do you have any other questions?"

Rosa did, unsurprisingly, and soon Gwyn found herself caught in another intensive discussion, much of it focusing on the book Rosa had mentioned. Which, it turned out, was an ancient midwifery manual, written by an orc healer an entire century before.

"Yes, of course I'd be happy to read it," Gwyn said, after she'd washed up in a nearby basin, and Rosa had thrust a neat, new-looking copy of the book into her hands. "There are so few informed resources on orc pregnancies, especially from an orc perspective, so I'm sure it will be invaluable. The only thing is"—she carefully flipped through the book's clean, crisp pages—"I can't be sure to keep it dry in the garden. Is there somewhere else I could safely read it?"

Rosa was again beaming at Gwyn with marked approval, as though she'd passed some sort of secret test. "Yes, of course," she said. "Have Joarr bring you to the library tomorrow afternoon, and we can read and discuss it together. And I'd love to have a follow-up exam too, if you don't mind? Perhaps once I've better researched these pain management options you've suggested? In a few days, maybe, or next week?"

Gwyn had been smiling back—Rosa's enthusiasm was contagious, somehow—but then she felt her smile falter, her eyes glancing uncertainly over her shoulder toward Joarr. Tomorrow? A few days? Next *week*?

Joarr had slipped slightly away from the general hubbub, in favour of leaning casually against the nearest wall, and observing the proceedings in silence. But now he strode forward again, shrugging, and gave Rosa a cool, careless smile.

"Ach, I shall bring her on the morrow," he said lightly. "Now come, woman, ach?"

There was another enthusiastic round of goodbyes as Joarr led Gwyn toward the door, and back out into the corridor. Back, too, into a rising, ringing silence, which suddenly felt both very welcome, and oddly, uncomfortably oppressive. *Could* Gwyn return here next week, somehow? Would she?

And perhaps more importantly, did Joarr *want* her to?

"Next, I take you to the Grisk," Joarr said, as the floor began to angle upwards again. "They are beside and above Ka-esh, to the north. They mayhap speak as oft as the Ka-esh, but no with so many questions, ach?"

It was a hint of a joke, or even a pinecone—but Gwyn somehow couldn't seem to meet it, or even manage a look toward him. Because maybe... maybe he *had* been telling the truth, this time. She *was* needed here. Wasn't she? And what did that mean, and what in the gods' names was she supposed to do next?

That uncertainty wasn't helped by her next consultation, this one with a lovely auburn-haired woman named Ella, who was remarkably outfitted in a variety of jewels and scanty furs, and also bore several sets of fresh-looking *teeth-marks* on her neck. And who seemed entirely unconcerned by these facts, and instead smiled at her hulking, similarly attired orc with surprising affection, and spoke with frank eagerness about their shared desire to have a hale, healthy son.

"And it's just *so* lovely to have another woman on hand to manage these things," Ella said warmly to Gwyn, once she'd finished her physical exam. "It's difficult for Natt to handle other orcs touching me—they leave such a strong scent behind, and Grisk orcs are especially sensitive about that. But another woman isn't nearly such an issue, right, Natt?"

She was smiling over at her orc, again with visible, almost tangible fondness, and the Natt orc's smile back toward her was just as warm, and surely relieved, too. "Ach, this is truth," he said. "I thank you, my sweet mate, for honouring me thus. And"—his eyes flicked toward Gwyn—"I thank you, Gwyn of Clan Bautul, for coming to us with this gift. I hope, mayhap, you shall stay here among us, and help to birth our son?"

His eyes felt oddly piercing on Gwyn's, even as he pulled Ella close, drawing her into the circle of his powerful arms. And for an instant, Gwyn could only seem to look back, while her heart thumped erratically in her chest.

"I'm sorry, but I'm—not sure, about staying," she said, hoarse. "But I'm committed to doing everything I can to help. No matter what."

The words felt painfully true, escaping out her mouth, and Natt gave her an inscrutable nod, before bending his head back into Ella's neck. Leaving Gwyn to blink uncertainly toward them, before stammering a goodbye, and turning for the door.

Joarr had been waiting out in the corridor this time, and upon seeing Gwyn he pushed off the stone wall, and fell into step beside her. Glancing sideways toward her with unreadable eyes, but not speaking, even as his hand slipped to its familiar place on her back.

"Where to now?" Gwyn finally asked into the silence. "Somewhere I could wash up, maybe? Or eat something?"

Much to her relief, Joarr instantly nodded. And after guiding her past many more strange orcs and doors—she was becoming rather inured to it all by now—he led her first down to the same latrine she'd used last time, and then to an actual *kitchen*. It was surprisingly well-outfitted, with a large stove, a roaring fire, and multiple tools and workspaces. And the two orcs working inside both greeted Joarr with warm-sounding black-tongue, and seemed to grant him leave to do whatever he wished.

"Our cooks make good supper for whole mountain each day," Joarr explained to Gwyn, as he led her toward a nearby pantry, where he began sniffing at barrels. "But no always use enough mushrooms, ach?"

With that, he triumphantly yanked a piece of salt pork out of a barrel, and next rummaged around for a few sprigs of thyme, and indeed, a surprising variety of fresh mushrooms.

And then, while Gwyn watched with increasing bemusement, he chopped it all up with a few deft strokes of an alarmingly large knife, and tossed it into a pan over the fire.

"How did you learn to cook?" Gwyn asked him, once she was standing close beside him, and the truly mouthwatering smell was unfurling under her nose. "You said you were a Chief *Scout*, right?"

Joarr shrugged, tossing the contents of his pan with a quick flick of his wrist. "I walk with the earth," he said, "and learn its ways. This means I no only grow green things, but I learn their use, ach? I watch, and see how they work. What they *are*."

Oh. Gwyn eyed him for a too-long moment, her brain catching oddly on the sight of him flipping the pan again, the lean muscles flexing in his forearm. "And you do it with people, too," she said, not quite a question. "And maybe that's part of why you're also a scout."

He inclined his head, his hand raising the pan toward her in a movement that meant, *Yes, just so.* And for an instant, standing here in Orc Mountain's kitchen, while this mystifying orc casually cooked her a delicious-smelling lunch, Gwyn felt something skip in her chest, circling around her ribs. Something that made her want to step nearer, to draw him against her, try to fight back the tightness gnawing at her throat...

"Here," Joarr said, as he produced an actual fork from somewhere, and thrust it toward her. "Eat."

He'd already pierced a piece of fried meat with his claw, and then popped it into his mouth, raising an eyebrow at her as he chewed. So Gwyn accordingly obliged, spearing a tender-looking mushroom with her fork, and taking a careful bite.

"*Gods*, that's good," she gasped, without at all meaning to—but Joarr's flash of a grin fired pure warmth into her belly, and he picked up another mushroom, and tossed it into his mouth.

"Ach, it is," he said lightly. "You like mushrooms, ach?"

She fervently nodded and speared another one, eating it

whole this time, while Joarr did the same. And while she watched him over their pan, his long lashes fluttering as he chewed, his throat bobbing as he swallowed...

She had to force her eyes back downwards, focus on eating, damn it—and all too soon the food was gone, and Joarr was calling out what sounded like a goodbye to the two cooks, the black-tongue fluent and rolling in his mouth. And then it was back to the corridor, to his warm hand on her arse, while Gwyn kept her gaze on the floor, and fought down the ever-swirling mess of her thoughts. She was here for a reason. She was here to save her garden, and to help these women. She was most certainly not here for *him*, especially when he still couldn't be trusted, and...

"One more, ach?" he said to her, his voice very smooth. "And then back to garden?"

Gwyn nodded, and Joarr accordingly guided her into another corridor, this one looking distinctly familiar. And then another one, the opposite way they'd gone last time, in the direction of...

"You're taking me to your old clan?" she asked him, the surprise too audible in her voice. "The Skai?"

That was surely surprise on Joarr's face too, but he covered it up with a quick nod, a cool smile. "Ach," he said, nudging her into another darker, twistier corridor. "Simon—who I have well known since I was an orcling—has of late gained a mate. Maria. I wish you to see her."

He wished. Suggesting that maybe Simon—or Maria—hadn't actually requested this particular visit. And Gwyn had just opened her mouth, about to point out the potential pitfalls of this plan, when Joarr drew to a halt before a nearby open door, and twitched a wry, tolerant grin at whatever was within.

Gwyn stepped closer, met his amused gaze, and then followed it inside the room. The room where—she froze in place, her eyes wide—a truly massive, fully bared orc was standing, close against a fur-covered bed. And before him on the bed was a kneeling, also-bared woman, her arse high in the air, her back arched, as the massive orc slowly slid his equally massive pole of a prick inside her.

Gwyn gulped for air, for conscious thought—good gods, that thing was a freak of nature, a *travesty*—but somehow, impossibly, the woman was taking it, bit by shocking bit. Until the orc had somehow seated it all the way within her, his broad hips grinding flush against her bare arse. His deep groan burning through the room, his head tilting back, while the impaled woman gasped and trembled beneath him.

The orc's drag back out was just as slow, just as deliberate, his thick length now coated in a glossy wet sheen. And as he held it there, just nudging it between the woman's parted legs, he glanced over toward Joarr and Gwyn, his mouth curving into a sharp, thoroughly terrifying smile.

"Ach, we have guests, woman," he said, deep and far too casual, as he slowly began easing himself back inside her. "Wish me to stop now? Greet guests?"

The woman's groan was pure frustration, and to Gwyn's astonishment, she didn't even try to look toward the door. Instead she shook her dark head toward the bed beneath her, her entire body shuddering as the orc gave a deep, approving chuckle, and again sank himself all the way inside.

"Good woman," he murmured, palming his big hand at her bare arse with obvious approval. "Then show them what more my brave mate can take, ach?"

With that, he shot another decidedly smug grin toward Joarr and Gwyn, as he drew all the way out again. Now bobbing fully free of the woman, his massive heft visibly dripping with thick white—and then he casually gripped that heft in his clawed fingers, and slid it higher up, delving between her full arse-cheeks. And then—Gwyn had to choke back her gasp—he again drove forward, breath by breath, until he was buried to the hilt inside her.

Gwyn couldn't help a shocked, dumfounded look up at Joarr's face—this couldn't actually be *possible*?!—but his glance back down toward her was still wryly amused. Almost as if he thoroughly approved of this little scene, of this orc and this woman so blatantly taking their impossible pleasure together.

And surely Joarr saw the disbelief in Gwyn's eyes, because he only shrugged as the massive orc slowly picked up speed, driving in and out of the woman with smooth, purposeful strokes. "Maria is good woman, ach?" Joarr murmured, under his breath. "Work hard to please her mate, in all ways. He deserve this."

Oh. So not only did Joarr approve of this, but he *expected* this of a woman. Of a... mate. This... freeness, this shameless-ness, to be eagerly taken and displayed, not even caring who was at the door. Not even when her orc was doing *that*, and while Gwyn had previously attempted such things with Roy, she'd surely never found such pleasure in it. And she'd surely never looked like that, either, her body tall and ample and rich with curves, her hair a lovely mass of tumbling waves, her orc's hands grasping at her generous arse as he drove inside faster and faster, his growls rising, his rapture etching into his face—

And when the orc finally finished, it was with a desperate, powerful roar, blending beautifully with the woman's husky moans as he ground himself even harder inside her. Clearly emptying himself deep within, into where this woman had so proudly and easily accepted him.

This *good woman*, Joarr had said. As though this, maybe, was what he truly wanted, rather than a skinny, plant-obsessed, self-destructive lord's daughter, who he only saw fit to laugh at, and manipulate, and lie to, and...

Joarr's hand had briefly grasped at Gwyn's chin, tilting it up toward him—but she couldn't seem to meet his eyes, and instead blinked intently at his chest. Until across the room there was a loud gasp, and then the sound of shuffling bodies and shifting fabric. "Simon!" came the woman's voice, thin and strangled. "You could have *said*!"

"Ach, I did say," came the orc's low, indulgent reply, and when Gwyn tore her eyes away from Joarr, the orc was smiling affectionately down at the woman, who had yanked on a gigantic-looking tunic. "You honoured me in this, ach?"

His accent was very similar to Joarr's, but his gaze sliding toward Gwyn was much warmer, his mouth curving into another true, sharp-looking smile. "It is honour to meet you, new woman," he said. "Joarr's scent smells sweet upon you. We have heard much of this Bautul blessing you gained him, ach?"

Gwyn couldn't seem to find an answer to that, and thankfully the woman lurched forward, her hand held out, a sheepish smile on her flushed face. "Yes, we're *so* happy to meet you," she said. "Though I do apologize for the circumstances. Joarr, I'd fully expect, but—"

She broke off there, her warm eyes flicking brief but familiar toward Joarr's face—confirming, surely, that this was a sight he'd often seen before. A sight he'd perhaps *wanted* to see. And it took considerable effort for Gwyn to swallow, to paste the smile to her mouth as she shook the woman's proffered hand.

"Please don't apologize," she said, too quickly. "I'm already becoming very accustomed to how things are around here, no trouble at all. I'm Gwyn, by the way, and I'm a midwife, and Joarr mentioned you might be interested in booking a consultation?"

Her voice had gone thin and high-pitched, her face sticky and hot, but thankfully the orc and the woman both kept smiling, the orc casting a bare, appreciative glance toward Joarr behind her.

"Ach, we should indeed wish for this, at once," the orc said firmly. "I thank you, Joarr."

A furtive look at Joarr showed him waving this dismissively away, though his eyes were still on Gwyn, his brow furrowed. And suddenly she couldn't bear to look at him, and she dragged her gaze back to the woman. The *good woman*, Joarr had said.

"Well, if now works for you, let's get started," Gwyn said. "I'd like to begin with a few questions, if you don't mind?"

No one minded, so Gwyn gratefully launched into her usual list, working through her questions one by one. Losing herself, finally, in the familiarity of it, the mental calculations, the needs of the patient above all else. It turned out that Maria was three months pregnant, just beginning to show, and though she'd experienced some fatigue and nausea so far, the physical exam, combined with her answers, suggested that thankfully, nothing serious was amiss.

"If you'd like to try a few herbal options to settle your stomach, just let me know," Gwyn said, once they'd covered her full list. "And ideally, I'd like to see you again in—"

She caught herself just in time, her face again furiously heating, her eyes glancing reflexively toward Joarr. Joarr, who'd pulled down one of the scimitars lining the room's walls—there was quite a considerable quantity of them—and had been sitting on a bench, sharpening the blade with a nearby stone.

"Ach, soon," he said now, as he smoothly rose to his feet, and hung the scimitar back up behind him. "We make sure all is good."

With that, he strode toward Gwyn, lightly punching the other orc—Simon—in the arm as he passed. But Simon abruptly reached a hand to catch Joarr, pulling him back, and clasping his huge arm around his shoulders.

"We thank you," Simon told him, his voice low. "You watch your way in this, ach?"

As he'd spoken, his big hand had grasped to tug at that tooth, still hanging around Joarr's neck. And then Simon added another stream of words in the black-tongue, all of them entirely unintelligible to Gwyn, but for the distinctive word *Bautul*.

"Ach, ach," Joarr said, with the cool, purposefully distant smile Gwyn now recognized all too well. "I ken, I ken."

His strides toward the door were quick, his hand on Gwyn's back firm and efficient. And Gwyn somehow even managed a series of bright-sounding pleasantries over her shoulder, to which Maria broadly smiled, and Simon only looked... troubled?

But at least Joarr had said that was the last appointment for the day, right? And as they strode through the corridor again, perhaps back toward the garden, Gwyn felt herself deflating, her shoulders dropping. Her thoughts fixating, foolishly, on good women, beautiful women, and how Roy had always preferred those, too.

And with that, even more lowering, somehow, was how all these orcs today had treated their women—all with obvious, open affection, and concern for their wellbeing. And while Joarr might cook for Gwyn, or show her fun in his garden, or even take his calculated pleasure with her, it still surely wasn't that. Not a good woman. Not a beautiful one. And most certainly not his mate, or a real Bautul, no matter what the rest of these orcs seemed to think.

"So look, that whole... ritual, on the altar, last night," Gwyn heard herself say, her voice hollow. "You didn't *mean* for it to go that far, did you? You didn't actually *want* everyone here to start thinking I'm a real Bautul, right?"

And beside her, suddenly, there was just... silence. Not even the sounds of Joarr's footfalls, or his breaths. She might have thought he'd vanished, but for the still-present touch of his hand on her back, now light enough to be almost imperceptible.

And of course, Gwyn knew what that meant. It meant that no, surely, Joarr hadn't meant that, or wanted that. He'd wanted to gain his own place among his clan, and that was all. Because of course it was all about him, everything was all about him, he was a selfish and completely manipulative *asshole*—

But the louder Gwyn tried to silently scream that truth, the more empty it felt. Because today, it *hadn't* been about him. He'd carted her all over his mountain, falsely advertising her as his true Bautul mate—surely to his own future detriment—so that she could help care for these women. So she could try to help save them from her father's horrible new law. And he'd waited patiently through hours of consultations, he hadn't once complained, he'd fed and supported her, and offered reassurances to his kin.

And gods, even before that—Gwyn's hands rubbed at her sticky face—he'd given her that tour of his garden. He'd offered her a prime location for her plants. He'd fully intended to keep giving her that day of fun he'd promised, even at the expense of what he'd obviously felt should be their true priority.

They'd finally reached the end of the corridor, the way to the garden. And Gwyn mentally grasped for that, clinging to the forthcoming vision of sun and green as he shoved the stone open—

But instead, the sky beyond was a deep grey, already somehow darkening into night. And not only that, but it was pouring rain, pattering in through the stone opening, pelting large drops of water against Gwyn's skirts.

"Wish to stay in?" Joarr asked, so cool, so casual, as if Gwyn wasn't already drowning in cold wet darkness, in rising clawing misery. As if she could bear another instant in this close cramped mountain, knowing all these bitter truths, knowing her own failures. Knowing this orc—this infuriating, devious, lying orc—didn't actually want her, and knowing she wasn't supposed to give a damn, and still feeling like she was about to weep.

"No," she said, or perhaps sobbed, as she slipped out past him, to stand under the raging sky. Into the beautiful, chaotic garden that didn't really want her, either, didn't belong to her, and never would. Just like him.

Stupid, stupid, *stupid.*

"No," Gwyn said again, to the streaming-wet darkness. "I think—I think maybe you should take me home."

19

The silence seemed to pound after Gwyn's words, pummelling into her like the driving rain. Like anger, or like... rage.

"You wish *what*?!" Joarr's voice demanded, and suddenly he was standing before Gwyn in the rain, looming tall and menacing over her. "I take you *where*?!"

Gwyn twitched and swallowed, wiped away the water streaking down her cheeks. "Home?" she said, the word nearly drowned by the rain. "To Varrahan? Where I *live*?!"

Joarr's growl rumbled through the air, his form bobbing back and forth on his feet. "Now?" he hissed at her. "After *this day*?!"

"Yes!" Gwyn's voice snapped, or maybe wailed. "And don't tell me Orc Mountain's Chief Scout can't find his way in the rain, because I surely won't believe you, *again*!"

Another growl hissed from Joarr's mouth, and he jerked even closer, his already-wet hair dripping onto Gwyn's face. "I never speak false to you this day," he barked. "No *once*."

"Yes, I know," Gwyn said, her voice badly wavering. "Which is why I finally understand exactly how things are between us. I might make you feel obligated, or aroused, or maybe even amused—but I'm also a lord's daughter, and my father's causing a hell of a lot of trouble for you, and I'm well aware I need to do a hell of a lot more to help clean it up. And obviously you don't ever intend to trust me—I mean, you told me that yourself—and you'd never want someone like me to actually *join* your new clan, or be your—your—"

Good gods, what was she even *saying*, and she squeezed her eyes shut against the rain, against whatever rubbish this orc might spout next. Because he would surely say *something*, cajole her, throw a measly pinecone or two, and Gwyn needed to stamp that down where it belonged, and face the empty, echoing truth in its wake.

"I'm not a *good woman*," she said bitterly. "I'm not beautiful, I'm barely even interesting. I'm a dotty, stupid, unfashionable, plant-obsessed lord's daughter, with a penchant for self-destruction, and an appalling ability to fix my affections upon males who couldn't actually care less about me!"

She could feel Joarr's stare, boring down into her, and she choked a laugh, and wildly shook her head. "And the more time I spend with you," she gulped, "the—the worse it gets. And the more I want to forget how you really see me. So I really should go now, before I—"

There was still no answer from Joarr, but his judgement felt like it was blooming, prickling, creeping down her neck with the cold rain. And wait, of course he was judging her, because he thought—

"And of course I'll keep doing whatever I can for these women," Gwyn added, her voice cracking. "They're welcome to come see me in Varrahan anytime, or perhaps I could return here on a regular basis. No charge, of course, though I'll still need to sort out Roy and my father, and..."

Her voice trailed away, her hands rubbing at her face. Because gods, she'd scarcely thought of Roy and her father this entire damned day, but they certainly hadn't gone anywhere, had they? She still had what, twenty-one days? To save her garden, her entire *future*? And how the hell was she supposed to keep helping these women, for possibly months on end, until she'd dealt with her own predicament for good?

There was the distinctive sound of a groan above her, deep and guttural and impatient. And when Gwyn blinked up through the pelting rain, Joarr was still glowering down at her, his mouth thin, his chest heaving with his breaths.

"You wish," he hissed, "to know truth of how I see you, woman?"

Gwyn grimaced, but felt herself rapidly, fervently nodding. Bracing herself for whatever he had to say, for finally getting this out between them. No convincing, no manipulating, no pinecones, no *fun*...

When suddenly, Joarr *grabbed* her. Snatching her bodily up into his strong arms, and then striding deeper into the garden with swift, controlled steps. And before she could even find her voice to protest, he'd jerked to a halt, and thrust her back down again. Onto something soft, and horizontal, and unexpectedly... dry?

And when she twisted around to stare, it was that distinctive flat stone. The one that stood in the middle of the garden, covered in moss, beneath the wizened old tree.

And Joarr was kneeling directly here before her, far too large and close, his fingers rapidly working at her buttons. Because yes, he was *undressing* her, his hands already yanking her dress open at the front, and shoving it off her shoulders.

Gwyn couldn't seem to follow, move, find thoughts to think—and in another jerk of movement Joarr tossed her dress aside, leaving her fully bared on a rock, outside in the pouring rain. While he loomed ever closer, high on his knees on the stone, his wet black hair streaking rivulets of water down his bare chest, his eyes glinting with vivid, vicious anger.

"You *never again* say you are stupid," he hissed at her, as both his clawed hands grasped at her bare thighs, yanking them brazenly apart. "Or all the rest of this. You no wish me to speak false to you? Then *you* stop this with *me*."

What? Gwyn had somehow slid back onto her elbows on the moss, and she struggled to pull up again, to fire off some kind of answer—but he silenced it with another growl, sharp and fierce. "No," he snapped. "I see. I learn. I *know*."

And before Gwyn could counter it, correct it, he shoved her legs wider, eased his body closer. And then he ducked his wet head low between her thighs, drew in a breath, and—

He *licked* her. *There*. Not light, not gentle—but bold. Blatant. Deep.

Gwyn jolted and gasped, her eyes shocked wide—and oh *hell*, he did it again. That long, strong, sinuous tongue dragging against her, slow and deliberate, in a steady, slippery stroke. And then again, and again, urging her to open for him, to falter and flutter against his onslaught, to flower for his taking...

Gwyn's groan wrenched from her throat, her back arching, her fingers fisting in the moss beneath her. While her knees somehow fell a little wider apart, opening herself further, silently welcoming him deeper...

And of course he instantly obliged, that twisting, torturous tongue already stroking deeper. Seeking its way inside, flicking and flaring as it went, his throat audibly swallowing over the sound of the pelting rain. As if he were brutally determined to drink all her nectar, to feed upon her fruit, to consume her until she was empty, broken, ravished...

But instead of taking, somehow, he just seemed to keep... giving. That seeking, stroking tongue finding new depths to drink, new petals to urge open, new secrets to unearth. Even slipping further down her crease, now, to tease and tickle and taste her most secret place—and at her choked, breathless gasp, he actually chuckled, husky and hot. And then held her eyes as he slowly, purposefully pierced her there, that tongue slick, alive, *impossible.*

Gwyn's head was thrashing back and forth on the moss, her fingers clinging painfully against it, the rain streaming onto her face, her breasts, her belly. As if covering her, cleansing her, while this orc drank her whole, driving her on, drinking so deep it felt like she was someone else, somewhere else, primed and plundered and pouring out more...

And then, oh gods, something *sharp.* His *teeth.* Scraping so light, so gentle, only teasing at his threat, his bite. While that slick, tortuous tongue slithered out again, following his slow drag of teeth upwards, finding the heart of her again—and then plunging back inside. Twisting and twining ever deeper, spurring her harder, gulping her down, impaling her whole on his greedy drinking mouth—

The release was trampling, relentless, pounding over her in flare after flare. Her invaded heat pulsing at him, milking him, perhaps even spurting at him—and he just groaned as he kept drinking, sucking, *giving.* More and more and more, until she was finally quivering, empty, sprawled and spent, and he pressed one last, painfully gentle kiss there, before slowly rising up over her.

And Gwyn couldn't breathe. Couldn't speak. Could only look at his blazing eyes, his dripping-wet face, his hanging hair pouring water all around her. And when she felt that telltale nudge, that dip of hungry hardness catching against where his tongue had just been, she shivered all over, opened herself wider. Yes. *Yes.*

And he knew, just like always. Not once breaking her gaze as he canted his hips forward, and sank inside. Skewering her in one single, powerful thrust, filling her flushed, opened flower with his fierce, stabbing strength. Watching her as she writhed and moaned beneath him, desperately dragging for air, her swollen, invaded heat clamping and clutching at him, more, more, more—

His yank out felt almost painful, the emptiness aching in his wake—but the slam back inside was breath, life, filling Gwyn's lungs, driving a harsh cry from her mouth. Her hands frantically gripping at his wet back—how hadn't she been touching him?—as he ground himself deep, making her feel it, watching, taunting, *knowing.*

And then out again, gone again, only for a breath—and slamming back inside. Hard enough to chatter Gwyn's teeth this time, her breached body clinging, crying out—and already he was dragging it out, taking it away. But then thundering back in, in perfect time with a distant rumble from above, the water pouring off his hair, his shoulders, streaming onto the moss all around Gwyn's trembling form. But under him it was almost dry, almost safe, held in the curtain of his hanging hair, in the strong arms closing her in, the flash of his watching eyes...

Gwyn's gasps and shouts kept rising, and in return he kept pounding ever faster, plunging himself into her again and again, driving her into the altar. Shouting back, without speaking at all, that she was his, always his, to open and drink and destroy as he chose. And the more she begged and screamed, the more he would feed her and fill her, he would drown her with his strength, with the furious swell of his seed—

And with one final drive of his hips, he reared up, his wet hair flying back—and the flood of his heat burst open inside her. Surging out in stream after stream, soaking her, filling her, *planting* her—and her own pulsing, screaming body drank it up, dragged it in deeper and deeper, while his straining form over hers lit up in sharp white relief, and thunder rumbled the very earth beneath them.

And for a breath, it was utterly, impossibly unreal. It was

the entire world shimmering away behind Gwyn's blinking eyes, and soaring down into the hidden depths of her body, her soul. Into where she'd been fully pierced and planted by an orc, driven into the throbbing earth, watered deep by the blazing sky. Where she'd been seen, known, filled, not only by the orc still covering her, but by...

"Ach," someone said, *he* said—and abruptly the world juddered back into place again, rippling out around them. And when Gwyn blinked up, again, again, she found Joarr's dripping-wet face, looking back down toward her, his eyes almost as stunned as she felt.

The lightning flashed again, followed a breath later by another peal of thunder, but surely fainter now, further away. And somehow Gwyn could breathe again, dragging in deep, gulping breaths, while above her Joarr did the same, the sound rattling like a burn in his throat.

"Ach," he said again, his eyes squeezing shut—and in a swift, jerky movement, he yanked himself away from her. Sparking a splutter of thick, molten heat in his wake, surging out from where he'd been inside her, pouring onto the moss below. Feeling, suddenly, far too familiar, the tree briefly blurring with a chimney, a fire, a room of watching witnesses...

And Joarr knew it too, his eyes still squeezed shut like that, his head twitching back and forth. His body shifting slightly away, sagging down to the moss beside Gwyn, his arm rigid and heavy over her bare chest.

And in the blare of her thundering heartbeat, the tingle in her fingers and feet, the light still dazzling behind every blink—it only felt right to slip her hand downwards, to feel the hot, sticky truth of what he'd given her. And perhaps, even, to coat her fingers in it, making it hers—and then streaking it upwards, onto her bare belly. Where the rain was still pattering, lighter now, tickling against her skin.

But it didn't wash her gift away, it wouldn't—and Gwyn

heard a harsh, husky groan beside her as she did it again. Streaking the slick warmth even higher this time, painting herself with it, while—she glanced toward him, caught—her orc watched with hooded, fluttering eyes, his teeth biting white at his bottom lip.

And then, oh gods, he did it too. His hand slipping downwards, swirling close and thrilling against her, and easing back up again. Palming gentle but purposeful against her breast, painting her peaked nipple, covering her in his scent.

And when her own tingling hands stopped, spent, he kept going. Covering her other breast, her neck, her cheek. And finally even slipping his long fingers into her mouth, wanting her to suck, to taste, to swallow. To *know*.

The rain was still pattering, but even softer now, and blended with the earth's fresh scent there was now Joarr's, too. Deep and rich and sweet, upon her, inside her, forever tainted, consecrated. And as bizarre, as unbelievable, as this was— whatever the hell it was—Gwyn somehow felt impossibly light, languid, alive. At peace.

"You know, Joarr," she murmured, once he'd finally stopped stroking, and gathered her close against him. "I think your new goddess really likes you."

His answering laugh in her ear sounded wry, oddly choked. "No," he said, with a strange lilt to his voice. "I ken she like *you*."

Gwyn's body gave a tingly shiver against him, as if savouring that truth—which was ridiculous, because she didn't even believe in deities, did she? Especially ones that required lewd, lust-driven sacrifices on ancient public altars?

"So you no go home," he whispered, very quiet. "No yet."

Oh. Right. Because yes, that had been Gwyn's intention before all this, hadn't it? And—another tingle snaked up her spine, less pleasant this time—even if this *had* been some kind of inexplicable sign from the heavens, it still hadn't answered even her most fundamental questions, had it? Had *he*?

"Ach, woman," Joarr added, just as quiet. "If you ken I no mate you in the mountain this day because I no wish to, you are wrong in this, ach?"

What? Surely that hadn't been the problem here, in any shape or form—right? But even so, Gwyn had shifted to better look at him, searching his eyes in the near-blackness.

"But you were all business, all day," she replied, her gaze dropping, her voice far too tenuous. "You went straight from that *fun* in the hammock—in which you barely touched me, by the way—to barely even *looking* at me, either. And then—"

She couldn't hide her wince, her thoughts darting back to that moment with Simon and Maria—that *good woman*—and suddenly Joarr's hand was on her cheek, dragging her eyes back to his. "I no mate you in mountain," he said, harder this time, "for there are few places where this is sure to be free of witness, ach? And when last I do this, you weep. You suffer. You make *pain*. I no risk again."

Oh. There were still important counter-points to this, surely—he could have damn well asked, for one thing—but instead Gwyn swallowed hard, and looked away again. Until Joarr's hand shook her chin, wanting her eyes on his, wanting her to listen. To know.

"And this morn, in my bed," he continued, even flatter, "If you wish for more from me, why you no say this, when I ask? I *seek* to grant what you long for, ach?"

Oh. Gwyn's bewildered brain was blankly flicking backwards, catching on how, yes, he *had* asked. Hadn't he? *You speak what you wish*, he'd said. *Speak more, and then I tend you, as you wish.*

And gods, what had she said? *Closer. Inside me. Again.* Telling him, maybe, that that was all she'd wanted. All she'd needed from him. Something casual, *fun*, and nothing more.

"And," Joarr added, with a sigh, "when I say Maria is good woman, I mean she is good for *Simon*, ach? My father whelped Simon beside me, after his own father's death—and thus, Simon is the nearest I have to blood kin. He was long alone, and long grieved this—so I find good woman for him. I bring her to him. I *wish* to see her kneel and plead and open for him, for he *deserve* this."

Gwyn swallowed again, and felt herself nod, short and furtive. While something that had still been prickling, hot and distant inside, seemed to somehow soothe, softening, settling. So Joarr *hadn't* wanted Maria, then. Hadn't thought her superior. But...

"But Maria is," Gwyn heard herself say, foolish, *shameful*, "very beautiful, don't you think?"

Joarr's brow furrowed, and he barked a hoarse, abrupt laugh. "Maria also need ceaseless tending," he said. "Simon work for many nights before she even mate him outside tiny room, or away from soft fluffy bed. She oft *reek* of fear for no cause, and next cling to Simon like helpless orcling until he soothe her. You ken I bear this in my mate?"

In his *mate*. A new, flickering warmth was pooling in Gwyn's chest, and she actually chuckled, the sound husky and low. "Do you even *own* a soft fluffy bed to mate in?" she asked, before she could stop it. "Or is it always tables, or trees, or sacred Bautul altars?"

Joarr's mouth had quirked up as she spoke—but then stilled at the last bit, his brow again furrowing. "This is *no*," he said firmly, "sacred Bautul altar."

"Of course not," Gwyn replied, but she couldn't seem to keep the smile from stealing across her mouth. "Just like this isn't an ancient Bautul garden, either."

It was almost too dark to see Joarr's eyes now, but that was surely a hint of a rueful smile, even as he shook his head hard enough to spray water drops at her. "No," he said. "*My* garden."

Something else nudged her as he spoke—that tooth around his neck, dangling down toward her. And suddenly seeming important too, somehow, and Gwyn felt her still-tingly hand move to catch it, stroking it in her fingers.

"Does this," she said, quieter, "have something to do with the Bautul, too?"

She could feel his exhale, heavy against her wet skin, and his head had ducked low, as though it was heavy, too. "Ach," he said, short. "It is a Bautul *tḳtem*."

A *tḳtem*. "And what's that?" Gwyn asked, careful now. "And why do *you* wear one, when none of the other Bautul do?"

He exhaled again, long and slow. "It is a Bautul pledge," he said. "Each young Bautul makes one of these, before his first battle. He bears this until he has come of age, and fulfilled its pledge. And once this has been done, it is burnt before all the clan. Only after this, is he claimed as a true Bautul."

Gwyn's head tilted, her eyes blinking, while a surprising indignation marched through her chest. Because despite being a fully grown orc, Joarr *still* had to fulfill some kind of absurd rite of manhood—or orc-hood—to actually belong in his new clan? Even after he'd supposedly gained this nebulous goddess' favour with that altar ritual?

"So the Bautul are truly treating you as though you're a *child*?!" she demanded at him. "How old are you again?"

Joarr shrugged, and stretched with deceptive casualness against the mossy stone. "Thirty summers, mayhap," he said. "But Bautul no break ancient rite for me, ach? Most of all with Silfast as their captain."

There was audible bitterness on his voice now, particularly on Silfast's name, and Gwyn considered that, felt her hand slip down to stroke at Joarr's slippery wet chest. "And what do you need to do to finish it? What's the *pledge*?"

He shrugged again, his exhale once more tickling across

her bare skin. "Its aim is always the same," he said slowly. "The Bautul must do his brother—or his clan—a great honour."

A great honour. Spoken with such heavy, brittle finality, echoing in Gwyn's ears, vibrating deep into her belly. A great honour.

And wait. *Wait.* Was *this* why Joarr had been spying on her? Why he'd come to her in Varrahan? He'd been trying to find a way to strike down that law... for his *clan*?!

Gwyn stared at him, her heart pummelling against her ribs, and surely that was a wince, tightening his mouth, *betraying* him. "The Bautul have suffered much of late from these men, and their laws," he said, even slower. "Their thirst for blood rises, and they begin to call for vengeance—but this risks all we have gained with this treaty, ach? This risks yet more war. More *death.* So after I find you, I *see* you, I see... way through this. For me, and Bautul, and all my kin."

Oh. So Joarr coming to Gwyn, seeking to seduce her—it hadn't only been about the law. It had been about slaking his clan's thirst for vengeance. About the war. About—*peace.*

Joarr had wanted to destroy her, to help save his kind. His *home.*

Gwyn's eyes felt trapped on his face, and her heartbeat was drowning out the distant thunder, resounding between her ears. Because what did that mean, what did he want from her now, was he still going to—

"Ach, woman," he snapped, jerking up to lean over her again, his eyes narrow and flinty on hers. "You hear me speak to Captain, ach? And to Silfast? I now seek new way, in this. I run with what the gods hurl upon me. And you—"

Gwyn blinked up at him, waiting, her heart still roaring, and Joarr's harsh expression seemed to falter, his mouth twitching into a grim little smile. "You are... witch, ach?" he said, his voice oddly tenuous. "You already alter much, in this. You learn my plan. You seek my help. You offer care to women.

So mayhap"—his smile twisted—"mayhap you are yet part of this. *With* me. Ach?"

Oh. Gwyn felt her breath catch, her head reflexively shaking—because Joarr was most certainly imagining this, there was no way she was part of some hazy future involving gods and spells and witchcraft, it was utterly ludicrous, wasn't it? Not to mention what he'd said—or hadn't said—about not wanting her as a Bautul. Or a true mate.

And maybe, oh gods, this was about him still manipulating her. Still using her, to help him gain his own ends. His pledge, his clan, his future...

But Joarr was frowning back down at her again, his brows pulled low, his forehead creased. "No," he hissed, his voice nearly a growl. "You no now think *this* is only what I wish from you. *No*, woman."

Gwyn kept blinking up at him, her breath still frozen in her chest, and he growled again, this time baring his teeth. "No," he said again. "Even if you have *naught* to bear upon all this, I still bring you here. Still"—his voice dropped—"wish to know more of you. Find more *fun* with you. Ach?"

Oh. The ice hardening in Gwyn's chest seemed to crack, just slightly, but her eyes were still fixed to his face, her thoughts swirling back to that still-dangling question of his mate. Of her not being a true Bautul...

"I only—I no yet see where this next lead," Joarr added, even quieter. "We only even *meet* these few nights past, ach? And after this, I only see—"

He stopped there, as if biting off the words, his head whipping back and forth. As if not wanting to tell her, again, that he didn't trust her. That maybe he even still expected she'd go back to Dunburg. To Roy.

And as much as Gwyn knew, with every breath of her being, that she would *never* return to Roy, she could still admit that Joarr wasn't wrong, either. They'd only actually known each other for a few days. And of course it was completely unreasonable for her to expect some kind of commitment, some kind of ridiculous declaration, especially when she wasn't even sure she wanted such a thing. If she'd accept such a thing. Most of all from an *orc*, who, she knew very well, she still couldn't trust, either. Who *still* might be trying to use her, to gain his own ends.

"Right," she said thickly. "Of course. I understand perfectly, thank you."

It was too dark to see Joarr's eyes now, but that was surely the sound of a slow sigh. And then the warm, unmistakable brush of lips to her cheek, soft, careful, gentle.

"You bear this *beauty* also, you ken?" he whispered, so quiet she barely heard it. "Now sleep, my comely witch. And stay."

Stay. Here, under the drizzling sky, on this altar, in his arms? Or here, at his mountain, in his life, his *home*?

And as the warm breeze tickled Gwyn's drying skin, swarming her with the scent of rich sweetness, the need to know somehow fluttered away, dancing off into the night air. Twisting, turning, toward her eyes sliding closed, toward quiet, warmth, *peace*.

She could stay, she thought drowsily, as she settled closer against him, safe. For now. She could see.

20

Gwyn awoke to a warm, reassuring brightness. Pooling soft across her face, flaring orange behind her eyelids.

She yawned and stretched, blinking her eyes open—and found bright blue sky above, scattered with puffy white clouds. And closer, the wizened branches of that old tree, stretching out high above her, and—she twitched, and huffed a laugh—dripping water down onto her bare belly, as if in some sort of backhanded morning greeting.

And wait. It was *morning*. Meaning that she'd slept all night on an altar, fully naked? While Joarr had gone—where?!

She sat up, her heart hammering, her eyes frantically searching—but no, wait, Joarr was there. Here. Rising up swift and smooth from where he'd been crouching, just at the edge of the clearing, his hands covered with fresh earth.

And when Gwyn peered closer, she realized he'd been *planting* something. Something that looked vaguely familiar, with its distinctive clusters of yellow flowers, and wait, wait—

"Is that a piece of my yarrow?!" she demanded, her voice shrill. "And my motherwort?"

Joarr flashed her an easy half-grin, his hands brushing off the dirt. "Ach," he said lightly. "My scouts begin this, last eve. I tell them to take good care, and bring only two to start, so you can judge their work, ach? They water all the plants in your house, also. And leave new note on table, in close copy of your hand, saying of new job. *And,* they bring more clothes."

With that, he nodded toward the north, to where Gwyn could just make out a few familiar-looking dresses, fluttering in the breeze. And a warm, convulsive shiver was whirling up her spine, and she felt herself slowly smiling back at him, her face heating. He was, once again, keeping his word. Keeping her safe. Bringing her plants here. *Helping* her.

And as she kept smiling at him, the memories of the night before seemed to swarm up in a rush, clenching deep and hard in her belly. He'd worshipped her on an ancient altar. He'd called her beautiful. He'd said he wanted to get to know her. *Her.*

And gods, Gwyn wanted to believe it. Wanted to trust him so hard it ached. And she still had twenty days before Roy came back, nearly a month, an *eternity...*

So she drew in breath, and twitched a little jerk of her head. Meaning, maybe, *Come here?* And in return Joarr's grin instantly broadened, showing off all his sharp teeth. Not smug, not mocking, but... warm. *Wicked.*

And as she watched, he brushed the rest of the dirt off his hands, and then sauntered over toward her. His steps smooth and prowling, his clawed fingers blatantly adjusting the thick, already visible ridge beneath the front of his cropped trousers.

Gwyn's gaze snapped to the sight, her breath catching in her throat. And in return, he breathed a low, knowing laugh, and then reached down inside the trousers, and smoothly drew himself out. And then began stroking that solid grey length as he walked, the motions brazen, arrogant, impossibly casual, flaring even more furious heat deep in her belly.

And as he approached, closing the space between them, Gwyn found herself somehow sliding down onto her back again, her legs easing further apart. And Joarr didn't slightly break his stride, didn't even blink, as his knees met the altar, and that hard dripping length bobbed down toward her...

And with one last step, an easy roll of his hips, he drove himself deep within her. Impaling her fully upon him, with a single sharp, shattering plunge.

Gwyn's cry tore through the air, her entire body curling up with the shock, the sensation, the sheer thrill of this orc suddenly sheathed to the hilt inside her. With the sight of him holding himself up high over her, his groin grinding hard against hers, his smirk curling across his mouth.

"You—*bastard*," she gasped at him, even as her trembling hands found his warm chest, slid up behind his shoulders. "Arrogant—*fiend*."

He was already drawing out again, his brows rising, his smirk quirking higher. "Ach, you wish for me," he replied, with infuriating coolness, as he slammed back inside. "And I wish to feel wet womb, gorged full of my seed."

Gwyn's harsh moan was half hunger, half shame, because gods above, he wasn't wrong, on either front. And this already felt far messier than it had the night before, far sloppier, and when he drove in again, faster now, she could feel the slick thickness oozing out between them, slipping out around him...

And damn him, but he *wanted* that. He was even watching that, his black lashes blinking downwards as he drew out again, and drove back inside. And then again, and again, sinking into his usual punishing rhythm, faster, harder, deeper. But not always at the same angle this time, not straight and true, because this way it only worsened the pooling, spluttering mess. The sounds rising thick and obscene from between them, the sticky liquid spurting out around him, streaming down from between their joined bodies onto the altar below...

And gods, it had no right to feel so good. To look so good. Joarr's lean muscled body over her flexing again and again in the sunlight as he furiously worked himself over her, inside her, his head bowed, his hair hanging over his eyes. While he blatantly drew up these sounds, dragged out this mess, wanting to make her sprawled and stretched and debauched beneath him, wanting to see her spurting his bounty...

And in one final, grinding thrust, a rasping bark from his throat, he poured her full again. Pulsing out more thick wet heat from the strength rooted inside her, emptying it as deep as it would go, watering her until she was sopping with his seed.

Gwyn's own hunger was flying, now, straining, soaring into the sky—and finally, finally, it shattered. Her entire form wracking and writhing, her ecstasy scraping from her throat, her pierced heat clamping for the strength inside it—

But it was gone, gone, *nowhere*—and even as she shouted in mingled relief and rage, her hazy, blinking eyes caught on the sight, the shame. On Joarr holding her knees wide apart, so he could watch his own seed fountain out from within her, flaring out toward him in surge after humiliating surge.

Fuck. Gwyn didn't know whether to laugh, or sob, or hide, her face painfully burning, her entire body trembling under his hands. The humiliation rising, roaring in her ears, what had she just done, *why*—

Until Joarr's eyes glanced up, and held. Caught. Stilled under his fluttering lashes, glinting with something she couldn't at all name. And tangling with the brief brush of his tongue to his lips, the visible bob in his corded throat.

"I—" he began, and then cleared his throat, swallowed again. "I like."

And surely—surely he even meant that, because there wasn't a trace of arrogance or triumph in his eyes. Only an odd, quavering intensity, as his warm hand reached to stroke down Gwyn's front, trailing from her shoulder to her breast to her belly, his long clawed fingers lingering, spreading wide over her navel.

"You like too," he said, still with that tenuous uncertainty on his mouth. "Ach?"

She blinked back at him, and found herself numbly nodding, and maybe even attempting a smile. Needing to see him smile too, somehow, and yes, there it was, tugging rueful at the corner of his mouth.

Her stomach flipped, fluttering in her belly, and she felt her own smile broaden, her fingers closing over his against her waist. "I don't suppose," she began, waving her other hand down toward the mess, "we could have a bath?"

Joarr's lips quirked again, and he reached to grasp her hand, easing them both up to standing. An action that instantly worsened the mess by multiple degrees, streaming it down her thighs, sweetening the air with its scent.

Gwyn's face burned even hotter, her mouth grimacing—and before her, Joarr actually winced too, his eyes intent on hers. "Is this pain?" he asked, his voice sharp. "You need herbs? Or my tongue?"

The sudden, powerful vision of that somehow sparked even more hunger in her belly—surely she was not already eager to go *again*?—and she heard herself bark a laugh, her hands rubbing at her hot face.

"I just—the bath would be lovely for now, thanks," she said. "And besides, you surely don't want to go there right now. With your tongue, I mean."

She grimaced again, shot him a chagrined half-smile—and his grin back was wolfish, dangerous, gleaming. "You wish to test me on this?" he purred. "You ken I draw no joy from this truth of my seed upon you? *Within* you?"

Gwyn's breath choked in her throat, the hunger pooling harder, and she had to scramble for thoughts, words. "Later, you messy menace," she managed. "*Bath.*"

He laughed at that, but accordingly nudged her toward the north side of the garden, against the mountain's sheer stone. Toward the little waterfall he'd shown her the day before, pouring down the side of the mountain, and gathering in a small stream below.

"Oh, gods, yes," Gwyn gasped, and instantly waded in. The stream was only up to her knees, and the water was bitterly cold—but it still felt utterly glorious, and she promptly set to scrubbing, cleaning the morning's mess away.

Joarr had been standing slightly to the side, unmoving, watching her with entirely unreadable eyes. But when Gwyn reflexively jerked her head toward the water—saying, again, *come*—he inclined his own head, and shucked his trousers to the earth.

And for a frozen, stolen instant, it occurred to Gwyn, far too late, that she'd never actually seen him fully undressed before. There had always been those ever-present trousers, hanging off his hips, hiding at least part of him away. And now—she stepped slightly out of the streaming water, in order to better blatantly stare—it was just... *him*. All smooth grey skin and lean rippled muscle, his shaggy hair brushing his shoulders, his face stark in the light of the rising sun.

And further down, that heft at his groin was casting stark shadows too. Already bobbing out half-hard toward her, and swelling even fuller as he came a fluid, graceful step closer.

Gwyn didn't even try to hide her gasp this time, and didn't look away, either. And when Joarr flashed her one of those sly grins, and stepped into the pool, she immediately reached for him, and drew him close.

"Thought you wish for later," he purred, taunting, mocking—but gods, Gwyn didn't even care. And when she shoved down on his shoulders, shameless, *appalling*, he dropped with instant, insolent ease, his eyes glittering on hers as he thrust her thighs apart.

It led to her standing on one foot under a waterfall, with her other leg hitched on an orc's bare wet shoulder, while he once again buried his face between her legs. That long tongue slurping and slithering up inside, dragging out her gasps and shouts, her body trembling, her hands fisting tight in his hair. Until the release screamed over her, for the second time in one damned morning, so strong that she nearly lost her balance, and toppled into the water below.

But Joarr was far too quick, his hands instantly snapping to catch her waist, holding her steady until she found her footing again. And without even thinking, Gwyn dropped her own still-trembly hands down to that heft at his groin, and milked it with fast, forceful strokes until he was the one gasping, and spurting out all over her breasts and belly.

This time, she couldn't seem to find the slightest shame in it—especially not with the water pouring over them like this, already washing it away. And before it could all disappear, she even found herself catching a thick drop on her shaky finger, and slipping it into her mouth. Revelling in its hot, slippery sweetness, and in the way Joarr's eyes instantly darkened as he watched.

"Witch woman," he murmured, and Gwyn actually heard herself laugh, the sound surprisingly warm and bright in the sparkling morning sun. And perhaps she would have even started all over again, if there hadn't been a loud, unmistakable scraping noise, coming from the mountain behind them.

It was the stone door opening, damn it—and Gwyn leapt out of the waterfall at once, lunging for the new clothes Joarr had brought. While he too tugged on his trousers, shaking the water from his hair like a dog, and then strode for the door.

The sound of speaking voices soon revealed that this new arrival was Stella, come to see the garden, as she'd promised. And when Gwyn went to greet her, still smoothing out her clean new dress, Stella was blinking uneasily up at Joarr, her dark eyes looking even more tired than before.

"Thank you so much for having me," she was saying. "I do apologize for Silfast's absence, but he had several crucial commitments that he just couldn't—"

"Ach, ach," Joarr interrupted, with obvious impatience, and Gwyn gave him a surreptitious elbow in the side as she stepped forward, smiling at Stella's wan face.

"We're so glad you came," she said warmly. "Now, where should we begin? Perhaps with a tour?"

Stella returned this with a relieved smile, but beside them Joarr was still looking distinctly unsettled, his mask already slipping over his eyes. Enough that Gwyn slid her hand up and down his back, and even squeezed his firm rear end, almost as if to... *comfort* him?

"I know Joarr had some work to finish up this morning too," she said. "So perhaps I'll take you around, Stella. And Joarr, we'll ask you if we have any questions, all right? And we certainly won't change anything without consulting with you first."

That seemed to help somewhat—Gwyn could feel him slightly relaxing against her—and he even patted her arse in return before turning and stalking off. Leaving her alone with Stella, who truth be told, was looking rather relieved, too.

"Well, let's get started," Gwyn said, as brightly as she could. "And just let me know if you need a break at any point, all right?"

Stella nodded, and soon she was trailing behind Gwyn through the garden's meandering paths, listening to her rambling commentary with shy attentiveness. Even asking a few questions here and there, and then exclaiming with genuine-seeming delight at the sight of the little clearing, and the moss-covered stone beneath the wizened tree.

"Oh, another altar!" she said, her face more animated than

Gwyn had ever yet seen it. "I didn't realize the Bautul had one of these out here. How *wonderful*."

It seemed like she truly meant that, her dark head lowering as one of her hands reached to touch the mossy stone. While her other hand clenched to a tight fist, and pressed close against her heart.

Gwyn watched her for a jolting instant, her face flushing, her thoughts darting with alarming vividness toward her own recent experiences on this altar. And when Stella finally raised her head, Gwyn swallowed hard, and heard herself ask a question that she'd never before imagined coming from her own mouth.

"Could you tell me more about your—our—goddess?" her voice said. "The Goddess of Bautul?"

She half-expected Stella to refuse, or point out that surely this was Joarr's responsibility—but instead she nodded, and flashed Gwyn an earnest, dazzling smile. "Of course," she replied. "Well, as I mentioned, the goddess is most often found in the moon, but she's actually the goddess of the earth *and* the sky. She speaks to us through the wind, the trees, the fire, the rain."

Oh. Gwyn's face burned even hotter, her thoughts again firmly caught on the night before, the sky opening over them as Joarr pounded into her. "And the altars?" she asked. "They're part of this?"

"Yes, very much so," Stella said, stroking the altar before them with a careful hand. "The goddess longs to see her Bautul sons and daughters sharing their joy upon them, and creating more sons for her beloved clan."

More sons. Gwyn's unhelpful brain was now flicking toward her multiple extra-strong doses of silphium, and to Joarr's original horrible plans for her—but thankfully Stella didn't seem to notice. "And as you've seen, there are also rituals to follow, especially around important times in the orcs' lives—births, coming of age, gaining a mate. But wise Bautul will often seek the goddess beyond these times as well—and in return, she will reward them with manifold strength, valour, vigour, and forbearance."

She spoke the words with palpable reverence, as though she'd memorized them, or perhaps even cherished them—and Gwyn made herself nod. "And is the, er, *joy-sharing* primarily how you seek the goddess?" she asked. "Or are there other ways, also?"

Stella shot Gwyn another knowing smile, and again brought her fist to her heart. "We often do this," she said, touching her other hand to the altar, and bowing her head toward the tree. "You can speak if you wish, or just be still and listen. But you can see how the tree is meant to represent her, right? How she's watching over you, and wanting the best for you?"

Right. Gwyn nodded again, her thoughts still oddly stilted, almost *appreciative*, somehow—and she took a breath, and searched for something, anything, to say. "It's unfortunate that the tree isn't doing so well, though," she managed, walking over to look up through its wizened branches. "But I've been wondering if we might still be able to salvage it. Try some heavy fertilizing, maybe cut back some limbs?"

Stella glanced up with unmistakable curiosity, and soon Gwyn was thankfully back on familiar ground, explaining the most successful tree-resuscitation practices, and talking through possible options. And before long, she and Stella were pitching the idea to a bemused-looking Joarr at his compost-pile, while Joarr's brows rose higher and higher on his forehead.

"You ken, woman," he said once she'd finished, his voice clipped, "that I am very busy orc, ach? I no need to spend free garden-time on tree that is already *dead*."

Gwyn winced, casting an uneasy look toward Stella, who

was looking distinctly crestfallen—but then Stella's eyes lit up again, searching Joarr's face. "Then perhaps we could ask Kalfr to help?" she asked brightly. "I know he's been wanting to learn more about gardens, and the old Bautul ways."

Joarr's expression had gone suspiciously blank again, but he gave a convincing enough shrug that Stella eagerly agreed to mention it to Kalfr later that day. And before things could devolve any further, Gwyn lurched to stand between them, putting a hand to Joarr's chest. "Hey, did you ever hear back from your captain?" she asked. "Does he still want that numbing salve for his son's teething?"

Joarr jerked a curt nod, and then waved at where Gwyn could indeed see some chamomile, growing just beneath a large willow. And then he strode off again without another word, leaving Gwyn to smile sheepishly at Stella as she steered her toward the chamomile, and launched into an impromptu lesson about its care and harvesting.

Stella again listened with genuine-seeming interest, and soon they were working side by side in the garden's hut. First crushing the flowers they'd harvested, and then mixing them with some lard Gwyn had found in one of the jars, and then slowly heating the concoction over the little burner. And by the time they were finished, they were easily talking and laughing together, and Stella had shyly asked if she might be able to return again tomorrow.

Gwyn angled a glance toward Joarr at that—he'd occasionally popped in and out of the hut as they worked, mostly swapping out tools—and his shrug looked slightly less pained this time, which was likely as much agreement as could be expected. So Gwyn willingly endorsed this plan, while also fighting to ignore the nagging realization that she'd just committed to spending yet another day here at this mountain, with this infuriating orc.

But once Stella had gone, taking the chamomile paste with

her—she'd promised to deliver it safely on her way past—Gwyn found herself searching for Joarr, and again finding him knee-deep in his compost-pile, shovelling dirt into a barrel. His back was gleaming with sweat, his muscles shifting with every movement, his grip on the steel shovel strong and easy and familiar.

And as Gwyn watched, she felt an odd, twisting tightness around her chest, knotting beneath her ribs. And when Joarr glanced over his shoulder toward her, she found herself coughing over the hoarseness in her throat, and giving him a slow, true smile.

"Thank you," she said. "I realize that wasn't easy for you. It must be"—she cleared her throat again—"deeply unpleasant, to have other people suddenly coming into a place you've always considered your own, and even making claims on it. Especially when the place is as lovely as this—and when you're not sure how you feel about those people to begin with."

Joarr gave his familiar casual shrug, but didn't meet her eyes. "Ach, I ken I have no true grounds to refuse this," he replied, with a too-dismissive coolness. "And I ken this help Stella today, also."

Gwyn definitely couldn't argue that point—Stella had certainly seemed in good spirits, and hadn't once complained of fatigue or pain. And it occurred to Gwyn, abruptly, that she'd actually enjoyed the morning, too. That in it, she and Stella had indeed almost felt like—friends.

"It was still good of you," Gwyn said to Joarr's back, quieter. "Toward me, too. Thank you."

Joarr kept shovelling for a long, dangling minute, not looking, not speaking—but then finally stabbed his shovel into the dirt, and strode toward her. "Ach, you shall no thank me," he said lightly, "when next I take you to the Ka-esh library, and they prattle at you until you weep."

Gwyn laughed, waving it away—but it soon turned out that

this was precisely what he meant to do. Leading her back into the dark mountain, deep down into the very bowels of it, to where Rosa was indeed reading in an actual, astonishing *library*. One with a lovely arched ceiling, multiple tables scattered about, and rows and rows of books lining the circular walls.

"You came!" Rosa exclaimed, leaping up from her table, clasping her hands to her chest. "You couldn't stay away from the orcling book, I'm sure! I have it memorized, of course, so perhaps we can discuss each section together as you go?"

Gwyn blinked, casting a quick glance up toward Joarr—who, despite having his mask firmly in place, still looked as though he might break into laughter at any moment. "Ach, I am sure you shall wish for this, woman," he said, his voice very even, as he gave her rear a decisive pat. "Mayhap I shall leave you here for a spell, whilst I go meet with some kin?"

Gwyn bit back the urge to make a face at the wily bastard—he was truly going to *leave* her here?—but made herself nod, and attempt a smile. "Right," she said. "Of course. See you then."

He gave her another pat before turning and striding off, leaving Gwyn alone with a bright-eyed Rosa. Who wasted no time in ushering her toward a table, thrusting the midwifery book into her hands, and then setting her up with a fresh quill, a bottle of ink, and a brand-new, hand-bound, never-before-touched book for taking notes. A surprisingly thoughtful gesture, and when Gwyn expressed her astonished gratitude, Rosa only waved it away, her cheeks flushing pink.

"It's just so exciting to have you here," she said, her hands dropping to her rounded belly. "You might—make the difference for all of us, you know? For our sons, and our very lives. Our *future*."

The weight of those words seemed to plunge in Gwyn's stomach, but she attempted another smile as she nodded, and opened up the midwifery book. And soon found herself fully absorbed in it, reading faster and faster, her thoughts whirling, her appreciation rising. The book's author had clearly had extensive experience birthing orcs, and had carefully documented multiple case studies, and written of multiple fascinating methods and treatments.

It was intriguing enough that Gwyn found herself actually wanting to discuss it, and Rosa soon proved to be an informed and interesting discussion partner. And by the time Joarr finally returned, what felt like several hours later, not only had Gwyn finished reading the entire book, but she'd also filled multiple pages with notes, and talked until her throat was raw.

"Come, woman," Joarr said, cutting off Rosa mid-sentence, and flicking an amused glance between them. "You must eat, ach?"

Now that he mentioned it, Gwyn *was* rather hungry, and after saying a warm farewell to Rosa—and even, gods curse her, promising to return again soon—she willingly accompanied Joarr back out into the corridor, and smiled up at his harsh face. "How was your meeting?" she asked. "Hopefully productive?"

He shrugged, and nudged her up a corridor to the right. "Ach, more of the same," he said. "You? You make friends? Learn more for work? Find fun?"

Oh. Gwyn blinked at him, and felt herself slowly nodding, even as her eyes kept studying his unreadable profile in the lamplight. He'd taken her there so she would... find fun? Support her work? Make *friends*?

And yes, surely, that was what he'd meant. And even though he personally didn't enjoy spending time with the Ka-esh, he'd still made it happen, for her. Just the same as with Stella in the garden.

That odd tightness had returned, clamping around Gwyn's chest, expelling her breaths. And she couldn't even seem to speak as Joarr guided her into the kitchen, and promptly began making her yet another glorious-smelling, mushroom-filled meal.

"Thank you, Joarr," Gwyn said, once they'd sat down together, and polished off most of the meal—which, once again, had proven to be delicious. "I can't remember the last time someone actually went to the trouble of—"

She broke off there, her fork halfway to her mouth, because what had she been about to say? The trouble of caring? Of trying? Of cooking her a meal? Or, beyond her midwifery mentors, of doing *anything* to support her, ever?

But a chagrined glance up at Joarr showed him only shrugging, tossing a mushroom in his mouth. "Your father never tend you?" he asked, with deceptive casualness. "Or this *betrothed*?"

His lip had slightly curled at that last bit, and Gwyn winced as she carefully speared another mushroom. "My father is far too preoccupied with himself—and his next fix of intoxicants—to notice anyone else's needs," she replied, her voice flat. "And Roy, he—"

She could feel Joarr's eyes on her now, intent enough to be a touch, and she heard herself laugh, hard and bitter. "Roy is actually very similar to my father, in many ways," she said, quiet. "He's just better at hiding it. At making you think he cares. Making you into a *fool* for him. Making you *stupid*."

She was frowning resentfully down at her fork, squeezing it so tight the metal was digging painfully into her fingers—until Joarr's hand covered hers, and gently tugged the fork away. "It is no *stupid* to care for others," he said, voice low. "We all long for this, ach?"

Gwyn barked another laugh, and snapped her prickling eyes back up to his. "It *was* stupid," she countered sharply. "I was a complete and utter *patsy* for Roy. Have you ever wondered how a lord's daughter ended up training as a midwife? How a lord's daughter would ever even *meet* a midwife?"

Joarr's eyes had shifted into something Gwyn couldn't quite read, his body gone very still, and she laughed again, gripping her hands to her knees. "Because I was sixteen, and a fool," she hissed at him. "My mother was dead, my father was chasing women all over town, my brothers essentially forgot I existed. But Roy was there, he was kind and funny and sympathetic, and *very* handsome and dashing and experienced, and he—"

And he'd poured Gwyn full of pleasure, of affection, of *life*. And even if it had never lasted, it had still been hers, in those shining, precious moments. Only hers.

Until that day, of course, when she'd discovered that her monthly courses were late. But even then, she'd still clung to it. Still borne it. Dismissed the questions, rationalized the uncertainty, accepted Roy's caresses and apologies and empty promises...

"You no... birthed this man a son?" Joarr asked, after an instant's silence, his voice very steady. "I no smell scent of this upon you, ach?"

Gwyn swallowed, shook her head. "I went to a midwife," she said, in a rush. "And she gave me herbs. It was the most hellish two weeks of my life, but it worked. It *saved* me. Because even then, I *knew* Roy wasn't going to settle down and marry me, right? Not even for that. And"—she gulped in air—"the midwife was *so* kind. She didn't shame me, or tell another soul. And she even let me keep working with her afterwards, and it turned out that I really love plants, and doing this was a chance to—to pass it on. To help other women, too."

And gods, Joarr's eyes. Looking so blankly toward her like that, hiding so deep behind his mask. Because surely, *surely*, he was judging her. That awful situation had happened a full decade ago, and here was Gwyn, *still* entangled with Roy and his constant rubbish. Which had now fully escalated into those appalling threats to destroy her garden. Her income. Her life's work. Twenty days.

"And yes, I kept going back," she said, toward the pan between them. "For *years*. And yes, if I'd been my own client, I would have told myself to throw him out the instant he 'forgot' to mention contraception. So if that's not stupid, then what the hell is?"

She couldn't even bear to look at Joarr now, not with the force of his judgement bearing down toward her, crushing her beneath it. Stupid. Stupid. *Stupid...*

"You are no stupid, woman," cut in his low voice. "I ken this man work hard to keep you caught in his web. I ken he oft make this good for you. Make this *fun*. *Safe*. Ach?"

Gwyn's eyes snapped up, searching Joarr's face—and suddenly, somehow, it didn't actually look like he was mocking, or judging. Just waiting, maybe. Watching. Wanting her to speak.

"I suppose it *was* safe," she whispered dully, down toward the pan between them. "I always knew exactly where I stood with him, didn't I? I knew he would always come back. I knew he was bound to me, because of the betrothal, and my father. I knew I always had that with him, no matter what."

Joarr didn't answer, didn't make a sound, but now that Gwyn was speaking, it seemed impossible to stop. "And because what if that's as good as it gets, for me? I'm well aware I'd only get male attention because of my father anyway, right? And you're right, maybe it *was* fun sometimes, Roy is gorgeous and charismatic and *very* good in bed, and"—she sucked back a strained breath—"and we both know I have *major* weaknesses around such things!"

Her voice had unexpectedly risen as she spoke, angry, *accusing*—and far too late she'd realized what she'd just betrayed. *We both know. Major weaknesses.*

As in, not only around Roy, but around *Joarr*. Suggesting that he, too, was charismatic. Very good in bed. *Gorgeous.*

And Joarr could have laughed. He could have mocked her. Even raised a cool eyebrow, let that superior smirk curl across his mouth. But when Gwyn risked another glance at his face, he was still only looking back toward her, his eyes very still, his breath unmoving in his chest.

"But I'm not going back to Roy this time," Gwyn choked out, and gods, why was she telling him this, why did it even matter? "I'm not. I'm *done.*"

There was another instant's stillness, a strange, distant flicker in Joarr's eyes. As if for a moment, he'd gone somewhere else, somewhere far away, lost so deep behind his mask...

"I ken," he said, quiet, abrupt. "I see. You find—own way. Away from all these cruel men, who no deserve you. Ach?"

The words came out with an odd, fervent certainty, enough that Gwyn's breath spasmed, her eyes frozen on his face. He was—agreeing with her? Supporting her? *Again?*

And clearly he'd caught that too, because he shook his head, harsh and quick, as if needing to clear it—and then he snatched for the lamp, and leapt to his feet. "Come, woman," he said, voice curt, his gaze not quite meeting hers. "Have one I wish you to meet."

Gwyn twitched, but accordingly obeyed, and Joarr's hand slid around her shoulders, guiding her toward the kitchen door. Back out into the cool cramped darkness, ushering her up and down and sideways again, until she saw a distant, flickering light.

The light grew steadily brighter, stronger, and Gwyn realized it was from a door, cut into the corridor up ahead. And when Joarr steered her through the door, she found herself faced with a large open room, illuminated by a sparking, roaring fire, burning bright in the opposite wall.

And clustered around the fire, there were orcs. Yes, more

orcs, but... their bodies seemed smaller, their backs bent, their hair grey or white. And Joarr's steps still hadn't faltered, his hand on Gwyn's back driving her straight toward a lean, wizened-looking orc at the very end of the row.

And somehow, Gwyn... knew. Knew, even before this orc caught sight of them. Knew, as she watched him shuffle up to his feet, his knobbly hand clutched to a wooden cane, his eyes bright and eager on hers.

"Gwynevere of Dunburg," he said with a bow, his voice warm and deep. "I am Ivar of Clan Bautul, your great-uncle. And I am ever at your service."

I var, of Clan Bautul. Her… *great-uncle.*

Gwyn's mouth had fallen open, her eyes flaring up and down this Ivar's wizened form. He was still tall, despite his bent back, and he still had all his hair, though it was wiry and pure white, hanging beyond his shoulders. But most powerful of all were those eyes, alarmingly aware in his wrinkled grey face.

Ivar. Her great-uncle. As in, her Great-Aunt Agnes' *mate.*

"Oh," Gwyn somehow said, her breaths choked, her hand clutched to her chest. "I—I'm honoured. To meet you, I mean. I—I—"

She couldn't even find words, her voice trapped in the orc's bright black eyes, and he flashed her a quick, half-toothless grin. "I am honoured also," he said. "Our wise Agnes wished oft for this day, ach?"

Our wise Agnes. Something seemed to yank on Gwyn's chest, drawing her closer, dragging another gasp from her throat. "Could you please," she whispered, "tell me everything?"

Ivar's eyes sparkled with warmth, perhaps even with *relief,* and he carefully lowered his body back into his chair. "Ach," he said, "I shall."

And then, to Gwyn's ever-rising astonishment, he did. Telling her of how he and Great-Aunt Agnes had met each other later in life, well after her childbearing years. How Agnes had been a suspicious but fair-minded woman, and how he'd spent months working to gain her trust, and then her heart. How she'd kept him secret, kept him safe, and how in the end they'd brought each other much peace and joy.

Gwyn had knelt at his feet as he'd spoken, her attention rapt on every word. And once he'd finally finished, his voice gone thready and thin, she found herself swallowing over the lump in her throat, and wiping at her wet eyes.

"I'm so glad Great-Aunt Agnes was happy," she said, the words audibly wavering. "I have so many regrets about her. I wish I'd written more, and made more of an effort to come see her. Even just to say goodbye."

But Ivar waved this away with a dismissive hand, and a casual shrug that was oddly reminiscent of Joarr's. "You no fret yourself over this, girl," he said firmly. "Agnes knew you had much to bear. She hoped in granting you her house, she might help you find your own way."

Find your own way. Again. Those words so familiar, so powerful, that for an instant Gwyn couldn't breathe, her eyes darting toward where Joarr had been waiting through all this, leaning against the nearest wall. "I—," she began, and gulped for air, tried again. "I hope so too."

Ivar's smile was far too knowing, his gaze following hers toward Joarr. "I ken you have," he said. "To find your way to Bautul, and our long-lost Seer—ach, this reeks of the goddess' blessing."

The goddess again. Gwyn felt her face heating, well beyond the radiating warmth of the nearby fire, and Ivar gave her a conspiratorial wink. "The goddess works in her own ways, ach?" he said. "But she always finds her own. And mayhap soon"—his bent body seemed to straighten slightly—"she shall find new Bautul son, also?"

The heat was truly smarting in Gwyn's cheeks now, and thankfully Joarr pushed off the wall and strode over, clapping a heavy hand to Ivar's shoulder. "You stop there, *gamli*," he said, "before you send woman running, ach?"

Ivar chortled with laughter, his eyes alight on Joarr's face. "She no run if *you* see her way, and treat her right," he said. "Keep her full of good Bautul seed, ach?"

Joarr rolled his eyes and reached to pull Gwyn up, his arm slipping easy around her back. "*You* keep loud mouth shut," he said over his shoulder, though there was no real anger in his voice. "And mayhap I bring her to you again, ach?"

Ivar looked disproportionately pleased by this, fixing them with his half-toothless smile, and waving his hand. To which Gwyn willingly waved back, her damp eyes still caught on his face, until Joarr steered her out of the room, and back into the corridor again.

And as they walked together, the light rapidly fading behind them, Gwyn scarcely even noticed the encroaching darkness, or the various orcs that passed. Not with her thoughts fully ablaze like this, flashing frantically between relief and disbelief, confusion and certainty, amazement and *awe*.

Great-Aunt Agnes' mate was still alive. He'd welcomed her, reassured her, comforted her. It even felt like he'd given her Great-Aunt Agnes back, somehow, given the memories warmth and fondness again, rather than the chilly, miserable guilt they'd somehow acquired these past months.

And even stranger still, Ivar had clearly wanted Gwyn to stay. He'd wanted her to have a son. *Joarr's* son.

And Joarr hadn't... *not* wanted that. Right? No, he'd wanted Ivar to stop talking. Hadn't wanted him to scare her away.

There was something in that, something new, bubbling unnervingly hot and close. Enough that there was the oddest urge to laugh, or maybe sob, and Gwyn gulped down a few breaths, shook her head, and clutched her arms against her chest.

Gods, what was she thinking. She was only here for another few days, at most. She was only... seeing how this went, and that was all Joarr wanted, too. Right? And she was on a strong dose of silphium, and she most certainly wasn't ready to have a child, most of all with an orc, with *him*. She could think about all this later, some other day, some other time, but until then...

Until then, she was once again faced with the truth that Joarr had been... kind. Considerate. *Generous.*

"Thank you," she said into the darkness, quiet. "Again. That... meant a lot to me."

She could feel his shrug, could almost see the dismissive wave of his hand. "Ach, it is naught," he said lightly. "I ken you need more friends. More kin-brothers who are no cruel heedless *fools*, ach?"

And blinking toward Joarr in the darkness, it occurred to Gwyn that yes, yet again, this was kindness. Consideration. *Care.*

Something hot was prickling behind her eyes, and she had to cough, clear her throat. And suddenly there was the strangest, wildest urge to—to reciprocate. To return this. To help Joarr, somehow, to support him, in the same way he'd just supported her. And what was there, what did he need, he needed...

"It's so strange that Ivar is Bautul too, don't you think?" she heard herself blurt out, into the silence. "And he was so lovely, too. Do you ever wonder—maybe—if the Bautul aren't as bad as you thought? Or even"—she swallowed hard, made herself keep going—"if you might have more in common with them than you realized?"

It didn't seem like a contentious question—did it?—but it felt like the air between them had shifted. Sharpened. And suddenly that was a growl, deep and feral-sounding, rumbling from Joarr beside her.

"No," he hissed. "No. *Never* wonder this."

Right. Gwyn grimaced, fought past the clutch of regret in her belly. "Of course not," she said quickly, her voice thick. "I'm sorry. I didn't mean to—to presume."

She could hear Joarr's heavy exhale, the sound still burning in his throat. "You no yet—see," he said, "other side of Bautul. *Horde* side. Ach?"

Horde side. Gwyn hadn't, she supposed—had she? Whatever she'd seen so far in their common-room, it hadn't felt *horde*-like, had it?

"No, perhaps not," she said carefully. "In truth, apart from Silfast, the Bautul have been..."

What? Kind? Decent, despite their brazen ways? *Welcoming*?

Joarr barked a short laugh, and without warning he steered her sideways, down what felt like a new corridor. Toward what sounded like distant deep voices, steadily becoming louder. Shouts, groans, even... screams?

"You no fear sight of blood, ach?" Joarr's voice asked, cool and clipped. "Or battle?"

Gwyn felt a dry chuckle rising—she was a midwife, of course she didn't fear blood—but then it faded at that telltale word *battle*. Surely Joarr didn't mean there were actual *battles* going on? Here, in Orc Mountain?

But the strange shouts and screams kept rising, clamouring ever closer in her ears. And when Joarr silently ushered her into an echoing, torch-lit room, she found herself standing at the top of a rough-hewn stone staircase, and staring down toward what looked like a pit, cut into the earth below. And within the pit, there was—

A battle. A *horde*. Dozens of huge, brawling, hollering orcs, hurling themselves toward one another in a chaotic, careening mess. Their mouths shouting and biting, their clawed hands punching and swiping, and even swinging large wooden weapons through the air. Weapons that didn't pull away at impact, but instead landed with dull, sickening thuds on backs, chests, *faces*.

And gods, the *blood*. Pouring out of the brawling orcs' noses, pumping from fresh wounds, spitting out their mouths. Pooling dark and thick into what looked like a metal *grate* below them, as if this appalling scene were a frequent enough occurrence to require actual *infrastructure*.

And the more Gwyn looked, the more horrifying it became. One orc had swung a wooden blade straight into another's mouth, breaking off several teeth with a nauseating *crunch*. Another had kicked his opponent in the groin, toppling him over—and then kept kicking, while the orc below him thrashed and screamed. And another was holding his opponent down, yanking out his black hair in chunks, when another one rushed forward and kicked him in the head, and—

And wait. That kicking orc had been... *Kalfr*. Hadn't it? The tall, charcoal-skinned orc, who Stella had mentioned as wanting to help in the *garden*? And that was the cheerful orc Eyolf, surely, crumpled on the floor in the corner, clutching his belly, and vomiting into yet another grate.

And standing there, in the midst of it all, was Silfast. Looking huge and horrifying, swinging a massive wooden axe in a vicious arc, and slamming another orc—Grum—so hard that he flew back into the nearest wall, and the distinctive sound of breaking bones cracked through the air.

Oh. *Oh.* Gwyn's clammy, trembly hands had snapped to cover her mouth, her throat choking down her own rising bile—and she had to squeeze her eyes shut, haul back deep breaths. Goddess above, this couldn't—they wouldn't—

"They don't," she croaked toward Joarr, without opening her eyes, "*kill* each other?"

Joarr's laugh was scornful, dry. "No on purpose," he said flatly. "This game is only to knock down. Winner is last to stand, ach?"

This *game*. Gwyn cracked an eyelid to look at him, at how he was watching the scene in front of them, mouth pursed. As though he wasn't even slightly shocked by any of this, or by the new set of bloodcurdling screams now tearing through the air. As if this were... *familiar* to him.

And as if he'd read her thoughts, his eyes angled toward her, his arms crossing over his chest. "You must no ken," he said, "I never draw blood, or battle thus against my kin. I oft do this. We all must. Ach?"

What? Gwyn's thoughts were floundering again, clutching for meaning, for mooring amidst the screams filling her ears. Thinking, hazily, of the men hunting in the woods, the way they'd wanted to catch Joarr, to *kill* him...

"So why," she choked, "do you not—then why aren't you—I don't—"

She couldn't even finish, her hand flapping at the nauseating sight before them, and Joarr frowned back toward it, his claws tapping against his arm. "I am only no such a fool, in this," he said, clipped. "I never take such risk. I never strike full at a brother's face, to break his nose or eyes or teeth. I never make wound that healer can no fix. I never brawl when I am no sure of my calm, or my control. I *never* battle young orcs thus, when they no yet have enough skill or mettle to meet this."

Gwyn's eyes had flicked back to Eyolf, who was still vomiting into the grate, now with his quiet brother Iyolf standing before him, determinedly blocking blows with his sword. "I never battle weak or broken orc," Joarr continued, his voice sharper, angrier. "I never make shame from defeat. And if I gain true wound, I send brother to healer, or take *self* to healer, so we stay strong enough to work more. To *help* more. To no *waste* us, or all we have fought to gain!"

It seemed to take Gwyn immense effort to follow those words, to find his meaning—but then it somehow struck all at once, thundering into her chest, into her bones.

"Surely you aren't suggesting," she breathed, "that these orcs don't even seek healing? For wounds like *these*?!"

Another spine-scraping scream had torn through the air, and Gwyn wouldn't look, couldn't. Just kept staring at Joarr, who was now jerking a hard, furious shake of his head. Saying... no? They *didn't*?

"It is great shame, among Bautul orcs, to show weakness," he snapped. "To claim pain, or wish for help. They shall no even allow medics to *watch* these battles, or pull wounded orcs away. They call this strength. They think this *valour*. They wish to be the horde, free of thought and care and fear, and thus"— he spat on the floor at his feet—"they *are*."

Oh. His contempt felt like a living, snarling thing, rearing inside Gwyn's chest—and swarming with it, somehow, were more memories. Visions of Joarr licking her, kissing her, working to take the pain away. *No. You no do this. No easy to heal. Find other way.*

And beyond that—Gwyn's blinking eyes darted back to the brawl, which was still being dominated by Silfast and his huge wooden axe—Joarr had brought a *midwife* to his mountain. He'd supported her in caring for his brothers' mates. He'd wanted to better support Stella, even when Silfast obviously didn't want that. When it meant *shame*, to show weakness.

"And you can't," Gwyn heard herself whisper, almost inaudible beneath the screams, "try to fix it? To change it?"

But Joarr's dark, disbelieving glance toward her spoke his reply, as loudly as if he'd shouted it into the maelstrom. He had no claim within this clan. No power. Not with that damned tooth hanging around his neck, marking him as not a real Bautul. All while he clearly hated this, hated that it had become part of him…

There was one more hoarse, horrifying scream from before them, grating against Gwyn's ears—and then silence. Silence, because—she risked another glance forward—Silfast had won. Looming huge and deadly above the heap of defeated, groaning orcs, many of them crawling away, coughing and spitting blood onto the floor beneath them.

Silfast's red-spattered barrel chest was heaving, his eyes swiftly surveying the room—and then catching, harsh and heavy, on Gwyn. And on Joarr beside her, standing tall and angry and contemptuous, his eyes narrow, his arms flexing over his chest.

"Ach, mark this," Silfast called out, his voice carrying over the surrounding orcs' groans. "After three full moons, our *Seer* finally blesses our work with his presence. But"—his lip curled, baring his sharp teeth—"he yet stands safe and whole to the side. He only *watches* as his brothers strive and bleed to build our strength, and save our mountain from our foes!"

Damn. Gwyn's eyes were darting between Joarr and the door, perhaps silently saying, *Go, let's go*—but of course it was too late, because multiple orcs' heads were turning, seeking, finding this truth. Their so-called Seer standing here, tall and safe and untouched, while they groaned and panted and streamed blood onto the floor.

And in their eyes, surely, was disapproval. Resentment. *Rage.* Digesting the fact that one of their own had somehow escaped this, and somehow saw fit to stand over them from afar. To perhaps even gloat in their defeat.

And Gwyn knew, without even meeting Joarr's eyes, how dangerous this was. What a precedent it established. It threatened to undo all he'd just gained with the goddess' blessing, with *her*. It threatened any chance he might have ever had of addressing this. Of *fixing* this.

And Joarr's glance toward her, brief and resigned, said he knew it too, just as much as she did. And he would face it, he would never walk away, he would run with whatever the gods threw at him...

"Ach, then, my brothers," he replied, his voice cool, carrying over the throng. "I shall fight."

22

He would fight.

Gwyn clenched her eyes shut, her heart erratically thumping. No. She couldn't watch Joarr become that. *No.*

But he was already giving her arm a squeeze, and striding away from her. Leaping down the large, rough-cut stairs two at a time, his movements deft, graceful, fearless.

"Ach, *now* you come to battle us," Silfast sneered at him, his deep voice booming over the orcs' ongoing pants and groans. "Now that your kin have already shed their blood for your gain!"

Joarr sprang down into the pit with fluid ease, landing in a low crouch before rising again. "I no yet smell *your* blood, *Captain*," he said, with deceptive pleasantness. "You no wish to fight me?"

Silfast hoisted his wooden axe over his shoulder, his chest still heaving with his breaths—and suddenly Gwyn realized that this was surely a provocation on Joarr's part. An attack. Because if the Bautul refused to admit weakness, of course a battle-captain like Silfast couldn't risk publicly refusing a fight. Even if he'd already just fought off fifty of his own orcs, and had to be exhausted as a result.

"I ken you have yet striven much this day," Joarr continued, just as pleasantly. "So mayhap you keep this weapon, whilst I bear none?"

Silfast's mouth thinned, his gaze darting briefly around at his groaning, bloody orcs. Many of them intently watching this little exchange, their expressions dark, shifting, skeptical.

"Ach," Silfast grunted, his eyes narrowing back at Joarr. "Ready yourself. Prepare to beg and *bleed* before your captain!"

Gwyn flinched at those words, her stomach twisting—but Joarr had raised a cool hand, his gaze sweeping over the orcs still sprawled and kneeling in the pit around them. "No wish to fight amidst this," he said. "First we grant our brothers leave to go rest and heal, ach?"

Silfast's disapproving bark was joined by several others from below, one loudly proclaiming that they'd rest when they were dead. All of which Joarr entirely ignored, his mouth pursed, his eyes cold on Silfast's face.

"We fight to keep safe our home," Joarr snapped. "You say this. I say this. But what if band of men now attack us, and all of Bautul is *bleeding*?! What then come?"

Silfast barked another reply, the words all in tangled black-tongue this time, and in return Joarr laughed, hard and brittle. "No," he replied. "Skai fight for you, *again*. Ash-Kai fight. Grisk fight. They all outmatch you, again, whilst you *waste* your blood and teeth!"

You, he'd said. Surely not on purpose, not with the chorus of growls now filling the air, with Silfast's carrying above them all. "And you *again* insult your clan!" Silfast shouted, his deep voice thundering. "You again show your ignorance and contempt. You show you do not belong among us. You show you are at heart still a Skai, with all your proud, selfish, slippery ways!"

Gwyn could see Joarr's shoulders slightly hunching, his hand reaching up to stoke at that tooth around his neck. "Then I also show you," he hissed back, "how a fool Bautul battle-captain shall *bow* before a lowly Skai!"

There was a collective intake of breath, as though Joarr had said something truly shocking—and then Silfast attacked. Charging directly toward Joarr, his axe swinging in a furious, devastating arc, straight for Joarr's head—

But in a flare of movement, Joarr dodged. Easing just out of the axe-blade's reach, his lean body bobbing on his feet, his hands loose at his sides. His mouth curling into a flat, chilly smile as he stood there, waiting, watching.

Silfast's next strike was even faster this time, his huge form barging toward Joarr—but Joarr again dodged backwards, leaping over the crouched bodies of two fallen Bautul orcs without even looking. And before Silfast could charge again, Joarr actually nudged one of them with his foot, hissing something in black-tongue.

It must have been some kind of order, because the orc— Arne, Gwyn now saw—began hauling himself away, toward the edge of the pit. Making just slightly more room for Joarr's shifting feet as he again leapt sideways, away from the next ferocious swing of Silfast's axe.

"Again, you show yourself a Skai, and a coward!" Silfast hollered, with another rush forward, another deadly arc of his wooden blade. "You run and hide, when you should attack. When you should meet your foe with bravery and honour!"

Joarr seemingly ignored this, in favour of barking out another command toward another fallen orc—but Gwyn recognized that telltale intensity in his narrow eyes, the tightness on his mouth. His feet circling around Silfast, his lean form rippling as he seemed to shake it out, shift it forward—

He flew toward Silfast without warning, his hair a black blur behind him. Charging not for Silfast's face, as Gwyn might have expected—but for his groin. His knee snapping up hard and powerful, making impact with an audible, sickening thud.

It was enough to knock Silfast back a step, straight into the space that had been occupied by Arne, only a moment before. And Silfast's answering axe-swing only met empty air, because Joarr had once again leapt out of the way. Nudging at yet another fallen orc with his foot, and then actually ducking to drag the orc away, while also somehow avoiding the next sweep of Silfast's blade.

Gwyn's frantically beating heart had seemed to settle some-what, and she belatedly sank her shaky body down onto the high stone step behind her. Realizing, distantly, that the steps were perhaps meant to be seats, intended for watching the shocking carnage below—but thankfully, in this instant, the only shock was just how impressive Joarr was at this. His attacks tight and strategic, his movements swift and effortless, his focus seemingly not even on Silfast, but on clearing the floor of fallen orcs, giving himself more room to move and dodge and strike.

Silfast's axe hadn't yet made one hit, and as Gwyn watched his ever-wilder swings, it occurred to her that Joarr almost seemed to *anticipate* them. To know when Silfast would strike next, and from where. And from what Gwyn could see, Silfast's attacks weren't linear or predictable, his axe-swings flying in both directions, his movements perhaps just as swift as Joarr's. And his breath was visibly panting now, the sweat streaking down his face, his huge body staggering as Joarr landed another vicious kick to his groin.

When Silfast caught himself again, his eyes were even narrower than before, his body poised for one more charge— but at the last possible instant, he dropped the axe. And instead, he hurled himself straight into Joarr's waist, toppling them both to the bloody stone floor below.

Gwyn's heart flipped, her hands clapping to her mouth, because oh gods, oh *gods*, there was no way Joarr could dodge now, no possible escape. Silfast was so much bigger, his bare fists driving down toward Joarr's face, and despite Joarr's whirling writhes and kicks, Gwyn could hear a punch landing, could hear the crunch of breaking bone—

"Not so proud now, are you, Skai?" Silfast gasped, shifting his huge body over Joarr's, gouging his knee deep into his belly, swiping his claws at Joarr's *eyes*. "Shall you now weep, and beg for my mercy?"

Joarr wasn't answering now, was only focused on avoiding the worst of Silfast's punches, his head whipping back and forth, his feet kicking desperately but uselessly at Silfast's back. While Silfast kept laughing as he punched, the sound carrying cruel and deep and scornful.

"You are *weak*," he snarled, his spittle spraying down into Joarr's now-bloody face. "You are defeated. You shall never make amends for your fathers' sins, or rise to lead my clan. You ought to run back to Osada and *hide* for the rest of your days, just like the *cowards* your fathers showed themselves to be!"

Gwyn's hands were clutched over her mouth now, her wide eyes frozen on Joarr's bloody face, on his *defeat*. And surely Silfast wouldn't permanently injure him, or incapacitate him, but now his clawed hand had found Joarr's thrashing neck, holding it tight to the earth. His other fist raising up, ready to slam straight down into Joarr's face, to *destroy* him—

When in an instant, Joarr's flailing hand clutched Silfast's *axe*. The axe that Silfast had previously tossed aside, and that— Gwyn blinked—*Kalfr* had just kicked over toward him, from where he'd been dragging himself away on the floor. And as Silfast's fist drove down, Joarr's surprisingly steady hand flipped the axe right-side up, and swung the flat of it straight for the back of Silfast's head.

It struck with a dull, decisive *thunk*, knocking Silfast's head forward, scattering his punch wide. And in the choked, fraught silence, Silfast's eyes slowly rolled back in his head—and then he slumped sideways, toward the floor, and was still.

For an instant, nothing moved or spoke—and then, suddenly, the sound of a single shout. Of Kalfr, bellowing what sounded like a cheer from the floor, his fist rising toward the stone ceiling above.

"For Bautul," he called. "For the goddess!"

And as Gwyn stared, still frozen with her hands over her mouth, another cheer rose to meet his. And then another, and another, until the entire room of fallen, wounded Bautul orcs had their fists raised, their deep voices shouting hoarse to the sky.

And amidst it all, Joarr finally, slowly, hoisted himself up. Pushing first onto his hands and knees, and then staggering to his feet. His face was scratched and bruised, his bent-looking nose streaking blood down his face—but his hands were rising above his head, his eyes bright and glittering as he tilted his face to the ceiling.

"For the goddess," he repeated, his voice thick. "She blesses your Seer!"

Your Seer. An odd thrill hurtled up Gwyn's back, sparking even sharper as the surrounding orcs bellowed their reply. As if they... *agreed*, somehow. As if this had been more than just a sparring-match, or a contest of strength. As if it had been a statement. A *claim*.

"Kalfr," Joarr's thick voice said, once the shouts had subsided. "You come to our garden on the morrow. I begin to teach you its ways. Ach?"

The look on Kalfr's blood-streaked face was pure delight,

and he instantly nodded, his fisted hand thumping against his heart. "Ach, Seer," he replied. "I shall."

Joarr nodded, his head still tilted back, his eyes fluttering closed. "And you, Eyolf and Iyolf," he said. "Should you wish."

Gods, Gwyn had nearly forgotten about them—but her searching eyes immediately found them, still in the corner of the room. However, they seemed to have been joined there by a number of other wounded orcs, and that was because Iyolf was... dragging an unconscious-looking orc over toward the rest, out of the way. And had perhaps been doing so the entire time? As Joarr had wished?

Iyolf's hand had come to Eyolf's shoulder, giving it a little shake, meeting his eyes—and then he looked back at Joarr, and jerked a curt nod. "Ach, Seer," he replied, his voice soft and heavily accented, his fist also bumping against his chest. "We shall."

Well. Gwyn suddenly felt like shouting, like doing a ridiculous victory dance right here on her stair. And when Joarr's gaze finally shifted again, and somehow caught on hers, she found herself grinning back at him—and then even mimicking the orcs' gesture, the *goddess'* gesture, her fist thumping against her heart.

And gods, Joarr's *eyes*. Dropping to that movement, watching it, holding it—and it was like something sparked between them, hot and bright and powerful. And when he abruptly strode toward the edge of the pit, toward *her*, it only seemed to flash brighter, unfurling stronger with each step, with every easy, graceful leap of his feet up the stairs.

And then, somehow, he was here. Whole, alive, standing tall on the stair before her. His nose far more crooked than it had been before, his face still streaming blood, his chest heaving with thick, dragging breaths. His body marred with multiple new scratches and bruises, and dripping with sweat, and still slightly twitching from the exertion.

But his eyes were steady, sharp, blazing on hers. Wanting, needing, piercing into Gwyn's belly, into her groin. Into her own eyes dropping downwards from his, trailing over his sweaty, banged-up, blood-streaked chest, his rippled abdomen, until she found—

That. The swollen, pulsing ridge of him, bulging out strong and shameless against his pulled-taut trousers. Speaking to her, shouting at her, with another sustained, visible shudder, a slowly growing spot of wetness at the tip...

And as Gwyn stared, that dark spot kept growing, the heft beneath twitching and swelling. While the sweet scent of him began curling into the air between them, blunting the thick smell of sweat and blood with its rising, swirling hunger.

Gwyn could feel her breath catching, her eyelids fluttering, her tongue brushing brief against her lips. Waiting, ensnared, *enthralled*, as Joarr reached his bloody, still-twitchy hand down into his trousers—

And then he drew himself out, slow, purposeful. His long smooth heft dipping down toward her, its wetness visibly leaking, as his clawed hand slid down to cup his heavy bollocks, caressing them, *displaying* them for her blinking eyes.

Gwyn's moan escaped on its own, loud and betraying, and in return that hand reached for her hair, fingers carding deep. And then giving her the slightest nudge forward, toward that dripping-white sweetness, the scent of him flooding her thoughts, her breath...

There was a distant, shouting voice at the back of Gwyn's skull, making very valid protests—but her eyes had angled back up to Joarr's face, to his glittering gaze holding so intent upon her. Wanting her. *Needing* her.

And Gwyn wanted to help. Wanted to return the kindness he'd shown her. And she felt herself nodding, again and again, quick, furtive, true.

Saying, *Yes. Whatever you need.*

In return, Joarr rasped a sound that might have been a laugh, or a groan. And in one smooth, fluid movement, he tightened his grip on her hair, drawing her closer—and then he slid his full, pulsing, dripping length between her parted lips, and deep into her throat.

Gwyn gasped and choked around it, dragging in air, fighting to breathe against the onslaught—but oh hell, he was already easing out again, bobbing fully free of her mouth. Showing the orcs—the *orcs?*—the long, shimmering string of wetness, stretching from her lips to his slit.

Gwyn froze in place, her mouth still half-open, her dazed eyes darting sideways. To where, indeed, several of the less-injured orcs—including Kalfr—had clearly dragged themselves up out of the pit, in order to—to *watch?*

Joarr's hand in her hair clutched even tighter—oh hell, his *claws*—and Gwyn's heated, humiliated gaze snapped back up to his eyes. To where he was watching her with unnerving, commanding intensity, as he deliberately slid himself back into her mouth, stretching her open around him, settling into her throat.

Gwyn's face was burning, her breaths dragging through her nose, her chagrined eyes again flicking to the watching orcs—but Joarr's pulsing, invading heft nudged even deeper into her throat, his fingers now gently tugging on their generous handful of her hair.

"You no look at them," he hissed, his voice sparking hot tremors beneath her skin. "You look at me, whilst I fill your mouth."

Gods. Gwyn moaned against him, gulping down the sweet liquid pooling in her throat, and somehow felt herself nodding, her eyes wide and earnest on his. Saying, again, *Yes.* And again he actually *laughed*, his head tilting back, the blood still streaming down his face.

"Good little witch," he purred, as he again dragged himself

fully out of her mouth, twitching wet and dripping before her. "You wish for yet more of my seed inside you. Ach?"

She *did*, oh hell, and she even tried to thrust forward, to catch him back between her lips—but his hand in her hair held her off, its grip almost painful, his laugh now full-throated mirth, brimming with hunger and lust and sheer breathtaking *greed*.

"Ach, I ken," he crooned at her, low and mocking, as his other hand joined the first in her hair, and drew her slightly forward. Just close enough to lick, now, her frantic tongue furiously reaching, dipping into his slick, dripping slit.

"What ought I do with her next, Kalfr?" Joarr asked as he watched, his eyes alight, his voice infuriatingly cool. "Grant her leave to suckle your Seer dry? Or tend her throat as she wishes?"

The bastard. Gwyn's disbelief was surging, soaring, and she felt herself glaring up at him, and betraying a sharp, frustrated growl. Even as her shameful, humiliating tongue kept licking at him, seeking for more, twisting as deep as it could go, his sweetness sparkling as it spluttered out to meet her...

"Do both, I ken," came Kalfr's breathless reply, with a low laugh. "But let her suckle first. See how hard she shall work for her sweet Bautul seed."

Joarr's smile was sheer vicious wickedness, his eyes on Gwyn so insolent, so *proud*. "Ach, you hear him, my witch," he murmured, as his hands promptly released her hair, and dropped easy back to his sides. "Suck me. *Show* me."

Fuck. The hunger was everywhere now, everything, thudding into the core of Gwyn's being—and she felt herself lunge straight toward him, driving him deep into her mouth. Earning a half-groan, half-laugh from above her, more bare approval in his watching, dancing eyes.

It meant he liked it, he wanted it, wanted *her*—and suddenly all that mattered was showing him, swallowing him.

Lavishing him with her eager tongue and lips and throat, sucking as hard as she could, caressing him with hungry, fervent fingers. Ignoring the lurid slurping sounds she was making, ignoring the approving murmurs of the watching orcs, ignoring the shocking dissipation in what she was doing. Her eyes fixed only to Joarr, only this, only his…

But he was giving her another wicked, impudent smile, and he casually raised his hands to his face. And then began *straightening out his bloody nose*, calm and collected, as if he'd fully forgotten the woman still desperately sucking him, choking herself on his heft.

"Is this yet bent?" he asked Kalfr, his voice utterly cool, his hand waving at his nose. And while Kalfr must have given some reply, Gwyn surely didn't hear it. Not with the heat rushing in her ears like this, her mouth sucking even harder, her lips tightening on the silken skin between them. *Rewarding* his rubbish, gods curse her—but here was her own reward, with the way his hardness leapt against her, his liquid pulsing faster, his breath hitching in his chest.

"Ach, I no forget you, woman," he finally said, his voice hoarser than before. "You now wish me to use you? Tend you?"

And in this instant, with the flashing flying hunger, with her orc so blatantly stretching her mouth, prodding at her throat—Gwyn could only nod, again and again. Holding those glinting, dangerous eyes as he studied her, as one of his hands again slid into her hair, the other curling around her neck. The movements so careful, so gentle, at unnatural odds with the intensity in his gaze, the deep, guttural growl in his throat…

His drive forward was everything, ecstasy soaring and swelling, skittering with pain and power and purpose. With her orc's hand now caught in her hair, holding her head still as he slammed into her throat again and again. Filling her, using her with devastating single-mindedness, hurling the tension higher and hotter between them. His sharp claw-tips nudging at her scalp, dragging against the sensitive skin of her neck, his sweetness steadily pulsing, leaking into her mouth, taunting her with its promise—

And with a shudder, a bark, a final fierce yank at her hair— he drove in one last time, and fired. His invading heft wildly spasming as it spurted, spraying its bounty deep into Gwyn's mouth, pouring it down her throat. Holding her firmly in place while he tended her, filled her, showed her his care...

And as she gulped and swallowed, her own hunger twisted and turned, wrenching between her clutched-tight thighs— and then exploded too. Flashing her full of sharp, throbbing pleasure, pulsing in time with Joarr's gasps, with his spurts deep into her belly.

And then, finally, it was still. Still, and also strangely silent, with Joarr's slowly softening heft still parting her lips, oozing onto her tongue. With the way his hand carefully released her hair, even as the other kept hold on her neck, and his finger trailed down her hot, sticky cheek with a gentle, quivering reverence.

But he didn't speak. Didn't offer any kind words, any approval. And after a heavy exhale, he tugged himself out of Gwyn's mouth with a lurid-sounding pop, and then yanked up his bloody trousers, hiding himself away.

"On the morrow," he said to Kalfr, his voice light and cool again. "But no too early, ach?"

Kalfr gave some kind of affirming answer, only partially audible over the ringing in Gwyn's ears. Gods, what had she just done. How many orcs had just watched that. And she couldn't even raise her eyes to look, but she could *feel* them, feel their prickling gazes on her hot face, on her swollen, sticky-feeling lips.

"Come, woman," said Joarr's quiet voice, his fingers circling her arm—and there was nothing for it but to nod, and oblige. Stumbling up to her shaky feet, and allowing him to usher her up and out of the room, back into the corridor's close blackness.

Joarr still didn't speak as they walked, as he guided her left, right, left again. As the shame kept rising higher, pooling on Gwyn's cheeks, in her blinking eyes. Why had she done that. Why had she given this manipulative orc that, when—

When without warning, he swerved before her, his long fingers grasping at her arse—and in a smooth flush of movement, he snatched her fully off the ground. Parting her legs around his hips as he hoisted her up against him, and then pressed her back to the corridor's solid stone wall.

And before Gwyn could speak, think, breathe, he was—*kissing* her. His mouth hard and desperate on hers, his long tongue slipping between her lips, his hand spreading wide against her cheek. Tilting her head so he could take her deeper, taste her, pour her full of his... reassurance. His... *approval*?

"You," he panted, as he slightly pulled away, his lips just brushing against hers. "Kind witch. *Kindred* witch. With *wondrous* mouth. Ach?"

Oh. The tension that had been gripping Gwyn's shoulders suddenly seemed to release, escaping in a choked, shaky laugh. Which abruptly broke into silence as Joarr caught her lips and kissed her again, strong, thorough, deep.

When he pulled away, they were both gasping, and she could feel his sweaty forehead settling against hers, his still-wet hair tickling at her face. "I... thank you," he whispered. "For honouring me thus, before them. Honouring my *triumph*."

His triumph. And yes, yes, that was what Gwyn had meant to do. To help him. To support him. To recognize his strength, his confidence, his cleverness. His force in the face of defeat.

"You deserved it," she whispered back, into the darkness. "You were"—she huffed a shaky laugh—"*extremely* impressive."

Joarr chuckled too, low and husky, and she felt him shake

his head, his hair again brushing her face. "I near suffer defeat," he breathed. "To Silfast. *Silfast!*"

Gwyn's trembly hands had fluttered up, stroking at his bare shoulders. "But you hadn't done that before," she said, her voice inexplicably certain. "Fought them like that before. Have you?"

There was an instant's stillness, and then another shake of Joarr's head, slower this time. "No. I knew this should only flaunt my... unlikeness. How I no belong."

Gwyn's head was shaking too, her hands tightening around his neck. "But you *did* belong," she said, quiet, fierce. "They listened to you, even when it didn't seem that way at first. They helped you. They *respected* you."

Joarr's shoulders rose and fell, his breath hot against her mouth. "Ach, mayhap," he said. "I no foresaw this. No until... you."

You. The warmth shivered up Gwyn's back, into her swelling heartbeat. "Well," she said, as steadily as she could, "clearly you should have. Because it seems quite obvious to me that Bautul could use someone like you. Someone with some new ideas. New ways."

There was another beat of silence, thudding out between them—and Gwyn felt Joarr's head ducking downwards, his face nudging against her neck. Or wait, *oh*, that was his mouth, his *lips*. Kissing her. Approving of her. *Listening.*

And suddenly Gwyn needed to keep speaking, following this, feeling this. "And it seems to me," she added, "that kind of... brutality, or bravado, or unthinking allegiance... it could multiply, right? Extend into the rest of the clan. Encourage them to hide their weaknesses, or their failures. To pretend that all is well, when it isn't."

Joarr's mouth was still kissing her neck, harder now—and that might have even been a furtive nod, brushing light against her. And Gwyn's fingers were spreading against his sweaty skin, her head tilting back against the wall, her breath shuddering from her exposed throat.

"And in your work as a scout," she whispered, "you'd probably have seen all that in the Bautul long ago. Probably much more than most. And you'd have a lot less patience with it. You'd need to escape, to your lovely garden. To your *fun*."

And oh, gods, that was the gentle, unmistakable scrape of his teeth. Dragging so soft, so dangerous, against the too-sensitive skin. And Gwyn's breath lurched, her fingers clutching tighter, her head even angling away, giving him more room...

"And now you're even allowing it into your garden, too," she continued, her eyes fluttering. "You're giving up your own space, your own peace, to help your clan. It's so"—she gasped for more air—"generous of you, Joarr. It's *magnificent*."

The hard caress of Joarr's lips on her neck was broken by a laugh, low and hoarse, and then a slight shake of his head. "You say this," he whispered back, pulling away from her neck. "But you no ken how I bear this. Mayhap they tromp on my huckleberry, and next I slit their throats in my rage."

Gwyn's laugh bubbled up on its own, the sound warm, bright, *affectionate*. "You wouldn't," she replied. "And besides, we'll strictly prohibit any and all tromping. We'll post signs. Set up traps. Maybe dig a pit full of stink-lilies to hold them in, until they learn."

Stink-lilies had a truly rank scent, not unlike that of rotting meat, and Joarr's answering laugh was merry and unfettered, his shoulders shaking beneath her hands. "Ach, my canny witch," he said, between chuckles. "I should give much, to throw Silfast into a pit of stink-lily."

Gwyn couldn't seem to stop grinning into the darkness, especially when Joarr ducked his face back against her neck, his mouth so warm, so *willing*. "Mayhap," he murmured, "*you* again teach them, to start. Head off the worst of their folly, and thus temper my rage. Ach?"

Oh. He was—asking. Asking? Asking her—to help him do this? To… stay?

Gwyn felt herself swallow, her hands tightening against him—and she heard him swallow too, felt another soft, scraping kiss to her neck. "Stay," he whispered. "A few days more. I show you more fun."

Something was quivering in Gwyn's belly, ramping up her racing heartbeat, and she tried for a laugh, high-pitched, hoarse. "You know, I'm starting to seriously question your sense of *fun*, orc," she said, as lightly as she could. "I mean, just now, you showed me a bloody *massacre*, and then completely ignored me while I sucked you off in front of your *friends*."

She punctuated that with a half-hearted elbow at his shoulder, but the bastard only chuckled, his teeth still scraping against her throat. "Ach, you like this," he purred at her. "You stay, and I grant you more. Mayhap"—he hesitated, dragging those teeth harder—"mayhap I fully pierce you. Drink you. Show you true taste of pain and pleasure."

Gods. Gwyn's shiver was unstoppable, undeniable, wrenching down her back—and this time, Joarr didn't laugh. Just opened his mouth wider, let those teeth settle sharper, deeper, their deadly points pressing against delicate pulsing skin…

"I make you scream for me," he breathed. "Make you spurt for me. Spark your bliss with no even a touch. *Again*."

Again. His voice so hot, so sure, so gods-damned arrogant. And wait, so *suspicious*, because—what if this was more manipulation? More of him using Gwyn for his own gain? *Especially*, her distant rational brain shouted, after he hadn't told her about his brutal clan, hadn't told her about… about…

But in this breathless, shimmering moment, with this orc's depraved, deeply dubious promises hovering between them, Gwyn somehow… didn't care. Didn't care what he was doing, what he was hiding, or even what else he was plotting. Not when this was on offer. Not when *he* was.

"You stay," he whispered again, so soft. "Few days more. Ach?"

Few days more. And she still had twenty days until Roy returned, an eternity...

So Gwyn... nodded. Again and again. Perhaps just to feel the tease of its tenuous truth against his teeth, scraping her raw beneath it.

"Yes," she breathed. "A few days more."

23

Gwyn slept easy that night, curled close against Joarr in his gently swaying hammock. Her body warm and sated, her breaths slow and deep.

And when she awoke again the next morning, blinking down toward the truth of his tall, sleeping body still entangled with hers, she couldn't deny something fragile and new, curling through her thoughts. Something like... temptation. Like *hope*.

Kind witch, he'd called her. *Kindred witch. Stay. A few days more.*

And what if—Gwyn swallowed, let her gaze linger on his sleeping face, his sharp cheekbones, his lashes long and black against his skin—what if she just... kept staying? If they could keep getting to know each other, supporting each other, learning to trust each other... what then?

And as if Joarr had heard her speak those betraying words aloud, he jerked awake beneath her, his eyes snapping open, and focusing on hers. On where she'd been blatantly watching him sleep, gods curse her—and she felt her face flush hot, her mouth twitching into a wincing, apologetic smile.

But there was no judgement in his lazy, half-lidded eyes.

Only an unmistakable rising hunger, as he slowly smirked at her—and as he slid his hand downwards, and pulled his already-hard length out of his trousers.

His brow hitched up—saying, perhaps, *You know what to do, don't you?*—and Gwyn huffed a short laugh, yanked up her skirts, and accordingly eased herself over on top. And then sank herself down upon him, bit by bit, until she was fully seated on his lap, his shuddering heft buried deep inside her.

Gods, he felt good. And looked so good, too, his lean body gleaming in the morning sun, his mouth curling up with slow, leisurely approval. And when he began rocking his hips against her, sharp and purposeful, Gwyn rode him with thoroughly betraying eagerness, her cries choking into the quiet air, while the hammock rolled and swayed beneath them.

By the end of it, their joined thrusts were frantic enough that the hammock was wildly jerking, nearly knocking Gwyn off onto the ground below—and Joarr laughed aloud as he gasped and poured himself out within her, his hands gripping strong and steadying to her hips.

"Ach, I no let you fall," he murmured, once his strength inside her had begun to soften again. "Most of all when you are stuck safe upon me."

Gwyn couldn't help a flushed, flustered smile, a deep thrill up her back at that telltale word *safe*. That hint, maybe, that she wasn't wrong to hope. To think about a new way. A new... *future*.

That hope only seemed to keep rising throughout the morning, as they again washed up in the waterfall together, and then looked over the new plants Joarr's scouts had brought overnight from Gwyn's garden in Varrahan. And then they headed for the trees, where Joarr once again taunted her into climbing and chasing him, and then rewarded her with a basket full of fresh, sweet-smelling fruit.

It led to them eating a companionable breakfast together

on one of the wooden platforms, passing fruit back and forth between them. While also discussing their plans for their new Bautul helpers, who—Joarr grimaced as he tossed a berry into his mouth—were sure to arrive and start tromping about his precious garden at any moment.

"I told you, I'll deal with them," Gwyn said firmly, half-smiling at him as she popped a berry into her own mouth. "Maybe I'll put them to work replanting what you've had brought from my garden. While you maybe start digging that pit of stink-lilies?"

Joarr's grin was warm and devious, but surely relieved, too. And when they heard the telltale scrape of the stone door, he even gave Gwyn's head a swift, appreciative-feeling scratch with his claws before turning and taking off, disappearing into the wall of surrounding leaves.

It left her to climb down from the tree herself, but it already felt easier than it had before—and perhaps rather satisfying, too. And once she'd reached the new arrivals—Kalfr, and Eyolf and Iyolf, and Stella, too—it also felt easy to smile at them, and wave them further into the garden.

"Good morning, and welcome to Joarr's garden!" she said brightly. "Joarr has some things to finish this morning, so I'll be showing you around. And perhaps putting you to work, if you—"

Her voice broke off there, her smile faltering—because wait, all three orcs were still visibly *injured*, surely from that vicious Bautul battle the day before. Kalfr's face and arms bore multiple deep wounds and scratches, and Iyolf's nose was badly bent, still dripping *blood*—and worst of all, Eyolf was awkwardly staggering with each step, and favouring his left side.

"Actually," Gwyn continued, her voice hardening, "maybe we won't be doing any work today. In future"—she cast a quick glance over her shoulder, but Joarr was nowhere to be seen, so she ploughed on anyway—"we'll expect you to be in excellent physical condition to work here, and to have any outstanding wounds properly dealt with."

For an instant, the three orcs looked bewildered—and then Eyolf flashed her a rakish, confident smile. "You mistake us, woman," he said, "for we are strong and hale Bautul, and always ready to work, no matter what wounds we bear. Ach, brother?"

This was said with a glance toward Iyolf, who silently but fervently nodded, and beside him Kalfr was nodding too, his big dark eyes almost pleading on Gwyn's. But she was not having their Bautul bravado, not in this—and she crossed her arms over her chest, and gave a sharp shake of her head.

"Open wounds are an infection risk, especially combined with earth," she said, "and it would be irresponsible of me to allow such a thing. Also"—she glanced at Stella, whose eyes were tired but warm on hers—"this garden is blessed by the goddess, who often speaks through the earth, and wants only the best for her Bautul seekers. So you need to bring your best here for her, too."

No one could argue with that, of course, and Gwyn felt herself smiling rather smugly toward them. "So you'll all go see that excellent healer of yours tonight, before you return tomorrow," she continued. "But for now, come along, and I'll show you around."

The three orcs and Stella meekly followed Gwyn deeper into the garden, their eyes already wide and wondering, drinking up the sights. As well they should, Gwyn rather thought—though she couldn't help grimacing at the realization that they'd surely never stepped foot in here before. Or, perhaps, had never even before *seen* a garden.

So she tried to make her tour as entertaining and informative as possible, often offering them food to eat, while incorporating what she hoped was a simple, straightforward gardening lesson. Focusing on the most crucial points—basic plant structure and maintenance, sun versus shade, and of course, the importance of not tramping on any plants.

Thankfully, it didn't take long until the three orcs were easily returning Gwyn's smiles, and answering her commentary with cheerful questions and comments of their own. And by the end of it, she was laughing along with them, and—as bizarre as it was—perhaps feeling almost *fond* toward them. Kalfr was kind, thoughtful, and surprisingly eager to learn, while Eyolf was a bundle of energy—the total opposite of his bashful brother Iyolf. But it was clear that the two brothers cared for each other very much, and Eyolf would often speak on Iyolf's behalf, even as he followed his quiet, subtle guidance.

However, Stella had remained very subdued throughout the tour, and perhaps rather distracted, as well. And once the three orcs had gone slightly ahead, Iyolf still visibly limping, Gwyn found herself thinking, abruptly, of Silfast. Of how Joarr had slammed him in the head with that axe, and surely humiliated him before his entire clan. And how surely, as much as Silfast had deserved it, a friend would care. Would ask.

"So how... are things, today?" she asked Stella, under her breath. "How is Silfast feeling? I hope he wasn't seriously injured yesterday?"

Stella twitched, her tired eyes suddenly snapped wide— and then she shook her head, very quickly. "No, of course not," she said, in a bright voice that didn't at all match her eyes. "He's already up and training again, and feeling quite all right. He's such a strong and vigorous Bautul. Nothing bothers him, really."

Oh. Gwyn bit back the first answer that came to mind, and instead smiled and nodded, and continued finishing up the tour. But she couldn't help the occasional worried glance toward Stella, or the uneasy twinge in her belly as they finally waved goodbye, all promising to reconvene the next morning.

Gwyn was still standing there when Joarr eventually reappeared from wherever he'd gone off to, a small blue huckleberry in hand. "This was good work, witch," he said lightly, as he popped it into her mouth. "I ken they all soon worship at your feet, ach?"

Gwyn gave a rueful chuckle as she ate the berry, savouring its glorious burst of flavour across her tongue. "I made them all promise to go see your healer before they returned, which they were *not* happy about," she replied. "And I provoked Stella into defending Silfast's honour, and his *excellent* health and vigour, too."

Joarr barked a low laugh, but his eyes were dark, and he shook his head. "I tell you, Silfast is a fool," he said flatly. "Either she believe this as truth—and some day learn this for the falsehood it is—or she no believe this, but yet feel bound to speak false of him. Ach?"

Gwyn winced, even as she nodded—both options seemed to again exhibit that same Bautul bravado, which surely couldn't be helpful for intimate relationships—and she attempted a teasing half-smile toward Joarr's watching eyes. "So you wouldn't want me to go around proudly proclaiming all your false virtues?" she asked. "Your honesty, perhaps, or your modesty, or your deep devotion to your goddess?"

Joarr's mouth twitched up, though his eyes had narrowed, his head tossing his hair over his shoulder. "I give much for this goddess. Even as she keep seeking to *curse* me."

Gwyn eyed him for an instant too long—did he truly believe that?—and then grasped his arm, and tugged him toward the altar. He didn't resist, but his eyes had gone even narrower, his forearm very taut under her grip.

"Seek her with me, for a minute," Gwyn said, over her shoulder. "Stella showed me how, yesterday."

With that, she assumed the pose Stella had taught her, one hand on the altar, one over her heart. While Joarr fully frowned down at her, his eyes glinting, his arms now crossed over his chest.

"*You* no follow this goddess," he snapped at her. "You no even ken she is truth. Ach?"

Gwyn shrugged, and felt her face oddly flushing. "Not really," she confessed, as she glanced guiltily toward the wizened tree. "But this is important to your clan, and therefore, important to you. And if it's important to you, I want to—"

She broke off there, twitching—gods, where had she even been going with that—but Joarr's eyes had seemed to still on hers, and she could see him exhaling, his chest hollowing. And finally he shrugged too, and shifted into the pose, bowing his head toward the tree.

Gwyn blinked, but then bowed her head too. And then just stood and listened, as Stella had suggested. Sinking into the rustle of the wind through the leaves, the bright calls of birdsong, the deep quiet beneath it all. And, beside her, Joarr's slow, near-silent breaths, moving with the slight brush of his arm against her.

When he finally twitched away, a few minutes later, his eyes were looking rather hunted, his hand dragging through his hair—enough that Gwyn instinctively reached for him, and hauled him close. And was rewarded with the feel of his body sagging against hers, his claws clutching against her back.

"I think *you* need some fun, after all this good Bautul behaviour," she said, muffled, into his chest. "Tell me, apart from the garden, what did *you* do for fun, back before you were a Bautul?"

Some of the tension had snapped back into Joarr's body, his chest unmoving—but then she felt him shrug. "Sparring, I ken," he said, far too casual. "In Skai arena, mayhap."

"Then let's go there," Gwyn replied, drawing back so she could meet his eyes. "I'd like to see it. Please?"

He visibly grimaced, but finally nodded. And soon they

were back in the depths of the mountain, and walking into yet another huge, echoing room that again seemed devoted to fighting. This one also had the stone carved seats rising up on each side, looking down toward a large circle below, which included a tall raised dais at its centre—but rather than fighting a massive brawl, like in the Bautul pit, the orcs here were all sparring one-on-one, within clearly delineated rings. And while it still seemed rather vicious—Gwyn winced as one orc kicked another straight in the groin—there was no visible blood, and no obviously wounded orcs, either.

"Joarr!" called a deep, vaguely familiar voice, and when Gwyn turned to look, she realized it was Simon, grinning toward them, while also swinging punches toward another orc—in fact, the captain's Right Hand, the sharp-looking orc named Drafli. And cheering from the sidelines was Simon's mate Maria, together with a young orc Gwyn didn't recognize, and again the genial-looking Baldr, who was again sporting fresh *teeth-marks* on his neck.

"And Gwyn!" Maria called eagerly, waving her over. "Come meet Bjorn, and watch with us. Simon's almost beaten Drafli, *again.*"

Baldr instantly returned this with a loud but good-natured growl, and beside Gwyn, Joarr made a noise that might have been a chuckle. And when she glanced up at him, he was indeed looking reluctantly amused, and even nudged her over toward them.

Gwyn willingly went, greeting Maria and Baldr with a genuine-feeling smile, and then introducing herself to the little orc. His name was Bjorn of Clan Skai, he proudly informed her, and Maria and Simon were his parents, and his father Simon was not only the biggest orc in Orc Mountain, but also the best fighter, too.

"Is that so?" Gwyn said, glancing over toward where Simon indeed pinned Drafli's thrashing form to the floor—but instead of going further, like the Bautul had, he instantly backed off again, leaping up to his feet. "Is Simon fast enough to even defeat Joarr, do you think?"

This was met with a chorus of jovial replies, and loudest of all was Simon's rolling laugh as he strode toward them, and clapped Joarr on the shoulder. "My brother likes to think he is faster than I," Simon said, his dark eyes dancing. "But it has been so many moons since he last faced me, or saw my ways. I ken his defeat shall thus be harsh and swift, ach?"

Joarr scoffed at that, and then spun and stalked into the ring, shaking out his own long limbs, snapping back something in black-tongue. To which Simon only laughed again, and then followed him in with slow, prowling steps.

They turned to face each other, and Joarr twitched a taunting smile, brows raised—and in a sudden flash of furious movement, he flew straight toward Simon. His hair streaking out behind him, his claws aiming for Simon's eyes, his knee slamming toward his groin—

But Simon ducked away, just as quickly as Joarr had ducked away from Silfast the day before. And as Gwyn watched the two of them settle into the match, dodging and weaving and flying at one another with ruthless, astonishing precision, she couldn't help noting the difference between this and the Bautul battle from yesterday. How this one felt—somehow— almost *fun*?

It was certainly helpful to have Maria and Bjorn and Baldr watching too, all alternately shouting cheerful complaints and praises. And even laughing good-naturedly as Joarr taunted Simon, at one point actually leaping to stand up on his *shoulders*, where he tried—and failed—to land a series of kicks on Simon's head before falling off again.

In the end, it turned out that no one won, because Simon was laughing too hard, his hands on his knees, while Joarr danced away from him, eyes glittering, his feet doing something that looked like an honest-to-gods *jig*. While beside Gwyn, Maria hollered an impressive series of curses toward him, and Baldr laughed so hard he collapsed into Drafli, who was reluctantly smiling beside him.

It was ridiculous enough that Gwyn couldn't stop laughing either, and she was still grinning once she and Joarr were back in the corridor again. He was all sweaty and panting, his skin shining in the light of the lamp, but his steps were easy and relaxed, his eyes warm and bright on hers.

"That was fun, right?" Gwyn asked him, clearly stating the obvious, but perhaps just wanting to hear him say it. "Maybe we can do it again soon?"

And wait, surely she was again implying more time, more days, more hope—but his smile down toward her felt open, true, *willing*. "Ach, mayhap," he said, voice low. "I have... missed this. I... no saw how this would be, among them."

Oh. He'd thought, maybe, that he wouldn't be welcome with the Skai anymore. And there was an odd tightness in Gwyn's throat, and she slipped her arm around his waist, pulling him close as they walked. "They were obviously delighted to have you there," she said. "And they were so welcoming to me, too. I'd love to see them again."

Joarr had settled his heavy arm over her shoulder, his claws clutching gentle through the fabric of her dress. "Ach, witch," he said. "You ken I—"

But he abruptly broke off there, his mask flicking over his eyes—and then he audibly exhaled, and drew her to a halt. "You ken I shall greet your kindness with yet more work," he said, his voice far flatter than before. "If you should wish to see yet more women today?"

Oh. Of course. He must have just smelled them, perhaps, and even as Gwyn instantly nodded, she felt herself searching his eyes. Seeing something that surely looked like wariness, or regret... or maybe even guilt?

"I don't mind," Gwyn told him, and she meant it. "I'm truly happy to help. We'll have time for more fun later, right?"

She flashed him what she hoped was a winning smile, and felt her stomach flip at his slow smile back, showing her all his sharp teeth. "Ach, witch," he said, his voice soft, almost affectionate. "I shall always have time for this."

Well. Gwyn felt her face heating, but she nodded, and accompanied him back through the corridor. Moving steadily downward now, surely toward the Ka-esh wing—and indeed, they soon stepped back into the little clinic where Gwyn had first examined Rosa. And where Rosa herself was already waiting, nearly bouncing up and down as she beamed toward them.

"We've cleared you a worktable, Gwyn," Rosa said brightly, giving an excited flourish of her arm. "And asked Joarr to send down some herbs that might be helpful. And we've brought clean rags, and disinfectant, and water, and some tools, and your midwifery book, and your notes! Is there anything else you need?"

Gwyn stared numbly at her newly stocked workstation—it truly had everything she could have possibly requested—and she had to drag her gaze back to Rosa's expectant face. "This is—wonderful," she said, her voice choked. "Thank you, Rosa."

Rosa immediately waved it away, and declared that she and the Ka-esh would arrange everything, if Gwyn would be kind enough to stay throughout the afternoon, and meet with anyone who needed it. To which Gwyn offered her earnest agreement, though she couldn't help again glancing at Joarr, who'd been watching all this in silence, his arms crossed over his chest.

"I wait and help, ach?" he said, jerking his head toward the corridor. "You must only speak, woman, for what you need. Herbs, or food, or aught else?"

Gwyn nodded, and gave him a grateful smile, a quick

squeeze at his arm. And then he strode out, and sent back her first client of the day—a pregnant woman named Hannah, who'd already been waiting outside the door with her orc, a tall, scarred, forbidding-looking Skai named Fulnir.

Gwyn launched into her list from the top, and proceeded through her usual consultation and examination. Discovering along the way that Hannah and Fulnir lived in a Skai camp to the west, and they already had one small son named Frothi. And that while Frothi's birth had been difficult, the most difficult part had been... the midwife?

"I didn't tell the midwife I was carrying an orc until I was in labour," Hannah told Gwyn, her eyes dark. "I couldn't risk it. But then, she refused to believe I wanted to keep my son, and tried to take him away. And when I wouldn't allow it"—Hannah took a shaky breath—"she threatened to confine me, and *report* me. And thank the gods Fulnir was hiding outside, because otherwise—"

She grimaced, and her body visibly shuddered, enough that Fulnir stepped closer, circling his arm around her waist. "This no happen again, *sæta*," he said, his voice deep. "We only see midwife here at mountain, ach? Keep you safe."

But Hannah was still twitching, her face buried in Fulnir's chest. "But those men will keep following us," she said, muffled. "They're already searching for women like me. They want to capture me. Make a public *example* of me."

Gwyn felt something cold flash up her spine, her eyes frozen on Hannah's bowed head—wait, she was talking about the lords' awful new law?—and she couldn't seem to move as Fulnir pulled Hannah closer, his clawed hands running firm up and down her back.

"You no fret over this, *sæta*," Fulnir growled. "Our brothers seek to face this law, and call off these men. They soon fix this."

His eyes had angled toward the corridor as he'd spoken— the corridor where *Joarr* was waiting—and he lifted Hannah off the table, and guided her toward the door. "More brothers wait to go home with us," he added. "You no fret over this also, ach?"

Hannah nodded, and gave Gwyn a misty-eyed smile as they left. While Gwyn blinked blankly after them, her head tilting, something cold and jagged crackling up her back.

Hannah had... been at risk. Then, *and* now. She'd been horribly betrayed by a professional who was supposed to have cared for her, to the point where she was afraid to seek care at all. And not only that, but Gwyn's father's new law was only making it worse. And was perhaps *already* making it worse?

The vision of those horrible men hunting Joarr was again swarming through Gwyn's thoughts, and she frowned down at the wash-basin as she scrubbed her hands clean, and then wrote out some notes for Hannah's file. And when she turned around again, it was to the sight of Joarr leaning in the door-way, his brows raised, his eyes flicking briefly toward the corridor beyond him.

Are you ready for another, it meant, and Gwyn drew in a bracing breath, and nodded. These women needed her. She had to help them. She *had* to.

Her next client was a tall, brown-skinned woman named Dania, who turned out to be only weeks away from giving birth. And she and her huge Bautul orc Rhon had apparently journeyed for two entire days from the south, leaving as soon as word had reached them of a midwife working in Orc Mountain.

"We're thinking of staying here until our son is born," Dania said to Gwyn, her eyes careful. "That is, if you think you'll still be here, and available to attend the birth?"

Gwyn had darted a reflexive glance toward the door, toward where Joarr was currently nowhere to be seen—and then squared her shoulders, and fixed her eyes back on Dania's. "I will do my absolute best to be here," she said firmly. "I would be honoured to attend your birth, and be one of the first to meet your son."

Dania's relief was palpable, lighting up her eyes, and behind her Rhon actually laughed, and swept her into his massive embrace. "We thank you, woman," he said to Gwyn, bowing his head toward her. "May the goddess pour out her blessing upon you."

Gwyn waved it away, though there was an odd prickling behind her eyes as they left, more cold ice swarming her thoughts. All of which only seemed to intensify as she met with her next client—a soft-spoken, fair-haired woman named Inga, who turned out to be very near to giving birth to her second orc son. And whose two huge Bautul orcs paced and twitched throughout the consultation, their clawed hands gripped tightly to their scimitars.

"No, we cannot stay here until the birth," one of them replied, with tangible regret, when Gwyn tentatively offered this as a suggestion. "Our other son waits for us at home, and we swore to him we should soon return safe. We do not dare linger, lest we are faced with more men, and more danger."

More men. More danger. Gwyn's stomach miserably plunged, but she gave Inga and her orcs detailed instructions on how best to manage a delivery on their own, should the need arise. She also gave them multiple packets of herbs— motherwort, yarrow, valerian—with more thorough instructions on when and how to use them.

And then, finally—and apparently the last client for the day—was the orc captain's mate Jule. The former lady of Yarwood, cradling her tiny, sleeping orc son in her arms. And Jule's broad smile toward Gwyn felt both genuine and reassuring, slicing through some of the shivering chaos churning through Gwyn's thoughts.

"You know, you're a very difficult woman to pin down,

Gwyn," Jule said cheerfully, with a conspiratorial wink. "Almost as though a certain orc *wants* to keep you all to himself."

Gwyn blinked at that—surely Joarr hadn't been doing any such thing?—but an uncertain glance over her shoulder showed Joarr now standing in the doorway, his expression distinctly forbidding, his eyes glinting on Jule's face.

"If you wouldn't mind, I'd appreciate some privacy, Joarr," Jule added, her voice light. "Grimarr actually asked me to send you to him, if you're free?"

Joarr's glower deepened, and Gwyn could see his jaw flexing in his cheek as his gaze flicked back toward her. "Wait here for me, ach?" he said. "I bring you food, also."

Gwyn replied with a silent nod, and Joarr nodded back before striding away. Leaving her alone with this unusual lady Jule, and her sleeping orc baby.

And Gwyn was here to work—to help—and with considerable effort, she shoved back the mess in her thoughts, and forced her focus to the baby. He was apparently named Tengil, he was almost six months old, and, Jule gratefully informed Gwyn, he'd already been sleeping better, thanks to the numbing herbs she'd sent.

Gwyn then proceeded with a quick examination of both Tengil and Jule, noting the baby's differing orc features for later reference. And then she and Jule talked through some considerations around Jule's desire to proceed with another pregnancy in the next year or two, and how it might differ from her first.

"Thank you for all this, Gwyn," Jule said once they'd finished, and she was again standing with Tengil in her arms. "It's so wonderful to finally have a supportive midwife here, and of course, we all hope you'll stay with us as long as possible. However…"

Gwyn felt her body stilling again, her eyes fixed to Jule's

face. Waiting, frozen, as Jule's gaze slid down to her sleeping son, and back up again.

"However," she continued, with a sigh, "there are some things you should know first. Before you make any lasting decisions."

The chaos was battering against the ice now, fighting to break out, to escape—Jule had sent Joarr away, she hadn't wanted him to hear this—and Gwyn could feel her heart thumping, far too loud and erratic in her chest.

"About what?" she asked, as smoothly as she could. "About Joarr?"

Jule sighed again, her brow creased. "Yes," she said slowly. "Do you know why Joarr first sought you out? And why he brought you here?"

Right. That. Gwyn swallowed, and attempted a careless smile at Jule's face. "Yes, actually, I do," she replied. "My father is Lord Anton of Dunburg, and together with his horrid lord cronies, he's been working to create an abhorrent new law targeting women who are pregnant with orcs. And in retaliation"—she swallowed again—"Joarr tried to seduce me, and have me become pregnant with his son. Thereby obliging me to take action on the new law, whether to try to sway my father, or to—to testify, and publicly humiliate him."

Gods, it sounded cruel, being spoken aloud like that—and Jule's chagrined wince suggested she thought so too. And as Gwyn blinked at Jule's face, her heart still thundering, it occurred to her that maybe there was... guilt there, too. Regret.

"I already know the captain—your mate—was aware of this plan," Gwyn added, her voice not quite steady this time. "I presume you were aware of it, too? Perhaps you all planned it together?"

Jule winced again, and rubbed a hand over her suddenly tired-looking eyes. "I'm so sorry, Gwyn," she said, with a sigh. "But yes, I knew. I strongly expressed my reservations, and was roundly overruled. It certainly didn't help that those lords have allowed armed men to run rampant over our lands—or that they've already been targeting women, rather than orcs. Because that technically doesn't break the treaty, right?"

She gave a wry, brittle laugh, at unnerving odds with the anger now flashing in her eyes. "Five orcs have lost mates this summer alone," she continued, her voice clipped. "Two women were forcibly 'rescued' and returned to their families, and then essentially imprisoned. Another woman ran away out of fear, and then disappeared. And two more women died after being detained by men—one after suffering a miscarriage, the other by her own hand."

More cold, vicious ice rippled up Gwyn's back, but Jule was still talking, her voice now flat and dull. "Two of those women left small sons behind," she said. "Both Bautul. The entire clan was ready to go on a rampage—in blatant defiance of the treaty, and Grimarr's orders—when Joarr stepped up, and suggested this instead. Suggested... *you*. And when the Bautul didn't believe him—didn't trust him—he then made one of those unbreakable Bautul pledges, to confirm it."

Oh. *Oh.* Gwyn's thoughts were swirling again, spinning, clanging together, and she had to grip at the table for balance, and gulp for breaths. Fight for the awareness that yes, Joarr had told her this, the other night on the altar—but he surely hadn't shared the breadth of it, the sheer *horror* of it. How women like Hannah were already being targeted. How women were already *dying*.

But gods, maybe Gwyn should have already known. She'd seen the men hunting Joarr in the forest. She'd heard Stella say it wasn't safe to go outside. And she *knew* her father, she knew men like Roy, she knew what they were capable of...

She felt her hands clutching at her hot face, her fingernails dragging down her cheeks. "So what now, then?" she heard her wavering voice ask, far too high-pitched. "Now that Joarr's plan is—now that I'm—"

She flapped a shaking hand at the clinic around her, at her new personal workbench. At all the promises she'd made to help these women. At all her hope for a new life, a new way. Maybe even a... a *mate*.

"I don't know," Jule replied, her voice heavy. "And I'm not sure Grimarr does, either. But"—she set her jaw, her eyes flinty on Gwyn's—"we both trust Joarr, and what he sees. And he seems to have held off the Bautul for now—between gaining you their goddess' blessing, and winning that brawl in their pit yesterday, and letting them back into his garden. Not to mention setting you up here, and spreading word that he's brought a midwife to the mountain. Probably all the cleverest things he could have done, really."

She gave a grim half-smile at that, as if Joarr had actually—*planned* all those things. But surely he hadn't, had he? Gwyn had been with him each time—gods, she'd even *suggested* most of them, she'd seen it all with her own eyes...

But her heart was still thundering, and she had to fight for air, for clarity, press it down deep inside. Joarr was rolling with what the gods threw at him. He'd wanted her to be part of this, with him. And surely he hadn't lied, not again, surely...

But he still hadn't told her the full truth, either. And Gwyn should have known he was still keeping secrets, still making plans around all this, stupid, *stupid*...

She swallowed over the thick lump in her throat, and blinked again and again toward Jule's watching face. "Hannah mentioned," she somehow said, her voice someone else's, "that she's already being pursued by men. Are you able to"—she swallowed again—"keep her safe? And other women like her?"

Jule grimaced, and her silence felt like it was crawling, creeping yet more ice up Gwyn's spine. "We're doing our best," she said finally. "But once this new law is sworn in, it will only give these men and mercenaries even more reason to harass us. To 'rescue' these women from us, and 'help' them. It's already been getting worse since the lords publicly announced it, and now that they've also committed to a date..."

Her voice trailed off there, her eyes dark, her mouth tight. While Gwyn's brain was shouting again, screeching, teetering on an edge...

"What do you mean, they've publicly *announced* it," she croaked. "And they've committed to a *date*? My father included?"

And it was like the room was crushing her, Jule was crushing her, with her regret, with the gods-damned sympathy in her dark eyes.

"Yes," she said, her voice quiet but firm. "We have a fortnight, before that law becomes truth."

24

After Jule left, Gwyn couldn't seem to stop pacing. Stalking from one side of the clinic to the other, over and over again, while her thoughts rattled ever-louder through her skull.

Her father was proceeding with that damned law. Pregnant women were already avoiding the help they desperately needed. They were already being targeted. They were *dying*. And in a fortnight, the situation would become even worse. Two weeks. Fourteen *days*.

And clearly, Joarr had known all this. He'd been fighting to deal with all this. And had he told Gwyn the extent of it? The urgency of it? No. No. *No*. Of course he hadn't, because she hadn't pushed it, she was so damned *stupid*, and he was—he was—

Here. Now. Suddenly standing tall and taut before her, his arms crossed, as though he'd always been there, all this time.

Gwyn reeled backwards, cursing under her breath, and furiously wiped at the wetness pooling in her eyes. "I would rather," she managed, "be alone right now. Please."

But Joarr didn't move, not beyond the sharp shake of his head, the flex of his black claws on his biceps. "No," he said, voice tight. "I no leave you alone thus. No when you taste thus. No here."

Gwyn gaped at him, at where his narrow eyes had flicked, brief but horribly telling, toward the workbench. Toward the *tools*. Toward the pointed steel scalpel, as though she would—

The craving surged through her thoughts in an almost staggering rush—gods, why hadn't she thought of that before he'd come?—and there was the overpowering urge to shout at him, to rage at him, to weep. Anything to make him leave, so she could dash over to that scalpel, find some trace of relief, no matter how painful or futile—

"No," Joarr hissed again, his eyes even narrower. "You no even try, woman. You find other way."

Gwyn kept gaping at him, and it felt like the room was slowly spinning behind him, like the rage was flashing bright red behind her eyes. "You," she gasped, "have *no right* to throw your orders at me. You have no right to judge me!"

"I no *judge* you," Joarr replied, his voice infuriatingly cool. "I ken you are wise woman. You find other way to face this rage, ach? To free this."

And gods, it was like Gwyn could feel the candlewood, the sharp steel, scraping against her skin, dragging down her throat. "If you would *listen* to me," she choked out, "and actually be *honest* with me for once in your life, my rage will be just *fine!*"

She was hollering by the end, her hands in fists, her heartbeat screaming in her skull—and the utter bastard just kept looking at her like that, arms crossed, mouth pursed. "No," he said, with enraging calm. "We seek other way."

And before Gwyn could even find a reply, his hands snapped out toward her, grasped her by the waist, and swept her up onto the edge of the nearest examination table. And then—her cry of outrage scraped through the room—he shoved her knees apart with easy, familiar hands, and stepped close between them.

"What the hell," Gwyn gasped, "are you *doing!*"

But of course she knew what he was doing, she always gods-damned did, and the bastard had the sheer audacity to *smirk* at her as he slid her skirts all the way up, exposing everything between her sprawled, trembling legs.

"You no ken?" he drawled at her, as he made a show of reaching down inside his own trousers, and pulling himself out. Already hard, full, and dripping, bobbing straight toward where her exposed, open heat was quivering, convulsing, craving...

"If you no wish for this," he said, so cool, as he eased a little closer, "you say this, ach?"

But as he'd spoken, that smooth, gleaming head had just brushed against her, just *there*, grazing her with its sweet slickness—and Gwyn's harsh, desperate gasp was utter, broken betrayal. How typical was it that she still wanted this, so gods-damned much, from this completely aggravating asshole, who'd betrayed her, lied to her, kept the truth from her, manipulated her, again and again and *again*—

But he was still waiting, the absolute prick, his brows raised, that smooth length shuddering, settling a little closer, finding its place. And gods curse it all, because even lost in the towering rage, she somehow found room to nod, quick and furious and ashamed. To say, *yes.*

"Wise woman," Joarr purred, and oh *hell*, he was pressing forward. Easing himself inside, slow but certain, his eyes dropped to the sight, lashes fluttering against his cheek...

And oh, it felt like power, like ruin. Like a beautiful devastating curse, pouring her full of poisonous, deadly pleasure.

Like this damned devious orc getting his way, again, again, again—

But then, it—stopped. He stopped, not even all the way in, and his eyes were back on hers again, brows still raised, while her traitorous, half-impaled body helplessly clamped and throbbed against him. Holding him there, wanting him, wanting this pain, wanting his poison to destroy her...

"Now speak," he said, his voice a strange distant bell in the screeching mayhem of her brain. "What spark this. What she say to you."

Gwyn gulped for air, flailed to find words—but there were none, not with him jutted up inside her like this, and still *speaking*. So cool, casual, so gods-damned *calm*.

"She say I speak false to you?" he continued, brows still raised, as he held himself there within her. "Or you no trust me? I am danger to you?"

Danger. Why was it so hard to think, to drag in air—but then Joarr sank in deeper. Slow, agonizing, utter destruction, until his groin was pressed tight against hers, his fullness finally buried all the way inside.

"Speak," he hissed, darker this time. "She doubt me? Rebuke me?"

Good gods, Gwyn couldn't *think*, and Joarr ground himself even deeper, while the chaos streamed through her thoughts. More ruin, more poison, speak, *speak*...

"None of that," she gasped at him. "But you still lied to me, *again*. You didn't tell me the true situation of your clan. How *dire* it is. That women are already at risk, and they're *dying*! That two Bautul sons are motherless. Because of *my father*!"

Joarr's forehead abruptly furrowed, and he drew slightly out again—the movement small, but still enough to wring another gasp from Gwyn's mouth. "I tell you Bautul clan suffers," he said, voice flat. "I no ken you wish to hear each tale of woe and death, ach?"

He punctuated his last sentence with another push inside, and Gwyn gasped again, even as she glared at him, her hands gripping to the edge of the examination table. "I *do* want to hear about it," she choked at him. "I want you to tell me the truth. *Everything.* Can't you see that I'm trying to trust you? That I *want* to be able to trust you?!"

Joarr kept frowning at her as he again slid out and sank back inside, a little harder this time. "I wish this also," he said, his voice still appallingly steady. "But you no follow why I no wish to burden you with this? You are no at fault for the deeds of your father, or these men. Yet here you seek to *right* this. You work with all strength to help us, and serve my kin. You honour us in this. You honour *me.*"

He'd picked up speed as he spoke, sliding in and out, the sheer sensation sending sharp flares of heat through her at every thrust. She honoured them. Honoured him...

"If I burden you with all this," he continued, his voice just slightly ragged now, "I ken you shall work yet more. You shall serve yet more. You shall cast away all you long for, all your hope for this *new way*, in seeking to right what these men have done. When these men have also harmed *you!*"

Gwyn's breaths were coming in short, scattered pants, her whole body trembling at every steady drive of that demanding hardness into her. "That is still," she somehow gasped at him, "*my* decision to make. Not yours, asshole!"

But Joarr was laughing, the harsh sound lacking all mirth, his hips slamming even harder against her. "Ach, no," he said, the coolness in his voice at unnerving odds with his bitter, glinting eyes. "This is no your choice. No even my choice. This is now the choice of my fool fathers, and these fool men, and this cruel Bautul goddess, who only taunt me, and mock me, and seek to *ruin* me! Ruin *you!*"

What? The anger was blazing bright in his eyes now, and Gwyn could feel him oddly quivering as he plunged in again and again, hard enough to make her teeth chatter, her body wrenching at each impact. Her hands finally fluttering to his shoulders, clutching painfully tight as he took her, pierced her, invaded her. As he somehow seemed to draw her anger into himself, into his flashing eyes, his growl burning through the air...

"You no deserve this," he hissed, his voice hitching with every plunge. "You no deserve your father. No deserve this betrothed. No deserve *me*. No deserve me making you my own. No deserve *this*."

This. He meant *this*, his coiled frenzied body ramming into her, claiming her, making her his. *My own*, he'd said, and somehow that was important, extremely important, his growls cracking into something like roars, his claws sinking through her dress, into her skin, as he kept hurling himself into her, flying together, soaring in a careening rush, plummeting into the depths...

His flood of heat blasted out in a furious charge, spurting deep and dark within her, pulsing again and again and again. While his bark tore from his throat, his eyes squeezed shut, his body otherwise frozen motionless, in utter thrall to the spray of liquid fire filling her, claiming her, *his*...

Gwyn's own shout tore through the room, the throbs of her release reeling hot and wild, clamping against the hardness still plunged to the hilt, pouring itself out inside her. Craving it, welcoming it, even if it, even if he...

And as the pleasure slowly ebbed again, in its place was... awareness. A strange, unmistakable certainty, teetering quiet and close between them. His. His own. Because...

His eyes were blinking downwards now, not toward their still-joined bodies, but just above. Because. Because...

Gwyn's hands fluttered for his face, tilting it up again, finding his eyes. His broken, betraying eyes, oddly bright on hers, glittering with all he wasn't saying. All he had done. All he had known...

"Am I..." she whispered, choked. "I'm not... *pregnant*, Joarr?"

And his slow, answering nod was a cruel, staggering blow from the gods, ringing deadly and devastating between them. No. *No. Impossible.*

"Ach," he said. "You are."

25

Gwyn was... pregnant. With an orc's son. With *Joarr's* son.

And as she stared at his dark, glimmering eyes—his guilty, *guilty* eyes—there was the strangest, wildest urge to laugh. Of course this would happen again. Of *course.* And of course Joarr would know about it before she did, gods curse all the world, gods damn her utter blazing *stupidity.*

Because she'd known this was a risk. Hadn't she? Even with the silphium, it had been a risk. She'd known all those stories about the power of the orcs' seed. She'd cared for all those pregnant women. She'd told them again and again to be safe, aware, because they couldn't trust men, surely they couldn't trust orcs...

"From... when?" Gwyn heard her voice say, distant, grating, someone else's. "Not just now, surely?"

Joarr shook his head, his mouth grimacing, his eyes squeezed shut. "From... the altar," he whispered. "In the storm. I ken."

The storm. So *days* ago. And surely he'd known before this moment—maybe he'd even known then?—and Gwyn's urge to laugh was swarmed with the desperate, all-consuming need to weep. He'd known. And he hadn't told her. *Again.*

But now it was his hands on her face, his fingers skittering on her skin. "I tell myself I... *dream* this," he breathed. "I long too much for this—fear too much for this—so thus I taste it in my scent. Same way I taste your care for me, ach? I ken I never gain such gifts, no after all I see. So I"—he swallowed, the sound thick in his throat—"I *savour* this. Revel in sweet scent of son, upon my quick, wise woman. I overlook how this grows stronger. How he tastes no only of me, but of *you.*"

Oh. Oh gods. And was Joarr telling the truth now, he couldn't be, so why was he blinking like that, why was his entire body twitching against hers, his breaths rattling in his throat. "Never wished to visit this upon you," he whispered. "No in truth. No after this first night I taste you, ach? When you keep me secret. When you *see* me."

Gwyn couldn't speak, caught in his choked words, trapped in his shimmering eyes. In eyes that were... guilty. Grieving. Perhaps even... *afraid.*

And that was because—Gwyn's breath expelled from her lungs in a rush—of her father. She was pregnant with—with an orc's son. Which meant that in two short weeks, she would now be subject to that awful new law. To testifying. To all the horror her father wanted to wreak upon women like her.

Just like the orcs had planned. Just like Joarr had... *wanted.*

Something kicked in Gwyn's chest, plummeted down her throat, and her heart was thundering, fierce and frantic against her ribs. Joarr *wanted* that. He had. Hadn't he? Wanted to spark his son upon her, and then...

And gods, the look in his eyes. The way he kept blinking, his hands hot and trembly on her face. "I no ask you to face this," he breathed. "I take you next to Efterar, and he *end* this before it grow. He even keep this from coming again. He has good magic, ach?"

Efterar would *end* this. With good… *magic*?! And even as the shock reeled through Gwyn's skull—surely no orcs had *magic*—it was as though something even darker had punched her in the gut, slammed her straight in the heart.

End this, he'd said. Joarr wanted to… end this? End their *son*?

And Gwyn didn't judge such measures. Had never done so, had always accepted them as one option among many, one way to help ensure women's safety, to save their lives. But the thought of doing it now, here, herself—with this son, his son, *her* son—suddenly it made her want to run, to weep, to vomit all over the floor at his feet.

"You *want* that?" Gwyn somehow croaked, at his glistening, blinking eyes. "Truly, Joarr?"

He stared back at her for a too-long instant, and then barked a sound that might have been a laugh. "Ach, no," he said, quiet, hoarse. "It is grief to even *think* of this. But if we no do this, I"—his voice broke—"I see what next comes, ach?"

He… *saw*. And oh gods, surely he didn't, he couldn't—and Gwyn wasn't believing it, wasn't even considering it, wasn't seeing that truth glimmering in his eyes. That… guilt. No. No. *NO.*

"No," she gasped at him, as both her hands clutched flat to his chest, her skin sticking hot and clammy to his. "No. You've changed your plans before. Haven't you? *I've* changed your plans, Joarr. And you… went along with it. You ran with what the gods dropped on you. You found a new way. With the Bautul. With *me*. Right?"

She could hear him swallow again, could see it bobbing in this throat. Could see his brow slightly furrowing, his head tilting. Considering it.

"So you do it again," Gwyn hissed at him, hard, fervent. "We do it again. Because I am sure as *hell* not sacrificing my son, out of fear of my father. That's what he wants. That's *exactly* what he expects this vile new law to accomplish. And I won't, Joarr. I *refuse. No.*"

Joarr's eyes on hers were unblinking, now, his head still cocked to the side, his body snapped to stillness. As if she'd struck him, shocked him, cracked something deep inside...

And he wasn't Roy. He wasn't. It wasn't the same. And curse her, but Gwyn would say the rest of this. Would say what had been rattling through her thoughts all day, beneath the rest of the mess. She would decide to trust him, one more time. Seek the new way. The—the *hope.*

"Look, I know I'm probably not"—she gulped for air—"not what you really wanted. Or planned. For your son. And we haven't known each other nearly long enough, and you wanted to take it slow, and you might not even want a mate, or one like me. But we've been"—she sucked back another breath—"figuring it out, haven't we? It's been—good. *Fun*, even. Hasn't it?"

There was another instant of choked, staring silence, waiting, waiting—because what if she'd horribly misread all this, what if Joarr truly didn't care, what if this was more lies, more plans, more stupidity...

But then, oh gods, he nodded. Nodded, again, again, and surely that was another laugh, rippling ragged out of his throat.

"Ach," he whispered, and he bent his head down, his forehead bumping gentle against hers. "No only fun, woman. It is—*hope*. A cruel taunt from this cruel goddess, ach?"

Hope. As if he'd read it straight from Gwyn's thoughts, and she heard herself laugh too, choked, high-pitched. "Then why can't we test it," she breathed back. "Take this goddess to task. Fight her for it. For our own future. For... *him*."

Her trembling hand had somehow slipped down to her waist, to this strange, tenuous truth, this bizarre, impossible hope. Him. Their son. An *orc*.

But as Joarr's clawed hand dropped to spread beside her own, there wasn't even a hint of what she surely should have felt—no panic, or dread, or fear, or rage. She was finding a new way. Finding hope.

And against her, Joarr was nodding again, again, again. His hair brushing against her cheeks, his lashes fluttering so close, as his slow, heavy exhale burned against her skin.

"Ach, my wise witch," he whispered. "We try."

26

For the next few days, it felt like Gwyn was flitting through a dream. A dream in which she'd somehow become not only Orc Mountain's midwife, but a busy gardener, a respected herbalist, a friend, a lover... and even an expecting *mother*.

That last one didn't feel even slightly possible, to the point where Gwyn hadn't yet told another soul—but she still found herself being struck numb with the truth of it, at the oddest moments. During a consultation with a new Bautul woman. In the middle of another delicious meal in the kitchen. As Joarr pushed her face-first to a corridor wall, grasped a thick handful of her hair, and drove into her from behind with fast, powerful strokes, while any number of random orcs strolled past.

"You just don't do slow and sweet, do you?" Gwyn asked him after, as she huffed a shaky laugh, her hands skittering against his chest. "Not even now?"

Joarr knew what she was referring to, of course, and she felt the briefest brush of claws over the waist of her dress. "Ach, no," he said, his voice light. "This is only more cause to make my witch scream and plead for me, ach?"

Gwyn rolled her eyes, but couldn't help another laugh, her body sagging into his. And into, for a fleeting instant, what must have been a kiss, pressed to the top of her head.

It was typical of how Joarr had approached this so far—not really speaking of it, as if perhaps he didn't truly believe it yet, either—but still giving her more, somehow, too. More of those sharp smiles, more hints of affection beyond the hunger. More answers to questions when Gwyn asked, more obvious attempts to keep her well-fed and well-rested. And even, to her genuine surprise, more insights into the rest of his life, and his work, and the *war*.

"Wish to come to meeting with me?" he'd asked her, perhaps two days after she'd learned of her pregnancy. "Hear more of war, and men?"

Gwyn had eagerly agreed, of course, and had soon found herself seated in a meeting-room with a variety of orcs, as well as many of the women she'd met these past days—Jule, Ella, Rosa, Maria. All of them not only listening, but actually participating, as the orcs discussed the latest threats from the men, the latest offenses, the latest attacks.

And even more astonishing, it was *Joarr* who seemed to know the most about the men's plans. About where they were currently searching for women, and where they were taking them. About how that new law would surely be signed in twelve short days, and how they needed to find a solution as soon as possible, before the attacks became an onslaught.

But to Gwyn's continued astonishment—and her genuine relief—no one seemed to assume that the situation was her responsibility. No one mentioned even a possibility of her testifying, or returning to Varrahan, or making a case to her father. And when she tentatively expressed her willingness to help— to share information about her father, or his men, perhaps— the orcs waved it away, and Grimarr gave her an indulgent, rather terrifying smile across the table.

"Ach, I ken we know far more of your father than you do, woman," he said. "Joarr most of all, ach?"

Really? Gwyn twitched to stare at Joarr beside her, who had very blatantly assumed his mask again, his eyes entirely unreadable. "You no offer more to us upon this, woman," he said, voice crisp. "You yet bear enough, ach?"

Gwyn didn't argue, but she had no intention of not trying, either. Of not doing her best to face this. To fix this. To take this—this *impossibility* growing all around her, inside her—and turn it into truth.

And as the next few days passed, she didn't push more on the meetings, or the men—and instead, she poured every breath of her focus into making this work. Being with Joarr, however he needed her. Becoming a true Bautul. Making her own way, and fighting for the future she suddenly, desperately longed for.

She kept working in the garden each morning, preparing herbs for anyone who wanted them, while continuing to teach Kalfr, Iyolf, Eyolf, and Stella. She spent her afternoons down in the Ka-esh wing, either meeting with women in the clinic, or reading and researching with Rosa in the library. And in between, she spent more time with Ivar, who turned out to be quite the resource on Bautul customs and culture, and was more than willing to offer his steady, cheerful wisdom, and answer any questions she asked.

And, of course, through it all, Gwyn threw herself into finding even more fun with Joarr. They explored the entire mountain together, going all the way up to the snow-capped peak, and deep down to the newest tunnels the Ka-esh were digging. They splashed and swam in Orc Mountain's huge heated baths, and chased each other through the trees until they were both sweaty and gasping, and yanking at each other's clothes. And almost every day, they went back to the Skai arena, where Gwyn eagerly joined Maria and Bjorn in watching Joarr and Simon—and often Baldr and Drafli—playing together like wild little orclings, and laughed at them until her stomach hurt.

And late one night, when Joarr abruptly shook Gwyn awake in the darkness, she grabbed her lamp and her bag, and accompanied him down into a deep, dark tunnel below the mountain. Moving faster and faster through the rough-hewn rock and earth, until Joarr finally threw her up onto his back, and ran at full tilt into the shadows. As if he could see—or perhaps smell—something Gwyn couldn't, and finally she heard the faint, distinctive sounds of a woman's cries, echoing against the stone.

It turned out to be Inga, who was well into her labour, and desperately clinging to one of her huge orcs, his harsh face crumpled and ashen. While her other orc had rushed over to Gwyn and Joarr, barking a stream of frantic-sounding black-tongue toward Joarr's face.

Joarr quickly translated for Gwyn—they'd been trying to get Inga to the mountain, but her labour had come on too rapidly—and Gwyn immediately set to work. Finding a position for Inga that seemed comfortable, perched atop her crouching orc, and then checking the baby's position and heartbeat. All while reassuring Inga that she was doing wonderfully, and everything would be well soon.

It was indeed a quick, unexceptional labour—the fact that it was Inga's second most certainly helped—and Inga's orcs proved to be a great help as well. Soothing her, massaging her with an oil blend that Gwyn had brought, and growling their earnest reassurances as Inga breathed and wept through contraction after contraction. Until finally, toward what felt like morning, Inga delivered a squalling, squirmy, grey-skinned son.

"He's beautiful," Gwyn said firmly, once she'd cleared out the little orcling's nose, and then settled his slick, twitchy body onto Inga's bare chest. "Congratulations, you three. Now Inga,

I'll just clean you up a bit, and keep an eye on things, while you get to know your son. And perhaps one of you"—she glanced between the two orcs—"would like to cut the cord?"

The two orcs seemed to silently communicate with each other—one was visibly weeping, the other rubbing the baby's back with palpable reverence—and seemed to agree that the weeping orc would handle it. So once the orc's hands had been thoroughly washed and disinfected, he carefully cut the cord with a gentle clip of his claws.

This led to more weeping, all three of them now clutching at their beautiful new son. And even as Gwyn kept intently working—watching for the birth of the placenta, and checking for any bleeding or tearing—she somehow found herself weeping too, wiping her eyes on her sleeve, while Joarr stepped close behind her, and squeezed his hand to her shoulder.

They ended up staying until what felt like late the next day, making sure Inga was rested and recovering well, and that the orcling was nursing properly. And though Gwyn strongly recommended that Inga come to stay at the mountain for a few days, she and her orcs again refused, pointing out—not incorrectly—that the danger from the men would only increase with every day that passed.

So Gwyn sent them off with multiple helpful herbs, including nettle and raspberry leaf, as well as extensive instructions for both Inga and her orcling. And Joarr—who had occasionally disappeared throughout the day, finding food and water, and meeting with a scout who was nearby—pressed fresh meat and mushrooms into the orcs' hands, and ordered them to send for him at once if anything was amiss.

By the time Joarr and Gwyn returned to the mountain, it was nearly nightfall again, and Gwyn could scarcely think through the towering, staggering exhaustion. But as she finally sank down beside Joarr in their hammock, there was only satisfaction, relief, and a raw, deep-seated gratefulness.

"Thank you," she mumbled into Joarr's neck, her eyes fluttering closed. "You were *wonderful*, Joarr."

His laugh sounded more like a scoff, his head shaking against hers. "I was naught," he said, husky. "*You* were this, woman. You ken one of these orcs is blood-brother to captain of southern Bautul, ach? This shall only build this trust, and bring many more women to you. Ach?"

Oh. Gwyn's heart felt like it was brimming, escaping out her prickling watery eyes, and Joarr pulled her closer, and wiped the wetness away. And sleep came so easily, suddenly, drawing her into Joarr's warm chest, into the slow rock of the hammock in the breeze. She was... content. *Safe.* Where she belonged.

And perhaps it was superstition, silliness, stupidity—but as the next few days slipped by, still seemingly without any breakthroughs regarding the men, Gwyn also found her thoughts turning more and more to the goddess. *This cruel goddess*, Joarr had called her, who they were fighting for their future. But the more Gwyn heard Ivar and Stella speak of this goddess, the more that didn't seem quite right. The more it seemed that maybe—maybe this goddess was important. Part of this. Of making this new way.

So one evening, after a delightful day full of gardening, meetings with clients, and a delicious supper in the kitchen, Gwyn pulled Joarr over to the goddess' altar, and nudged him down upon it. He didn't need convincing, especially when she shoved down his trousers, and began making thorough use of her mouth—and afterwards they even slept there again, tangled in each others' arms. But when morning came, and Gwyn once again paused to stand beside the altar in the pose Stella had shown her—one hand against it, the other to her heart—she could feel Joarr's eyes watching her, heavy with unease, or maybe even disapproval.

"You no need to do this, woman," he said, with a gentle

scratch of his claws to her head. "You yet do more than enough. We shall find other way to face this, ach?"

His voice was light, but it still seemed to grip at Gwyn's belly, her throat. Because he was implying, of course, that the situation still wasn't even close to being dealt with. The men, the attacks, the new law. And while Gwyn hadn't been attending all Joarr's meetings these past days, he'd kept her consistently informed about the orcs' progress, and their ongoing plans against the men. Which so far included increased patrols, an astonishing amount of tunnel-digging toward the most heavily populated orc camps, and multiple letters and statements of protest sent off to lords like her father.

But the tales of the attacks had kept swirling ever higher, too. And the women Gwyn cared for—indeed including a few more from the southern Bautul clans—had also seemed more anxious, more fearful, with each day that passed. And as much as Gwyn kept fighting to ignore it, the days until the law's ratification seemed to keep slipping away faster and faster, counting down with unnerving, relentless rapidity. Six. Five. Four.

And adding to the mess, of course, was the looming question of Gwyn's house in Varrahan. Joarr's scouts—most of whom Gwyn now knew by name—had continued to bring back plants and cuttings from her garden each night, while also leaving more notes explaining her ongoing absence, and even spreading word of her various travels. But that house, that *life*, was still there, still empty, waiting—and that deadline was counting down, too. And there were now only nine short days until Roy returned to drag Gwyn back to Dunburg, or burn her house to the ground.

And while Gwyn hadn't properly spoken of it—to Joarr, or to anyone—it almost felt as though that fate was already set. If she truly wanted to embrace this new way, to become Joarr's true mate, a true Bautul, Orc Mountain's midwife, a mother to an orc—that house was already lost. That entire life was lost.

They would likely end up needing to stage Gwyn's death, in an unnerving echo of what Joarr's grandfather had done decades before. And she would never see her own father again, and would he even care, and…

"I want to," Gwyn belatedly told Joarr, over the thick lump in her throat, as she raised her eyes to his, her hand still on the altar. "To get to know the goddess, I mean. I think it could—help."

Joarr made a sound that might have been a scoff, but his eyes on hers looked rueful, or maybe even resigned. And Gwyn was still fighting for this—she was—and she squared her shoulders, and attempted a smile up at his face. "And speaking of things that might help," she continued, "Kalfr said yesterday that Silfast is holding another big brawl in the Bautul pit this morning. And as loath as I am to suggest this, maybe we should make an appearance?"

Joarr audibly groaned this time, though Gwyn didn't miss his hand reaching to stroke at the tooth around his neck. "Ach, my wise witch," he said, with a sigh. "You ken you may come to rue this plan, ach?"

However, it turned out that the brawl was slightly less painful than the previous time, mostly because Joarr again refused to wield a weapon, and again sharply ordered—or dragged—any wounded orcs off to the side. And in the end, he drove a raging Silfast to exhaustion, without striking him once. And then he loudly reiterated to the room that the goddess didn't bear blood in her garden, and that any Bautul wishing to spend time there had to see a healer first.

To Gwyn's genuine delight, this led to multiple more Bautul orcs in the garden the next morning, wandering carefully through the paths, and blinking at its beauty with wide, appreciative eyes. And thankfully, Kalfr and Eyolf and Iyolf had already learned enough to offer some direction, and Gwyn couldn't help chuckling at the sound of Eyolf's proud voice carrying clearly through the air, reminding the new orcs not to step off the path.

"Ach, time for meeting, I ken," Joarr said, with obvious relief, as he rose up from where he and Gwyn had been sitting and eating breakfast in a tree. "You herd these orcs for me? Throw them into pit if they step on huckleberry?"

Gwyn grinned up at his disgruntled face, while an increasingly familiar warmth seemed to unspool in her chest. Joarr still didn't enjoy having other people in his garden, she well knew—but he'd still borne it with surprising grace, and had continued to treat the orcs with creditable politeness. Again sacrificing his own wants for others', which was something Gwyn had kept noticing from him more and more—even down to the way he always cooked her meat to perfection, when she now knew that he much preferred to eat it raw.

"Of course," she said lightly, and she impulsively leapt up, and pressed a quick kiss to his cheek. "See you soon, love."

Love. It had slipped out before she'd even noticed, and she belatedly froze in place, her eyes wide—because despite how things were going between her and Joarr these days, she certainly hadn't gone there yet, and neither had he. Gods, even that loaded word *mate* hadn't again been spoken, perhaps because Gwyn still couldn't bear to risk it, not yet, not until...

And Joarr was looking just as frozen as she felt, his eyes unblinking on hers. And gods, this was so foolish, Gwyn was pregnant with his son, she was probably going to stage her *death* for him. And she was fighting for this, for this life, for their son. For their new way.

"I mean," she made herself say, her face furiously heating, "I—I love you, Joarr. And I hope you"—she swallowed hard—"I hope you have a most productive meeting?"

He still hadn't moved, hadn't even blinked, and Gwyn's cheeks felt hot enough to be painful, her eyes wide and chagrined on his. And maybe this had been more of her infinite stupidity, maybe she should just turn around and climb down this tree, before the humiliation swallowed her alive—

But then Joarr dragged her close, and pressed a hard, bruising kiss to her mouth. His teeth scraping, his tongue twining deep, his claws digging into her back. And Gwyn sagged into it, melted into it, clutching her hands in his hair, drinking up his hunger, his strength, his... *affection*.

When he finally pulled back again, his cheeks were flushed, his eyes glittering, his trousers visibly tented. "After, witch," he murmured, as he reached a hand, and scraped its claws purposefully against her neck. "Make you screech and wail for me, ach?"

Oh. Well. Gwyn's full-body shiver was surely visible, her face still hot and flustered—but that was just what he'd wanted, the bastard, as he shot her a teasing, genuine grin, and then leapt down out of the tree. Leaving her standing there alone, breathing hard, her determination swirling even louder than before.

She would face this. Fix this. Fight for her future. Find her own way.

So she climbed down to the ground, and met the Bautul orcs with staunch cheerfulness, and set them to work on their current projects. Eyolf and Iyolf with the new orcs on the goddess' tree—they were in the process of carefully cutting off the dead limbs—and Kalfr on more of Gwyn's own plants, placing them in the best possible locations around the clearing's edges.

"Oh, and have you seen Stella today?" Gwyn asked Kalfr, as she finished smoothing earth around her newly replanted fennel, and then brushed off her hands. "Do you know if she's stopping by?"

Gwyn had been coming to rely on Stella's kind, calming presence each morning—her friendship had been a true gift, and a true help as well. And of all the Bautul orcs, Kalfr had generally seemed the most aware of Stella's mood and whereabouts, perhaps on Silfast's orders—though, from what Gwyn had seen so far, it rather seemed that Silfast disliked Kalfr almost as much as he disliked Joarr.

"Ach, I smell her now," Kalfr said now, his voice low, his dark eyes angling toward the mountain. "But I know Silfast is yet enraged over how Joarr defeated him in the pit yesterday, and thus did not wish Stella to come here."

Right. Gwyn swallowed down her waiting reply—her opinions on Silfast had certainly not improved these past days—and thanked Kalfr before heading off to meet Stella at the door. Stella was indeed looking rather morose, her shoulders hunched—but she visibly straightened as she caught sight of Gwyn, and gave her a wan smile.

"Sorry I'm late, Gwyn," she said. "Just one of those mornings, you know?"

Gwyn roundly dismissed the apology, and then accompanied Stella to the cool shade of the hut, and pulled over the stools Joarr had scrounged up from somewhere. And as had become their regular habit, they reviewed the day's list of herbs together, and made plans for their preparation and delivery. Peppermint for Hannah's nausea, motherwort to send off to Inga, heavily diluted henbane for several injured orcs' sleep, more chamomile for Tengil's teething.

Stella had shown a genuine aptitude for it all—not only in remembering various herbs' names and uses, but also their preparations, dosages, and possible side effects. She also seemed to truly enjoy the work, and despite her chronic-seeming fatigue, she hadn't once complained, or failed to finish a task.

But today, she was looking almost alarmingly pale, and her trembling hands suddenly slipped on the mortar and pestle, scattering ground henbane across the floor. And though Gwyn

swiftly rescued them—and most of the henbane as well—
Stella's hands were still trembling, her eyes rapidly blinking.
As if she were about to begin *weeping*, over a few dropped
herbs?

"Hey, it's all right," Gwyn said, her voice soft. "No harm
done. Maybe you'd like to take a break? Go watch the orcs work
for a while, or go back inside?"

"No, I'm fine," Stella replied, unexpectedly sharp. "I only
need a moment. I am *not*"—she dragged in a thick breath—
"ready to go back in there yet."

Oh. It was perhaps the first negative comment Gwyn had
ever heard Stella speak, and after an instant's considering that,
she intently returned her attention to the mugwort she was
chopping. "It's so dark in the mountain, isn't it?" she said, as
lightly as she could. "It really bothered me at first, but it's
gotten a lot better with time. Starting to feel more like a cozy
den, instead of being trapped in a crypt."

She attempted a quick grin toward Stella as she spoke—
and then froze in place, her smile instantly fading. Because
Stella's hunched shoulders were shuddering, her dark head
still buried in her hands—and suddenly she was sobbing, the
painful sounds tearing from her throat.

"But it *is* like being trapped," Stella gasped. "Like it's never
going to end. Like this baby is trying to *destroy* me."

Something twisted in Gwyn's belly, and she choked back
the almost overwhelming urge to demand more details about
Stella's symptoms, or suggest possible solutions. Because she
still wasn't Stella's midwife, and Stella hadn't once shown any
interest in changing that, either. And while Gwyn strongly
suspected that was entirely Silfast's doing, she'd made a
concerted effort to respect that boundary, and give it a generous
berth. To be a friend, and only a friend.

But Stella was gulping for breaths now, her hands clutching
against her face. "We used to be so *happy*," she choked. "Before.

When I felt like myself. When I didn't know how much Silfast wanted a son. When I thought he actually wanted *me*."

Gwyn winced and shook her head, about to point out that surely Silfast wanted Stella—but again swallowed down the words. Because she *had* seen Silfast and Stella together around the mountain multiple times now, and despite the orcs' ongoing freedom regarding such things, she hadn't yet witnessed any actual intimacy between them. Had she?

"I'm so sorry, Stella," Gwyn said finally, helplessly, and she felt her hand reaching out, rubbing against Stella's shoulder. "And I'm sorry if this is overstepping, but I know from experience that pregnancy can be so, so hard—not only on women, but on their relationships, too. It's *so* common, but no one ever wants to talk about it. Fearing that they'll call down the gods' wrath upon their pregnancy, or their child's life, or some other such *bollocks*."

It came out far more scathing than she'd meant—her patience for such superstitions remained very thin, especially when they affected women's health—and Stella gulped another sob, her head twitching back and forth. "But what if the goddess *does* see how I feel," she gasped. "What if she's decided I'm too weak? And not worthy? Of Silfast, or the Bautul?"

Gwyn bit back the curse that was bubbling in her throat, and kept rubbing Stella's shoulder. "Not a chance," she said, as firmly as she could. "You told me yourself that the goddess wants the best for her Bautul followers, right? And Ivar believes that too, and he's the wisest person I know. Which means that you certainly wouldn't be punished for suffering, or seeking help, or being honest about the difficulties you're facing. The goddess would want you to be healthy, and safe, and *content*."

Stella didn't protest, but didn't raise her head, either. And too late, Gwyn realized she was probably on shaky ground speaking so authoritatively of the goddess, whom she'd only just begun to know—so she pulled in another breath, and searched for something else. Something not a midwife would say, but a friend. A friend who'd also been trapped and frightened. A friend who understood.

"You know," she said slowly, "have you ever thought that perhaps a change of scenery might help? My house in Varrahan is still empty—for another week or so, at least—and it's not a long journey. You'd be welcome to spend some time there—and Silfast too, if you like? It's bright, and clean, and the garden is walled in, and would offer you a chance to continue getting some activity, too."

Stella didn't reply, but she hadn't refused, either, and Gwyn kept talking, feeling the idea take shape in her thoughts. "The house likely won't be mine after next week anyway," she said flatly, "so someone might as well use it until then. Perhaps you could even take a look through my plants, and see if there's anything Joarr's scouts have missed bringing here?"

Stella's face had actually turned toward Gwyn at that, her wet eyes wide with surprise. "But—it's *your* house," she said, her voice thick. "Surely you'll want to go look it over yourself? Especially if you're planning to—to sell it?"

Her forehead had briefly furrowed, and Gwyn felt herself grimace, her mouth twisting. She hadn't yet told Stella about Roy and his horrible threats, and she wasn't sure she could bear to, either. Great-Aunt Agnes had left that house to her, for her midwifery practice, her new home. And as much as Gwyn had chosen her new path here, it still hurt to think of her cozy little house burned, or sold, or lost, forever.

And clearly Stella had followed at least some of that, because she shook her head again, burying her face back in her hands. "It's a lovely offer, Gwyn," she gulped, "but I couldn't. And even if I could, it's surely not safe. Not with all these men crawling over the forest, seeking to capture us. To— to *destroy* us. That law is coming in three days, and there's *nothing* we can do about it. Nothing the orcs can do. Even Silfast, he—"

Her voice frayed as she spoke, breaking into more harsh, gasping sobs. And Gwyn's useless, helpless brain couldn't seem to produce any kind of reply—at least, nothing beyond herbs, sedatives, some attempt at an easy fix. But this surely wasn't an easy fix, Stella wasn't a client, she was a *friend*, she was terrified, she was *suffering*—and suddenly Gwyn just wanted to start sobbing, too.

"I'm so sorry, Stella," she whispered, her hand almost frantically stroking at her shoulder. "I'm so, so sorry. I wish I could help. Wish I could make it end. Take this all away for you."

And at that awful, perfect moment—with those incriminating words coming out of Gwyn's mouth—something new rushed into the hut. Something huge and deadly and growling, looming tall and terrifying over them, and nearly spitting with rage.

Silfast.

"How dare you, woman!" he barked down at Gwyn, his eyes alight with black fury. "I *knew* you meant no good for my mate, or my son. But this is beyond all reason! Beyond *forbearance*! You threaten to *kill* our *son*?!"

What? The urge to cringe backwards, to cower, was almost overpowering—but Gwyn's sheer indignation held her in place on her stool, her eyes blinking up at Silfast's outraged face. "I threatened no such thing," she snapped back. "I was only seeking to—"

To comfort her, she was about to say, but good gods, that would surely betray Stella's confidence, wouldn't it? Or perhaps even put her at risk, from this huge enraged orc? And behind Silfast, Stella was indeed looking deeply horrified, her hands clasped over her mouth, her head shaking back and forth— and Gwyn clamped her own mouth shut, and searched for something, *anything* to say, to help...

"I would never suggest termination at this stage," she gritted out, finally, around her shallow breaths. "Unless the situation was dire. It's far too dangerous for the mother."

But surely that was the wrong, *wrong* thing to say, because Silfast's deep, vicious bark seemed to shake the hut around them. "And what of the danger to our son!" he hollered at her. "How dare you speak of such foul deeds before him, and thus tempt the goddess' judgement!"

And wait, *wait*, this orc was actually *espousing* this nonsense, in front of his pregnant mate, who was already miserable?! And Gwyn could have *thrown* something at the bastard, and she abruptly leapt off the stool, away from his rage, his appalling *stupidity*.

"Your son doesn't care about a damned thing we say, and neither does your goddess," she snarled back at him. "And the only person tempting judgement here is *you*, because I'm feeling an *extremely* strong urge to spike your next drink with henbane, so maybe you'll finally be obliged to smarten the hell up, and shut your damned foolish mouth!"

Silfast's answering growl was truly terrifying, his huge body advancing toward her, his claws and teeth bared—when somehow, out of nowhere, there was *Joarr*.

And Gwyn hadn't even seen him come in—how had he come in?—but she had perhaps never been so relieved to see him, or to feel the close, coiled stillness of his tall body against hers. Or, even, to see that cool mask slipped over his eyes, that chilly, deadly smile curling across his lips.

"You touch her, fool," he said to Silfast, his voice clipped, "and I kill you where you stand."

27

For an instant, Gwyn was certain there would be another battle. More blood, more agony, tainting this precious garden, defiling it, while she and Stella helplessly watched.

"No," Gwyn gasped, and whether it was to Joarr, or Silfast, she didn't know. "Not here. Not now. *Please.*"

But her frantic eyes weren't looking at either orc—but rather, at Stella. Stella, whose tear-streaked cheeks had gone even paler than before, her eyes turned to wide, dark hollows in her suddenly gaunt-looking face.

And perhaps Silfast had finally remembered Stella too, his furious gaze darting back toward her—and Gwyn could see his big body stilling, his shoulders sagging. His clawed hand reaching out, as if to touch her rounded belly—but Stella flinched away, and Gwyn saw Silfast's hand jerk back too, as if he'd been stung.

"Ach, we settle this later, *Seer,*" he hissed over his shoulder toward Joarr, his voice heavy with contempt, his eyes again flashing with dark, miserable rage. "And this time, you shall crawl and weep at my feet, begging for my mercy!"

Joarr's laugh was loud and harsh, scraping through the too-small space. "You again waste your breath, fool," he hissed. "You dishonour this garden, and forget your sacred vows to your mate. Now go, before I *shout* your grave folly to our goddess!"

And to Gwyn's genuine astonishment, Silfast actually betrayed a faint but unmistakable wince, his eyes guiltily glancing back toward Stella. Stella, who still hadn't spoken a single word, and who still looked... sick. Worn. Empty.

"Come, woman," Silfast said now, his voice rough, his hand again reaching toward her. "You ought to further rest. After we go again to Efterar, ach?"

Stella's eyes had dropped to the floor, but she gave a small, short nod. And she hadn't flinched away, either, and Silfast steered her out the door, casting one last dark, furious look over his shoulder toward Joarr and Gwyn.

"And you shall *never* come to this garden again," he said to Stella, his voice hard, authoritative, *final*. "This is no more safe for you, or our son. Ach?"

And Stella, walking away with her head bowed, once again—*nodded*. And didn't even look back, or say goodbye, and Gwyn felt her own eyes prickling as she watched, her hands clutching to fists at her sides. Her gaze abruptly seeking downwards, finding the knife on the workbench, so close, relief, please—

But once again, Joarr almost seemed to read the thought aloud. His tall body easing swift and certain before her, his clawed fingers closing around her wrist. "No," he said. "Find other way."

But suddenly Gwyn just wanted to scream, to curse herself, to weep. She'd made all that so much worse, she'd driven her miserable friend away from the one thing that had clearly comforted her. Gods, she'd shouted that she'd wanted to *poison* her friend's partner—

"No your fault," Joarr's terse voice cut in, his hand catching on her chin, tilting it up to make her look at him. "I tell you, Silfast is a fool. No even ask his own mate to *speak*, in this."

Gwyn wasn't about to argue, but the urgency kept clawing, craving an outlet, an escape, anything—and Joarr's eyes on her were watchful, glittering, unrelenting. "Wish to work?" he asked, voice low. "Take herbs to women? Or study?"

It was what Gwyn would have usually done at this point in the day—making her rounds, meeting with her clients, delivering the day's herbs, then reading in the Ka-esh library with Rosa—but even the thought of smiling, speaking, thinking through this mess was impossible, abhorrent, she—

"Then visit Ivar?" Joarr continued, clipped. "Ask his wisdom? Or ask him what Great-Aunt say?"

And yes, Gwyn would usually have done that, perhaps with Joarr, but some days on her own, too. Just enjoying his cheerful, surprisingly astute company, and laughing at his often-ribald jokes, and seeking his advice and guidance. But Gwyn didn't want to end up gossiping about Stella, either, didn't want to betray anything, didn't want to think about it for another damned instant—

"Then I ken," Joarr said finally, "what help. Come?"

Gwyn numbly nodded, and allowed Joarr to guide her out of the hut, and back toward the mountain. His voice calling something over his shoulder toward Kalfr in black-tongue—wait, he was actually leaving the orcs *alone* here?—as they stepped into the mountain's close, quiet darkness.

Joarr hadn't brought a lamp this time, but even as Gwyn's brain kept churning, she instinctively settled closer into his familiar touch, following the silent signals she'd somehow learned these past weeks. Left, then right, then left again. Into the Skai wing, surely, and then more twists and turns, the floor tilting steadily downwards. And when they finally stopped,

Gwyn could actually hear Joarr's breath, could feel his chest rising and falling against her.

"This is," he said, strangely stilted, "my—other garden. My other—home."

His... *what*? The words, and the way he'd said them, seemed to slice through Gwyn's frantic thoughts, catching her own breath, stilling it in her throat. Because clearly this—this *garden*?—meant something to him. Something important.

So she swallowed, and nodded, and attempted a smile toward where she knew his face to be—and when he again nudged her forward, she willingly went. Into his... garden. His garden of...

Mushrooms.

Gwyn felt struck to the floor, her hands clamped over her suddenly hammering heart, her eyes gaping wide at the sight all around her. Because, yes, yes, it was a room full of mushrooms, and it was—

Spectacular. Glorious. A *marvel.*

There were mushrooms clustered on the ground. Mushrooms climbing up the walls. Mushrooms growing out of large logs and branches, mushrooms tucked under little cliffs and stones, mushrooms even growing out of *other* mushrooms. Too many varieties for Gwyn to even name, but she saw the distinctive orange stalks of stinkhorn, the intricate clusters of pearl oysters, the flowing white tendrils of lion's-mane—and even a rare, deadly *webcap,* close enough that she could reach over and touch it.

Impossible. *Impossible.*

And even more impossible was the fact that Gwyn could... *see* them, even without a lamp. Because of the honey-mushrooms, which were glowing at regular intervals throughout the room. Almost as if they'd been purposefully planted like this, ensuring the room's full illumination with their pale, blue-green light.

Gwyn truly couldn't stop staring, couldn't remember how to speak. Couldn't do anything but stand there, and feel her heart fighting to break free from her chest.

"You... like?" came Joarr's voice from beside her, quiet, unusually tentative—and when Gwyn finally managed to drag her eyes back to his face, it occurred to her that he looked... uncertain? Uneasy?

She blinked, coughed, gulped desperately for air—and then heard herself bark a laugh, bright and shrill, echoing in the small, wonderful room. "I *like*?!" she croaked at him. "Good gods, Joarr. It's impossible. It's *magnificent*. How"—she had to gulp for more air, flapping her hands in front of her face—"*how* long have you been doing this? How have you managed it without any sun? And how many varieties do you even *have* in here?!"

Joarr's mouth had twitched up, and something shifted in his eyes, glittering in the greenish light. "I make this since I first come to this mountain as an orcling," he said. "And mayhap I... show you, should you wish?"

He sounded tentative again, almost *shy*—but Gwyn couldn't fathom why, and she was nearly bouncing on her feet, her hands gripping tight to his arm. "Yes," she breathed. "Gods, yes. You utter devious *fiend*. Show me *everything*."

Joarr huffed a husky, strange-sounding laugh, but he nodded, and again guided her forward, along a narrow, winding stone path. And then he began to speak, to *explain*, his voice still unusually thick. Telling her how he'd explored the entire mountain when he'd first come here—and how he'd run across this room with a few mushrooms growing in it. How he'd then discovered—he leapt up at the wall as he spoke, clinging to a little ledge with his fingers—this crack in the wall, which led to a tunnel, which led up to the surface. Which, thanks to some luckily-placed light-coloured stones, had reflected bits of sunlight into the room, just enough for the mushrooms to grow.

And then, how he'd worked to propagate the mushrooms that were already there. How he'd next sought out new varieties in the forest, and worked to propagate those, too. And how it had kept growing, and he'd kept working away at it, adding bits here and there over the years, until... this.

And *this*, it turned out, included not only this room, but a second room deeper below, also illuminated with the honey-mushrooms' greenish light. And this room felt far larger than the one above, sprawling wide beneath the earth, and it was chock-full of massive posts and boulders, and rough-cut stone pillars that rose from the floor to the high ceiling above.

"Up is for growing," Joarr told Gwyn, his eyes sparkling as they flicked toward the ceiling. "But down is for playing, ach?"

With that, he crouched and leapt into the air, landing lightly atop a nearby boulder—and with another flying leap, he soared over to another one, an astonishing distance away. And as Gwyn again stared, her mouth agape, he darted all the way to the opposite wall, without once touching the floor—and then spun around, and made his way back. But this time, he hurled himself at the tall, jagged stone pillars, clinging and climbing with his claws and his legs as he flew from one, to the next, to the next.

When he landed back beside Gwyn again, he'd barely broken a sweat. And once she'd croaked some kind of weak, ineffectual response, he grinned down toward her, flashing her all his sharp teeth. "Wish to try?" he asked. "Come. Hold me."

There was no refusing an offer like that, and Gwyn eagerly climbed onto his back, and held on tight. And then, as she peered over his shoulder, he did it all over again. His fluid powerful body crouching and leaping beneath her, his laughter ringing through the room.

It was pure, whirling exhilaration, swooping through

Gwyn's belly, thrumming in her hands and feet. And when Joarr finally put her down, and next coolly informed her that she had to try to find him, she instantly raced after him from boulder to post to boulder, doing her damnedest to catch the sneaky bastard, while he taunted her from a distance, and even threw mushrooms at her with infuriating and hilarious accuracy.

He finally stopped when Gwyn was laughing so hard she couldn't breathe, her hands on her knees, the tears streaming down her face. And when Joarr swaggered back toward her, all twinkling taunting insolence, she couldn't seem to stop drinking up the sight of him, her heart furiously swerving in her still-wheezing chest.

"You are a menace," she gasped at him, as she snatched up one of the nearby mushrooms he'd thrown at her, and hurled it back toward his face. "And a dirty rotten *scoundrel.*"

He easily caught the mushroom with a quick flick of his fingers, and then tossed it up into his mouth. "Ach," he said, as his teeth snapped down, followed by a single gulp in his throat. "You like. Wish for more."

And yes, good gods, she did. Even if he was tormenting her with it, she still couldn't stop staring at him, smiling at him, needing him closer, here, under her hands. And as usual, he somehow just knew, closing that last space between them, and again snatching her bodily up into his arms.

"Wish for me," he murmured, his voice low in her ear, as he strode back toward the far side of the room. "For *me.* Ach?"

Gwyn rapidly nodded, circling her arms tighter around him, inhaling the scent of his neck. So caught in its rich, lovely sweetness that she scarcely noticed where he was taking her— at least, until he deposited her on something soft, and flat, and... familiar?

Gwyn blinked hazily around her, rubbing her hands at the softness—the furs—beneath her. They were surrounded by a ring of tall, looming boulders, almost as though this were a little room within the room—and here, in the middle of the boulders, was this large, flat stone, perhaps waist-height, covered all over with furs...

"Joarr," Gwyn said, her voice strangled, even as he put his knee to the furs, nudging her own knees apart. "*Why* do you have another Bautul altar in your secret shroom-room?!"

Joarr stilled, brief but unmistakable—and then leaned back to frown mightily toward her, his forehead furrowed. "This is no *altar*," he countered. "This is bed. *My* bed. *I* make this. For *me*."

But he surely hadn't made the ring of boulders around them, that was clear, let alone this stone itself. Without question a highly similar size and shape as the others, and Gwyn could see Joarr's eyes looking at it too, and then narrowing back at her face.

"Canny witch," he muttered, under his breath, dragging a hand through his hair—and then he gripped her chin, gave her head a little shake. "You *never* speak to Bautul of this. No Stella, no Kalfr—most of all no Silfast. *My* garden. *My* bed. *Our* secret. Ach?"

A shiver of warmth trilled up Gwyn's spine, and she felt herself smile back at him, slow, affectionate. "Of course," she said. "I'm honoured that you shared such a delightful secret mushroom-room with me."

But there—wait, there—was something, in his eyes. A twitch, oh so brief, of his mask. His... *hiding* something.

Gwyn's breath stuttered in her chest, and she searched those eyes, searched beyond the mask—and somehow found truth. Heavy, cold, dragging up darkness she'd desperately wanted to keep deep below...

"Oh, so it's *not* a secret room, then," she heard herself say, her voice damnably uneven. "You just—kept it secret from *me*."

Joarr's eyes closed, brief but thoroughly betraying, and

Gwyn fought to ignore the sudden, awful plunge in her belly, the rapid-fire beat of her heart. The clear, devastating realization that he *still* didn't trust her, not even after all she'd done, all she'd sought to prove to him. She'd helped him, she'd understood him, she was even pregnant with his child. She'd committed to a life here. To him. And maybe this meant—maybe—

"No, woman," Joarr's voice cut in, fervent and low. "I only—wished to be sure. Of you. Of *us*."

Us. His eyes were glittering on hers, hard, bright, even as his hand reflexively reached up, stroked that tooth around his neck. "Wished to be sure," he whispered, "of all I saw. How you no curse me. No betray me. You... *love* me. You are mine. *Always*."

Oh. Gwyn's heart was still thundering, her throat swallowing, her eyes fixed on his face. On what he was admitting, what he was confessing.

And most of all, on *his. Always*.

And gods, it was so close, waiting here on her tongue. *Yours? As your mate? Always?*

But the words wouldn't seem to come, not yet, not yet—he'd still hidden this from her, concealed the truth, *again*—and after another instant's choked silence, Joarr reached down, and plucked something up from beside the altar. Two little brown mushrooms, looking deceptively innocuous, with their thin white stems and peaked caps. But Gwyn had seen these before, had *prescribed* these before, when she'd been able to acquire them—and they were excessively rare, and deeply valuable, and extremely powerful.

Joarr silently handed the smaller of the two toward her, brows raised, and Gwyn swallowed as she spun it in her fingers, inhaled its distinctive, unpleasant scent. "Um," she said, "you know, for a woman in my situation, I wouldn't generally recommend—"

But Joarr had already bitten off half of his mushroom with a sharp snap of teeth, and shook his head as he tossed the rest into his mouth. "Mayhap with human son," he said firmly. "But you ken there is *naught* human can eat to harm orc-son, ach? Even when human *wishes* for this."

It was an excellent and very valid point, and even moreso when Joarr gave her a slow, wicked smile, and leaned in to nibble at her neck. "And this is only tiny one," he murmured. "Just enough to grant you more fun, ach?"

And Gwyn's breath was half-laugh, half-groan, the heat already coiling in her belly. And she should have still been focusing on that secret, on how he'd hidden something so important, how he still didn't trust her, after all she'd done— but it was so much easier to pop the little mushroom into her mouth, and swallow it back. To meet the eyes of her orc, her lover, she would fix this, she would...

"Wise woman," he purred, his voice dark and dangerous, his eyes alight on hers. "And now, we mate."

28

Now, we mate.

They were the same words he'd spoken to her their very first time, heavy with hunger, with promise—but this time, it felt as though there was even more weight to them, more meaning. *We mate.*

We *mate.*

And as he crawled toward her on the altar, nudging her down onto her back beneath him, Gwyn's body was already shivering, her head nodding, her eyes desperately searching his face. Finding the intensity in his gaze, the shimmering heat, the bare, beautiful hunger.

His hand was moving efficiently between them, shoving down his trousers, yanking off Gwyn's dress—and then, oh gods, he was already there. That smooth, slippery head of him finding her quivering heat, parting her around it, feeling her pulse and pant against him...

His slam inside was sudden, brutal, *wonderful*, and Gwyn cried out as she arched up, as he ground himself deep within her. Holding her eyes as he did it, watching her, weighing her—

and then dragging out, slow, intent, before driving back in again.

The feeling was so familiar now, the furious fluid rhythm, the pulsing, primal power. And as he picked up speed, plunging into her again and again, Gwyn somehow felt the strength of it coiling, sharpening, swirling even more vivid than before. Speaking, without a single word, of how he needed it like this, craved it like this—the power, the control, the certainty. The *safety*.

And Gwyn saw him, understood him, *loved* him—and so she met him, welcomed him, drew him harder and faster with her own gasps and groans and pleas. With her hungry, writhing body meeting his every slam forward, her hands and feet tingling, the room slightly stuttering behind the strength of his watching, glittering eyes.

"Yes," she gasped at him, clawing at him, wrenching him closer. "More, Joarr. *Everything*."

His eyes fluttered, gone briefly distant, his gasp choking from his throat—and oh, oh, it was here already, that thick molten heat of him, pumping out deep inside her. Filling her full of his truth, his vulnerability, perhaps even his *weakness*—and even as Gwyn moaned, twitched, revelled in the feel of its slick warmth within her, she knew it wouldn't be enough, not for him now, not like this.

And when he drew back, his eyes still blazing, the room now slowly spinning behind him, Gwyn felt her shivery finger reach up to touch his face, tracing down the sharp smooth lines of it. Her orc. So distant, so lonely, for so long, so carefully hidden beneath...

"More," she whispered, her tongue slipping out, brushing at her lips. "Tend me. Please."

He groaned close in her ear, nipping it with his teeth—and Gwyn shivered all over as she yanked him upwards, hard and purposeful. And with another deep groan, a quick little flick of his graceful limbs, Joarr was kneeling up over her, his legs straddling her chest, his slippery length bobbing over her mouth, dripping a long string of thick white from the tip.

Gwyn opened her mouth to catch that dangling white, to feel its sweetness spark on her tongue. To hear the heat of his growl as his hand wrapped around his swollen strength, and then pumped up, milking out more, drizzling it down between her waiting, parted lips.

Gwyn eagerly drank it, swallowed it, the glorious taste of him sweeping into something almost like colour, like bright light sparkling over her skin. Into the strange, surreal ecstasy of her powerful orc pinning her to an altar, feeding her the very essence of him, easing that dripping slit ever closer…

She licked for it as it came, kissed it, sank her tongue deep into that oozing, bubbling source of him. And when he kept driving forward, bearing down deeper, she could have sobbed her relief, her *greed*. Revelling in the reality of an insolent orc impaling her by the mouth to an altar, pulsing his bounty straight down her open, gulping throat.

Above her, his eyes were fluttering, his head tilted back— and it was like he was radiating that heat and hunger and loneliness, or perhaps even… *fear*. And Gwyn couldn't follow it, couldn't bear it, and she felt her fingers skittering up to find his gasping chest, to offer some small comfort, stroke it all away…

But his hands were far too quick, catching her wrists, his eyes flashing—and in an instant, he had both her arms pinned to the altar over her head, his body now leaning over her, his heft still jutted deep into her mouth.

"Witch," he growled at her, as he ground a little deeper, gods, yes—and then slowly drew himself out again, away. Lingering at Gwyn's lips, letting the thick white smear against them, watching her kiss and suckle him, as that reckless hunger again shot up sharp between them—

Gwyn fully expected his slam downward, welcomed it,

needed it—but she didn't expect the frustration of his growl as it came, the low streak of curses in black-tongue. Or how he yanked himself out again, all the way, his body twitching back onto his heels between her knees, his clawed hands rubbing against his face.

It was like Gwyn was being pulled up too, like he had her on a string—and she crouched between his legs, stroked her trembling fingers up his hard thigh. "Not good?" she whispered, her voice sounding utterly foreign in her ears. "Not enough?"

His laugh wasn't a laugh at all, and his hand slid down to his still-leaking slit, catching a bulging bead of white—and then he brought it up, slipped it between her parted, swollen lips. "Always good," he breathed, as he watched her suck and gorge on it, his eyes swallowed in darkness. "Always this spell upon me, ach? Make me forget duty. Even forget *fun*."

Oh. Gwyn's swirling, scattering thoughts couldn't seem to settle, couldn't stop searching those eyes. Those secrets. Her *spell*, he'd said, and he'd said that before, too, hadn't he? After that first time on the Bautul altar, he'd called himself bewitched, *ensnared*...

He abruptly twitched all over, shaking his head, as if to thrust the thought away—and when he met her gaze again, he was smiling, though the darkness seemed to linger in his eyes. "For you are hungry witch," he said lightly, in a voice that sounded more like his. "*Greedy* witch. Wish me again inside you, ach?"

Gwyn fervently nodded, following his pinecone wherever he wanted, supporting him, adoring him—and in a sudden, shocking swath of movement, he flipped her over on her knees, shoving her thighs wide apart. And then he slammed himself back inside her, with a rising, curdling howl that nearly drowned out her own.

The room was fully dipping and swirling now, the colours

of their craving and longing streaming before Gwyn's eyes. Joarr's hand curling tight in her hair, yanking her head back as he rammed in again and again, driving her, spurring her, *fighting* her. And then halting, howling more agony as he again emptied himself inside, the surges of hot liquid flooding her even fuller than before—

But even as he slightly softened, he didn't stop. Kept grinding, circling, prodding, his claws now dragging down Gwyn's shuddering back, until he'd fully swollen again. And then he did it all over again, and then again. Pushing her, filling her, growling his frustration over her while Gwyn gasped and shook and welcomed it, pleaded for more, more, more, while his red flashed in her vision, his pain become her own...

And when he finally yanked out, his breaths audibly straining, Gwyn could have shouted at him, begged at him, wept— but instead she only held herself still on her trembling hands, waiting, feeling his thick hot bounty pulse and spurt from within her. Pooling from her used, inflamed, stretched-open heat, streaking down her spread thighs, pouring onto the altar below.

And was Joarr watching, or had he even noticed, because that shuddering, swelling hardness was now... sliding up. Searching for—for *there*, for the one part of her he hadn't yet taken, not today, not ever. And Gwyn was already shivering, nodding, spreading herself wider, needing him inside, needing to show him...

He moaned as he nudged it open, as that slick searching head carefully breached her—and then slowly, surely impaled her. Plunging her full and deep and utterly glorious, conquering her very innards with his swelling, shuddering strength. Holding her there, locked and trapped, full of his seed and his son, whole, safe.

And as he steadily drew out, and then pushed back inside, it was like the colours juddered, and then shattered apart. The red shimmering into white and yellow and purple, into Joarr's body sagging down over hers, covering hers, driving it into the altar. His hand yanking her hair hard and powerful, pain flickering and tickling as her head jerked sideways, exposing her neck toward him. As she felt—his *teeth*.

And as much as he'd often teased her with his teeth these past weeks, taunted her with the promise of their danger, he'd never once followed through on those threats. Not wanting her to need it, her distant thoughts pointed out, or misuse it—because oh, it felt so good, their sharpness scraping close, his breath inhaling deep—

The pain flashed hard and bright as his teeth sank down, firing red back into the rest of the colours streaming before Gwyn's eyes. But it was beautiful, it was perfection, it was utter, sheer relief. And she nearly sobbed with wonder as his hips again drove down, his mouth sealing tighter against her skin, his hard swallows gulping in perfect time with every plunge of his furious strength within her.

It was beyond thought, beyond reality, it was like galloping high into the starlit sky beneath the driving fervour of her beautiful, raging rider. Like all of the colour, all the power all the anger all the ecstasy was streaming into her at once, her orc desperately gulping her lifeblood even as he sought to bury himself ever deeper within her, to flood her with his truth and his weakness and his life, to fill her so full of him she would burst—

And then she did. The light and the rapture pouring out of her like a sun, flaring wide in the bright orange scream, in the pulsing, devastating surges of agony, ecstasy, *divinity*. Of all the world's rages and miseries rushing away, leaving only light and beauty behind, and a clarity that shone so strong it rang aloud, resonating in Gwyn's ears, in the very core of her impaled, flooded-full soul.

She was here. She was his. She was... *herself*.

And then Joarr poured her full one more time, his growl against her neck so deep it seemed to thunder within her already-bursting body. And Gwyn was both sobbing and laughing as she welcomed it, became it, *adored* it.

She could feel his breaths heaving against her, his mouth slowly releasing its hold on her throat, his tongue briefly skittering against the wounds he'd made. And then he shifted behind her, as if to pull away—but they were somehow still clamped together, as if Gwyn couldn't bear to let go.

It meant she was up on her knees again, on all fours on the altar, as Joarr's hands finally held her still, and drew himself out. And as the hot molten proof of what they'd done again poured out from inside her, streaming and spurting from both gaping-open places this time, anointing the altar beneath her, while her silent, watching orc bore witness.

And then, all at once, quiet. A hushed, soundless stillness, broken by not even a breath. Until Gwyn somehow remembered she could move—*herself*—and slowly shifted around, and met Joarr's eyes.

And he looked—*shocking*. His hair all on end, his mouth streaked with red, his face both flushed and deathly pale. And his eyes, his eyes were empty black hollows, drowned alive by his hunger, his misery, his... *guilt*?

And here, still swimming in the glory, the euphoria, Gwyn couldn't bear to see him like this—and before she'd even realized it, she was tucked close against him, circling her arms around his waist. "Hey," she murmured, soft. "It was fun. Right?"

He didn't reply, but his hand stroked up and down her sticky back, and she felt what might have been his face, pressing against the top of her head. And his body was still twitching, perhaps with aftershocks, and Gwyn clutched him tighter, felt him slightly settle beneath her touch.

"You no," he said finally, his voice so hoarse, "feel pain, from this?"

He'd leaned back as he spoke, not meeting her eyes—because his gaze was intent on her neck. On where—Gwyn's shaky hand lifted to touch it—it did still sting a little, but not nearly as much as she might have expected, or perhaps even wanted.

"No," she whispered back, smiling ruefully up at his face. "It was *wonderful*, Joarr."

But he didn't smile back. Didn't meet her eyes. And as Gwyn blinked at him, she realized that this was his mask. His gaze so still, so empty—and her thoughts had flashed, sudden but certain, back to their first night together. How he'd looked exactly like this. How she'd pushed at it, seen through it—and then ordered him to leave, and never come back.

But this time... this time she couldn't even bear to follow it. To call it out, to learn where it led. To allow that low, bubbling whisper to finally surface, to breach her, to ruin everything. No. Not yet. Not after this. *No.*

So she didn't try to meet his eyes, and instead nudged him back down on the altar, away from the mess. And thankfully he didn't argue, exhaling as he settled against it, and then dragged Gwyn close. One arm strong and rigid around her back, the other resting so casually—too casually—against her still-flat waist.

He didn't speak again, and neither did she. But she was still herself, and he was still here, hers, in this moment. Still the father of her son. Still maybe—maybe—her mate.

And that had to be enough, had to be, for now. So Gwyn finally took a long, shuddering breath, closed her prickling eyes, and sank into a dark, dreamless sleep.

29

Gwyn snapped awake to a twitch, a curse, a choke of inhaled breath beneath her.

She blinked her bleary eyes open, and found herself still sprawled on the fur-covered altar, still entirely unclothed. While Joarr—who must have still been lying down with her—was sitting up, cursing under his breath, and rubbing at his face.

Gwyn's heart was suddenly hammering, and she swiftly sat up too, reached a hand to touch Joarr's back—but he actually flinched away from her, his shoulders hunching. Firing a sharp, shivering ache deep into her belly, and she felt herself gulp for breath, her arms curling around her cold-feeling body.

"What is it?" she whispered at his back. "What's happened?"

Joarr's shoulders rose and fell, his clawed hands dragging through his hair. "It is—" he began, and then inhaled again, exhaled. "Stella. She is gone. *Run.*"

What? *Stella?* Was... gone? Run?!

And no, no, that was ridiculous, this was ridiculous. First of all that Joarr was even saying this, that he seemed genuinely upset about this, when he surely had no way of even knowing such a thing. Not with them ensconced down here alone all night, and, and...

And Gwyn swallowed hard as she stared at Joarr's back, her heart now thundering against her ribs. As all those hidden thoughts, those hints and suspicions, churned ever closer, higher, stronger...

"Where?" she asked, her voice a croak. "Is Stella safe?"

Joarr flinched again, and he abruptly leapt off the altar, his movements jerky, uncontrolled. "I no ken," he said, as he yanked up his trousers, his back still turned toward her. "Must go learn more, first. Mayhap then"—he again dragged his hands through his hair—"see more."

See more. Because down here, deep in this isolated darkness, he had... *seen* this. He'd *known.*

"You... *saw* that Stella ran away," Gwyn whispered, wincing at the sound of her own voice, because she didn't want to know, she couldn't bear to, she had to. "From down... *here*?"

Joarr still wasn't looking at her, his body so unnaturally stiff—and then he twitched a single nod, quick and curt. Saying... yes.

Yes. He had. *The Seer*, the Bautul had called him, *Silfast* had called him, with that mingled awe and envy and fear. *The Seer.*

And even as something seemed to clutch and crumple in Gwyn's chest, her thoughts screaming white agony through her skull—there was still, somehow, a dull, deadened awareness, thundering deep beneath it all.

She had... suspected. Guessed. Known.

Or, rather, she would have. If she'd ever allowed herself to think of it. To face the little, nagging questions, all the things Joarr had somehow known, without ever being told. Inga's delivery. Gwyn's fight with Silfast. Even the chasteberry gift, the men hunting him in the forest, the Bautul women come to meet with Gwyn. Gods, even the way he *fought*, like he knew his opponents' actions long before they did. Not to mention all that talk of *seeing*, not only from him, but from the captain, from Jule, Stella, Ivar, Simon...

Joarr had finally, slowly turned toward Gwyn, holding out her limp dress—and there was nothing on his face now, nothing but the mask, hiding everything. *Betraying* everything.

How he'd known. How he'd... *lied*. Because...

And suddenly Gwyn couldn't bear to take that thought further, couldn't bear to even look at him, to feel him look at her like that—and she trembled as she stumbled off the altar, and reached to snatch her dress from his hand. He'd lied about this, because...

"You wish," he said finally, his voice so hoarse, "to go to Efterar now?"

To Efterar. To that damned healer orc—with his gods-damned deadly *magic*—who Gwyn had never actually met. Because she hadn't wanted to meet him, came another dull realization, thudding into her belly. She hadn't wanted to even think of it. Of this. Of *magic*. Of what Joarr was saying, because...

"No, you utter prick," she choked at him, as she somehow yanked on her dress, and then pressed her palms to her hot, prickling eyes. "No. We need to"—she had to haul in air, dig harder into her eyes—"find Stella. Make sure she's safe."

And with that, without warning, came another shock of agony, sharp and sickening. Stella had run, perhaps alone. The woods were crawling with men, hunting women just like her. And Joarr had spoken, many days ago now, of Stella being at risk. Of, maybe, what he had *seen*.

She is no better off when she is dead.

Gods, Gwyn wanted to weep, to scream, to tear her hair out until it bled—but before her, Joarr had nodded. And then waved his shaky-looking hand beyond them, clearly saying, *Come, let's go.*

Gwyn felt herself nod too, and staggered forward so fast she would have stumbled, if not for Joarr's strong grip, clamping on her arm. But she couldn't bear to feel him touch her, couldn't even bear to see his face, and she kept her head ducked low as she bolted away, toward the stairs that led up, back into that beautiful glowing room.

But it had been just one more secret, one more thing he'd hidden from her, and Gwyn rushed through it as quickly as she could, keeping her eyes on the floor. Forcefully shoving back the memories of yesterday—yesterday!—when she'd explored and marvelled and laughed here with him. When he'd spoken as though he'd cared, as though this had been something he'd truly wanted to share with her.

Gwyn wiped a betraying tear from her cheek as she darted out into the corridor, away, away—and then snapped to a halt, squeezing her eyes shut. Because it was pitch-dark, of course, and she therefore needed this bastard to guide her, to touch her, take her wherever they needed to go. Whatever he'd... *seen.*

Thankfully he didn't speak as he settled beside her, as his painfully familiar hand nudged against her back. As he guided her swiftly through the corridors, back over toward the Bautul wing. As he briefly halted mid-step, wanting her to wait—and then disappeared and re-emerged, clearly from the Bautul trading-post, holding a flickering lamp.

It meant Gwyn had to see him again, his body tall and lean and agonizing before her, but at least he didn't need to touch her anymore. And she tightened her arms around her chest as she followed behind him, his steps long and urgent, his gaze intently ahead.

And then, finally, he turned toward a door. One of many doors in this corridor, in what Gwyn knew was still the Bautul wing. But it was a room she'd never entered before, and she felt her breath catch as she stepped inside, and blinked around at the sight.

It was a bedroom, and it was—*lovely*. It was small, with the ever-present stone walls and floor—but here, the walls were covered with patchwork quilts, and the floor was scattered with soft furs and bright, homespun rugs. There was a little table in the corner with two chairs—one noticeably larger than the other—and in the middle of the table was a bunch of bright wildflowers, only starting to wilt in their chipped vase. And on the opposite side of the room was a large, cozy-looking bed, piled high with pillows and furs, and close beside that was a small, wooden rocking *cradle*.

Gwyn's prickling eyes blinked at the cradle, which was entirely empty, but for a downy little fur lining the bottom. And while the sight shouldn't have been unusual—not in her line of work, anyway—there was still something about it that seemed to hold her there, struck still and stunned, her hand clutched to her own waist...

But beside her, Joarr had lurched forward. Striding around to the end of the bed, which was just out of view behind the cradle. But suddenly Gwyn realized there was something moving down there, something *alive*—

"Srrrr," it slurred, its voice gravelly and deep—because wait, wait, it was *Silfast*. And his huge body was sprawled on the floor at the end of the bed, his legs sliding unnaturally against the floor, his head lolling slightly to the side. As though he were... drunk? Or... *drugged*?

Gwyn rushed forward to kneel beside him, feeling for the pulse in his neck, searching the dazed emptiness of his eyes. And then she leaned in toward his face, inhaling deep—and then flinched, and silently shouted a furious stream of curses.

He *reeked* of henbane. Of precisely what Gwyn had threatened to shut him up with the day before, and what—she squeezed her eyes closed—Stella had been working on, when Silfast had arrived in the garden. And then Gwyn had left too, without finishing her work, clearly without noticing that the henbane had gone missing...

Damn. *Damn.*

"You," Silfast growled, his unfocused eyes narrowing on Gwyn's face. "*You* do this!"

His big clawed hand flailed up, swinging out wide toward her head—but before it could make impact, something kicked it away. *Joarr* kicked it away, before dropping to crouch beside Gwyn, and grabbing a strong handful of the front of Silfast's tunic.

"You *no touch her*," he hissed at Silfast, as he gave him a hard shake. "She do *naught*. Now what you last eat. Or drink."

Silfast's mouth curled up, but his eyes had glanced, brief but telling, toward a chipped cup sitting on the table, in front of the larger chair. And before Gwyn had moved, Joarr was already over there sniffing at it, and then placing it back onto the table with a firm thunk.

"*Stink* of henbane," he said, clipped. "And your mate, fool. Now, where she go? You follow her scent?"

Silfast moaned and shook his head, rubbing at his nose—and Joarr's expression was pure irritation, and contempt, and... *unease.* "I can no trace her scent amidst this," he said, with a fluid wave of his hand—meaning, perhaps, this part of the mountain, which surely was already crowded with Stella's scent. "No with speed. I go find Grisk to help. Baldr, mayhap."

But Silfast was suddenly groaning again, and he swiped his huge hand toward Joarr, missing his leg by a large margin. "No," he gasped. "No tell. *Shame*, if Bautul hear. *Disgrace.*"

Gwyn gaped down at him—surely this complete asshole was not rejecting help finding Stella, on account of it being *embarrassing* for him?—but Joarr actually seemed to be considering this as a valid point, his fingers pinching at his nose. Until his eyes blinked open, flicking toward Gwyn, almost as though he'd felt her frustration, her disbelief.

"He no mean shame for him," Joarr said, quiet, his eyes dark. "He mean for Stella. Bautul no again welcome her here, if she scorn Bautul captain thus. Most of all if she carry Bautul son, and next... lose him."

Lose him. Spoken with meaning, with a surreptitious glance toward Silfast—but despite his condition Silfast seemed to catch it, his eyes again fixing on Joarr's face. "She lose son?" he demanded, his voice still slurred. "You see this?"

And Gwyn was again staring at Silfast, because that wasn't anger in his eyes, or grief. It was... relief. It was... *hope*?

"You see this?" he repeated, his eyes wide, unblinking, *hopeful* on Joarr's face. "She well again? *Free* again? Happy?"

Oh. Oh. He meant he... he wouldn't grieve his son? He was thinking of Stella... being well again. Free. *Happy.*

But then something seemed to strike him, his seated body swaying, his head dropping into his hands. "Then mayhap," his slurred voice said, "no follow. Keep her free. Keep happy. Only"—his shoulders sagged—"send coin. Food. Pie. She need pie."

And as Gwyn stared at this huge, deadly orc, she realized he was... *weeping*. His sobs coming in harsh, dragging gulps, wracking through his massive body, shaking his big head in his hands. "Sought to keep strength," he gasped. "Give help. She need this from me, ach? But I fail. I *fail*."

Something thick was choking in Gwyn's throat, her own misery threatening to bubble up, to escape, to *explode*—and it seemed to take immense effort to shove it down again, find focus amidst the mess. Think. *Speak.*

"Stella didn't run away because you weren't strong enough, you fool," she heard herself snap, her voice hollow. "She likely ran because you were being a rigid, overbearing bastard, who thought you knew what was best, instead of actually listening to her, or being *honest* with her!"

Silfast raised his head to blink toward Gwyn, his eyes wide, wet, wounded. "She wished this from me," he said, thin, uncertain. "Always wished this, since our first night. I know this. Tasted this. Saw how she *thrived* from this. How she *bloomed* for me, like fairest flower ever I see."

But Gwyn shook her head, swallowed down the lump blocking her throat. "But can't you see," she replied, her voice just as thin, "how pregnancy could change that. How months of constant illness could change that. How women could suffer from depression, from the severe changes in their bodies, from all the uncertainty around their future, the *danger*. And how they might not even realize the extent of it themselves, especially if they haven't been informed, or properly supported, or permitted to do healthy activities that they clearly *enjoyed*!"

Her voice had nearly risen to a shout by the end, enough that Silfast actually shrank away from her—and gods, it felt like she'd just kicked a cowering puppy, like her own misery was reflected in his bright, desolate eyes.

"Then how I fix this," Silfast pleaded, again clutching mournfully at his nose. "How we find her. Where she *go*."

And despite the misery, the sheer curdling mess, Gwyn's helpless, blinking eyes searched for Joarr. Joarr, who was looking straight back toward her, as if he'd been searching for her, too. Searching for an answer from her, even, because she'd been the one to give Stella that thought about the henbane, and...

"My house," Gwyn whispered, to his waiting eyes. "Goddess curse me, I told Stella she could stay at my house."

Silfast barked some kind of outraged sound from the floor, but Gwyn fully ignored it, and kept her eyes on Joarr. Seeing how his own eyes shifted, changed, slipping behind his mask. Not hiding, perhaps, not like Gwyn had always thought, but... seeing. *Magic.*

And when his eyes refocused on hers, they were sharp and hard, glinting with purpose, with urgency. With the truth of something learned, known, from just standing here, and breathing. And if Gwyn hadn't felt so bereft, so *destroyed*, she might have almost been tempted to marvel at it, demand details of it, *revere* it.

"Ach, your house," Joarr said, his voice stilted. "But at your house…"

He grimaced, and that was surely guilt flashing across his eyes, and regret, and *rage*. The sight already far too familiar today, too meaningful, too painful. The things he'd known. All he'd seen. His plan for her, because…

There was… danger waiting at her house. *Destruction.*

And gods, Gwyn had been so stupid. So stupid to offer such a thing to Stella, to think it would still be safe. With all the men, all the threats, the impending law. How could she have thought her house would be free of it? How could she have possibly thought it was a good idea to send Stella there?

"There are—men at my house, aren't there?" Gwyn finally said, numb, empty. "Or there will be. Men come… for *me*. From Roy, and my father."

And she should have fought it, railed against it, sought to change it—she was supposed to have another week of freedom, they still had *time*—but maybe that had always been a futile, foolish hope. And maybe Joarr had seen that, and known that, too. Maybe that was why he hadn't said he'd loved her. Why he hadn't made her his mate.

And once again, Gwyn had been a fool. A patsy. A *pawn*.

Stupid. So, so damned *stupid*.

"Very well, then," she whispered, or perhaps sobbed. "Let's go."

30

They left the mountain via a twisty, circuitous, underground route. Following paths Gwyn had never before seen, many of them rough and narrow, their walls jagged and shadowy in the light of her lamp.

The goal had been to avoid encountering any other orcs, and so far, it had seemed successful. Aided, no doubt, by the way Joarr would sometimes stop at a fork in the route, his eyes shifting—and then choose one, without hesitation, without looking back.

It should have been shocking, maybe, impressive, *astonishing*—but Gwyn's whirling brain seemed to accept it with the same deadened, empty resignation that had swarmed her this past half-hour. Her orc lover had magic, the father of her child could see the *future*, and he'd lied to her again and again, and she should have seen it, she *had* seen it, stupid, stupid, *stupid*.

She'd been trailing along behind him, blinking blankly at how he was holding up a still-staggering Silfast, and taking slow, controlled steps. His lean body tall and unyielding under Silfast's added weight, his shaggy head fixed straight ahead.

Not once glancing back at Gwyn, not speaking to her, because he'd wanted—he wanted—

"Brothers!" called a voice, deep and familiar. "Silfast. Wait!"

Gwyn dully turned to look, and her blank eyes found... Kalfr? His grey-skinned form jogging up the corridor toward them, his narrow gaze fixed to Silfast's teetering bulk.

"What has caused—" Kalfr began, sliding to a halt before them—but his voice broke off as he leaned toward Silfast and inhaled, slow and deep. "Ach," he said, flatter than before. "Is Stella safe?"

Silfast was glaring at Kalfr, a garbled-sounding growl burning from his throat—and beside him Joarr visibly exhaled, and then bodily shoved Silfast away, toward Kalfr. "For now," he replied, clipped. "We must reach her before nightfall."

Silfast's staggering body had reeled toward Kalfr, and Kalfr braced himself to catch him, even as Silfast kept growling down into his face. "You sh'll no speak of this, *traitor*," Silfast spat at him. "No to *any* other. *No* Bautul."

Kalfr seemed to be expending considerable effort to keep Silfast upright, and he shoved him against the nearest wall, and repositioned Silfast's huge arm over his shoulder. "I wouldn't do that to her," he said, his voice thin. "Or to you."

Silfast growled again, but didn't seem to resist Kalfr's handling, either. And soon they were hobbling along again, with Silfast's massive form pinned close to Kalfr's side, his head occasionally lolling toward Kalfr's shoulder.

"You two ought to go ahead," Gwyn heard Kalfr's low voice say to Joarr, who was now striding unencumbered in front of them. "Seek to speak to Stella first. Learn if she wishes to see him."

Silfast barked another furious growl, which no one paid any heed to, because Joarr was nodding over his shoulder at Kalfr—and then, finally, glancing back toward Gwyn. His eyes fully hidden behind his mask again, but his brows raised, his head angling her forward. Toward him.

Gwyn's breaths were coming shallower, the constriction clamping tighter in her chest, but she made herself nod, and lurch around Kalfr and Silfast. To where Joarr had actually stopped to wait for her, and once she'd caught up, he instantly fell into step with her, his gaze prickling on the skin of her neck.

Gwyn reflexively reached her hand to her neck, as if to rub the feeling away—but there, of course, was a telltale twinge of pain beneath her fingers. Because Joarr had used his *teeth* there, last night. He'd marked her, for the first time. Because... because...

A sob suddenly caught in her throat, the choked sound echoing against the stone around them, and Gwyn felt her feet moving faster, rushing away. Away from Joarr's watching eyes, away from where Silfast and Kalfr were already a good distance behind them. Away from Orc Mountain, the place she'd stupidly thought could be an actual home, where she'd thought she could *belong*, be helpful, be needed, be safe. When in truth...

Gods, she was stupid. So, so *stupid*.

Joarr had easily caught up with her again, striding tall and silent beside her, but not looking at her now, not speaking. Not acknowledging any of his guilt, his deception, his gods-damned *cruelty*.

"So was it funny," Gwyn finally breathed, long after Silfast and Kalfr had fallen out of view, "to watch me throwing myself at you? Trying to please you? To help you? To gain your *trust*?"

Her voice came out sounding tenuous, shrill, and she could hear Joarr's hoarse inhale, perhaps about to reply—but she cut him off with a loud, broken laugh, her head whipping back and forth, her feet nearly jogging beneath her.

"Because you saw it all, with your *magic*," she gasped.

"Didn't you? You *knew*. You knew exactly what to do with me. What to say to me. How to seduce me, have *fun* with me, make me trust you. And then how—"

She flapped her hand forward, toward Roy, her *father*—and another sob tore from her throat. "You knew how—how lonely I was," she croaked. "How Roy treated me. How relieved I was to—to finally escape. To find—*hope*. And you still—you still—"

She rushed ahead even faster, scrubbing at her hot, tear-streaked face—but Joarr kept up so easily, why was he still here, why was he still *doing* this—

"Woman, I—" he began, but Gwyn kept pushing beyond him, almost running at full tilt now. Her lamp bobbing, her feet sliding on the wet stone below, get it the hell over with, please, *please*—

"You never had another plan, with this law," she gasped over her shoulder. "Did you? I was always the plan. Getting me pregnant, and then sending me back, was always the plan. You just had to drag it out long enough, keep me dangling after you, until you knew I'd give you exactly what you wanted. Exactly like Roy did."

And gods, she couldn't breathe, her ribs were crushing her, her heartbeat roaring through her skull. And curse her, she was still doing it, still going back there, because she cared about Stella, cared about the Bautul, cared about *him*—

"No," Joarr said, his voice cracking. "No. Wait. Gwyn. I *beg* you. *Please*."

It wasn't him, wasn't something he would ever say—and it seemed to slice through the chaos flooding Gwyn's thoughts. Enough that her feet skittered against the stone, her betraying eyes darting back toward him—

And suddenly Joarr was here. Everywhere. Hovering tall and close and dangerous over her, his long fingers clamping around both her wrists, holding her still. His eyes flashing, his mouth pressed tight, his skin deathly pale over the harsh lines of his bones.

"No," he rasped again. "I no foresaw all this. Had I seen this, I should never have sworn this pledge to the Bautul. *Never* come to you. Never touch you, or seek to spark son upon you."

But he *had* done all that, he'd *meant* to do that, it was what he'd wanted all along. And Gwyn couldn't even stop the tears from streaking down her face, while the sobs choked bitter and anguished from her throat.

"You... *break* my sight," Joarr continued, a little louder, his hands giving her wrists a hard, jolting shake. "You surprise me, again and again, with all I never see. I no see how you spurn me, when first we meet. I no see you learn my plan. I no see how you seek *fun* with me, or gain the goddess' blessing with me. I no see"—his eyes closed, opened again—"how you help me face Bautul. How you work amongst my kin, and make their cares your own. I never see you *happy* to spark my son. I never see you happy to... *stay*."

Another sob escaped Gwyn's mouth, and she felt her body swaying against the words, the heat in his voice, the truth in his eyes. Like they were all striking at her, stroking at her, pleading with her to understand. To know. To follow his damned pinecone. To—*forgive*.

But it was cruel, impossible, *unfathomable*. Because how could Gwyn ever know if he was telling the truth again? Or if he was only saying what needed to be said, to gain his own ends? To make his visions real?

"You are witch, ach?" Joarr breathed now, his voice low, fervent. "*My* witch. You catch me in your spell, with your wisdom, and hunger, and kindness, and *fun*. You are surely the goddess' own. You bear her blessing. Her *favour*."

The goddess' own. Her *favour*. Those words striking strange and deep, plunging in Gwyn's belly, as her thoughts abruptly flipped, sharp and jolting, toward the day before. The altar. The light. The ecstasy, the divinity, the mingled longing and grief glimmering in his eyes. His. *Hers.*

"Wished to tell you all this truth," Joarr whispered, blinking, shaking his head. "Wished you to know. Thought, mayhap, you did."

And curse him, curse *her*, because again—maybe she *had*. He'd dropped so many hints, he'd known so many things he shouldn't have known, he'd spoken of *seeing* so many times. Gods, even that whole bit about him being the Bautul Seer, the tale of his grandfather failing to predict a future danger, of him now wanting to make amends to the clan. And why had Gwyn never asked him, never sought deeper...

But no. *No.* She was done fooling herself, done pretending not to see what was right before her face. And in truth, she... she...

She hadn't *wanted* to know. She hadn't wanted to face it. She'd ignored all the hints, all the signs, on *purpose.*

Because Joarr seeing the future, knowing what was to come—it destroyed *everything.* It destroyed their happiness, their work together, their *hope.* Because it meant that all that time, in all he'd done—he'd still known it would ultimately come to this. To a lord's stupid, *stupid* daughter, running home afraid and alone, and pregnant with an orc's son. So that...

"Should you," Joarr cut in, his voice so quiet, "wish now to turn back, you—you ought to do this. You shall always be welcome among us. Even if you forever spurn me, or my son, I shall always seek to honour you. Keep you safe."

And it should have helped, it should have been an option, an answer—but Gwyn just kept blinking at his pale, drawn face, her eyes swimming, the misery pulsing deeper with every frantic beat of her heart.

"But what happens if I turn back?" she asked, hollow. "You know, don't you?"

His grimace was hard and ugly, twisting at his mouth, and

Gwyn wasn't looking away from the truth this time. She wasn't. Not anymore.

"I was right, wasn't I?" she heard herself whisper. "There is no other viable plan with the men. No other way to stop my father's new law, or keep all those terrified women safe. No other way"—she had to force out the words—"to fulfill that pledge you made to the Bautul. To regain your place as Seer among them."

Her bleary eyes had dropped to that tooth around his neck, that damned symbol of her doom. Just hanging there so innocuously, so constantly, between them. Sharp, silent, deadly, waiting to bite her, break her apart...

"I no care for this pledge, or this place amongst the Bautul," Joarr said finally, hoarse, fierce. "I should forsake all this in a breath, if this should keep you with me. And we *have* sought new plan. Fought for new way. But..."

But. Gwyn's heavy eyes lifted up again, finding his angry, bitter gaze. And then following it as it flicked, grim and purposeful, toward the yawning corridor ahead. Toward—the men. Toward *Stella*.

And what had he said, that day in the garden, what felt like an age ago? *You ken Stella is only one?* he'd snarled at her. *Only woman who shall meet death at the hands of this?*

And yes, this was precisely what he was talking about. What he was doing here. What *Gwyn* was doing here. Saving these women's very lives, in the face of her father's cruel short-sightedness. In defiance of all the power of the realm.

A lord's dotty, unfashionable, plant-obsessed daughter... pregnant with an orc's son. And ready, in her stupidity, to fight for that, with everything she had. Even if it meant testifying. Even if it meant public humiliation. Even if it meant losing everything she'd fought for. Everything she'd ever longed for.

"You must no ken," Joarr said, his voice halting, "I no care for you. Ach? I *never* know care like this. Never know hunger or peace like this. You are"—his hands skittered on her face, tilted it back toward him—"true goddess. Kind. Kindred. *Magic.* Worthy of deep fealty. Of *worship.*"

The truth was far too close, too vivid, flashing in his too-bright eyes—but it only made it worse, wrenching the agony hard and tight and cold. He *had* cared for her, and he'd still done this. Still trapped her to save those women, and his people. And Gwyn saw it, knew it, *understood* it—and gods, maybe she would have even done it, had she been in his place.

But it still destroyed everything. It still meant Joarr had lied, again and again. It still meant she'd been second best, not good enough, not worthy enough. She hadn't fought hard enough, done enough. She hadn't been able to prove it, to change it, to defy the whims of that damned goddess. She'd been a pawn all along, and she'd *known* it.

Stupid. So, so damned *stupid.*

"No," she whispered, dropping her eyes, her voice wretchedly wavering. "No. You don't get to give me your empty praise or your platitudes anymore, Joarr. You're getting what you want from me, and then"—she gulped down breath—"you're getting the hell away from me. *Forever.*"

Joarr's hands twitched on her face, his eyes squeezing shut, his mouth opening to speak, to try again—but this time Gwyn ripped herself away from him, wildly shaking her head. No. No. *No.*

"No," she gasped at him. "No. I helped you. I trusted you. I gave you so, so many chances. I listened to you again and again, I put my whole future in your hands. All my hope. And this is how you repay me? *This*?!"

Her voice was ringing through the corridor now, and she didn't care if Silfast or Kalfr heard, if the entire blasted mountain heard. "You don't come to me again," she hissed. "You don't touch me again. You don't even *speak* to me again. I am finally done with being your plaything, your target, your fool! And as stupid as I am, I am never, *ever* falling for your rubbish, *ever again!*"

And as the words rang out around them, Joarr actually *flinched.* His entire body recoiling away from her, as though she'd slammed him in the face, or kicked him in the groin. And even as he shook his head back and forth, as if to thrust it away, he was opening his damned lying mouth, about to speak again, to try again, he was, he *was*—

But before Gwyn could hear it, could break apart beneath it, she shoved away with all her might, and ran into the darkness.

31

Gwyn ran and ran through the dark corridor, her feet sliding, her breaths straining, her thoughts screaming through her skull.

Stupid, they shouted, with every slap of her boots against the stone. *Stupid, stupid, stupid.*

And even stupider—she reeled to a halt, glared in tearful disbelief at the sheer, rocky wall blocking the path before her—was the reality that Joarr was still *here*. Jogging close and silent behind her the entire damned time, as if he hadn't heard a single damned word she'd just said.

And she wasn't giving him the satisfaction of acknowledging his existence, she wasn't—even as he strode past her to the wall in front of her, and then slowly, deliberately, began to climb it.

He was taking his time on purpose, Gwyn's raging thoughts noted, showing her where to hold on, where to put her feet, like he'd done so many times before. And once he'd reached the top, he shifted something above—and suddenly light streamed down, blinding her blinking, leaking eyes.

Joarr leapt up into the light with one final quick, fluid

movement, and then spun back around, and reached a hand down toward her. His fingers making a familiar come-here motion, and Gwyn fervently fought to ignore that awareness as she slung her lamp over her wrist, and followed him.

However, of course it wasn't nearly as easy as he'd made it look, and once she was halfway, his strong hands grasped both her arms, and hauled her up. Up and out into cool fresh air, into a circle of surrounding trees, into the rich dappled light of the low, setting sun.

He helped her to her feet, and then plucked the lamp from her wrist, snuffed it out, and then placed it back down into the hole behind them. All of this without speaking a word—like she'd asked, Gwyn's miserable thoughts pointed out—even as she could feel the heavy weight of his eyes on her, raising gooseflesh over her skin.

But she only waited, her gaze downcast, until he finally turned, and started walking again. Striding along a narrow path through the trees, heading due north. Toward Varrahan. Toward her house. Toward Roy, and toward Stella.

Gwyn silently followed, keeping her eyes on the earth, fighting to ignore that telltale, too-frequent prickle of Joarr's gaze upon her. Focusing only on her steps, her purpose, the flat, deadened resignation hollowing out her chest. She would save those women. Save Stella. This was all the orcs had wanted from her, all she was good for, and she would do it. She would.

And the fact that Joarr was still walking, still taking her there—that had to mean something, at least. Had to mean she could do at least this. That even if her own future was destroyed, there was still hope for all the other women affected by this. For women like Inga and Dania and Hannah, and Jule and Ella and Rosa and Maria. For Stella.

Gwyn kept silently repeating that with every dogged step, louder and louder, as if to drown out her ever-wailing heartbeat. So loud that she didn't even notice when Joarr abruptly halted in front of her—not until she strode straight into his back. Into that lean, shifting strength, its sweaty sweet scent swarming her lungs, his hands snapping out to catch her waist—

And gods, he was touching her, holding her, *lingering*. And Gwyn wanted so desperately to curl into him, to gulp up deep swallows of his strength. To hear him say whatever empty words he could, to tell her she mattered, to make it all go away—

But when she found his eyes, there was only her own desolation reflected in them, shimmering black and bitter. And she had to look away before she started weeping again, before she betrayed the agony, the anguish, the *grief*.

His hands on her waist briefly clenched, his claws nudging into her skin—and then one hand gave her a brief, purposeful pat before moving away again. Saying, surely, *Stay here*, and Gwyn nodded even as she hated it, berated it, braced against the black battering despair.

She didn't look up again to see what Joarr was doing, but she could feel him moving nearby, could almost sense the strength of his presence. And when the smell of cooking meat wafted through the air, making her stomach rumble, she numbly strode toward it, and accepted the fully laden skewer that he silently held out toward her.

It was delicious, of course—some kind of roasted fowl, seasoned perhaps with nettles this time—but Gwyn could scarcely seem to taste it, couldn't raise her eyes as she ate. Couldn't even manage a thank-you once she'd finished, not even when Joarr plucked away her empty skewer, or stamped out the fire, or then—*threw* something at her.

Gwyn twitched to catch it, her tingling hands desperately fumbling, needing it—at least, until her fingers finally clutched it safe, her eyes blankly fixing upon it. It was—a *pinecone*.

The misery and rage seemed to snap alive at once, streaming through Gwyn's gasping thoughts, surging to the darkening sky. A pinecone, like they were playing a *game*, like this was supposed to be *fun*. Like he wanted her to forgive him, even as she walked straight to her *doom*?!

She hurled it back toward him, as forcefully as she could—and the audacious, infuriating bastard just caught it, with a sharp flick of his claws. And then carefully closed his fingers around it, as if to hide it, to keep it, to *treasure* it.

Gwyn's eyes had jerked to his, her mouth snapping open to curse him, to rail and scream at him—but then the words choked away, because Joarr was...

Weeping. Yes, this audacious, infuriating orc was just standing there and *weeping*, his shoulders slumped, his heavy-lashed eyes brimming with wetness, streaking it down his harsh cheeks. And he wasn't even looking at her, he was looking at the pinecone in his hand, and the sudden sound from his throat wasn't like anything Gwyn had ever heard before, like a strangled, guttering death-cry.

"I ken," he choked, without looking up, "you no wish me to speak. But I wish you to know, I—I am—"

He gave another of those awful-sounding barks, his head shaking, his free hand rubbing at his face. "I am sorry," he whispered. "I shall never forget you. Shall never stop grieving what I have brought upon you. What I have *stolen* from you."

Gwyn couldn't move, couldn't even shout or curse, trapped in his regret, his grief, his desolation. In the stark, staggering certainty that he... meant this. He... mourned this.

And surely it didn't matter, surely Gwyn should have raged at him anyway—but she still couldn't even muster a breath. Not through all the sudden, swarming memories, the gardens, the trees, the mushrooms. All the people she'd helped, the true friends she'd made. And all the times Joarr had grinned at her, made her laugh, given her his tongue, his teasing, his *taking*.

Cooked for her. Stayed with her. Held her against his heart, helped her sleep, heard her, *understood* her.

You need more friends, I ken. You find other way. Kind witch. Kindred witch. We try. It is—hope.

And finally, there was just sadness. Loss. Loneliness. The truth that Gwyn had had this, she'd *known* this—and now it was leaving her. Slipping away from her, now, forever.

And without at all meaning to, she clutched for it, one last time. Clutched for Joarr, dragging him close—and feeling his warm, familiar body instantly catching her in return. Folding her into the tight circle of his arms, cradling her against the thundering drum of his heart.

"You ken," he choked above her, into her hair, "I wished you for my own since that first night. Should have made this truth long past, were the goddess no so cruel. Ach?"

And Gwyn was nodding, gulping for air too, her eyes streaking their wetness against his skin. Because yes, somewhere deep down, she had known that, all that time. And perhaps that was the knowledge she'd clung to, amidst all the rest of her weakness. Her stupidity.

"And you were no *stupid* in this, ach?" he continued, the unnerving awareness of those words shuddering deep. "You were kind. You were *wise*. And in this, you"—he drew back from her, gripping her face in his hands, blinking at her with molten eyes—"you have yet gained this safety for your garden. I shall always keep this and tend this for you, until you pass from this earth. I *swear* this."

And within the swath of devastation, it was... something. It was one thing, not lost. One thing kept safe. The one damned reason Gwyn had gone to Orc Mountain in the first place.

And maybe it was foolishness again, believing him like this. Maybe it was more of her sheer stupidity. But maybe she could choose to trust it, to trust him, one last time.

So she nodded as she squeezed him tight, drew up breath,

strength, courage. And kept nodding as she finally, reluctantly stepped back, wiping at her eyes. "Thank you, Joarr," she whispered, the words stilted, thick. "I wish you all the best with your clan, and your gardens. And with—"

Her hand had somehow found her waist, gripping close against it, and oh goddess, what had she been about to say? With your next mate? With your next... *son*?

And it was the last, worst blow, the final terrifying reality that Gwyn couldn't bear to face. No. No. No.

And it was pure denial that made her square her shoulders, and attempt a wavering, pathetic smile before she turned, and walked away. Toward Stella. Toward Roy. Toward her future. Her doom.

"It was fun while it lasted," she whispered, confessed, *truth*, into the darkening night. "Goodbye."

32

Gwyn walked the rest of the way to her house in silence, her shoulders straight, her eyes fixed ahead. Knowing, maybe, that Joarr was still somewhere behind her, but he didn't approach her again, didn't try to speak.

It was for the best, surely, because the misery was still clawing inside her skin, along with the yawning, looming loneliness. Feeling far more real than it ever had before, and Gwyn had to choke it down, keep moving, keep walking. She needed to find Stella. Needed to face this.

When her gaze finally settled on the familiar sight of her house through the trees, it was nearly nightfall, the sun just dipping below the horizon. And despite everything, Gwyn felt her feet faltering, her eyes casting a furtive, uneasy glance over her shoulder. Toward where, yes, Joarr's tall shadow was still here, still following her, hesitating at a careful distance behind her.

His face was unreadable in the dim light, and Gwyn grimaced as she turned back to look at the house, scanning the empty-looking road, the dark, gaping windows.

"Is Stella there?" she asked, her voice cracking. "Or any men?"

There was an instant's silence, and then the familiar feel of Joarr's body, halting close beside her. "Ach, I smell her within," he said, quiet. "And I ken the men soon come."

Right. Gwyn drew in breath, rubbed her shaky hands on her dress. "So I should rush her out of the house," she said, "and do it as quickly as possible, so you can take her somewhere safe, right? And then you can decide to meet up with Silfast and Kalfr, if she's comfortable? And then I'll stay here, and wait for Roy?"

She was fighting not to envision what Roy would do, what he might demand from her. And when Joarr didn't immediately answer, she kept going, kept facing it, the words sounding shriller with every breath.

"Is there anything that you think will improve my chance of success?" she asked. "Anything I should do, or say? Should I try to fob Roy off, or surrender? And should I tell him about my pregnancy at once, or keep it secret? Should I try to stop the law before it's final, or wait and then make a show of publicly testifying afterwards in Dunburg? Or, do I need to be considering more drastic measures, like"—she gulped down air— "like poisoning my father?"

The bile was churning in her stomach—for all her father had done, the thought of killing him was suddenly a thoroughly sickening one—and she dragged her hands at her hair, felt the pain hiss and splinter in her scalp. Why in the gods' names hadn't she been thinking of this all this time, making plans, drilling Joarr on every damned possible outcome, not wasting her only opportunity, her sacrifice, so *stupid*—

But again, abruptly, Joarr was here. Here, *again*, his hands clamping on her wrists, because apparently she would never be able to rid herself of him—and she couldn't even pretend to resist as he drew her hands downward, away from her hair.

"Ach, woman," he said, so quiet. "I wish I have all this truth to tell you. But it no work thus, ach? I no oft see such ways, such depth. Such *choice*. I most of all... *feel* this. I feel you must come here, in the path of these men, and face this law. I feel you are only way to save Stella. I feel she need *friend*."

Oh. Gwyn's shoulders sagged, her eyes dropping, her arms slackening in his grip. "But I thought you were the Seer," she whispered, disconsolate. "You have visions. Dreams. Plans. *Magic*."

But Joarr choked an odd sound, his hands clenching against her wrists. "It is no like dream, ach?" he said, his voice brittle. "It is no oft *vision*, also, and it is no even always true. I tell you, you oft break this, ach? But yet—"

Gwyn twitched to blink up at him, searching him, and he exhaled, heavy and slow. "I yet feel I must be near you," he breathed. "I feel you are *hope*, for the Bautul, and our women, and this war. I feel"—his hand still holding her wrist drew it sideways, his claws brushing against her waist—"my son upon you."

Oh. Gwyn was still gaping at him, unmoving—and Joarr jerked another shrug, exhaled another thick breath. "I feel you suffer for me," he whispered. "I feel you give all for me, and my kin. I feel all your grief, and your *loss*, at my hands."

Her grief. Her *loss*. Gwyn's body shuddered, her stomach roiling, her thoughts reeling away in a dark, desperate stream—but then, somehow, catching again. Hesitating, and then whirling back toward this, wondering, comprehending...

Because wait. Wait. Joarr hadn't actually had dreams, or visions of this? He just... *felt* these things? And she had truly changed his *feelings*, before... hadn't she? Hadn't she?

And even as her brain kept hollering, Gwyn's heart seemed to lurch and settle again, finding a new, steadier thud in her chest. And where the emptiness had been, the aching aimless agony, there was suddenly something that felt more like... determination. Like... *hope.*

She was. She *was.*

You break my sight. Make me forget. Always good. Kindred witch. Stay. We try. Break this.

Mine.

And before it could fade, or gutter out, or get lost in the grief in his eyes—Gwyn spun on her heel and strode away, toward her house. Not saying goodbye this time, not even looking back, because maybe—maybe it wasn't goodbye.

Not yet.

And with a breath, a whisper, a *hope*, she raised her hand, and rapped on the door.

33

For an instant, there was only stillness beyond the door. Empty, echoing stillness, as though perhaps they'd mistaken this, perhaps there was no one here at all.

But then, soft but certain, was the distinct sound of a sob. Muffled, strained, as if someone were seeking to hide it—and curse Gwyn, but that was no doubt because her knock on the door had surely suggested men, soldiers, danger, *death.*

"Stella," she called, as loudly as she dared, casting an uneasy glance around at the still-empty road behind her. "It's me. Gwyn. May I come in? Please?"

There was another choked, muffled-sounding sob—and then, the sound of movement, of the bar sliding back. And finally the door swung open, and behind it, there was Stella. Weeping, trembling, but alive. Safe.

"Oh, thank the *goddess*," Gwyn breathed, and without even knowing that she'd moved, she'd slammed the door shut behind her, and clasped Stella close in her arms, squeezing her tight. "How—how are you feeling? Is anything injured? You weren't pursued, were you?"

She yanked back to look Stella over, to search her pale, tear-streaked face and bloodshot eyes. She appeared unharmed, at least, no visible scratches or injuries, but she was still sobbing, the sounds harsh and broken. "Nothing like that," she gulped, "but it's still been so awful, I feel so wretched and afraid, I should never have even *thought* of such a foolish thing—"

Her voice badly cracked, and she sank into sobs again, burying her face in her hands. While Gwyn's own misery and guilt felt like an ever-tightening vine, clamping close around her chest.

"I'm so, *so* sorry I put you onto this, Stella," Gwyn said, her voice hitching. "I should have come up with a better option for you. Should have told you that it was—risky, coming here. Should have been a better friend."

Stella glanced up, her wet eyes wide, her shivers briefly stilling—and then she flapped both hands toward Gwyn at once, the tears still streaking down her face. "Goddess, Gwyn, you've been a *wonderful* friend," she choked. "It's me who's ruined everything. I knew it wasn't safe, I *knew*, and it just—it just felt like something broke, inside me. Like I didn't even care anymore. Like it would be better for—for everyone—if I just disappeared, and—"

The words sank away into sobs again, her whole body convulsing, her hands now clutching at her rounded waist. "W-what's wrong with me, Gwyn?" she gasped, her eyes molten, desperate. "Why did I do this? Why am I so *stupid*?!"

Gwyn was fighting back the urge to sob too, and she yanked Stella close again, rubbing her hands firmly up and down her trembling back. "You are *not stupid*," she said, her voice hard, her brain shoving down the odd, horrible familiarity in those words. "And I know I'm not your midwife, but I can absolutely assure you that acute anxiety and depression are very, *very* common in pregnancies, especially difficult ones. And any added stress will only make it that much worse. Like this awful new law we're dealing with, the way it's changed your life, and put you in constant danger. Or—or your relationship with Silfast, surely that's been a major stressor too, and—"

But that was without question the wrong thing to say, because Stella burst into tears again, her body stumbling backwards from Gwyn's, her hands clutching at her face. "Oh goddess, *Silfast*," she gasped. "Do you know what I did to him, Gwyn? I knew he wouldn't let me leave, not without him, or at least a dozen warriors flanking me, so I—I *drugged* him. With the henbane. My own *mate*. And he's been so patient, so strong, so—so attentive to my every need, while I keep pushing him away, and turning into this—this *wraith*. And I repay him like this? When I know how much he's been struggling too, what with the long-lost Bautul Seer suddenly showing up to take his place, and making a *mockery* of him before his entire clan? After all Silfast has done for them? Everything he's sacrificed?!"

Her voice had nearly risen to a shout, the broken words ringing through the room, shuddering into Gwyn's belly—and then Stella visibly snapped to stillness again, her wet eyes wide and chagrined on Gwyn's face. "Oh, Gwyn," she gasped. "I'm so sorry. I don't mean to insult your mate. I know you love him, and I'm sure he didn't want any of this either, he was *such* a Skai, before all this, and—"

She broke off there, her eyes shimmering, her lips pressing tightly together—and blinking back at her, Gwyn suddenly felt oddly far away, her thoughts swimming in a fog. "I—Joarr's not my mate," she said, her voice hollow. "It was actually all just a—a ploy. To get me pregnant, and send me back to testify against the law. Using me, and—and then throwing me *away*."

And goddess, perhaps she was finally going to start weeping here, too—but Stella's sobs had actually stilled, her forehead creased, her head twitching back and forth. "N-no, Gwyn," she countered. "That's not right. I mean, m-maybe that was Joarr's original plan, but then he—he told everyone he'd changed it. I mean, he claimed you as his mate at our hearth, and g-gained the goddess' blessing on your union. Even if he hasn't spoken vows to you yet, he might as well have, because after that—"

She flapped her hand at Gwyn again, as if this shocking statement were entirely self-explanatory—and Gwyn found that she couldn't move, couldn't think. "What?" she heard her distant voice say, so thin. "No. Joarr—he—he even made that unbreakable pledge to the Bautul about me. The *great service*."

But Stella's head was shaking again, the confusion still palpable in her wet eyes. "Yes, but then—then he set you up as our midwife. And he sent word to every Bautul camp—even the far south—that you would help their women, and treat them with only acceptance and kindness. Which you *have*, Gwyn. It was a great service, on his part. And on yours."

What? No. *No.* Surely Joarr hadn't done that. Surely. Right? Claiming Gwyn as his mate? As Orc Mountain's midwife? Changing the plan, changing his pledge?

But wait, he *had* spoken again and again about changing things, hadn't he? He'd said it again and again. *I seek new way. I alter my means. You break my sight. We try.*

But then—Gwyn's scrambling brain was flipping, searching, scraping—Joarr had never said anything about her being his mate. And surely she had even asked him that night in the rain, about him not wanting her for a—a real Bautul, and he'd said... what? Had he said anything? That quip about Maria, maybe? *You ken I bear this in my mate?*

His... *mate?*

"I mean, he adores you, Gwyn," Stella said now, with a loud hiccough. "How could he not? You're so... so poised, so clever, so *confident*. And we've all seen how he's always cooking special meals for you, and chasing you around the mountain, and guarding the Ka-esh corridor while you work. Not to mention moving your entire garden into his own—you realize he never let anyone step *foot* in there before you?—and showing you off in public all the time, and flaunting how much you enjoy each other. And now even"—her voice broke, her eyes dropping, her hand waving frantically toward Gwyn's neck—"even *marking* you, like a true mate should. You're so *lucky*, Gwyn. The goddess has *blessed* you."

Gwyn stared blankly at Stella, her body fully frozen again, while her fingers skittered up to touch against her neck. Against that still-present twinge of pain, of his teeth, of the way he'd felt, looked, tasted.

And what had he said in the forest? *I never know care like this. Never know hunger or peace like this. You are true goddess. Kind. Kindred. Worthy of deep fealty. Of worship.*

Mine.

"But," Gwyn said, her voice so strange, so far away, almost pleading, "he never—he never—*said.*"

But Stella only flapped another dismissive wave of her hand, gave a jerky shrug of her shoulder. "Sometimes they'll wait, to speak vows," she said. "Silfast, he—he waited for *weeks*, even after we'd earned the goddess' blessing. It was set for him, you see, but he—he still wanted to make sure I was ready. That I would be happy there, with him, and—"

Her voice had been thinning, rising, her eyes welling up—and then the sobs tore from her again, wracking her taut body, dragging down her head. "And I *was* happy," she gulped. "I *was*, Gwyn. For the longest time. Until—"

Her hands clutched again at her waist, her misery like a battering punch to Gwyn's gut. And goddess, Gwyn had to do something, be a friend, be a Bautul, fight this, face this. She was. She *was.*

"You *will* get through this, Stella," she said, as resolutely as she could. "You are a Bautul. You bear the goddess' blessing. You're so kind, and thoughtful, and hardworking, and you have the makings of a top-tier herbalist. You have friends who care for you, and want the best for you. And Silfast, he—"

Stella's desolate eyes had snapped back to Gwyn's, her head shaking. "Silfast will *never* be able to forgive me," she whispered. "Not after this. Not after I've put his son at risk like this. He wants a son so much, it's been the only thing bringing him happiness, and I've been one constant disappointment to him, he'll be better off once I'm away from him, and—"

And behind Gwyn, there was the sudden boom of a rough, rumbling bellow. A *roar*. And then shouts, and a flurry of movement. Coming closer, closer—

Oh goddess, it was the men, it was *Roy*—and Gwyn leapt into motion, and yanked Stella away from the door. Just in time for something to barge through it, banging it against the wall, flooding the room with wind and cold and fear. With a huge, vicious, deadly body, covered in mud, crawling on all fours, and *roaring.*

Gwyn bit back a shout—it was a beast, something feral and lethal, the men were sending dogs again, it was going to hunt them, *destroy* them—but it was too late, the beast was already here, inside the house, rising up to its staggering feet.

"You shall never escape," it growled, the words shuddering into Gwyn's bones. "For you are *mine.*"

34

Gwyn's fear felt like a hammer, a deadly strike to her already-raging heart. This couldn't be it. This couldn't be happening. Not yet. Not now. She had to keep Stella safe, had to run, to fight this—

When behind her, Stella choked out a strangled sob—and then dodged away from Gwyn. Around her. Toward the door, straight toward the beast, Stella was going to end this, she was going to *die*—

"NO!" Gwyn yelled, too late, too late—but it was already done. Stella rushing into the beast, straight into the deadly danger of his huge arms, as he—

Hugged her?

"I'm so sorry," Stella gasped, her voice muffled, her head buried in the beast's muddy fur. "I'm so, *so* sorry."

And wait. The beast was... that wasn't... was that *Silfast*?!

But yes, oh good goddess, beneath the mud and the sweat and the fur—no, the *hair*—it did look like an orc, an orc who'd perhaps been beaten and battered and left to drown in a swamp. And rushing into the room behind him was the unmistakable form of Kalfr, his grey face sweaty, his hands in fists, his tall body also streaked with muck. And his dark eyes flashed with both frustration and relief as they settled first on Stella, still wrapped tight in Silfast's huge arms, and then upon Gwyn, standing motionless before her kitchen table.

"I tried," Kalfr said, with an exasperated grimace. "The fool fought me off, and then *crawled* here."

Gwyn's relief bolted through her, strong enough that her feet staggered, her hands gripping at the table for balance. And she somehow managed a nod, an attempt at a smile, her traitorous eyes oddly searching beyond the open door, to where maybe—maybe—

But no. There was no sign of Joarr, no twitch of his amused grin, no familiar comfort from his solid presence. No, no, of course not, because what had Gwyn told him, before all this, back in the trees?

You don't touch me again. You don't even speak to me again. I am never, ever falling for your lies, ever again.

She clutched harder at the table behind her, gulping down heavy breaths—surely Joarr still wouldn't have *left*, would he?—and fought for balance, for focus. She was Bautul. She was fighting this, fixing this. And she was supposed to be helping Stella, who had still almost disappeared within the embrace of the massive, muddy, hairy creature before them.

"You shouldn't have come," Stella was gulping, into his filthy chest. "You must hate me, Silfast. You ought to punish me. You ought to forget me, and take a new mate. A braver one. A stronger one. A better Bautul."

But Silfast's deep bark sounded just as feral and vicious as he looked, vibrating through the room. "There is no better, woman," he growled at her. "There is no braver. I did not"—his huge shoulders rose and fell—"listen, or seek your truth, or speak my own, as a true Bautul mate should have done. And so you have struck back at me, with all your strength, to make me see this. To help me *learn* this. This is just what a Bautul should do."

Stella was sobbing again, protesting, wildly whipping her head against him—until Silfast's next bark snapped her back to stillness again. "No, woman," he hissed at her. "I swear to better hear you, but I yet shall *never* bear affront against my sweet mate. I shall strike down *any* who speaks ill of her, with all my strength."

It sounded like a threat, burning from his cruel mouth—but in his arms, Stella had indeed seemed to stop weeping, her shoulders shuddering, her breaths dragging in slow. And as Gwyn blinked, blank, bemused, Silfast's huge, muddy hand slid down Stella's back, and gave her arse a firm, audible little slap.

And to Gwyn's rising astonishment, Stella—shivered. *Gasped.* And then clutched Silfast even tighter, smearing herself in more mud, inhaling deep. "Then I must require," she whispered, "*excessive* correction, my lord, don't you think?"

Against her, Silfast's huge body had gone strangely, suddenly still—and in his eyes, dark but unmistakable, was the unease. The uncertainty. The... *fear*.

And in that instant, as Gwyn kept blinking between them, so many things about their relationship made full and infuriating sense. Had they truly not talked to their healers about this? Or worse, had they been told to *stop*? In the middle of all the other stresses going on in their lives?

"All right then," Gwyn said loudly, to the room at large. "Just so everyone is aware, many games of intimacy are *fine* to continue throughout pregnancy, as long as both partners are careful. Everyone *is* aware of this, right?"

But there was only an abrupt, choked stillness, in which both Stella and Silfast had wrenched to stare at Gwyn, their eyes wide and stunned, *waiting*—and Gwyn groaned, and sighed, and dragged a hand through her hair.

"Right then," she said again, her voice harder. "So. Here's

the list. Pregnant women will scar more easily, and nipple play can lead to contractions, so all that's best avoided. Circulation will also be reduced, so you'll need to avoid any overly tight restraints, and watch for dizziness or fainting. And, you need be able to check with each other regularly, so no gagging. I'd be careful with any claw penetration, too, but anything that isn't sharp is fine. And obviously no impact on her belly, but I'm sure you're aware of that anyway. Does that"—she paused, pulled in a breath—"cover the main points, for now? Any further questions?"

Both Stella and Silfast were still staring at her, both gone entirely immobile, so Gwyn kept talking, giving an uncertain shrug. "If, at some point, you'd like to bring me on as your midwife," she said, "I'd be happy to go through a breakdown of your usual activities, and make recommendations. Or check Stella over, after an encounter."

There was still no movement from either of them, just those wide staring eyes, as though Gwyn had said something truly shocking—and she shifted uncomfortably on her feet, and glanced toward Kalfr, who was looking as nonplussed as she felt. And goddess, maybe she'd horribly overstepped, maybe that hadn't been the issue at all, and—

"You are *sure* of this, woman," Silfast's voice cut in, his eyes unnervingly sharp on Gwyn's face. "I shall not harm my sweet mate in this? I shall not worsen her weariness, or push her into an early birth? Efterar says mating is good for her health, but in this"—he grimaced—"I must be only, always *gentle*. Most of all with my mate so unwell, and humans so delicate."

Gwyn blinked at him—good goddess, she needed to have a word with this Efterar, pronto—and jerked a hard shake of her head. "You'll be fine," she said flatly. "If anything, making drastic changes to your relationship dynamic during a stressful time is a far greater risk. You just need to be careful, and check in with each other—and your healer—on a regular basis."

Silfast's shoulders had visibly sagged, his head bowing down toward Stella's, his eyes fluttering closed. While Stella just kept staring at Gwyn, her eyes so wide and dark, her hands trembling against Silfast's muddy, hairy chest. "You're sure, Gwyn," she whispered. "You're *sure*."

Gwyn fervently nodded, and didn't miss how Stella seemed to collapse into Silfast's muddy body, how his huge clawed hand had again given a sharp, heavy slap at her arse. And how Stella again shivered all over, her lashes fluttering, her mouth letting out a hoarse, broken gasp.

And Gwyn was probably going to regret this, but she squared her shoulders, and twitched her head toward the half-closed door of her bedroom. "You're welcome to make use of the bedroom, if you like," she said. "Though I'd be very grateful if you'd wash the bed-linens afterwards."

Stella was eagerly, frantically nodding, and already tugging Silfast toward it. And after one last, oddly penetrating look toward Gwyn, Silfast staggered after Stella, and then slammed the door shut with a piercing, resounding *thud*.

It left Gwyn still standing behind her table, and blinking at Kalfr, who was still hovering near the front door—and she could see his exhale, his hand rubbing at his mouth. "Silfast likely will not say thank you," he told her, quiet. "So, thank you."

Gwyn tried for a shrug, a dismissive wave of her hand—but then something occurred to her, and she felt her eyes studying Kalfr's face. "It was kind of you, too," she said. "Without Silfast, maybe—"

Maybe Stella would have turned to you, she was about to say, but instead she grimaced, her eyes angling toward the closed bedroom door. But Kalfr had clearly followed her meaning, and he shook his head, twitched a wry little smile.

"I could not give her *that*, the way she wishes," he said, as the sound of a loud slap—and Stella's answering squeal—

filtered from beyond the door. "But her soft, ripe sweetness—*ach*. Mayhap I find this some day, in my own mate."

Right. Gwyn nodded, and attempted a smile of her own. "I'm sure you will, Kalfr," she said. "And she'll surely adore you."

Kalfr's smile twitched higher, and that was an unmistakable flush, darkening his cheeks. "Thank you, woman," he said, with a slight duck of his head. "Now, I shall wait close by, with your mate. Only speak if you need us, ach?"

Her mate. *Close by.* And Gwyn's heart had skipped a beat, her breath catching, her eyes pinned to Kalfr's face. To his wry, knowing smile tugging even higher before he turned away and strode out the door, shutting it tight behind him.

And then Gwyn was alone—or mostly alone, barring the rising sounds of gasps and growls coming from her bedroom. And her thoughts were swimming again, her eyes oddly fixed to the closed front door, her breaths dragging in, out, in again.

Joarr was truly... still here? Still waiting? Intending to *help* her? Her... *mate*?

It still didn't feel possible, it couldn't be possible. He'd lied to her, he hadn't told her, that pledge, *You break my sight, kindred witch, stay...*

And it was as Gwyn was considering it, perhaps even accepting it, that she heard a sudden clamouring commotion, thundering up the road. Surging toward her house, toward *her*, rising hoofbeats and voices and *chaos*.

No. No. Her body froze all over, her heart hammering, her eyes darting around the room—but oh goddess, it was already too late. And that was surely a familiar voice, and then firm footsteps coming closer, and then...

The rap on the door was sharp, sure of itself, enough to make her flinch. But she didn't move, couldn't move, couldn't breathe. Couldn't make herself take a single step forward, toward whatever was behind it, her *doom*...

And when the door banged open, slammed against the wall, it was like the rest of the world slammed shut. Flattening Gwyn with its devastating strength, crushing the breath from her lungs, driving the hope from her heart.

It was Roy.

35

For a long, curdling moment, Gwyn stared at Roy, while her heartbeat fought to pound out of her ribs.

He was here. He was armed. And he was... *angry.* His handsome face staring back at her like that, like she'd both repulsed and astonished him, like he wanted to rush across the room and throttle her.

"Where," he growled, "have you *been*, Gwynevere."

Gwyn's stomach lurched, her thoughts scrambling—how did he know she'd been gone?—and her eyes darted down to the table before her. The table where, just as Joarr had promised, there was a small collection of notes, written in script that looked astonishingly like hers. And she could still read the first one she'd written, still innocuously sitting there, from so many days past.

Gone to care for a client, she'd written. *May be complications.*

She blinked at it for an instant, at its odd, unnerving truth—and then snapped her eyes back to Roy's furious face. "I was working," she said, as coolly as she could, with a wave toward the note. "As a midwife. As I told you I was coming here to do. Remember?"

Roy loudly scoffed, and came a swift, angry step closer. "You were gone for *weeks*," he hissed. "My men searched for you everywhere. You weren't anywhere in Varrahan, or Ashford, or any of the smaller villages. People had heard of you, sure, but no one could ever remember actually *seeing* you!"

Wait. Roy's men had been here? Searching for her? *Spying* on her? After he'd *told* her he was leaving, and giving her the month her father had promised?

Gwyn's mouth had dropped open, her eyes wide on Roy's angry face—and yes, yes, clearly he'd done that. He'd kept his men here. He'd told them who she really was. He'd lied to her, *again.*

"Really, Roy?" she demanded, her arms folding tightly over her chest. "Even after you promised me that day that you were *leaving*, and going back to Dunburg? And, that you wouldn't betray my identity to your men?!"

Roy barked a harsh, bitter laugh, his smile not even touching his furious eyes. "I was worried about you," he snapped. "I was *helping* you. And if you really thought I was going to leave my betrothed alone here to get kidnapped and knocked up by orcs, you're even stupider than I thought!"

His voice had risen to a shout, that awful word *stupid* scraping up Gwyn's spine, and she swallowed hard, lifted her chin. "My father promised me a month of freedom here," she replied, as smoothly as she could. "You had *no right* to secretly spy on me, let alone barging into my house like this, and demanding detailed reports of my whereabouts. *Especially* before my month is even finished!"

Roy laughed again, even harder this time, and gave a slow, deliberate shake of his head. "I have every right, Gwynevere," he countered. "You're my *betrothed*. And now that you've had your chance to live out your stupid little commoner fantasy, you're going to grow the hell up, and come home with me, and *marry* me. Like you're damn well supposed to!"

Marry him. *Marry* him?! It felt like a slap, like being struck straight across the face, and Gwyn gaped blankly at Roy, at his enraged, glittering eyes. After a full *decade* of his nonsense—of him constantly putting off their wedding, brushing her away, giving careless laughing excuses—now he wanted to get married? *Now*?

And as Gwyn kept gaping at him, it occurred to her that her father had been... right?! *Leave Roy here to stew without you,* he'd told her that day in her apartment, with that knowing look in his eyes. *Light a much-needed fire under the boy...*

And goddess, Roy was *smiling* again, and it even looked genuine this time, curving rueful at his mouth. "Yes, you're going to marry me," he repeated, his voice low, as if Gwyn had shouted her disbelief across the room. "I know I've been putting it off for long enough. And look, I don't even blame you for giving me a hard time over it, or trying to give me a good scare. If you'll just let all this go, and come home, I'll forget this even happened. And you can start visiting dressmakers, or make plans to overflow the chapel with pretty flowers or some-thing, all right?"

Unbelievable. *Unbelievable.* Gwyn couldn't stop staring at him, her heartbeat ringing in her ears. "You do *not*," she somehow choked, "want to marry me, Roy. You *just* said you think I'm stupid! You've consistently disrespected my interests, my choices, and even my misplaced affections for you! And, last time I saw you, you threatened to burn down my *house*, and completely destroy my irreplaceable garden!"

Roy blinked at her, once—and then gave an uncomfortable little chuckle, a quick shake of his head. "Look, I just lost my temper, all right? Because I was worried about you. Because I *care* about you. Because you're going to be my *wife*."

Gwyn was shaking her head too, the incredulity jangling through her thoughts—but Roy only came a step closer, that smile still tilting up his mouth. "And I *knew* you probably wouldn't believe me," he said lightly, "so I've already set a wedding-date for next month, and sent off the announcement to the papers. The news will be public next week."

Next month. Next *week*? Gwyn seemed utterly incapable of movement, of speech, and she just stood there, her mouth agape, as Roy came another step closer. "So come along, then," he said, a little impatient, his head tilting sideways. "Unless you want to spend some time catching up first?"

His eyes had angled purposefully toward the closed door of Gwyn's bedroom—toward where Silfast and Stella were still inside, oh goddess, and how had Gwyn forgotten that? They'd clearly had the sense to stay quiet, at least, but what if Roy walked over there right now? What if he saw them, and saw *Stella*? He had soldiers outside, they could *capture* Stella, it would be a complete catastrophe, why couldn't she *think...*

"No," Gwyn choked, and she felt herself desperately clutching to that word, to the solid truth beneath it. "No, Roy. *No.* I told you it's over between us, and I meant it. You are not stepping *foot* in my bedroom. You are not taking me anywhere with you. And, most of all, you are *not* marrying me. *Ever!*"

Roy's body betrayed a faint but unmistakable twitch, his jaw flexing in his cheek. "Yes, I am, Gwynevere," he said, with enraging calm. "We have been betrothed for decades. I have your father's permission. And I am only looking out for you, and supporting you, when you have clearly become increasingly unstable. Your father should never have allowed you to come here, and given even more credence to your make-believe commoner *delusions!* And you can either come voluntarily, or I'll drag you kicking and screaming behind me, and tell everyone I meet that you've had a full-on nervous *collapse!*"

Oh, so now he was going there, the utter swine. Of *course* he was. And Gwyn didn't know whether to laugh, or spit at him, or curl up in a corner and sob, because what the hell was she supposed to do with this? Why hadn't she come up with a better plan? Would he truly just make her go, was there any way to salvage this, to make him see, make him leave...

"Even if you drag me out of here, Roy," she said, her voice wavering, "I still won't marry you. Because I—I met someone else. Someone else I... want to be with. Someone I... care about."

The words seemed to flare through the room, ringing, reverberating—but Roy didn't flinch. Didn't even blink, his eyes gazing at her like that, cool and distant and hard.

"You met someone else," he repeated, slow, very steady. "Someone *else*."

"Yes," Gwyn said, her voice harder now. "I've gotten to know him very well these past weeks. And not only does he under-stand me, but he—he respects me. He supports my work, and my goals. He *helps* me. He would never call me stupid, or even *think* of burning down my garden!"

Roy was still staring at her, not moving, not speaking, and Gwyn hauled in another breath. "And unlike you," she contin-ued, and was she going there, yes, yes, she was, "even if he meant for me to become... pregnant, he would offer me options. He would want me to do what's best for me, even if that wasn't what he wanted. He would *help* me, and be there for me. He would *never* leave me to deal with it on my own, like you did!"

Her voice had risen, ringing through the room, resonating with a strange, swirling certainty. Yes, perhaps Joarr had started out just the same as Roy, with perhaps even the exact same plan—to trap her, for his own purposes, his own gain. But Roy had gone one way, ended up here, while Joarr had done the utter opposite. He'd tried to change the plan. He'd tried to make amends. He'd supported her. Stayed with her.

And yes, yes, he'd stayed. From the very first night, he'd always been there. Always. And even now, he'd followed her here, he'd refused to leave, he was surely still out there listening to every damned word she said...

While Roy kept staring at her like that, his eyes slowly narrowing. And then flashing with something new, something... understood. As if he'd... *suspected*. That he... *wait*.

Roy hadn't *known* where she'd been. He hadn't known she'd gone to Orc Mountain. Had he? *Had* he?

"And let me guess, Gwynevere," Roy said, his voice silken, deadly. "This new paramour of yours. Tall fellow, is he? Lanky and sneaky? *Green*? Hair to about"—he cut his hand against his throat—"here?"

Ice was suddenly pouring down Gwyn's spine, freezing her feet to the floor, her eyes fixed to Roy's—and out of nowhere, he *laughed*. Loud and long, grating against her ears, while his glinting gaze lit up with cruel, wicked satisfaction. With *fury*.

"Oh, I know you think you're so *clever*, Gwynevere," he said, every word a sickening thud in her belly. "Now make yourself useful for once in your life, and tell me the *truth!*"

The truth. Gwyn couldn't breathe, her heart battering her ribs, her thoughts whirling up higher, higher, no, goddess, help, please—

But there was no help, only Roy stepping closer, his mouth still smiling, his eyes on fire. "Tell me," he said. "*Where is he?*"

36

W here is he. *Where is he.*

Gwyn's heart plunged in her chest, and she twitched a step backward, away from Roy, away from that terrifying look in his eyes.

"I have," she gulped, "*no idea* what you're talking about, Roy."

But Roy's laugh felt like more ice, dragging, shivering. "Your *orc*, love," he drawled at her. "The one who's been following you for *months*. The one who's apparently knocked up *my* betrothed with his disgusting orc spawn!"

What? Impossible. *Impossible.* And Gwyn's shock was thankfully firing heat to her frozen body, her frozen brain, think, *think...*

"You're the one who's imagining things, Roy," she managed, as steadily as she could. "There's no way you could possibly even *know* such things!"

But that glint only sharpened in his eyes, that laugh again scraping ice up her spine. "Isn't there?" he asked, so cold. "If you must know, love, my best men have been tracking that sneaky orc bastard all over Dunburg for *months*. Until he suddenly disappeared, about three weeks ago. Which, in retrospect, is precisely when *you* left!"

Wait. Roy had been tracking Joarr? And Joarr had been in Dunburg? For *months*? For... *her*?

Gwyn's shock surely read true on her face, her head wildly whipping back and forth—and Roy laughed again, and came a smooth step closer. "We tracked him down here," he continued, "and my men *nearly* caught him on his way to Orc Mountain. Which was, oh so coincidentally, on the same day that *you* first disappeared!"

Good goddess. So not only had Roy's visit to Gwyn that day been about hunting *Joarr*—but those men in the forest had been specifically chasing him, too? And had Joarr—had Joarr *known* that?

Something new plummeted in Gwyn's belly, shouting more chaos in her thoughts, and Roy's laugh abruptly faded, his eyes darkening on her face. "But obviously, I gave you the benefit of the doubt," he said thinly. "There was no sign of the bastard having someone with him, and no sign of struggle at your house. And there was word of you in various villages, and"—his eyes flicked down to the table—"all these damned notes. And I would never have dreamed that my *betrothed* would voluntarily join forces with a vile, vicious orc!"

Gwyn was not speaking, was *not* replying to that, and Roy came another step closer. "Do you know the shit that foul orc has caused, Gwynevere?" he demanded. "That orc—that lanky creeping spy of theirs—gets into *everything*. He was a *crucial* contributor to Lord Norr's untimely death. He broke into Duke Warmisham's house in broad daylight, and *drugged* him with a deadly mushroom. We're quite sure he let a flock of wild *geese* into the lords' last Council meeting in Wolfen. And last time my men nearly caught him, he set their horses loose, went for a joy-ride on a *priceless* stallion, and then dumped their supply-wagon off a *cliff*!"

And curse her, but even in the midst of the constantly rising chaos, Gwyn felt her traitorous mouth twitch up, an irrepressible bubble lurching in her throat, while the all-too-vivid vision of that—of Joarr doing all that—flashed across her thoughts. And Roy caught it, the utter bastard, his eyes widening, his hand jerking down to clutch at the sword hanging at his side.

"So that's how it is, is it, Gwynevere?" he continued, his voice soft deadly danger. "I'll grant you, it's been total silence from that brute for weeks now—and now we know why, don't we? He was holing up in Orc Mountain with *my* betrothed, and making *damn* well sure he knocked her up with his spawn! But believe you me, Gwynevere"—he snapped one step closer, his lip curling—"his leavings will be dealt with by morning, and so will he. And so will *you*!"

The last of Gwyn's mirth had thoroughly vanished, and flooding its place was more ice, more cracking pouring fear. And she had to say something, Roy was waiting for her to say something, what, what would escape this, what would save this, goddess, please...

"You have," she began, halting, "no right to speak to me like this, Roy. No right to *threaten* me. And no matter what you say, I am still Lord Anton's daughter, and he will *not* take kindly to you harming me!"

And was that true, that had to be true, her father did still care, somewhere—but Roy was laughing *again*, the sound curdling in Gwyn's belly. "Luckily, fair Gwynevere," he purred, "your father is on his way here as we speak. And I assure you"—he stepped toward her again, now standing just on the other side of her table—"he will be fully on my side in this. Not only that, but he will give me *anything* I want, to make sure I keep this quiet, and follow through on actually *marrying* you!"

No. *No.* Goddess, please. *Please.* But Roy was still talking, more dead light firing through his eyes. "And," he continued, cold, terrible, "just on my way here, I received word that my men made another capture. Another pregnant chit, whose disgusting orc barely escaped our clutches. Woman by the name of Hannah. Sound familiar, Gwynevere?"

Hannah. They had *Hannah*?! No. It wasn't possible. And it wasn't possible that Roy's men had been orchestrating those attacks against women, supporting those attacks, leading those attacks?!

The hell. The *gall.*

"Yeah, I thought so," Roy continued, his voice thin, merciless. "And when we haul up this Hannah before your father—maybe make a few threats about that little *vermin* she's growing inside her—what's she going to tell us, Gwynevere? What's she going to say about you, and what you've been doing these past weeks?"

The swine. The complete and utter *scum.* And Gwyn was shaking all over with shock, with rage, with the rising, jolting urge to hurl her kitchen table at Roy's smug, mocking face. But he had a weapon, and she didn't, and she could *not* afford to expose Stella and Silfast, how would she escape this, how would she rescue Hannah, what the *hell* was she supposed to do—

"You will *not*," she gasped, without thinking, the words hitching from her throat. "He won't let you."

He. *He*, meaning not Gwyn's father, not even Hannah's mate Fulnir—but Joarr. Joarr, who had to still be listening. Joarr, who had to help. Who had to save Hannah. Please, goddess, please...

And Roy's eyes, Roy's harsh rolling laugh, said that he *knew* that. He *wanted* that. And wait, he wanted *Joarr*, he wanted to draw him out, he'd been hunting him for *months*, he'd said...

"*He* won't let me?" Roy asked now, brows raised, that dreadful smile still curling at his mouth. "Surely you don't mean your slippery orc lover is *here*, fair Gwynevere? And if he is"—she could see the thought collecting, hardening—"he must be listening, don't you think? I wonder what he'd do, if I were to remind him who you really are? Of who *really* owns you?"

Of who *owned* her? The shock flashed again, dark and dizzying, and Roy was still coming closer, now moving to step around her kitchen table. "What would that brute do," Roy continued, his voice lowering, "if I decided to have my way with my own betrothed? If I made her scream for me, while he listens?"

No. *Never*. But Gwyn was trapped in ice, in sliding deadly cold, in bitter frozen fear. She couldn't move, Roy was walking toward her, he was going to touch her. He was going to goad Joarr into breaking the treaty, she was backing away toward the stove, please, please—

And she—stepped on something. Something that crunched, oddly, beneath her foot. And when her frantic eyes flicked down toward it, there was...

Heat. Life. Hope. Because it was a pinecone. A *pinecone*.

And there was no way a pinecone could have appeared in here. Impossible, *impossible*, except—her eyes darted left, right, up, around—for the window. The small, glass-paned window, just over her stove, and below the window was—

Her *crossbow*?!

But yes. Her crossbow. Sitting there, silent and innocuous, as though it had been lying there, all that time. But Gwyn had taken it to Orc Mountain, it and all the bolts, and then entirely forgotten about it. But two bolts were lying there beside it, waiting...

Gwyn had again frozen in place, staring down toward it, for a breath too long—long enough that Roy finally looked, too.

His eyes swiftly widening, his body suddenly lurching toward it, his gloved hand reaching for it, no, goddess, no, no, *no*—

And Gwyn didn't think, didn't hesitate. Just snatched for the bow, loaded the bolt, and aimed it straight for Roy's heart.

"Like hell, asshole," she said, and fired.

37

Luckily for Roy, he had passable reflexes. Enough that he dodged sideways, toward Gwyn's table—and her crossbow-bolt speared him in the shoulder, rather than nailing him in the heart.

"Ahhhhhhh!" he screamed, his body rearing up, his voice echoing horribly through the too-small house. "Owwwww!"

Gwyn flinched and ducked backwards, waiting for the almost-certain onslaught of soldiers, barging through her front door—but nothing happened. Not beyond Roy's stiff body, taking one staggering step toward her—and then collapsing down onto her kitchen table with a dull, heavy *thunk*.

Gwyn stared down at his limp form, his rolled-back eyes—and then reflexively reached a hand to his throat. To where his pulse was still fluttering, but he surely wasn't awake... and that was most certainly the first trickle of his blood, pooling out from his shoulder onto the table.

"Gwyn!" said a familiar voice, and when she blankly blinked up, it was—Stella? Yes, Stella, rushing out of the bedroom door, with only a shawl hastily thrown around her shoulders. And behind her, there was Silfast's huge bulk, striding out fully naked into the kitchen, until they both halted by the table, staring down at Roy's sprawled, bleeding body.

"You didn't," Stella gulped, her eyes wide, "*kill* him. Did you?"

Gwyn was feeling curiously distant, detached, her eyes now fixed to that crossbow-bolt still embedded in Roy's shoulder. "No," she heard herself say. "But he captured Hannah, and he's been pursuing our women, and our orcs. And, he threatened to attack me. To terminate my *son*."

Gwyn could hear Stella's faraway gasp—perhaps she'd neglected to mention about her son?—but she ignored it as she turned and picked up the second bolt, lying so innocuously, so conveniently, beside where the first had been. "So," she continued, her voice someone else's, as she set the bolt in place, pulled the lever back. "I really ought to finish the job, don't you think?"

Stella hitched forward, her hands clutching Gwyn's arm, her head wildly shaking. "Y-you don't need to, Gwyn," she said. "You can—think about it."

But Gwyn wasn't thinking, didn't want to think, wanted to fight back, face this, finish this. And she drew in a hard breath as she raised the bow again, should she shoot Roy in the heart, or maybe the neck—

"Woman," cut in a deep voice, Silfast's voice—and when Gwyn's eyes darted up, he was frowning down toward her, his huge arms crossed over his still-muddy chest. "You are Bautul. And thus"—his eyes hardened on hers, dark, challenging— "you must first ask. Does this serve the Bautul. Does this serve our mountain. Does this serve your mate, your son. Does this honour the goddess."

Gwyn twitched, shook her head—surely getting rid of Roy would help, surely it would keep him from harming anyone else, ever again—but Silfast barked a low growl, vicious enough to raise the hairs on her arms. "You must ask," he insisted. "Does this honour your goddess."

Something was distantly shouting, somewhere in Gwyn's head, and she thrust it away, gritted her teeth. "You're a fine one to talk," she hissed back at him, "especially with the reckless way you run your training. You think maiming half our *clan* honours our goddess either?"

Silfast loudly harrumphed, but his brow had also furrowed, his mouth thinning. His eyes flicking back to Roy, who was still gazing empty-eyed toward the ceiling, the blood still trickling from his shoulder.

"I should never kill one who cannot even *see* this," Silfast said flatly. "This does not honour the goddess."

The distant shouting was rising again, whirling, struggling to escape, and Gwyn grasped for thought, for truth. "Well, then what about maiming orcs who aren't ready!" she shot back. "Orcs who might develop lasting injuries, that then prevent them from fighting at full capacity against horrid men like *him*"—she glared down at Roy—"in the future! Does that serve Bautul? Or the goddess?"

Silfast kept frowning, his eyes now sweeping balefully between Gwyn and Roy. While his huge shoulders rose and fell, his folded arms shifting against his chest.

"I shall speak to the goddess upon this," he said finally. "But only if *you* now speak to her upon *this*."

He angled his head down toward Roy, toward Gwyn's crossbow-bolt pointing at his heart. And Gwyn was staring again too, as the distant shouting in her skull seemed to come closer, rattling against something important. The Bautul, those injuries, the blood, Eyolf and Iyolf, Joarr...

So she somehow jerked a nod, and clutched her hand at the table. Much the same way she would have touched the altar back in the garden, and she closed her eyes. Breathed. Listened.

There was nothing at first. Only the urgency, the chaos, the *rage*, the combined breaths and shifting bodies around her. But this felt so familiar now, the inhale and the exhale, the way her thoughts sifted and settled—and behind them, the distant shouting seemed to be suddenly audible, screeching through her skull.

I hate Roy, for what he's done to me. I hate him for trying to take this life away from me. I'm trying to make my own way, I'm trying to fight you, to defeat you...

To fight. To defeat. To be that kind of Bautul. But... there was another kind too, wasn't there? There was Joarr's kind. *I seek new way. I alter my means. I run with what the gods drop upon me. I shall no throw this man's death into the fray...*

And wait, Gwyn had forgotten that, somewhere, hadn't she? She'd all but asked Joarr to kill Roy, all those weeks ago—and he'd refused. On account of his kin, he'd said. Maybe even his clan.

He's found a new way. He had. And maybe—maybe Gwyn could trust him, one more time. She could trust the goddess. Trust *herself*. She *was*.

She felt her hand lowering the bow, felt her breath shudder out slow. And felt both Silfast and Stella exhaling beside her, and yes, surely that was relief, flaring through their eyes.

"Wise woman," Silfast said firmly. "Now we shall again hide in this room, whilst you, mayhap, tell these men"—he cocked his head toward the door—"how your betrothed has assumed grave falsehoods of you, and sought to harm you. Mayhap speak of how you maimed him for your safety, but you yet bear no wish to cause him lasting harm. Mayhap you also tell them how they have captured a woman you care for, and how you shall not bear such affront against the women you serve. Ach?"

Oh. Gwyn blinked at Silfast, at his glinting black eyes, because that was... a good plan? A sensible plan. Trust the goddess. Trust herself. Trust... the *Bautul*?

She eyed Silfast for another strange, stilted instant, but then nodded, and waved him and Stella back toward her bedroom with a shaky hand. And once they'd gone, closing the door tightly behind them, Gwyn took one last look at Roy's immobile form, and then strode to her front door, and yanked it open.

There were a dozen-odd men waiting outside, chattering and brushing down their horses. And when they looked up toward Gwyn, their voices fading, it was far too easy to put a trembly hand to her heart, to bring the genuine fear to her eyes.

"I need help," she told them, her voice hoarse. "There's been an—an accident. Is there a medic here? *Please*."

She braced herself for their questions, their censure, their certain accusations—but the grey-haired man who must have been Roy's second-in-command immediately jogged toward her, and gestured for the other men to follow. And soon they were all rushing inside her house, taking stock of Roy's unconscious body on the table, and launching into frantic, furious action. Assessing the wound, pouring painkillers down his throat, extracting the crossbow-bolt, binding him up again.

And throughout it all, Gwyn pointedly ignored her own considerable knowledge of wound care, and instead stood there wringing her hands, and answering the men's questions with astonishing honesty. *Roy was angry with me. He threatened me. He attacked me.*

Roy thankfully didn't once awaken to offer his own side of the tale, and his second-in-command seemed grimly unsurprised by it all, gravely shaking his grey head. "I've told that boy his foolish ways will come to haunt him someday," he said, frowning as his men finally dragged Roy's limp form out the door, and strapped him to a horse. "And to attempt such wrongs against our lord's own daughter. I'll be sure to report this to your father when he arrives here tonight, Lady Gwynevere, and I assure you, he'll not be pleased to hear it."

Wait. So Roy really had been telling the truth about her father? Lord Anton was coming? Here? *Now?*

"My father's really on his way here?" Gwyn echoed, her voice rising, her heart reeling in her chest. "Tonight?"

"Yes indeed," the man replied, with a smile that was surely intended to be comforting. "He means to escort you back to Dunburg himself, I believe."

Oh. Oh, goddess. Back to Dunburg. *Tonight.*

And whatever relief Gwyn might have found in this—whatever hope she'd still been clinging to—seemed to plummet all at once, clenching hard and cold in her belly. Because yes, her father's one-month deadline was nearly up, wasn't it? And she still hadn't found a way out of that, had she? Had she?

No. No, she hadn't. Because even if she'd managed to get rid of Roy, her father's awful new law was still looming, still waiting. Still just as deadly as ever...

"Why don't I leave you to rest for a spell, Lady Gwynevere," the man said, patting his hand to her shoulder. "I'll stay with a few men outside, and wait for your father's band. Just call if you need anything more."

Gwyn twitched a nod, and somehow even managed to express her thanks. And then the man was shutting the door behind him, leaving her alone again, while the panic kept ringing louder and louder through her thoughts.

Her father was coming. Her father was going to take her back to Dunburg, to her old life. Away from Orc Mountain. Away from Joarr.

And in Dunburg—Gwyn's hands fluttered to her still-flat waist—she would still need to testify. To make as public a scene as possible. To fight as loudly and vehemently as possible against that horrible law. Lord Anton's dotty, unfashionable, plant-obsessed daughter... pregnant. With an orc's son.

And she would do it. She *would*. She would serve the Bautul. Serve all the women she'd met, all the new friends she'd made. She would serve Joarr. Serve... her son.

An odd gulp choked from her throat, and she felt her head bowing, her hands clutching to fists. She'd been fighting so hard to forget about the truth of her son these past days, to pretend he didn't truly exist—because if he *did* exist, what then? What if she started thinking about a little, bright-eyed Joarr, scampering about a garden, climbing trees with his tiny claws? What if she started thinking about rocking him in their hammock, or chasing him all over Orc Mountain, or teaching him about herbs and mushrooms? What if she started thinking about—about a *family*?

But no. *No*. It didn't matter. Because their son was just another pawn in this war, and always had been. And Gwyn had always known that returning to Dunburg would seal his fate for good. She couldn't think about it. She *couldn't*.

And without even seeing it, knowing it, she'd stumbled toward her candlewood. Her candlewood, that was still here, one of the few plants left. And that was surely because—she stilled, even as her hands were already reaching for its sharp spines—Joarr hadn't meant to bring it. Hadn't wanted to add that temptation into her life.

Find other way, he'd kept saying, over and over again. *Seek other relief. Stay safe.*

Gwyn's stomach twisted, her face crumpling—and somehow, *somehow*, she shoved away from the candlewood, back toward the table. Gripping it so hard it hurt, bowing her head, squeezing her eyes shut. Listening, seeking, choked and desperate, for her own heart, her own altar. Where Joarr had first found her, taken her, made her scream under his tongue. *You are quick. Sharp. Wise. Now we mate...*

And she clung to it, dragged it in with breath after strangled breath. Seeking, waiting, praying. Finding a new way. Seeking one more favour, upon one more altar. Please. *Please.*

And when the next commotion finally came beyond the door—the familiar hard rap against it, the familiar voice—Gwyn's eyes were dry, her jaw set. And she lurched toward the door with staggering steps, and yanked it open.

"Father," she said, with her best attempt at a smile. "You're here."

38

Behind the door, Gwyn indeed found Lord Anton of Dunburg, in the flesh. Looking distinctly hot and sweaty and ruffled, his corpulent body hunched in the doorway, his brow heavy and furrowed.

But then—he blinked at Gwyn once, twice—his shoulders sagged, and that was surely warmth, flashing across his bloodshot eyes. *Relief*.

"Gwynnie!" he exclaimed, as he stepped inside, and dragged her into a tight, sticky hug. "You're here! And alive, and *safe*, thank the gods. And looking so well, too! And"—he yanked back, frowning, as his eyes darted up and down her form—"what's all this I heard about you up and disappearing? And now, about you *shooting* Roy?!"

Right. Straight to that, then. And Gwyn drew in breath, lifted her chin, held her father's watching eyes. "I didn't disappear in the least, Father," she said. "I was busy *working*, just as I'd planned to do when I moved here. As for Roy, he insulted me, tried to attack me, and threatened to burn down my *house*, and"—she felt her anger genuinely rising, sharpening—"he publicly announced our engagement, and even booked a wedding-date in Dunburg, without *once* consulting with me!"

Her father blinked toward her, his frown deepening. "Now, now, Gwynnie," he said, in a soothing, conciliatory voice. "You've been betrothed to Roy for *years*, and you're the one who came here with the sole intention of winding him up. Surely you can't be upset, now that he's doing exactly what you wanted!"

Gwyn's own irritation kept rising, and she whipped her head back and forth. "No, Father," she countered. "That's what *you* wanted, remember? *I* wanted to escape Roy, and break our engagement, for good. I wanted to start my own *life* here, away from him."

Lord Anton was looking genuinely bewildered now, his gloved hand rubbing at his reddened face. "But *Gwynnie*," he said earnestly. "Roy will take good care of you. He'll keep you safe, and give you a good life. A good *home*."

His eyes had darted darkly around the room, clearly suggesting that this house was no such thing—and Gwyn felt her breath rushing out, her anger snapping even stronger. Because she—she'd *had* all that. Hadn't she? A good life. A good home. *Safety*.

She'd had all that, with *Joarr*.

And she was finding a new way. She was. She *was*.

"No, Father," she replied, her voice curt. "I will not marry Roy. *Ever*. And if you want the truth"—she squared her shoulders, she was facing this, she *was*—"I met someone else. Here. And I want to make a life with *him*."

Her father kept blinking at her, astonishment flaring through his eyes—and then he exhaled a heavy, exasperated sigh. "Someone new?" he demanded, as he pulled off his gloves, and used them to fan his face. "Someone well funded, I hope? With decent holdings and property? Any titles? Hopefully no children?"

The tightness in Gwyn's belly had oddly flipped, because wait, surely her father wasn't actually—*agreeing* to this? Asking? *Listening*?

"No, no children yet," she replied, her voice sounding thin, strange. "But he runs some excellent properties, with very valuable yields. And he's very clever, and holds a high position, and frequently travels, and"—her distant thoughts flicked back to what Roy had said—"often goes up to Dunburg. So I'd still be able to visit you, too."

And her father was still—*listening* to this. Listening, watching her, and... and *nodding*? And then giving another worn, resigned-sounding sigh as he fumbled for one of her kitchen chairs, yanked it out, and sank his heavy body onto it with obvious relief.

"You realize I'm not paying for a *copper* of this, Gwynnie," he said, though there was no heat in his voice. "So who is he, then? Who's this miraculous man who's managed to steal away my precious daughter?"

Well. Gwyn swallowed hard, her eyes held blankly to her father's face, while her stomach kept swerving, her heart galloping harder and higher in her chest.

Goddess, she wasn't going to do this. Surely she wasn't. Finding a new way. Rolling with whatever the goddess threw at her...

"I'd be honoured to introduce you," she said. "Joarr, will you please come, and meet my father?"

39

For a fraught, frozen breath, there was nothing. Only the increasing uncertainty in her father's wary eyes as he glanced around the kitchen, twisted to look behind him—

When on the other side of the room, Gwyn's bedroom door swung open, silent and sure. And from within, out strolled *Joarr*.

He looked cool, relaxed, utterly at ease—goddess, he'd even put on a *tunic*—and he calmly shut the bedroom door behind him, and then strode over toward them.

"Lord Anton," he said, with a fluid little bow. "I am Joarr. Of Clan Bautul."

Gwyn's father had badly startled, his mouth dropping open, his hands clutching at his heart. "Gwynnie!" he shouted, leaping up from his chair, and rushing over to stand before her. "There's an *orc* in your house! *Run!*"

And twisting in Gwyn's furiously thundering chest, there was something—new. Her father was—afraid for her? Protecting her? Telling her to *run*?

"N-no, Father," she managed, grasping both her hands

against his bulky shoulders. "This is who I was talking about. He's—an orc. And he's—he's my—"

Goddess, she couldn't even say it, because what if it wasn't true? What if she was still horribly misreading all this, what if she still couldn't trust him, still—

But Joarr's eyes had flicked up, over her father's shoulder, to hold on Gwyn's face. Quiet, steady, intent. True.

"I am Gwyn's mate," Joarr said, very smoothly. "I shall tend her, and honour her, and worship her. For as long as I am able, and as long as she should wish."

Oh. Oh, *goddess*. Those words soaring deep, curling up warm and close, quelling Gwyn's screaming thoughts, quieting her rampaging heart. Joarr was her mate. *Hers*.

But before her, her father was twitching, spluttering, staring back and forth between them—and then he lunged, with surprising speed, toward Gwyn's crossbow. Which had been lying fully armed on the table beside them, and her father was sweeping it up, aiming it toward Joarr's heart—

"No!" Gwyn shrieked, clutching at his shoulders, yanking him away—and luckily, the shot went wide. Firing straight toward the closed front door, even as Joarr had already flashed into motion, dropping and rolling well out of its path.

And when everything shuddered still again, there was another crossbow-bolt embedded in Gwyn's door, her father was cursing and trembling, and Joarr was standing tall again, smirking toward Gwyn, and clearly trying not to laugh.

"You can't shoot him, Father," Gwyn said firmly, giving his quavering shoulders a harsh, forceful shake. "He won't harm us. He's my—my *mate*. And"—her gaze flicked back to Joarr, whose eyes had sobered, holding on hers—"he's the father of my child. My son. To be born in the spring."

That, of course, set her father sputtering and shouting again, but Gwyn mostly ignored it this time, and kept her eyes on Joarr. Lifting her chin a little, as if even challenging him. Saying, perhaps, *Are you sure, you really still want that…*

But Joarr nodded, once, again. And his throat was convulsing, his eyes steady and watchful, liquid, deep enough to get lost in…

Yes, it meant. *Yes. Mine.*

Something fluttered in Gwyn's belly, something warm and light and *home*—and she felt herself smiling up at him, slow, genuine, relieved. And he was smiling back, all sparkling eyes and sharp white teeth, and she wanted to hurl herself toward him, curl up against his heart—

"Gwynnie!" her father was hollering between them, wildly waving his arms. "You can't be serious. You can't be *sane*! What in all the gods' holy names have you *done*? Do you not realize what this *means*?!"

But Gwyn was rolling with this now, with her *mate*, with the warmth and the courage now pooling strong and deep in her belly. "Yes, I do realize what this means, Father," she said, her voice surprisingly calm. "It means I'll now be subject to that horrid new law of yours. And that I will happily come to Dunburg with you, and testify about it before *everyone* you know."

Her father flinched all over, his eyes frozen wide on her face—but Gwyn wasn't done, not even close. "Your law wanted to hurt women like me," she continued, harder now. "You wanted to humiliate us, and destroy our lives. So if you don't find a way to stop that law, I will walk straight into this. I will *run* with this. I will take my destruction—and yours—all over the damned *realm*. To *anyone* who will listen."

Her father's face had gone very pale, and his big body suddenly staggered, tripping sideways. But before he could collapse onto the table, Joarr had swiftly grasped his arms, and half-guided, half-dragged him back to his chair. And to Gwyn's vague surprise, her father didn't even try to fight him, and just sank down into the chair, and buried his face in his twitching hands.

"But an *orc*, Gwynnie!" he moaned. "Good gods. You can't. You *can't*. And look, *I* can't. I even tried with the other lords, all right? After I saw how upset you were, before you left. But"—his shoulders shook as he hauled in air—"they've already pushed ahead with it, Culthen and Warmisham most of all. They have a lot to settle with these orcs, but they also think they have the right of all this. They think they're *helping* those women, with that law."

Of course they did, the rich complacent bastards. And wait, this couldn't mean Gwyn was still trapped, still stuck with this, still lost... could it? Not now, not after everything she'd done, please, goddess, please...

She'd somehow clutched desperately at the table, squeezing her eyes shut, dragging in deep breaths. Needed to roll with this, needed to find a new way, *please*...

A new way. New *hope*.

"Then—then you *change* the law," Gwyn heard herself gasp, breathless, her eyes snapping back up to her father's bowed head. "You *fix* it, Father. You stop hunting these women. You drop the public testifying part. And if and when those women come to you, you send them *only* to midwives who will actually support them. You send them to *me*."

And yes. *Yes*. This could work. This *had* to work. And when Lord Anton's head slightly lifted, his brow furrowed, Gwyn kept talking, following it, thinking it through. "If you can do that, Father," she said, "you could truly *help* those women, instead of hurting them. You'd give them the care they need, and the choice. *Please*."

Her father blinked at her for one uncertain, halting instant—maybe, *maybe*?—but then he moaned again, and buried his face back in his hands. "This is just too much, Gwynnie," he said, high-pitched and plaintive. "Orcs?

Changing *laws*? Especially right now? Because ever since Roy sent me that damned urgent message—three days ago!—I haven't had a moment's proper rest. Let alone a good stiff drink, or a half-decent *meal!*"

Gwyn's heart was fiercely pattering, her eyes held to her father, her thoughts twisting, tangling, twirling. He had honestly tried to change the law. He'd tried to protect her. And he was thinking about this, he was considering it, he *was*...

"Joarr," Gwyn heard herself say, not quite steady. "Do you think—could you please make my father some supper?"

And goddess bless him, because Joarr was already nodding, his eyes warm and appreciative on her face. "Ach, I shall," he said lightly. "But first, mayhap, this help?"

With that, he'd reached into his trouser pocket, and plucked something out. Something small, brown, familiar. A... *mushroom?*

But yes, yes, it was a mushroom, of precisely the same rare, valuable variety he'd given Gwyn in his mushroom-room. And Lord Anton's wary, mulish, frowning eyes had flicked up toward it—and then snapped wide, while an audible gasp choked from his mouth.

"Is that—" he began, and his hand reached out with astonishing eagerness, and snatched the mushroom out of Joarr's hand. "It is! Where did you find this?!"

He shot Joarr a dark, accusing look—goddess, as if Joarr had *stolen* it—and Gwyn loudly cleared her throat, crossing her arms over her chest. "Joarr *grows* them, Father," she said flatly. "He's an accomplished mushroom specialist. Now"—she squared her shoulders—"have you had any adverse effects with these before? Any unmanageable hallucinations or terrors? Any mental difficulties over the next days, or weeks?"

Lord Anton was already shaking his head, eyeing the little brown mushroom with a hushed, blinking reverence. And before Gwyn could speak another word, he popped it into his mouth, and swallowed it whole. And then closed his eyes, his face smoothing, his body sagging back into his chair.

Oh. Well. Gwyn stared blankly toward him, entirely nonplussed—and an uncertain glance toward Joarr showed him looking highly amused again, his mouth twitching up, his eyes dancing on hers.

"Grouse for supper?" he asked. "Mayhap you make fire, witch? And"—his gaze darted around at the few plant-pots still remaining in her kitchen—"harvest herbs for us? Rosemary, mayhap?"

Gwyn nodded back, her face unaccountably heating—and after a surreptitious pat of his hand to her arse, Joarr spun toward the window behind them, and yanked the sash open. And after a little leap, a fluid slither sideways, he was gone out the window, leaving Gwyn standing stock-still behind him, and foolishly half-smiling at where he'd gone.

"I cannot *believe* you, Gwynnie," cut in her father's voice, and when she turned back around, he was eyeing her darkly, his mouth curling. "You *like* that fellow. That *orc*. Enough to"—he shuddered all over—"*reproduce* with him?!"

But Gwyn was rolling with this now, running with this, and she somehow even nodded, and pulled over her pot of rosemary and her shears. "Yes, Father," she said, as she began clipping. "Joarr and I have a lot in common. We have a lot of fun together. He's very supportive of me. He"—she swallowed, took a breath—"he takes care of me. In a way no one has done since Mother died."

Lord Anton at least had the grace to wince, though his eyes were looking distinctly unfocused now, his body sagging heavier into his chair. "But he's an orc, Gwynnie!" he protested. "I don't want to lose you to an orc! And their spawn are *deadly*, and this could very well *kill* you! And, hasn't it occurred to you"—his gaze sharpened on Gwyn's face—"that he's playing sweet on you because of *me*? Because of this *war*?"

Gwyn bit back the sudden, surging urge to laugh, and shook her head as she turned to light a fire in the stove. "It has occurred to me, Father," she said, "but I'm now confident that's not the case. As for my safety"—she blew on her little fire, and turned to meet his still-sharp eyes—"you can be assured I will use my own midwifery knowledge to the best of my ability, and also seek out the best prenatal care possible. And if you'd like to further improve my prospects, you can deal with that horrid law, and *help* me."

Lord Anton sighed, rubbing a hand at his face, but didn't speak. And at that very moment, Joarr leapt back through the window, now with multiple skinned grouse gripped in his clawed fingers. "Hungry?" he said cheerfully, as he rummaged around for a pan, and set it on the stove. "You like mushrooms in food also, Lord Anton?"

Gwyn's father twitched, but then gave a slow, wary-looking nod. And soon the room filled with the delicious scent of frying poultry and mushrooms, seasoned with a generous helping of light, fragrant rosemary.

And when Joarr finally plunked an overflowing plate down before Lord Anton, he blinked suspiciously down toward it, and carefully poked at its contents with his fork. And then speared a chunk of meat, and took a slow, reluctant nibble, his head tilting as he chewed.

"Oh," he said, his eyes brightening, and he took another bite, much larger than before. And soon he was tucking in with astonishing eagerness, his body leaning close over the table, his dazed eyes fluttering with visible approval as he swallowed.

Joarr quickly made up plates for Gwyn and himself too, and soon they'd joined her father at the table. And it felt utterly, impossibly surreal, to be casually sitting around a table with her father and her orc, eating a delicious meal here in her cozy new house.

"This really wasn't bad," Lord Anton finally said, once he'd polished off his entire plate, frowning wolfishly down toward it. And before Gwyn could even ask, Joarr had already stood and refilled the plate, and set it back down before him again.

By the time they'd all finished eating, Lord Anton was looking rather dazedly contented, rubbing both hands at his rounded belly, and vacantly smiling toward the opposite wall. "I don't s'pose," he said, in a somewhat sing-song voice, "you've got any more of those lovely little mushrooms on hand?"

His hazy gaze had flicked toward Joarr, narrowing with visible effort on his face—and to Gwyn's astonishment, Joarr reached into his pocket, and produced two more little brown mushrooms. "You help daughter, and keep me secret," he said coolly, "and I keep you in mushrooms, ach? Send you new supply for each moon, mayhap?"

Wait. Was Joarr—was Joarr offering to become Gwyn's father's regular *supplier*?! And wait, was her father actually *considering* it? Studying Joarr across the table, his mouth tight, his clouded eyes shifting...

"One for each day," he countered, as Gwyn stared at him in utter disbelief. "And a few extra for friends."

But Joarr's brows had lifted, his head shaking back and forth. "I can no grow so many," he said. "Two for each week. And some for friends, when I can do this."

Gwyn's father returned this with a counter-offer, which Joarr returned with one of his own. Leading to a full-on haggling session over Gwyn's kitchen table, which she watched with ever-increasing bemusement. Until her father and Joarr had settled on an amount, a delivery schedule, and even a comprehensive plan for keeping it all secret from her father's guards and servants. And by the end of it, Joarr had even thrown in a demand that Lord Anton quietly cancel Roy's engagement-notice, and call off his betrothal to Gwyn, as well.

When Lord Anton finally stood to leave, the extra mushrooms were safely ensconced in his pocket, along with a rough handwritten agreement he and Joarr had drawn up on the back of one of Gwyn's notes. And while Lord Anton's eyes on Joarr weren't at all approving, they weren't quite disapproving, either—and he even reached over toward Gwyn, and yanked her into a painfully tight embrace.

"You make sure you take care of yourself, Gwynnie," he said, his voice surprisingly choked as he rocked her back and forth. "And send me letters, with that mushroom supply. And come see me, too, when you can. All right?"

Gwyn's eyes were unexpectedly prickling, and she hugged her father back, as tightly as she could. "Of course," she said thickly. "Th-thank you, Father."

If she wasn't mistaken, her father even wiped his own eyes as he backed away, his hands on her shoulders, his gaze flicking up and down her form. "You really are looking well," he said, with a sigh, and a resigned glance toward Joarr. "See that you keep her that way, orc."

And with that, he turned for the door, pulled it open, and slipped out into the darkness beyond.

40

Gwyn and Joarr stood in place behind the closed door, staring at one another. Not moving, perhaps not breathing, as they stared at one another, and listened. Hearing first voices beyond the door, and even a few easy laughs—and then horses walking, hooves clopping, fading off into the distance.

There was one last gulp of stilted silence, an odd-looking quiver on Joarr's mouth—and then he suddenly burst into laughter. His shoulders shaking, his eyes dancing, his body nearly bending double as he staggered sideways, and sank down into a chair.

"Mushrooms," he said, between guffaws. "Mushrooms! Powerful Lord Dunburg defeated by *mushrooms*?!"

All Gwyn's tension seemed to drain away at once, and she felt her own mouth twitching up, her body instinctively following his—and Joarr let loose another howl as he reached and dragged her close, down onto his lap. "And this *betrothed*," he gasped, shaking his head. "I *never* see you *shoot* him, witch. You hear how he *squeal*?"

The laughter was stealing over Gwyn now, too, convulsing

her belly, shuddering through her shoulders. "*Ahhhhhhh!*" she said, in her best impression of Roy's voice. "*Owwwwww!*"

Joarr's hoot of laughter echoed through the room, his head thrown back, his fist banging at the table. "I shall hear this in my *dreams*, witch," he choked, and those were actually tears, streaking down his cheeks. "*Owwwwww!*"

Gwyn was laughing too hard to speak now, her hands wiping at her wet eyes, her whole body collapsing back into Joarr's. Into the sheer contagious joy of him, the rolling convulsions of his chest, the bright warm comfort of his arms.

And when their laughter finally settled again, breaking into the occasional shaky chuckle, Joarr yanked Gwyn even closer, his head buried hard in her neck. "Ach, my witch," he said, his voice hitching. "This was well met. You are so quick. So wise. Make me so proud."

The warmth furled deeper into Gwyn's belly, her fingers lacing together with his. "I couldn't have done it without you," she replied, quiet. "Thank you for staying. For helping."

He shrugged against her, and that was surely a soft, lingering kiss, pressed to the tender skin of her throat. "Always," he said gruffly. "But"—he pulled away slightly, leaned around to meet her eyes—"mayhap you no welcome me keeping your father in mushrooms, ach? Mayhap you no wish to keep him so close?"

His eyes were serious, suddenly, searching hers with careful intent, as if he were truly worried about this—and this time it was Gwyn who shrugged, and huffed a hoarse little laugh. "It was brilliant," she said. "And of all the vices he pursues, this is probably one of the milder ones. And you know"—her head tilted as she considered it—"I actually think it'll be nice to still stay in touch with him. In controlled doses."

She was surprised to find that she meant it, and that the anger that had so often surrounded her dealings with her father seemed unexpectedly, curiously absent. Yes, he was selfish, and heedless, and infuriating—but he did care for her, in his way. He'd tried to protect her from Joarr. He'd tried to change the law. He'd agreed to help women, and help her.

"I think getting some distance from him lately really helped, you know?" she said, settling back into Joarr's arms. "And having more friends, and more support, away from him. I mean, I don't feel even the *slightest* urge to poison him anymore."

She felt Joarr chuckle again behind her, his mouth still kissing at her neck. "This is good," he murmured. "Though if this *betrothed* dares to come back again, we yet poison *him*, ach?"

"Oh, most definitely," Gwyn said, with a bubble of laughter. "With something *very* nasty. One of your webcap mushrooms, maybe."

Joarr laughed too, though it sounded rather viciously satisfied this time—and Gwyn twisted around to look at him again. "By the way," she said, "did you *know* Roy was tracking you? And hunting you? Even back in Dunburg?"

Joarr's eyes shifted, but he nodded, and exhaled a slow sigh. "Ach, I knew," he said. "I may have... taunted him in this, more than was wise. And I ought to have spoken of this to you also, I ken. But I no trusted you at first, and I no wished to stoke your fear after. And I no wished you to wonder why I was in Dunburg, for this was—"

He stopped there, running a hand through his hair, and he seemed strangely flustered, with an actual *flush* creeping up his cheeks. But before Gwyn could prod further, there was the tell-tale sound of movement, across the room—and then the bedroom door eased open, and Stella's mussed-looking head poked out.

"Is it safe now, Gwyn?" she asked. "You sent them all packing?"

Gwyn flashed Stella a rueful smile, and waved her out

toward them. "Yes, thank the goddess—and thanks to Joarr, too," she replied, with another glance back at his still-flushed cheeks. "How are you two faring? Hopefully you weren't too bored in there all this time?"

Stella took a tentative step out the door, a blanket clutched around her shoulders, a fresh set of large teeth-marks visible on her neck. "No, not at all," she said, as her shining eyes darted up to where Silfast's fully bared form was now looming close behind her. "We've been... catching up, haven't we, Silfast?"

Silfast was looking darkly pleased, and he gave an affirmative-sounding grunt as he swatted Stella on the arse. "Ach, and we have only just begun," he said smugly. "You yet have *much* chastening to bear, my sweet."

Stella shivered, her eyes dropping to the sight at Silfast's blatantly exposed groin, which was now obviously *twitching*—and behind Gwyn, Joarr loudly coughed, and then nudged her sideways on the chair, so he could stand to his feet. "You hunger?" he said, toward Stella and Silfast. "Like mushrooms?"

Silfast's eyes had sharpened, watching as Joarr strode over to the stove, and flipped the remaining meat and mushrooms in his pan. "Ach," Silfast grunted, and then he stalked toward the table, and dropped his huge body into a chair across from Gwyn. "Mushrooms are good."

Stella had followed him over, sinking into the chair beside him, and then flashed Gwyn a warm, conspiratorial smile. "He can scent them from a half-league away," she added. "Once, he nearly got himself shot, trying to pick some of those ruffled yellow ones. The ones that grow on trees?"

"Sulphur shelf," Gwyn said, over the irrepressible swell of mirth in her chest. "Joarr loves those, too."

Neither Joarr nor Silfast deigned to reply to this, though Silfast's wary eyes were still fixed to Joarr at the stove. And when Joarr finally turned and plunked a steaming plate of meat and mushrooms in front of him, Silfast blinked, and took a long, careful sniff—and then immediately began eating, with thoroughly betraying relish.

"This is really good, Joarr," Stella said, once Joarr had handed her a plate, too, and she'd taken a cautious bite. "Thank you. For this, and for—for everything."

Joarr shrugged and waved it away, his eyes narrowing back down at where Silfast had already polished off half his meal— and in a quick flick of movement, Joarr grabbed for the pan again, and dumped its remaining contents onto Silfast's plate. An action that Silfast returned with a wary-looking nod, before immediately tucking in again.

"Do you know, Seer," Silfast said finally, hesitating long enough to frown over at Joarr, "if any of the men shall return here tonight?"

Joarr had dropped down to sit on the last empty chair around the table, and shook his head. "No tonight, I ken," he said, with astonishing certainty. "And the men have now freed Hannah also. She is yet with Fulnir, and they run back to the mountain now."

Wait, *Hannah*. A belated flare of guilt shot through Gwyn's belly—good goddess, she'd forgotten all about Hannah—but Joarr's hand had already snapped out toward her arm, stroking smooth and reassuring against it. "Hannah is safe, thanks to your wise demands, woman," he said. "And also"—he betrayed a grimace, his gaze again flicking to Silfast—"your wise counsel, Captain."

Captain. Silfast shrugged and resumed eating, not looking up—but the tension in his shoulders seemed to relax, some of the wariness slipping from his face. And in that instant, it almost felt as though something had... shifted, in the room. Something... changed. And across the table, Stella clearly felt it too, her eyes darting back and forth between Silfast and Joarr, a soft smile curving at her lips.

"This house," Silfast said abruptly, his eyes still fixed to his plate, "speaks to me. It tastes of meaning. Of... the goddess' blessing. Ach?"

Gwyn blinked, and glanced toward Joarr—who was now leaning back in his chair, his arms crossed, his mouth pursed. "You ken?" he said. "I ken Ivar oft came here. Other Bautul, also."

Wait, *other* Bautul had come here too? But yes, good goddess, way back at the start, Joarr had said the house reeked of Bautul, hadn't he? And now the images of Great-Aunt Agnes and Ivar *and* multiple Bautul were swarming Gwyn's brain with alarming vividness, and she was almost grateful when Silfast loudly rapped at the tabletop, nearly startling her out of her chair.

"Ach, this fits," Silfast replied, his head bending down low, sniffing at the table. "Ivar is wise Bautul, who oft tastes the goddess' blessing. And this"—he rapped at the table again, a look of undeniable satisfaction flashing through his eyes—"is surely one of the goddess' altars, ach?"

What? Gwyn felt herself sputtering, staring between Silfast and Joarr—surely her kitchen table was *not* yet another ubiquitous Bautul altar—but Joarr seemed to be giving this claim actual consideration, his head tilted, his brow furrowing, his claws tapping against his arm.

"Ach, mayhap," Joarr said finally. "I ken I... I tasted the goddess' blessing, when I claimed my mate here."

Oh. He... had? And he was actually... *believing* Silfast on this? As if Silfast perhaps... *did* know this goddess, after all?

"Ach, this fits also," Silfast said, settling back in his chair. "Your mate then brought us great blessing, just as the goddess proclaimed. And thus"—his flinty gaze slid toward Gwyn—"you must not sell this house, woman. You must keep it safe, and all of Bautul shall support this. Ach?"

A sudden, shivery warmth was swooping in Gwyn's belly—

the Bautul would really help defend her *house*?—and Silfast nodded sharply at her, as though the matter were already settled. "I am sure you shall wish to spend many of your days with our Seer, either at our mountain, or whilst he scouts," he continued flatly. "Thus, when you are elsewhere, you shall allow other Bautul to come here, and tend your garden, and worship at this altar. If you yet wish to serve the women of this town, we shall also help arrange this."

Gwyn's mouth had fallen open, her eyes unblinking on Silfast's face—he truly meant all this? But yes, yes, surely he did, his jaw set like that, his eyes imperious and commanding on hers, clearly expecting her immediate compliance.

The warmth flared even higher in Gwyn's belly, escaping in a bright, delighted peal of laughter. The Bautul would guard her house, and tend her garden, and help her keep supporting Varrahan's women? And even if that surely meant orcs would be regularly copulating on her kitchen table, she was frantically, fervently nodding, and wiping away the wetness brimming in her eyes.

"That's—very generous of you, Silfast," she said, with another bright choke of laughter. "Of course I would be honoured. *Thank* you."

Silfast nodded too, his expression smugly satisfied. "You are Bautul," he said. "We fight for our own."

Well. Gwyn couldn't seem to stop smiling, or wiping at her eyes, or glancing around at her cozy little house. It would still be hers, after all. She could still be Varrahan's midwife, and Orc Mountain's, too. She could be Bautul. Fight for her own.

But that was bringing up something else, something important—and Gwyn felt her smile slightly fading as she glanced between Stella and Silfast, and drew in a deep breath. She would fight for her own. Her clan. Her friend.

"In that case," she said, "if Stella's not opposed, I would also like to work with her as her midwife, to help her through the rest of this pregnancy. Not as a replacement for Efterar and the Ka-esh, of course—but *with* them. And while I'll do my best for your son, my focus will always be on Stella. On *her* health, and *her* needs."

Silfast visibly flinched, his mouth grimacing, but his gaze had snapped to Stella's uncertain eyes, and held there. "Ach, this should be... good, I ken," he said, his voice stiff. "I was not... wise, in this. In my anger, I did not listen to my own mate. And I did not show her how I also care for *her* more than all else, even more than a son. I have"—his hand stroked at the table, his head briefly bowing—"sworn to the goddess to right this."

Oh, Gwyn felt herself flashing a relieved grin at Stella across the table, and Stella smiled back, slow and stunning. "Thank you, Gwyn," she said earnestly. "I'd be so happy to have you as my midwife."

The warmth was bubbling again in Gwyn's belly, more wetness pooling in her eyes, and she gave Stella a twitchy little nod. "But I'll warn you now, though," she said, "as part of that, I think you two need to talk to someone. Someone you trust, who can be impartial, and help you work through some of this. You've both been through a lot, and there's still a lot to come with pregnancy—not to mention a child. You both need to be prepared, and that means working together, and communicating honestly with each other. About your desires, your fears, your hopes for your future together. All right?"

Silfast was looking rather disconcerted by this, but thankfully didn't argue—and Stella was already nodding, her eyes grateful on Gwyn's. "Of course, Gwyn, if that's what you recommend," she replied. "Did you have anyone in mind?"

Gwyn mulled that over for a minute, her own hand now reflexively rubbing at the table. "Maybe someone like Ivar?" she said slowly. "He's very fair-minded and generous, and has given me a lot of helpful guidance these past weeks. And"—she glanced at Silfast—"if you feel he often knows the goddess' blessing, that would be helpful, too, wouldn't it?"

A dangling silence seemed to echo after her words, in which Silfast frowned at the table, his claws absently drumming against it. "Ach, we shall think upon this," he said finally. "But first"—his eyes narrowed back on Gwyn—"I feel I must seek the goddess' blessing here with my mate, upon this altar. *Now.*"

His claw had jabbed down at the table, his brows high on his forehead. Challenging her, Gwyn realized, by brazenly announcing that he was going to get busy on her kitchen table, at this very moment, and what the hell was she going to do about *that*?

And surely it was ridiculous, it was completely absurd—but Gwyn somehow... nodded. And then even felt her head bowing, one hand still clutching at the table, the other slipping into a fist against her heart.

"As you wish, Captain," she said, her voice quiet, sure. "I pray that you'll both find the goddess' blessing here tonight."

With that, she pushed her chair back, rising to her feet—and then found that Joarr had somehow already done the same. And his eyes on hers were warm, approving, as his arm slid around her waist, and drew her close.

"We shall sleep in the garden," he said over his shoulder toward Stella and Silfast. "I shall watch for danger. Call if you need us, ach, Captain?"

And when Gwyn glanced back at Silfast, he was blinking toward them, his eyes unreadable—but then he slowly nodded, and brought his own fist to his heart. As if he'd acknowledged them. As if they'd begun to fix this.

And as if—Gwyn carefully touched the door as Joarr swung it open—the goddess was indeed here, among them.

As if she was truly home.

41

Gwyn walked around to the garden in silence. Caught, somehow, in the truth of Joarr's hand on her back, the stars twinkling in the black sky above them. The peace, perhaps, of knowing she was here. Safe. Bautul. Joarr's. A midwife, to both humans and orcs. Maybe even a lord's daughter.

She just... was.

And it felt so easy to lean into Joarr's warm strength, to allow him to guide her through the garden, and over to the wooden bench. The bench he'd sprawled on that morning so long ago, watching her, mocking her.

But he certainly wasn't mocking her now. Not as he sank onto the bench, and then drew her down to straddle his hips. Not when he gently cupped her face in both hands, blinking at her with something much like adoration—and then pulled her into a slow, succulent kiss.

"Ach, my witch," he breathed as he drew back again, his throat convulsing, his eyes glittering. "You are a fierce, wondrous prize. A gift. *Joy.*"

The heat again bubbled in Gwyn's belly, and she shook her

head, tried to wave it away—but both Joarr's hands circled strong around her wrists, a soft growl hissing from his throat. "No," he said. "You are. You honour me again and again. Grant me so many boons. Beyond *all* I saw of you, when first I hunted you."

Gwyn swallowed, her head tilting—when first he'd *hunted* her?—and she could feel him exhale, his grip loosening on her wrists. "Ach," he said, with a wince. "This. This is the last truth I hide from you. This I *swear* to you."

Gwyn had gone still over him, blinking uncertainly at his face, and he exhaled again, his gaze dropping to where his hands were now skimming up her arms. As if he were bracing himself, finding the words, for whatever this last truth might be.

"I... hunted you," he said in a rush. "Many moons past, in Dunburg. No to harm you, but to... seek you. Claim you. In the way of the Skai."

Wait. Joarr had wanted to... seek her? *Claim* her? Many moons past? In the way of the *Skai*?

"But," Gwyn protested, her voice weak. "But you—you were spying on me because of my father. Because you wanted to *compromise* me. To use me against that law."

Joarr twitched a shrug, his eyes still intent on his hands stroking up and down her arms. "This *was* truth, after," he said, quiet. "After I learnt of my true clan. After the Bautul almost break our mountain's treaty, and I seek way to face this. But before this"—he shrugged again—"I was Skai. And I worked oft in Dunburg, to watch your father and his men. And when a Skai finds a woman he wishes for his own, he... hunts her. This is how Skai take a mate, ach? No goddess, no altar. Only the hunt, and then... the claiming."

With that, his eyes had darted, brief but far too betraying, toward Gwyn's house. And now her thoughts were tumbling with it, flooding with memories, with comprehension. Roy had known about Joarr, because Joarr had been *hunting* her in Dunburg. Joarr had... *wanted* her. He'd... *claimed* her, like a Skai, on her kitchen table, and he'd said, he'd said...

Now we mate, he'd said that night, with that truth burning in his eyes. *I claim, tonight. Mine.*

A tremulous little shudder rippled up Gwyn's back, a gasp escaping her mouth—but then she shook her head, hard. "But—but *after*," she countered, flapping her hand toward this very bench. "Here. You said you only felt guilty. You tried to *leave* me. You certainly did *not*"—she hauled in air—"suggest in any way that you now considered me your *mate*, in the ways of the Skai!"

Joarr's grimace felt more like a flinch, his shoulders slightly hunching. "But I could not, you ken?" he said, his voice thin. "I—broke my pledge to the Bautul, in this. I was no to make you my mate, I was only to—to *use* you. So all this night, and in the days after, I fought against what I had done, ach? I sought new ways. Sought to make walls against you, push you away, make you think I no care. Make sure you no trust me, and thus I no trust you. Find way—any way—to keep my pledge to the Bautul, and keep away this war. Ach?"

Oh. Gwyn's stomach had plummeted again, her gaze desperately searching his—and he was looking back, his eyes hard, molten, blinking. "I was wrong," he said, hoarse. "This was wrong. I had made you my mate. And the more I fought to deny this, to push this away, the more it found me, ach? *You* found me. You see me. You see past all my falsehood, into the truth beneath."

She couldn't seem to move, let alone speak, and Joarr's warm hands slid up her arms again, over her shoulders, her neck. Until he was again carefully cupping her face in his fingers, as if she was something fragile, beyond price.

"You seek my truth," he breathed. "You seek fun with me. Seek to help me. Seek new ways with me. You break all my sight. And you even take me on Bautul altar, and make me your mate in the ways of the Bautul also. And next you help my clan, and seek to bear my *son*, and I am"—his chest hollowed—"I am undone. Forever under your spell. My witch. My *mate*."

There was still no way to speak, to answer this, and Joarr's eyes kept holding hers, a single streak of wetness slipping down his harsh cheek. "I am sorry, for all the ways I fought you, and failed you," he whispered. "I long to face this anew. Long to find new ways with you. If you should see fit to grant this gift to me, after all I have brought upon you."

Gwyn's eyes were suddenly leaking wetness too, and she desperately gulped down air, clutching her hands at his stiff shoulders. "You—you did a lot of good things too, Joarr," she managed. "You showed me fun. Found me friends. Believed in me. Supported me. Helped me find a way to get rid of Roy, and—"

Her voice broke off there, because Joarr had slipped his warm hand over her lips, his head twitching back and forth. "No, my witch," he breathed, a ghost of a smile on his mouth. "You no give me yet more kindness in this, ach? Ought to cast dark spells. Make cruel demands. Make me suffer."

But goddess, Gwyn couldn't, not with the warmth so close, whirling with relief, with *hunger*. He'd wanted her. He'd come for her. And she was revelling in that truth, and dragging in the hot close scent of his hand over her mouth, perhaps even flicking out her tongue to taste it...

His response was instant, his body gone utterly still—so Gwyn tasted him again. Dragging her tongue slow and meaningful against his palm, and drinking up the sudden answering heat, flashing sharp and beautiful in his watching, blinking eyes.

And in a flick of fluttering movement, his hands dropped to the front of her dress. Undoing the row of buttons with astonishing speed, and then tugging the fabric off her shoulders, and hurling it away into the garden. Leaving Gwyn utterly naked upon his lap, her bared groin spread apart over his. Over where he was already hard, hungry, pulsing up against his trousers...

So this time Gwyn's hands fluttered down, yanking at the trousers' waist—and oh, he was kicking them off entirely, too. And now there was nothing left separating them, no lies, no clothes, no secrets. Nothing but skin and hunger, and the hot crackling craving in Joarr's watching eyes.

"Mine," he breathed, his voice catching, his hand sliding down Gwyn's front. Stroking first over her breasts, and then lingering against her belly, fingers spreading wide. And then easing down to caress soft between her thighs, to where she was already swollen, slick, waiting.

He held her eyes as his hand briefly slipped to his own groin, guiding himself up, nudging that familiar, heated hunger against her. Where it wanted to be, where it *belonged*. And Gwyn felt it, clutched at it, revelled in it—and then sank down, slow and smooth, driving him deep inside.

His groan was harsh and rasping, tangling with her own breathless moan, and she could feel him swelling even fuller within her, lighting her from the inside out. And she was shuddering all over, clamping and convulsing upon him, needing him there, needing him to stay, to mean this, to prove this...

But already he was nodding, his eyes shimmering on hers, his strong arms gathering her close against his warm, solid chest. And then—surely for the very first time since they'd met—he rocked into her, slow. Gentle. Reverent. No driving, no taking, no conquering. Just—quiet. Sweet. His. Hers.

Oh. *Oh.* It felt so strange, so tenuous, so... vulnerable. As if this was something he'd never done before, something that was only hers. Something... new. A new feeling, a new way, with this orc's hungry hard power willingly caught, trapped, in her thrall. In her strength. In her spell.

But he wasn't fighting it anymore. Only staying, only giving, rocking into her again and again as she gasped, shivered, clung desperately at his shoulders. As his warm hands kept stroking up and down her back, his face buried deep in her neck, his mouth kissing soft and worshipful against her skin.

She... was. His. Hers.

The proof of it was already building, already rising, twisting higher and tighter with every grind of his hips, every swell of his strength inside her. With the scrape of his teeth against her neck, the gentle prick of his claws into her back, his raw, guttural groan as she felt him shudder to stillness, his heat rooted as deep as it could go—

He shouted as he sprayed out, flooding her with his furious truth, his affection, his *pledge*—and then Gwyn was shouting too, breaking apart around him. The release and the relief screaming out from her pierced core, streaking to every breath of her soul. His. Hers. A new way.

It wheeled again and again, circling and juddering between them, until Gwyn finally collapsed against his chest, her breaths heaving from her lungs. While his heart frantically thundered beneath her ear, his hands still spread wide on her back, his head bowed against hers.

"Mine," he whispered, so soft she barely heard it—but she twitched a nod, pressed a light little kiss against his skin.

"Yes," she breathed. "And mine. Ach?"

He huffed a choked laugh, his fingers spreading wider, pulling her tighter against him. "Ach," he said, gruff. "Always."

Always. Gwyn felt herself nodding again and again, feeling it, believing it, letting it settle deep and rich and true. And when Joarr slowly shifted around sideways, sinking down onto his back on the bench, she easily went with him, curled close upon his chest, with his truth still tucked half-hard inside her.

And goddess, it felt good. Felt so right. Felt like one last truth settled, a final question answered. Like peace. Like a... a blessing.

Gwyn's head abruptly jerked up, her eyes searching for Joarr's—and finding them already on hers, his brow furrowed deep. About to ask if she was in pain, no doubt, and she swiftly shook her head, and felt herself half-smiling down at his harsh, beautiful face.

"This bench," she said. "It is *not* another long-lost Bautul altar. It *can't* be. Right?"

But Joarr's mouth was twitching, his shoulder giving a far-too-casual shrug against the suddenly ancient-looking wood. "If this is what you ken," he said lightly. "I no more fight my wise witch on such things, ach?"

Gwyn groaned aloud and rolled her eyes at him, and then dropped her head back down onto his chest with a snort. "It is, isn't it," she said, muffled, into his skin. "Oh goddess. One of these days I'm going to *hex* you, you slippery fiend."

Joarr's laugh was throaty and warm, rumbling through his chest. "Ach, I ken," he said, as his arms wrapped tighter around her back. "I shall await this with all hunger, my greedy witch."

Gwyn couldn't resist laughing, either, even as she nudged a halfhearted elbow into his ribs. And then settled even closer against him, into this quiet, calm certainty. They were blessed. *Mated.* At home. At peace.

And as her mate's scent curled closer around her, wrapping her just as safe as his arms, she closed her eyes, and drifted off to sleep.

42

On the night of the next full moon, Gwyn and Joarr stepped out of Orc Mountain, and into their familiar, beloved garden.

And into a raucous, rioting *party*.

The rhythmic pulse of drums thudded through the trees, and there were dozens of Bautul drinking, dancing, and talking all at once. A large fire sparked and crackled in the clearing, the scent of cooking meat swarmed rich in the air, and hanging from multiple tree-branches were little burning torches, looking rather like fairies flitting through the darkness.

"What do you think?" Rosa demanded, as she bounded up to hover before them. "We followed the instructions we found in *four* different ancient Bautul sources, so it's an authentic Bautul coming-of-age and pledge-keeping garden-party! Joarr, you must be shocked and thrilled, I'm sure!"

Joarr was indeed looking rather stunned—and also unquestionably wary, his narrow eyes darting around toward all the garden's priceless, precious plants. But before he could say something that would surely cause offense, Gwyn squeezed his arm, and returned Rosa's expectant smile with a sincere grin of her own.

"It's lovely, Rosa," she said. "And so thoughtful of you, too. And I presume you've put precautions in place around keeping the garden safe?"

"Yes, of course," Rosa replied brightly. "We've blocked off most of the paths, and are keeping everyone in the clearing. And if anyone *dares* to step on even *one* plant"—she waved grandly off to the right—"our strong, vicious Bautul guards will immediately toss them out, won't you, boys?"

The vicious guards turned out to be none other than Eyolf and Iyolf, who both obediently trotted over, looking abashedly pleased at Rosa's praise. "You can trust us, Seer," Eyolf said, with a flourishing little bow. "We know how precious this garden is. We shall guard it with our lives."

That seemed to slightly relax Joarr's stiff-looking shoulders, and he nodded, and even brought his fist to his heart. "I... thank you, brothers," he said. "And the Ka-esh, also, for this kindness."

Rosa beamed up toward him, and then bounded off again, to where Gwyn could see a cluster of Ka-esh lounging beneath a plum tree. And once Iyolf and Eyolf had also gone back to their posts, Gwyn instinctively leaned into Joarr, and inhaled the familiar warm scent of his bare chest.

"You're such a generous orc, Joarr," she murmured. "This mountain is lucky to have you."

Joarr returned this with a typical shrug, but one arm had tightened around her waist, the other slipping down to spread against her belly. To where he still so often caressed her, his hand curving over the slight swell of their son with careful, quiet reverence.

Gwyn had dropped her hand to cover his, her face nuzzling into his chest—or rather, into that ever-present tooth, still dangling around his neck. And poking at her cheek sharply enough that she drew backwards again, and jabbed a finger against it.

"And it'll be nice to get rid of this tonight, won't it?" she said, meeting Joarr's eyes. "Proclaim all our crushing victories before your clan, once and for all?"

She could feel him exhaling, nodding, his mouth twitching into a wry little smile. Because truly, over the past several weeks, they had indeed made remarkable progress together. Not only had Joarr begun his regular mushroom deliveries to a still-grateful Lord Anton—but Lord Anton had also kept his own end of the bargain, and neutered his fellow lords' new law with astonishing thoroughness. Requiring that women report their pregnancies to an approved list of certified midwives, who would then offer care and guidance as needed, without any outside interference. He had even halted the plans for public shaming or testifying, and had put in place stiff penalties for hunting, as well.

And to Gwyn's genuine surprise, her father had also decisively dealt with Roy. He had blocked the planned public wedding announcements, and—according to Joarr's scouts' reports—he had loudly and irritably castigated Roy, in front of all his guards, for causing such distress to his beloved daughter. However, it had also been recently reported that Roy was accompanying Lord Anton on his next hunting trip—no doubt involving a generous quantity of mushrooms—so Gwyn was reserving judgement for now, but held full trust in Joarr's scouts to keep a close watch on the situation.

In other excellent developments, Gwyn's house in Varrahan had already become something of a Bautul retreat, and she'd begun to offer regular consulting hours there each week, serving any local women who needed it. She'd also had several solid orc-forged locks installed on the house's front door, ensuring that no one barged in unexpectedly, and discovered orcs copulating on her kitchen table.

"Joarr!" cut in a deep, familiar voice, and when Gwyn spun to look, it was Simon, striding over toward them, with Maria tucked close by his side. "So we are to honour you tonight, ach?"

Joarr shrugged again, but Simon fully ignored this, and dragged him into a crushing, bear-like hug. "I shall not be sad to see the last of this pledge, brother," he said, once he'd pulled away again, tugging at the tooth around Joarr's neck. "Though I am glad"—his warm gaze flicked toward Gwyn—"that you have gained such a quick, hungry mate in this, ach?"

Joarr twitched another rueful smile, his eyes following Simon's toward Gwyn. "Ach, she is a good, greedy little witch," he replied. "Always seeking out new altars to anoint with my fresh seed."

Gwyn tried to elbow him, but he easily avoided it, and Simon's loud, rolling laughter carried through the trees around them. "As she should," he said, with a staggering clap of his huge hand at Gwyn's shoulder. "You keep worshipping my brother thus, woman, and your goddess shall keep you flooded with blessing."

Gwyn made a noise that was half-laugh, half-scoff, and rolled her eyes at where Joarr was now grinning down toward her. "Thanks, but I'm afraid Joarr's the one who'll be doing the worshipping," she said to Simon, as sweetly as she could. "On his knees where he belongs, making thorough use of his slippery tongue."

Simon's roar of laughter at this was loud enough to draw over several more friends and well-wishers. Ella and Natt, Hannah and Fulnir, Baldr and Drafli, Grimarr and Jule, and even a smiling Inga and her two orcs, who had brought an entire Bautul band from the south for the party—including their beautiful new son, who Gwyn had last seen being fawned and fussed over by multiple orcs in the newly restored nursery.

"Congratulations, you two," cut in another familiar voice,

and when Gwyn turned to look, it was Efterar, of Clan Ash-Kai. Orc Mountain's big, scarred, irritable Chief Healer, together with his sly, smiling, handsome orc mate Kesst.

Gwyn smiled back with genuine warmth, and soon fell into easy conversation with them both. Because now that she'd finally met Efterar—after all that time spent avoiding him—it had turned out that they were utterly in accord, and had become instant allies. Efterar was a stubborn, no-nonsense kind of healer, who did wield truly spectacular skills—but he thankfully wasn't fool enough to refuse correction, either, and he'd tolerated Gwyn's lengthy tongue-lashing about Stella with tolerable grace. After that, he'd even worked with her to create a comprehensive treatment plan for Stella and Silfast—which had indeed included regular counselling sessions with Ivar, who'd of course been delighted to offer his services.

"I'll need you to send more mugwort down to the Bautul pit for tomorrow, Gwyn," Efterar was saying now, his eyes narrowed on Gwyn's, his arms folded over his chest. "That fool Silfast nearly decapitated four of his fellow Bautul with that axe yesterday, and then sent me and my medics down there to clean up his mess. I couldn't even risk moving the poor bastards without breaking something. That prick is a *menace*."

Joarr, who had also participated in that Bautul brawl the day before—with precise but deadly enthusiasm—was suddenly wearing a mask of utterly blank innocence, and carefully inspecting his claws. While beside them, Kesst was stroking Efterar's shoulder, and giving an exasperated but affectionate roll of his dark eyes.

"We're supposed to be here *relaxing*, Eft," he said firmly. "Not raging against Bautul for being Bautul. Now come. Is there somewhere we can actually have some fun around here?"

This was said with a beseeching glance toward Gwyn, who after an instant's silent communication with Joarr, waved up at the row of trees along the mountain's wall. "There are platforms up in the trees, if that might help?" she replied. "It'll be quieter there. With fruit to eat, too."

"Ooooh, fruit to eat, Eft," Kesst repeated, with satisfaction, as he instantly steered Efterar off toward the trees. "Maybe you can think of some other tasty sweets to offer me, too?"

Efterar certainly wasn't arguing, and allowed himself to be herded away—which was just as well, because now here was Silfast himself, with the aforesaid axe in his hand, striding through the crowd toward them.

"Seer!" he called, his deep voice carrying through the clamour all around. "Come. The goddess awaits you."

Joarr squared his shoulders and nodded, brushing Gwyn's back with his hand—*you too*, it meant—and she readily accompanied him and Silfast toward the clearing, and into the depths of the crowd. Which seemed to part around them as they went, the loud voices slightly quieting, the drums softening to a slow, rhythmic rumble.

Silfast didn't stop until he'd reached the altar, in the very middle of the clearing. The goddess' wizened old tree still stretched out over it, but now—thanks to the efforts of Gwyn and her helpers—there were clusters of budding green on multiple branches, flickering orange in the light of the nearby cook-fire. And more of the little lanterns also hung throughout the tree, twisting in the breeze, almost as if they were dancing to the beat of the drums below.

"The Bautul have come together this night," Silfast announced, his deep voice booming through the crowd, "to welcome a new Bautul among us. We do this under our goddess' eye, so that we may seek her blessing."

His head had tilted up toward the full moon above them, his fist clenched over his heart—and in the watching, rippling thrum, the Bautul around them all did the same. Raising their eyes, seeking their goddess, their hands pressed against their hearts.

Gwyn had already assumed the pose—it had become so familiar these past weeks—and a glance at Joarr beside her showed that he'd already done so, too. His head high, his gaze unflinching on the moon, his face bathed in silvery light.

"Our new brother is the Seer of the Bautul," Silfast's deep voice continued. "His truth was long lost to us, his fathers' names spurned and forgotten. But to make amends for this, our Seer swore the Bautul coming-of-age pledge, and vowed to offer a great service to us, and our clan."

The drums kept rumbling, the moon silent and serene, the world hushed and watching all around. Awaiting Silfast's words, his wisdom, his judgement.

"Our Seer honoured his pledge," Silfast said, every word slow, solid, certain. "He broke this cruel new law from the men. He crushed our enemies with his speed, strength, wit, and will. And not only this, but he brought us a midwife. He brought our women the help we did not see they needed."

Gwyn's stomach was flipping, her skin prickling—and when she glanced toward Silfast again, he was watching her, his gaze fierce and firm. "You have saved us," he said, perhaps to her, or Joarr, or both. "And in this, you have honoured our goddess. You have earned her blessing."

It was a gift, a prayer, maybe even an invocation—and in its wake, there was a breathless, rolling stillness. Even the drums now fallen utterly silent, as the Bautul held their faces to the moon. Waiting, watching, seeking as one, until...

The sudden gust of wind swirled through the clearing, caressing Gwyn's hair, fluttering the dangling, flickering torches above. And the tree over them loudly creaked, its new leaves rustling, as if it were a living, watching presence, saluting its waiting sons and daughters below.

There was a low shout behind Silfast—it was Olarr, the Bautul's other captain, his gaze still on the moon, his fist punching up into the air. And now Gwyn recognized Kalfr's voice calling out behind her, and then Stella's, close behind Silfast. And then more and more and more, the drums rising to join them, until it was a chorus of warmth and gratitude, swelling and soaring to the sky.

Gwyn was shivering all over when it ended, and she could feel Joarr twitching beside her, too. And when she glanced up toward him, his throat was convulsing, his eyes rapidly blinking, his fingers clutching at that tooth around his neck.

"Now come to your goddess' altar, brother," Silfast's voice called out. "And kneel, to fulfill your pledge."

Joarr nodded and obeyed, his steps unusually jerky as he strode the rest of the way to the altar, and then sank to his knees before it. One hand on the mossy stone, the other again over his heart, his head bowed low. Showing his trust, his acceptance. His worship.

Silfast had moved to stand over Joarr, the huge axe still gripped in his hand. And as Gwyn stared, her heartbeat skipping, Silfast shifted his stance, and raised his axe high—and then swung it downwards, its gleaming blade slicing straight toward Joarr's exposed neck.

Gwyn's heart leapt, her shout nearly escaping her throat— but she'd somehow choked it back, just in time. Because Silfast's axe had halted, frozen in place, its sharpened blade just kissing against Joarr's bared neck. While below Joarr, the tooth fell to the earth, its cord cut clean.

Silfast swung the axe back up again, as his other hand snatched down for the fallen tooth. And then he tossed it over to Olarr, who easily caught it, and then strode to the nearby burning fire, and dropped it in.

The fire sparked and cracked, the tooth already consumed within—and there were more loud shouts and whoops, ringing through the air. And Silfast had reached toward Joarr, roughly hauling him up to his feet, and then actually even clasped him close, his huge hand clapping against his back.

And suddenly Olarr had piled on too, and Kalfr, and Eyolf and Iyolf, and that was surely Simon's massive form, sending the whole lot staggering. And as more and more orcs rushed in, shouting their welcomes and congratulations, Gwyn felt a hoarse, joyous laugh bubbling from her throat, while the pooling wetness finally escaped her eyes, and streaked down her cheeks.

It was some time before Joarr was freed from the orc pile-up, and once he emerged he looked like a ruffled mess, his hair all on end, his face flushed. And there was even *blood* smeared on his chest and shoulder—from where Silfast's axe had nicked him, no doubt—but despite all that, his grin was broad and genuine, his stance easy and relaxed, his eyes catching warm and wicked on Gwyn's.

She grinned back at him, her eyes still blinking, her hand still fixed over her heart. And when he twitched his head toward her—clearly saying, *come*—she immediately stumbled over toward him, and threw herself into his waiting arms.

"Congratulations, love," she breathed, into his warm, familiar chest. "You did it. You *deserved* it."

She could feel his shrug, dismissing it, even as his strong arms crushed her tighter against him. "Should never have gained this," he whispered into her ear, "without you. Ach?"

Gwyn shrugged too, but clutched him even closer, inhaled the sweet rich scent of him. Felt his lean solid strength, the steady thud of his heartbeat, and—she shivered all over—that hard, familiar ridge in his trousers, jutting out thick and demanding against her.

She drew back, searching for his eyes—and found them dark, half-lidded, hungry. And as she kept blinking at him, her heart picking up speed, the audacious bastard casually dropped a hand down into his trousers, and pulled himself out.

Gwyn's breath choked, her gaze now furtively darting around them—but the party had already resumed in full force, the assembled orcs once again talking and laughing and drinking. One pair of orcs—Baldr and Drafli—were grinding up against the goddess' tree together, their bodies fully bared in the firelight, and she could see Natt leading Ella away behind a rose bush, his hand slipping up her short skirt. Which meant that Gwyn was the only one watching Joarr do this, his hand now blatantly pumping up and down his swollen length, while his other hand slid down to caress his full bollocks below.

"Altar, you ken," he said to Gwyn, his eyes lazy and mocking, as he kept brazenly stroking himself, flaunting himself for her. "You wish to be bared and used upon this, ach? Wish to bow and beg for your Seer, where all Bautul shall see?"

Oh, *hell*. Gwyn's breath choked again, her face hot, her eyes darting between Joarr's groin and his smug, taunting face. And would she really volunteer for this, *again*, with all these orcs indeed sure to start noticing at any moment, and...

"Ach, you yet have much to learn, Seer," cut in a hard voice. It was *Silfast's* voice, goddess curse him, and Gwyn whipped around to discover him standing close beside her, his eyes watching Joarr, his mouth pursed. "Should a Bautul wish to have his mate upon the goddess' altar, he ought to do this with all speed, before another orc chooses to take his place."

With that, Silfast spun around to where Stella was standing behind him, her eyes bright with amusement—and she squealed aloud as Silfast grasped her by the waist, whirled her around, and plopped her on her hands and knees on the altar.

"See?" Silfast said, as he swiftly snatched off the flimsy shawl Stella had been wearing, and tossed it up onto an overhanging tree branch. "Too slow, Seer."

Stella was gasping and shivering on the altar beneath him, her lush curves fully bared to the moon—but at Silfast's light swat to her bare arse, she instantly stilled. And at the next swat of his big hand, she even arched her back, and lifted her arse, almost as if... presenting herself. Offering herself for his taking.

"Please, Silfast," she breathed, her voice choked, pleading, entirely unashamed. "Please, grant me your favour."

Silfast loudly harrumphed, his brows raised triumphantly toward Joarr—and then he reached down, yanked his huge, veined, blunt-tipped heft out of his own trousers, and coolly turned toward Stella's bared, waiting body. And then, keeping his eyes on Joarr the entire time, he sank himself deep inside her, while she moaned and shuddered upon him.

Joarr was wearing an almost comical expression, of something between thwarted lust and pure bristling rage—and before Gwyn could breathe, or think, he'd grasped her by the waist, too. And an instant later, she was on her hands and knees on the altar beside Stella, with Joarr's sharp claws digging into her hips.

"I am *never* too slow," Joarr said from behind her, his voice clipped. "I only wish to spur my mate's hunger, ach? Wish her wet and longing for me."

Silfast's laugh was low and arrogant, rising over the hard, steady slap of his hips against Stella's arse. "You cannot think mine does not long for me?" he replied. "Look how her sweet juices already cling to me. If you watch, mayhap you shall even see her spurt for me, ach?"

Joarr scoffed at that, his hands clenching tighter against Gwyn's hips. "Mine oft does this," he said thinly. "You can no scent this, all over *my* altar?"

Silfast laughed again, and did something that made Stella startle and moan beside Gwyn, her head rearing back. "I can only scent my own sweet mate," Silfast said, with satisfaction. "Whilst yours"—he snorted, loud and jeering—"is yet *dressed.*"

Gwyn's own indignation was sharply flaring, whirling up against her own hot, lurching hunger. And when she snapped around to glare at Silfast, he was smiling smugly toward her, even as he gave Stella's arse a firm, purposeful slap with his huge hand, and plunged himself harder inside.

The bastard. And before Gwyn had even realized quite what she was doing, she'd fumbled for the buttons of her dress, and yanked it off over her shoulders. Leaving herself bared and exposed on an altar, in the middle of a party, beside her equally bared and exposed friend—and goddess, she didn't even care. She only cared about the look of vague surprise in Silfast's eyes, and—she exhaled, shuddering—the look of pure, potent hunger in Joarr's. The *pride.*

"Ach, for I wish her to long for me," Joarr said, his eyes not once leaving Gwyn's as he shucked his trousers, and kicked them off to the side. "Wish her to meet me. See me. *Need* me."

And Gwyn was fervently nodding, needing him, *adoring* him—and she somehow even arched up toward him, just like Stella had. Raising her bare arse, exposing herself, opening herself wide for him. Waiting.

Joarr's hands had once again found her hips, his body leaning close, his eyes still glinting on where she was watching him over her shoulder. But instead of driving into her, as Silfast had done—as Silfast was *still doing,* grunting with each heavy thrust—Joarr slid a finger to trail down Gwyn's open crease, his claw sharp, teasing, tantalizing.

"Wish my witch to beg for me," he purred, as that claw lightly pricked against the swollen, too-sensitive skin. "Wish her to plead for my tending on her knees, where she *belong.*"

Oh *damn* him, this was such a devious ploy on his part, surely meant as revenge for what Gwyn had said to Simon earlier—and Joarr's grin was sheer, insolent wickedness as he yanked her legs wider apart. Exposing even more of her, for Silfast, for the orcs that she could *feel* now watching them, for his own greedy, glinting eyes...

And then he knelt down, and—*licked* her. Impossible, unthinkable, and Gwyn's cry of shocked pleasure tore from her mouth, her body reflexively opening wider for his tongue— and oh, it was brilliant, the deceitful wonderful *fiend.* His glorious tongue shamelessly flicking and tasting and drinking, sinking into all her most secret places, wheeling the hunger higher and hotter with every slick, slippery touch.

"Oh goddess," Gwyn gulped, her breaths heaving, her eyes squeezing shut. And suddenly it didn't matter who heard, who saw, her orc feasting upon her in the middle of a party, kneeling and worshipping her on his altar, while their friends flagrantly mated beside them. "Oh, please, Joarr. More. *More.*"

He was dragging his teeth now too, skittering up the pain alongside the pleasure, his claws gripping at her trembling thighs, holding them apart. "More what, witch?" he asked behind her, between licks, over her gasping groans. "Speak, and then I tend you."

And *then.* Goddess curse him, bless him, because Gwyn couldn't think, couldn't possibly stop the words tumbling from her mouth. "Yes, yes, yes," she babbled. "Tend me. Take me. Fill me. Let me worship you. Seek blessing with you. *Please.*"

And when her frantic eyes again found his, he was already standing tall behind her, his eyes glittering with hunger, his long tongue slowly licking at his slick-wet lips. "See?" he said to Silfast beside him. "It is all the sweeter, when they plead."

Silfast's hooded gaze had been fixed on Stella's bare arse, on his own heft slamming inside—but he paused his rhythm as he glanced over, his eyes assessing. As Joarr finally leaned closer, and nocked his slick swollen head against Gwyn's clenching, craving heat. Pulsing against her, gently parting her around it, making her feel it, please goddess *please*—

She howled as he slammed inside, burying himself to the hilt. Spewing the hunger fierce and furious, trampling beneath her skin—and then ramping it even wilder as he circled himself hard within, grinding against her, gouging himself deeper. While behind her his groan burned through the air, his claws piercing sharp against her hips, his breath hot against her bare back.

"Ach, this is fair," said Silfast's voice, though it sounded hoarse, faraway. "But *my* mate's screaming is better. Mark this."

With that, he did something that indeed had Stella shrieking, her whole body shuddering on her hands and knees—but Gwyn scarcely noticed, not with Joarr now sliding back out of her, all the way. Until he'd slipped fully free again, his slick head just brushing against her swollen, convulsing crease.

"Ach, ach," Joarr said to Silfast, his voice appallingly smooth. "But you wish to hear good scream? Mark *this.*"

His drive inside was more like a charge this time, skewering Gwyn in one powerful stroke, impaling her whole upon him. And her sharp scream indeed rose on its own, tearing out of her throat, carrying high and shrill over the noise of the party and the drums around them.

Joarr's laugh behind her was dark and satisfied, his body again grinding hard against her invaded, helplessly clutching heat. While beside Joarr, Silfast made a grunt that sounded reluctantly *approving*, even as that was surely the sound of another slap of his big hand against Stella's arse.

"Ach, but mine is so meek and sweet," Silfast said, his voice unmistakably breathless now. "And her form so full and soft. See how her pretty rump trembles whilst I plough her."

Joarr had briefly gone silent, as if he was in fact looking, oh goddess—but then Gwyn felt the hard prick of his claws again, digging into her bare hips. "Ach, and mine is lithe and sleek and quick," he countered flatly. "She now climbs trees better than most orcs. And"—she felt his hand slipping up her back, gathering up her hair—"she *sees* me. Follows what I wish, so I no even need to *speak*. Ach?"

With that, he gently yanked on her hair, the pressure steady and sustained, wanting her upright on her knees—so Gwyn instantly pushed herself back, and felt his strong arm clutch close around her front, holding her tight against him. And when his hand on her hair tugged sideways, her head immediately tilted, baring her neck with appalling ease. Almost as if begging him to taste, to drink...

And yes, those were his teeth, scraping hot and close, sharp deadly *ecstasy*—and Gwyn screamed again as they clamped down, sinking deep. As he again ground and swelled within her, his throat now greedily gulping, his hand clutching hard against the swell of her waist.

When he released her she was shuddering all over, trembling on her hands and knees, her only support the heft still plunged deep inside her, and his hand's strong grip on her hair. Holding her head high, flaunting her, while he slowly picked up speed behind her, sparking more heat, more hunger, more furious fiery *pride*...

"She longs for me," Joarr hissed as he slammed in again and again, scraping his other hand's claws down her side. "She is fierce and loyal for me. She shall destroy all my enemies, to honour me. *Me*."

Oh hell, oh goddess, the need and the ache burning, spiralling, rushing hot and white. Gwyn's orc praising her, claiming her, firing her through with impossible pain and pleasure, his hand yanking on her hair, his claws dragging hard enough to score against her skin...

"She is mine," Joarr gasped, slamming harder, now in perfect time with Silfast's steady grunts beside him. "She shall milk me dry, spurt out her juices, and anoint this altar with our fresh seed. She shall bear our next Seer, and gain us all the goddess' deep blessing, ach—"

It was like he'd choked on the words, driving desperate and careening toward the edge. Spurring Gwyn on, yanking her up and back, racing past Silfast, his body locking and pulling up hard, catapulting toward the cliff—

The fall was sheer, sharp, shocking, their shouts soaring as one—and then they were flying. Gwyn's rapture screaming through her entire self, her *soul*, thundering again and again and again, as the hot powerful prod inside her finally burst apart. Pumping out its rushing surge of seed in hard streaming torrents, while Gwyn's own body flooded out her release, and dragged yet more from him in clutch after greedy clutch. Making it her own, making him hers, hers, *hers*.

When they finally settled again, found earth again, Joarr was bent double over Gwyn's back, his breath coming out in heavy, dragging gulps. And beside them, Stella was finally shouting too, her face flushed and alive with pleasure, while behind her Silfast bellowed and roared as he emptied himself inside her.

And then, somehow, silence. Or rather, the sounds of the ongoing party around them, the steady pulse of shuddering drums. And when Gwyn risked a furtive glance upwards, it was to the realization that they'd indeed had an eager audience, multiple Bautul watching this—this *competition*, damn it—with hungry, wondering eyes.

But in it, too, there'd been... trust. Peace. *Fun*, even. And as Gwyn raised her eyes to the ever-watching moon, she found that there wasn't the faintest hint of regret, or shame. Just satisfaction, maybe, or even an odd, lighthearted smugness.

"We won," she murmured, toward where Joarr's head was still close beside hers, still breathing hard. "The winners probably get most of the goddess' blessing, don't you think?"

Joarr's laugh was throaty and low, his mouth nibbling approvingly at her neck, even as Silfast huffed a harsh, husky growl beside them. "There is no *winning*, with the goddess," Silfast grunted. "She blesses all her own. Most of all those who have known her longest, ach?"

Joarr loudly scoffed over Gwyn, and abruptly jerked himself up and back, dragging her with him. And of course she didn't resist, just followed the easy lead of him like always—at least, until he kept his hands on her hips, tilted her sideways, and yanked himself out. Which meant—Gwyn gasped, her face flooding with heat—the heated, slippery mess he'd made inside her was surging out of her in spurt after spurt. And spraying directly onto Silfast's hairy bare flank, painting him with thick ropes of Joarr's hot, sticky seed.

"Ach, ach," Joarr said, his voice dripping with coolness, with mockery. "Raining again, I ken. This is what comes, Captain, when you seek to steal your Seer's altar, and his blessing."

Silfast's growl was hard and vicious this time, raising the hairs on Gwyn's neck—and thankfully Joarr whisked her back and away, standing her to her feet, well out of Silfast's reach. With good reason, too, because Silfast was spitting and snarling with terrifying ferocity, his eyes alight on Joarr's face.

"You skinny, sneaking *snake*," he hissed. "You shall *pay* for this in the pit tomorrow, ach?"

With that, he spat at Joarr's feet, and then—with surprising speed—snatched up Joarr's discarded trousers, and made a show of using them to wipe himself off. While Joarr himself made a show of shrugging, and using a casual hand to shake off the worst of the wetness from his still-bared heft. And then he coolly turned his back to Silfast, and guided Gwyn's also-bared body through the crowd of watching, wide-eyed orcs.

His mess was still streaming down her thighs, but surely that was exactly what he wanted—and once he'd led her over to the trees, he even snickered as she climbed up, leaving an obvious messy trail behind her. And then he leapt up too, striding straight toward her—until he suddenly crashed close against her, dragging her down to the platform with him.

And then, without a word, they both burst into laughter. Shaking all over as they roared, gulping for air, the mirth careening back and forth between them.

"You skinny, s-sneaking, s-*snake*," Gwyn gasped, clutching at his thigh, as water streamed from her eyes. "I can't believe you actually *sprayed* him, you fiend. You've been wanting to do that for—for—"

"For *moons*," Joarr gulped, between guffaws, his hand slapping Gwyn's knee. "Ach, this was even better than I dreamt, witch. You see his *face*?"

Gwyn only laughed harder, shaking her head, wiping at her wet face. "He's going to *murder* you tomorrow," she gasped. "He really is."

"Ach, he shall try," Joarr said, and his eyes were leaking too, the guffaws rolling from his chest. "And I shall say..."

"'*Is it raining?*'" Gwyn supplied, in her best impression of Silfast's deep voice—and Joarr's instant, cackling howl set her off again, collapsing into his chest, as she laughed until it hurt.

"Oh goddess," she finally gulped, clutching at her aching stomach. "I hope you didn't insult him beyond repair. Or risk your place in the clan. You didn't. Did you?"

Her chuckles had finally subsided, her head twisting around to search Joarr's eyes in the faint flickering firelight— but he shook his head, whipping his hair in his face. "Ach, no," he said. "We are kin now, and shall always lead the clan together. These feuds shall only make this more *fun*, ach?"

Right. Gwyn grinned up at him, and then sagged closer into his warm arms. "Good," she said lightly. "Though did you *really* need to make such a spectacle of me in the process?"

Joarr's hands were stroking at her hair now, and she could feel his mouth, gently kissing at where he'd pierced her neck. "Ach," he murmured. "Wished to flaunt my fierce little witch, stuck and screaming upon my prick, and spraying my seed. But should you no wish for this, you need only speak, ach?"

Gwyn settled even closer against him, and gave a slow, shivery exhale. "No, I... I like it," she whispered, confessed. "Even though that still feels... wrong, sometimes, you know?"

Joarr's teeth nipped a little against her skin, his disapproval gentle but certain. "No wrong," he whispered back. "Blessed by goddess. At peace with father. Helping many women. Bearing strong son. Marked only by me. Ach?"

His claws had skated softly up her arm, where all those old scars were still visible—but where they'd faded, too. And the more they'd faded, the more Joarr had made new ones of his own. Pricks and scrapes of his claws, marks of his teeth not only on her neck, but on her breasts, her thighs, her arse. Careful, but steady and certain, too. Still making sure it was different, marks made not in pain or shame, but in pleasure. In *pride*.

And it hadn't always been easy—even now, that temptation sometimes still lingered at the back of Gwyn's thoughts—but knowing she would lose this, if she returned to that, was an astonishingly powerful deterrent. And so was the truth, too, that there were other ways. And if she couldn't find another way on her own, Joarr would help her find one, and stay with her until the temptation had passed.

And goddess, she adored him, her sly, devious, and impossibly generous orc. Her partner. Her conspirator. The father of her son.

His hand had again found her waist, spreading wide against it, as he so often did. And Gwyn was caught on that, considering that, as something from earlier twined back into her thoughts.

"You said, down there," she began, twisting back around to look at him, "that I would bear the next Seer."

Joarr's eyes had very slightly stilled, perhaps slipping behind their mask—but Gwyn watched, waiting, until they came back again. Until he stopped hiding, or seeing, or both.

"Ach," he said finally, quiet. "You shall. Is this no... no good?"

Gwyn blinked, and then elbowed him in the stomach, huffing a soft laugh. "Of course it's good," she said, just as quiet. "I—I'm just surprised, is all. And honoured."

She could see the relief in his eyes, could almost taste it in the air around him. "I ken some day," he murmured, "you shall be weary of all my seeing, ach? Shall no more wish to know these things."

But Gwyn knew very well, now, that Joarr didn't always like it either. That what he saw was sometimes still wrong, too, and that—oddly enough—it was still her that broke it the most. And that part of the reason he hadn't told her about his seeing, all that time—even as he still hadn't once tried to justify it—was that he hadn't wanted to take her freedom away from her. Her choice.

But it was him, it was part of him, and Gwyn loved him so much it ached—and more than that, she was indignant. Down-right piqued, in fact, because wait, Joarr knew things about their son, and he hadn't yet *told* her?!

"You sneaky, underhanded *fiend*," she snapped, as she squirmed fully around to face him, glowering at his surely shifty eyes. "Tell me everything. What's his name. What's he like. And will he defeat his devious father in combat?"

Joarr's mouth twitched, and his eyes were wry, a little pained. "You are sure," he said, "you wish to know."

"Yes," Gwyn replied, with an exasperated roll of her eyes. "I am. *Tell* me, Joarr."

His chest rose and fell against her, his hands sliding down to once more circle against her waist. "We call him Joakim," he whispered, "after my father's father. And I see him as sharp little orcling, ach? Always watching, always learning. He run away and hide in mountain, and we no find him for days. He try to fight Silfast, and then his son, when Silfast and I are back in bitter feud again. And he adore his quick witch mother, and you laugh at his wicked ways, and feed him all my best berries. And worst of this"—his mouth quirked up—"*you* teach him how best to defeat me in battle."

Oh. Oh. Something was quivering, suddenly, far too strong and close in Gwyn's throat, and one of Joarr's hands had come up to skitter against her cheek. "He is best son," he whispered, "and you, best mother. Ach?"

And goddess, Gwyn was weeping again, the wetness streaking freely down her cheeks. And Joarr was wiping it away, shaking his head, giving her another twitchy little smile. "See, this is no good, ach?" he murmured. "You ken, this may alter. He may be stuffy orc who only sleep in soft bed. May never stop speaking. May need to be thrown in pit of stink-lily."

But Gwyn was laughing now, even as she was still sobbing, and throwing her arms around his neck. "You fiend," she choked again, with no heat in it. "How long have you seen this?"

He shrugged beneath her, which surely meant it had been quite some time, and Gwyn kissed his neck, his jaw, his clever, willing mouth. Realizing, with a flood of heavy, grateful affection, that he'd surely known this back before they'd dealt with her father and Roy. And that even then, he'd still wanted to give her the choice. He'd still offered Efterar's services. He'd kept his seeing abilities secret, maybe for himself—but also, surely, for her.

And he kissed her, and held her as she wept, until she felt whole and calm again. And when he eased her down onto her back on the platform, she willingly went—at least, until she winced at the feeling of something prickly, poking into her spine.

But before she could reach for it, Joarr had already yanked her slightly up, his hand snatching it out from behind her. And then they both stilled at once, staring down toward it.

A... pinecone.

Gwyn heard herself laugh, soft and choked, and she circled her fingers close around it. And Joarr let her have it, his eyes shifting lights and shadows as they flicked up, brief but certain, toward the moon.

There was another instant's silence, Gwyn's hand reflexively touching the pinecone against her heart—and she could feel Joarr's heavy exhale, burning against her skin.

And then, without warning, he plucked the pinecone away from her. Tossing it up into the air, and flashing her a swift, wicked grin as he easily caught it again.

"You, my witch," he purred, "are *mess* of fresh orc-seed. Need good strong cleaning, with strong orc tongue. Ach?"

Oh, hell yes, that was *exactly* what Gwyn needed, and she fervently nodded—but Joarr's grin only cocked higher, the mocking smugness curling over his mouth. "Mayhap I grant you this," he breathed, "if you catch me. And if no one else see my witch, dripping such mess all over my garden."

And even as Gwyn groaned at him, she couldn't seem to stop grinning, the warmth bubbling and blazing through her chest. And when Joarr smoothly rose up, and then soared down out of the tree in one graceful leap, she immediately rushed for the nearest rope, and clambered down after him.

He was waiting at the bottom, standing tall and beautiful before her, his eyes alight, his sharp teeth bright and vicious in his shadowy face. Her orc, her mate, her love. Smiling at her like that, like she was a goddess, his own goddess, come to earth to give him life again.

"Good little witch," he murmured, so soft, so proud, as he beckoned her toward the garden. "Now come."

With that, he spun and whirled away, disappearing behind a raspberry bush. And with a laugh, a shiver, a furious hope in her heart, Gwyn kicked off, and chased him into the darkness.

BONUS EPILOGUE

I t was a cool, crisp night. The sky was clear, the trees were bare and still, and the full moon shone high above, painting the garden in silvery white light.

And throughout the garden, the Bautul had gathered. Praying, seeking, waiting. While all around them, the low rumble of drums thudded through the air, broken only occasionally by Stella's ragged gasps and groans.

"Oh goddess," she choked, clutching at her swollen belly, as she writhed back and forth in the steaming tub of water, placed just before the goddess' altar. "Oh please, oh help, please…"

But Silfast, who was waist-deep in the pool behind her, was already rubbing firm at Stella's naked back, growling into her ear. "Good woman," he rasped. "Brave woman. Breathe deep for me. Ach?"

Stella fervently nodded, dragging in a harsh, hoarse breath. And close beside the large steel tub, Gwyn was nodding too, and giving Stella her most reassuring smile. "You're doing wonderfully, Stella," she said. "Just a little longer. Keep breathing with the drums, make as many low powerful sounds as you like, and feel Silfast hold you and massage you, all right?

Feel how safe you are here. And maybe Efterar can check you again?"

Stella nodded again, sucking in air through her teeth. And on the other side of the pool, Efterar indeed dropped his big hand into the steaming water, resting it against Stella's belly. "Ach, almost," he said, his eyes briefly unfocusing before he drew his hand away. "Your son is eager to meet you, Stella."

Stella barked a laugh, even as she groaned again, her eyes squeezing shut. And behind her, Silfast kept growling into her ear, his hands still rubbing against her back, while his own eyes had once again darted to Joarr, who was pacing back and forth in front of the nearby crackling fire.

"Ach, still good," Joarr replied, without being asked. "I see... cord around neck, mayhap? But no risk from this."

Gwyn nodded, and quickly explained this to Stella—how she would ask her to stop pushing for a moment once the head was out, so she could slip off the cord—and then flashed a genuine, grateful smile over toward Joarr. Who accordingly flashed her a swift grin back before starting to pace again, his eyes gone distant too, his head occasionally tilting to the side.

He was Seeing, Gwyn knew—and as always, she felt herself relaxing into the surprising, soothing reassurance of it. Over the past few months, Joarr had proven to be a most excellent midwifery assistant, using his Seeing to great effect—not only flagging when labour was forthcoming, but also calling out any complications in advance, and thereby giving Gwyn, Efterar, and the Ka-esh medics as much extra time to respond as possible.

It had been an important factor in Ella's birth several months before, which had come on very suddenly, and might have been devastating, if not for the combined frantic efforts of their entire team. And after that, Joarr had been a significant help in Rosa's birth, too, pointing out the likelihood of back labour far in advance, and thereby allowing Rosa and Gwyn to prepare an extensive lineup of expanded pain management options.

But in the end, Ella and Rosa had both borne healthy, happy orclings, and they had both made full physical recoveries. Not only that, but Dania and Hannah had both had successful births also, and Gwyn and Joarr had even travelled south several times, delivering three more Bautul sons to women there. And of course, Gwyn had continued to serve women in Varrahan as well, and had attended multiple human deliveries these past months. Along with one surprise orcling, birthed by—oddly enough—the very first woman Gwyn had ever served in Varrahan, a plump blonde weaver named Annie.

And it was a true relief to know that Stella's birth would proceed without complication, and Gwyn took a brief moment to thank the goddess, before returning her attention to the situation at hand. Focusing on counting between Stella's contractions, reassuring her that all was well, and encouraging her to trust her body, to breathe with the drums, to push whenever she felt ready.

Things proceeded quickly from there, and soon Stella's groans were tearing through the garden, drowning out the drums. And once Gwyn had dealt with the cord—indeed around the orcling's neck—Stella choked one more broken moan, her eyes shocked wide. And then Silfast clasped their new little orcling in the water, and brought him out into the pale morning light.

And of course, he was *beautiful*. Big and hearty and hale, and sporting a thick thatch of black hair atop his head. And though his eyes were still squeezed tightly shut, his tiny fists and feet were already flailing at the air as he squealed and squirmed in his father's hands.

"Our son," Silfast whispered, hushed, into the caught silence—and all around them, a chorus of joyous Bautul voices suddenly soared to the sky. The drums wildly thudding again, whirling with laughs and shouts and stomps. With an entire clan united in celebration, shouting its gratitude to its goddess.

Stella had been staring at her son, her eyes bright and wondering—and when Silfast carefully settled the orcling's squirmy body against her chest, she gave a raspy laugh, and clutched him close. While Silfast's hand stroked her wet hair again and again, his eyes wide, blinking, reverent.

Gwyn was blinking too, wiping her wet face with her equally wet sleeve, and she belatedly dragged her focus back to the cord, and guided Silfast as he carefully cut it with his claws. And thankfully the placenta birthed quickly as well, with no signs of bleeding or tearing, and once Efterar also seemed satisfied, Silfast eased himself out of the water, and then swept up both Stella and their son into his huge, powerful arms.

"You have honoured me, woman," he told her, as he strode over to the nearby altar. They'd covered it with a pile of warm, cozy furs, for just this purpose, and Silfast thoroughly dried off Stella and the orcling before wrapping them up in furs, and settling them back against his broad chest. And after a quick lesson from Gwyn, the orcling was soon nursing happily at Stella's breast, his tiny hand clutched tight around Silfast's finger.

"Ach, look how hale and hungry he is," Silfast said proudly, his gaze fixed to their son, his big hands again stroking Stella's slightly shivery body. "Just as strong as you, ach?"

Stella smiled and shook her head, even as her tired eyes streaked wetness down her cheeks. "He *is* perfect," she whispered back. "And it's finally over. Thank the *goddess*."

Silfast nodded, his gaze lifting above them, to where the moon was still just visible in the brightening morning sky. "Ach, we thank you, Goddess," he said, his voice resonating against the surrounding trees. "And we seek your blessing upon our son."

The words were met with a moment's shuddering stillness,

broken only by the still-steady beat of the drums. Waiting, watching, worshipping—until the little orcling abruptly released Stella's breast, and *sneezed*. The sound surprisingly loud, slicing sharply through the wondering silence.

And once again, it was as though a spell had broken—and the garden erupted into a chorus of shouts and laughter. While the orcling, now unexpectedly deprived of his new favourite treat, immediately launched into a loud string of frustrated wails, as he bonked his little head back against Stella's breast.

Gwyn laughed as she helped Stella get the orcling latched again, his little body squirming closer into her arms. While behind Stella, Silfast's mouth had curved into a rather terrifying smile, his smug gaze now glancing over toward the clusters of Bautul, who had all been waiting at a respectful distance around the edge of the clearing.

"Come, and meet your new brother," Silfast called. "He is sure to be a fierce and proud Bautul warrior, ach? He shall surely defeat *all* the other orclings in battle."

This was said with a pointed glance toward Joarr, who was blinking back with blatant disbelief in his eyes, and then a rapidly increasing outrage. And thankfully, Olarr had quickly lumbered over between them—probably on purpose—and loudly coughed as he settled his big hand to the orcling's fuzzy little head.

"Welcome, little brother," he said firmly, his deep voice carrying. "We are honoured to meet you."

"Ach, we are," interjected Eyolf, who had bounded excitedly up behind Olarr, pulling Iyolf along after him. "We shall find much fun together, ach?"

Iyolf was nodding his agreement to this, his hand gently resting against the little orcling's back. "Ach," his soft voice said. "Welcome, little brother."

After Iyolf came Kalfr, his tall body gone strangely still as he blinked down at the orcling, his throat bobbing, his hand brushing against the orcling's head with cautious, uncertain care. "You bless us, little brother," he finally said, his voice thick. "May we be worthy of you, ach?"

Next in the line was Ivar, who enthusiastically greeted the orcling, and offered a short, heartfelt prayer on his behalf. And then came Egil and Thorvald, and Arne and Matuk and Grum, and Magni and Thrand and Leif. All giving their congratulations and best wishes, while Stella smiled misty-eyed up toward them, and Silfast grunted with ever-increasing satisfaction.

Once everyone had finished saying hello—and Gwyn, Efterar, and the Ka-esh were all satisfied with Stella's physical state—Stella profusely thanked them all, and then admitted that she was still chilly, and quite tired, too. So after a moment's conferring, Silfast once again gathered both Stella and the orcling up into his arms, and carried them off toward the mountain. "My sweet mate shall now rest in our room with our son," he announced over his shoulder. "You shall bring your pies and gifts to us there, ach?"

To Gwyn's vague surprise, the Bautul all called back their eager assent to this plan, their fists thumping against the hearts. While Silfast looked even more smugly pleased than before, casting one last proud look over his shoulder before stepping into the mountain.

Which meant, finally, it was over. And Stella was healthy, and happy, and *safe*. And once Gwyn had finished washing up in the ice-cold waterfall, she found herself instinctively turning and reaching for Joarr, sagging into his waiting arms, her head burrowing into his chest.

"Thank you," she breathed, against his familiar scented skin. "You were wonderful. As always."

Joarr huffed a laugh and shook his head, his claws pricking gentle into her back. "Ach, no," he breathed back. "This was all you, witch. *As always.*"

Gwyn exhaled a long breath, sinking closer into his reassurance, his sweet, solid safety. Into his hands now stroking at her back, his mouth pressing a light kiss to her hair. "You wish to rest also?" he murmured. "You must be weary and cold also, ach?"

Gwyn was indeed feeling excessively damp and chilled, but her brain still felt far too full to rest, careening unsteadily between exhaustion and elation, tension and relief. Seeking some kind of escape, pain, peace...

"I *am* cold," she mumbled into Joarr's chest, her body slightly twitching against his. "But I definitely can't sleep yet. I just... I need..."

It was still difficult to say it some days, to admit that still-present weakness—but thankfully Joarr was already nodding against her, his comprehension curling close between them. And when he nudged her back toward the mountain, she willingly went, settling under his warm, heavy arm as he led her through the familiar dark corridors.

He was taking her to the Bautul hearth, Gwyn soon realized—and even at this early hour, it turned out to be already packed full of Bautul orcs. All dancing and mating and carousing together, continuing to celebrate the birth of their newest Bautul son. But the goddess' altar before the crackling fire was entirely empty, and Joarr led Gwyn straight toward it, his steps quick and purposeful, his hand firm on her back.

He didn't speak as he plucked her up, settling her on her knees upon it. But goddess, Gwyn knew that look in his eyes, could taste it in his scent—and she gasped aloud as his familiar clawed hand caught her chin, tilting it up toward him.

"Only me, ach?" he murmured, his brows lifting—and Gwyn instantly nodded, leaning into his touch. Watching with rapt, rapidly rising hunger as he flashed her a devious, approving grin—and then swiftly, efficiently shucked his trousers. Exposing the already-hard heft at his groin, jutting out toward her over those full, bulging bollocks.

"See how naked I am for you, witch," he purred, as he dropped his other hand to that swollen length, and began smoothly, casually stroking it. "How shall I first tend you? In your throat, mayhap? Feed your hungry belly?"

Gwyn's hoarse groan escaped on its own, her face flushing hot—and Joarr's mouth curved into another smug, wicked smile as his hand on her chin slipped up, tugging her lips wide apart. And then, with damnable coolness, he drew her head forward, and smoothly fed his hard, twitching prick deep into her mouth.

"Better, witch?" he crooned, as he flared and swelled between her lips, his leaking head digging into her gulping throat. "You need good fat Bautul prick to suckle upon, ach? To *feast* upon?"

There were a few amused chuckles from around them—oh gods, the orcs were already watching—but Gwyn kept her eyes on Joarr, *safe*, and even found herself nodding, around the thick flesh blocking her throat. Earning an approving little nod in return as he slowly drew back out, holding his glossy head just at her lips, watching with half-lidded eyes as she kissed and lavished him—and then he rammed deep again, plunging her throat full of his hard, delving heft.

But this was so familiar now, the force and the rhythm and the craving, the fierce, commanding affection behind his cool eyes and gently scraping claws. And Gwyn frantically, eagerly met him in it, driving him deep again and again, needing her lithe, virile, beautiful mate to use her, to tend her, to pour her full of his approval, his *pride*—

But instead of flooding his release deep down her throat, as he so often did, this time he yanked himself out entirely. Blatantly ignoring Gwyn's groan of sheer frustration as he caught his finger on her lower lip, holding her mouth open—

and then smirking down toward her as his other hand firmly milked his erupting length, shooting thick ropes of hot white heat into her waiting, open mouth.

And curse her, but Gwyn kept groaning aloud as she eagerly tried to catch it, to swallow, to gulp down as much slick sweetness as she possibly could. But goddess, he was making a mess of her on *purpose*, sweeping himself back and forth, his spurts of sticky seed catching and clinging to her cheeks, dripping down her chin.

And Joarr liked this, the smug bastard, he *wanted* this—and once he'd finished with his softened length, he made a show of caressing Gwyn's face with both hands, streaking his mess against her burning cheeks. Wanting to flaunt her like this, his kneeling, pregnant mate willingly being painted with his fresh seed, his scent rich and sweet upon her...

"Good little witch," he finally murmured, as he dropped his hands again. "Now show me—and all my clan—the rest of what is mine, ach?"

Oh goddess, of course he would want that, the utter *fiend*. But his devious ploy was assuredly working, because Gwyn was already giving another fervent nod, and her previously frenzied, tattered thoughts had thankfully drawn in, caught only on this. On the pure power in her mate's eyes, the heady, glorious clarity of it. Of obeying him, pleasing him, *trusting* him.

She barely felt her hands dropping, skittering against the buttons on her dress, undoing them one by one. Baring herself for her orc, and yes, for the watching eyes of all his clan—but she kept her gaze on him, only on him, as she tossed the dress aside. As his hooded eyes flagrantly raked up and down her naked, kneeling body, his previously spent length already twitching and filling again.

And whatever secret fears Gwyn might have harboured about her pregnant appearance—the extra weight, the many obvious stretch marks, the new heaviness of her breasts—they had long ago been dashed, thanks to moments like this. To the way Joarr had proudly continued to flaunt her, embrace her, *worship* her. To how—her breath choked as his hand dropped, his claws gently tracing the intricate red lines on her breasts— he'd whispered, more than once, that it was just like his witch to transform herself as she wished, while keeping him utterly caught in her thrall.

And he did look rather enthralled now, his hazy eyes lingering on his hand stroking her breast, and then flicking lower, to the swell of her belly. At nearly twenty weeks, her pregnancy was now very visible, and Gwyn twitched a self-conscious smile up toward him as she dropped both hands to her rounded waist, and began caressing it, displaying it, for his watching, glinting eyes.

His low growl hissed harsh from his throat, his hungry heft bobbing ever higher before Gwyn's eyes. Wanting this, wanting more—so she took a breath, and then slipped a trembly hand down lower, between her parted legs. Just stroking herself at first, tentative, careful—but Joarr was brazenly licking his lips now, his prick fully hard again. And somehow, Gwyn found the courage to part herself with her fingers, opening herself wide— and then she slowly sank a finger up inside, into her own throbbing, clenching heat.

She could feel the orcs avidly watching now, could almost scent the appreciation rising in the air around them. And as she began sliding her finger in and out, her wetness slick and shamefully audible against it, Joarr only groaned again, his expression gone markedly pained. And his own hand had snapped back to fist around his swollen, straining prick, pumping it up and down with reflexive, forceful strokes.

"*Mine*, witch," he hissed, low and hot, as his other hand dropped to grasp her wrist, tugging her finger out again. And before she could think, *breathe*, he'd yanked her hand up to his mouth, and sucked her slick finger deep inside. Licking and caressing it with his long, sinuous tongue, while his eyes wildly fluttered, his other hand jerking even harder against his swollen, dripping-wet prick.

When he finally released her finger again, he was looking almost predatory, his teeth bared, his eyes dark, vicious, dangerous. "On your knees, witch," he growled. "Show us the rest. Show us *my* wet womb, wide open and ready for me. Ach?"

And goddess, yes, Gwyn could do that, she *had* to—and she desperately nodded as she shifted around onto her hands and knees. Willingly spreading her legs, arching her back, and tilting out her flushed, swollen, dripping-wet heat toward him. Making herself wide open for him, just as he'd asked. And yes, yes, she could feel him looking, breathing, *approving*.

"Please, Joarr," she whispered. "Please, fuck me."

There was another dark, guttural growl behind her, and finally, the feel of her mate's warm, solid strength, easing powerful and close. His fingers carefully catching up a thick handful of her hair, his hand gently stroking down her flank. While his hot, swollen head finally nudged up against her, nocking into its rightful place, waiting...

His drive forward was like a battering ram, thudding fierce and deep inside her. And Gwyn screamed as she arched up, pierced, impaled, oh goddess, *oh*—

"More," she gasped, but the astute bastard was already doing it, dragging out, holding it just at the edge of her, making her feel it—and then ramming in again, while her frantic shouts tore through the room around them.

And as Joarr settled into his usual punishing rhythm, slamming her full of him again and again, it was sheer, stark relief, bright blazing euphoria. Driving away the last dregs of the tension, the tiredness, the *fear*, and filling it with utter, unadulterated hunger. With two bodies crashing together, finding their mutual understanding, seeking release together in the night. Being known, *seen*, wanted, *loved*.

Joarr's urgency was firing faster and faster, wheeling them closer, closer. The world swerving and tilting, shouting and shuddering, his body locking deep inside her, almost about to burst—

But just before he did, his hand pulled up a little harder on Gwyn's hair, meaning something—and when she twitched around to look at him over her shoulder, his hazy eyes briefly sharpened on hers, his rhythm slightly hesitating.

"You no find relief yet, witch," he ordered her, his breath hitching, his prick furiously swelling inside her. "You wait, for—"

And oh, oh fuck, he was bending double, squeezing his eyes shut, as he emptied himself into her. Pumping her full of his hot, surging seed, flooding her with jet after jet of his bright, burning approval.

But it indeed left Gwyn quivering, uncertain, almost undone, still pierced and craving upon him. And she nearly wept as he yanked himself free of her, *depriving* her, his thick seed already streaming through the sudden close press of his fingers—

But wait. *Wait.* He was keeping his hand there, even as he'd abruptly twisted around, dropping onto his back on the altar. And then—Gwyn stared, and froze all over—he shoved himself back up beneath her, between her still-spread legs. Meaning that she was now kneeling over—over his face. His *mouth.*

And yes, oh goddess, that was exactly what he was doing, because in another swift movement, he'd released the hold of his fingers against her, and instead clutched her thighs, and dragged them down toward him. So that her trembling, wide-opened, sopping-wet heat was splayed close against his face, pouring his own hot seed back down into his open, gulping, licking mouth.

"*Fuck*," Gwyn gasped, her eyes rolling back, her heart nearly galloping out of her chest—and when Joarr tugged a little harder, pulling purposefully against her thighs, she felt her shaky body again obeying him. Shifting her weight back even more, so that she was now sitting fully upright over him, like he'd surely wanted her to do.

But this meant—she gasped again as her head arched up— she was naked, and pregnant, and sitting on her mate's face on the goddess' altar. Feeding his own hot, surging seed straight back into his own mouth, just like he'd fed it to her, while his entire clan watched.

And goddess, Joarr knew it too, his dark, dazed eyes fluttering closed beneath her rounded belly, as he sucked and licked and swallowed, plunging his long, slippery tongue into her again and again. As if he wasn't only accepting this bounty, but actually *seeking* it, drinking it out from inside her with gulp after ravenous gulp.

It was impossible to follow, to *think*, and when Gwyn's badly trembling body somehow rocked against him—*riding* him, oh fuck—his groan only rumbled loud and deep against her, his clawed hands on her thighs clutching her even closer. Wanting her to do this, to ride him like this, and she shook all over as she did it again, fucking her mate's mouth, driving herself deep onto his hot, voracious tongue.

There was nothing like this, *nothing*, and she moved harder and faster, fully lost in the thrill, the sensation, the trampling, head-spinning hunger. Joarr's tongue plunging deeper and deeper, her plundered heat streaking and slipping against his face, the clutch trembling ever tighter, higher, she was losing it, she was going to break—

Her release felt like it shattered her apart, her entire body wrenching and wracking against it, writhing against that greedy, licking mouth. And flooding out even more hot fluid into it, spurting it out with raging, reckless fury, while her hungry mate's hard, sustained growl vibrated her whole, his throat audibly gulping as he eagerly, desperately swallowed.

Oh, oh, goddess. *Oh.* Gwyn was trembling all over, her entire body tingling and shivering, her breaths dragging like she'd been drowning. So hard that she nearly fell forward onto her face, and she caught herself on shaky hands, hauling more air deep into her lungs.

And it was then, finally, that Joarr's eyes slipped up, meeting hers. Looking hazy and dark, and blinking hard, his lashes oddly heavy, perhaps even downcast, against his harsh, stark cheekbones. As if he were just as stunned, just as overcome, as she was. And as if this, maybe, was true, unadulterated worship, sealed and sworn, before all his clan.

Gwyn swallowed hard, blinking back down toward him, while something wildly knocked within her chest. And without thinking, or even quite knowing what she was doing, she reached a trembly hand down, and tilted his head sideways, toward the inside of her thigh. And then watched, her own lashes frantically fluttering, as he accordingly leaned up, settled his teeth sharp and close...

His hard bite down was more sheer, shouting ecstasy, this time spiked with sweet, succulent streaks of pain. And Gwyn could only seem to stare, her body struck still and silent over him, as he once again drank his fill from her. As if this was perhaps her own worship, feeding her mate with her very own lifeblood, returning his gifts with her own.

She kept watching until he finally, carefully released his bite, and drew slightly back again. And then, without looking up, he stroked his tongue over the wounds he'd made, lapping soft and careful, already easing the pain into a quiet, thrumming warmth.

And before Gwyn could move, or find ways to speak again,

Joarr abruptly slipped himself further upwards under her, while also drawing her down over him. So that she could finally, *finally* collapse her weakened, quivering body down onto his, and feel the strength of his solid chest, the fierce thunder of his heart.

"Was this pain?" he whispered, as he so often did, after such things—and Gwyn somehow shoved herself up onto her elbows, blinking down into his face. And then froze again all over, because good goddess, Joarr looked utterly *feral*. His hair all on end, his face streaked with slick seed and blood, his sharp teeth rimmed with red. And she couldn't stop staring, swallowing, even as she slowly bent down, and met his reddened lips with hers.

He returned the kiss with warm, swift eagerness, his clever tongue instantly slipping against hers, teasing their combined flavours into her mouth. His heady sweetness, her sharp tanginess, the metallic salt of her blood. And there was no way it should taste this good, dragging out Gwyn's low groan, her tongue sliding deeper into his beautiful mouth...

And when he shifted her over him, and that familiar hardness again prodded against her, she easily opened up, and sheathed herself down upon him. Locking herself back onto his hard, powerful safety as she kept drinking him, tasting him, *worshipping* him.

His release up inside her felt softer this time, sweeter, like he was bathing her with him, refilling her with everything he'd taken. And goddess, Gwyn needed it, craved it, milked it out from him in long, shuddering pulses, until they were both thoroughly, utterly spent.

And this time, there was no crack of fire, no thunder, no wind. Just their own heaving bodies and gasping breaths—and that familiar, steady peace. Stealing over Gwyn all the same, curling her ever closer into her mate's beautiful body, into her goddess' deep blessing. And even though there were still voices and groans around them—and perhaps a few approving comments—Gwyn was certain that there was nothing else but this. Nothing but quiet, and peace, and *home*.

"Better?" Joarr finally whispered, and Gwyn felt herself earnestly nodding, her breath exhaling, her hands clutching even tighter against him.

"Goddess, yes," she breathed back. "So much better. You brilliant, devious *fiend*."

His chuckle beneath her was low and indulgent, his claws gently scraping down her spine. "Ach, only wish to serve my goddess," he murmured. "Wish to make her scream and weep for me, whilst all my clan marvels at my great skill."

Gwyn elbowed halfheartedly at him, but she was already chuckling too, burrowing even closer into his chest. "Thank you, Joarr," she whispered. "I love you."

He shrugged beneath her, but she could feel his slow sigh, rustling her hair. "I... love you, also," he said, quiet. "My witch. My Gwyn."

And somehow, it felt like yet another blessing, rippling rich and raw into Gwyn's belly, her heart. And with one last, contented little sigh, she settled into her mate's safety, his warmth, her home—and closed her eyes, and drifted off into sleep.

THANKS FOR READING

AND GET A FREE BONUS STORY!

Thank you for joining me for this tale! I had SUCH a blast following Gwyn and Joarr as they found their new ways together, and I hope you did too.

Next up in the Orc Sworn series is *The Maid and the Orcs*! Drafli is devastated and furious when his beloved mate Baldr accidentally builds a scent-bond with a woman. And Drafli would never, *ever* fall for this awful interloper too... right?

And for even more orc fun, sign up at www.finleyfenn.com. You'll get lots of bonus treats, including artwork from this book, and a free Orc Sworn story. I'd love to stay in touch with you!

FREE STORY: OFFERED BY THE ORC

The monster needs a sacrifice. And she's on the altar...

When Stella wanders the forest alone one fateful night, she only seeks peace, relief, escape. A few stolen moments on a secret, ancient altar, at one with the moon above.

Until she's accosted by a hulking, hideous, bloodthirsty *orc*. An orc who demands a sacrifice—not by his sword, but by Stella's complete surrender. To his claws, his sharp teeth, his huge muscled body. His every humiliating, thrilling command...

But Stella would never offer herself up to be used and sacrificed by a monster—would she? Even if her surrender just might grant her the moon's favour—and open her heart to a whole new fate?

FREE download now!
www.finleyfenn.com

ACKNOWLEDGMENTS

First of all, I'm so deeply grateful to my fabulous readers, advance reviewers, and supporters for your kindness, enthusiasm, and generosity. Thank you!!!

I'd especially like to thank the alpha and beta readers who provided feedback on this book: Amy, Jennifer N., Erin, Jen R., Ann, Serena, MK, and the truly brilliant Eris Adderly. I was also honoured to have guidance from three midwifery and health care professionals: Line Vienneau, Rianna Nisbet-Roth, and Twilla Love. Their wisdom and knowledge really helped bring Gwyn's character and career to life, and gave me even MORE appreciation for the incredible midwives among us!

I also need to rave about my highly entertaining friends at my Facebook group and Discord (if you're not already there, you can find both via Finley Fenn Readers' Den)... they're so much fun! And special thanks to Elizabeth, for the spectacular art commissions; Katie, for the staggering support (and Kalfr's name!); Angie, for sharing all the orc love; MK, for managing everything; and Coco, for all the fanart and adorable orclings.

I also remain profoundly grateful to so many of my fellow authors on this journey—your kindness has been truly life-changing. Thank you for the laughs, the moral support, and the excessive patience with my incessant random questions. ;)

Finally, as always, all my love to my own quick, clever mate, who also cooks all the delicious meals, provides the much-needed snark, and makes everything so much more fun. I adore you, my wise one.

NEXT IN THE ORC SWORN SERIES

THE MAID AND THE ORCS

She's fallen for an angel... but he's mated to a monster.

In a realm of orcs and powerful men, housemaid Alma Andersson is drowning—in grief, debt, and drudgery. And when her awful employer makes his darkest demand yet, she flees for the forest, and tumbles toward her doom...

Until she's snatched to safety by a **huge, vicious green beast.**

An *orc.*

He's utterly terrifying, with his towering bulk, sharp teeth, and deadly black claws—but his touch is gentle, and his eyes are kind. And his scent is a deep, decadent sweetness, sparking a furious flame between them...

But it's only more disaster, because **Alma's shy, soft-hearted rescuer is already mated... to another** *orc.* A tall, silent, snarling monster named Drafli, who loathes Alma on sight, and clearly longs for her death.

Yet Drafli will do anything for his sweet mate, even if it means tolerating a weak, worthless human. So he makes Alma a cold, calculated offer: **he'll share his mate with her... but only on his terms.**

He wants her silence.

Her surrender.

Her servitude.

And with Alma's fate firmly in Drafli's ruthless hands, how can she face her own dark desires—or all the secrets hidden behind Orc Mountain's walls? **Can a lost, lonely housemaid come between two orcs... without being crushed?**

ALSO BY FINLEY FENN

THE HEIRESS AND THE ORC

Once, he was her dearest friend... but now he's a brutal, terrifying monster.

In a world of recently warring orcs and men, Ella Riddell is determined to ignore it all. She's the wealthiest heiress in the realm—and soon, she's to wed a lord, and become a real lady.

Until the night her engagement-party ends in utter *disaster*, and Ella runs for the forest—**and straight into the powerful arms of a hulking, deadly orc.**

And it's not just any orc. It's *Natt*. The orc Ella made a secret, foolish pledge to, many years past...

He's huge and shameless and vicious, not at all the gangly, laughing daredevil Ella remembers. **And he's here with one shocking, scandalous aim: to wreak vengeance on Ella's betrothed. With** *her*.

With her hunger.

Her surrender.

Her undoing.

Ella knows she should run, even if this deadly enemy was once a friend. Even if his scent drags up a dark, forbidden longing. Even if his kisses are the sweetest, filthiest thing she's ever tasted in her life...

But will Ella truly risk her perfect future, for an orc? Will she face the bitter truths of the past, and brave the terrifying Orc Mountain, before more war rises to destroy them all?

THE LIBRARIAN AND THE ORC

He's a cruel, terrifying orc. And he's reading a book in her library...

In a world of recently warring orcs and men, Rosa Rolfe leads a quiet, scholarly life as an impoverished librarian—until the day she finds an *orc*. In her library. Reading a *book*.

He's rude, aggressive, and deeply terrifying, with his huge muscled form, sharp black claws, and cold, dismissive commands. But he doesn't *seem* truly dangerous... at least, until night falls. **And he makes Rosa a shocking, scandalous offer...**

Her books, for her surrender.

Her ecstasy.

Her enlightenment...

Rosa's no fool, and she knows she can't possibly risk her precious library for this brazen, belligerent orc. Even if he *is* surprisingly well-read. Even if he smells like sweet, heated honey. Even if he makes Rosa's heart race with fear, and ignites all her deepest, darkest cravings at once...

But surrender demands a dangerous, devastating price. A bond that can't easily be broken. And a breakneck journey to the fearsome, forbidding Orc Mountain, where a curious, clever librarian might be just what's needed to stop another war...

ALSO BY FINLEY FENN

THE DUCHESS AND THE ORC

She just traded herself to a new lord. And he's the most brutal orc in the realm...

In a world of recently warring orcs and men, Maria is desperate to escape her gilded cage, and her cruel duke husband. So she plots the perfect plan: she'll run away to Orc Mountain, and offer herself to the first orc who agrees to keep her safe.

But the first orc she meets is *Simon*. The huge, hostile Enforcer of Orc Mountain. The biggest, most dangerous orc in all the realm.

Worst of all, Simon hates humans. Especially wealthy, pampered women like Maria. And when she makes him her offer, he answers with vicious fury, and a proposal of his own...

He'll protect her, and share his home with her. But only if she gives him *everything* in return.

Her defeat.

Her dignity.

Her devotion...

Surely, a duchess wouldn't dare agree to such a shameful deal... or would she? Especially if her surrender to Orc Mountain's mighty Enforcer might spark another war... **or break both their hearts?**

ABOUT THE AUTHOR

Finley Fenn is "the queen of dark orc romance" (Virgo Reader), and her ongoing Orc Sworn series has been praised as "sexy, romantic, angsty, and captivating ... utter brilliance" (Romantically Inclined Reviews).

When she's not obsessing over her stories, Finley loves reading, drooling over delicious orc artwork, and spending time with her incredible readers on Patreon, Discord, and Facebook. She lives in Canada with her beloved family, including her very own grumpy, gorgeous orc husband.

For free bonus stories and epilogues, special offers, and exclusive Orc Sworn artwork, sign up at www.finleyfenn.com.